WHISPERS OF WINTER

Whispers of Winter

TRACIE
PETERSON

BETHANY HOUSE PUBLISHERS

Minneapolis, Minnesota

Published by Bethany House Publishers
11400 Hampshire Avenue South
Bloomington, Minnesota 55438

Bethany House Publishers is a division of
Baker Publishing Group, Grand Rapids, Michigan.

Printed in the United States of America

Paperback:	ISBN-13: 978-0-7642-2775-2		ISBN-10: 0-7642-2775-0
Hardcover:	ISBN-13: 978-0-7642-0235-3		ISBN-10: 0-7642-0235-9
Large Print:	ISBN-13: 978-0-7642-0236-0		ISBN-10: 0-7642-0236-7

Library of Congress Cataloging-in-Publication Data

Peterson, Tracie.
    Whispers of winter / Tracie Peterson.
        p.   cm. — (Alaskan quest ; 3)
    ISBN 0-7642-0235-9 (alk. paper) — ISBN 0-7642-2775-0 (pbk.)
    1. Survival after airplane accidents, shipwrecks, etc.—Fiction. 2. Alaska—
Fiction. I. Title.
    PS3566.E7717W57   2006
    813'.54—dc22

                                                                    2006019508

To Sarah Long for all you do;
the books are better because of you.

Thank you for being a blessing to me.

Books by Tracie Peterson

www.traciepeterson.com

A Slender Thread
What She Left for Me
*I Can't Do It All!***

ALASKAN QUEST
Summer of the Midnight Sun
Under the Northern Lights
Whispers of Winter

BELLS OF LOWELL*
Daughter of the Loom • *A Fragile Design*
These Tangled Threads

LIGHTS OF LOWELL*
A Tapestry of Hope • *A Love Woven True*
The Pattern of Her Heart

DESERT ROSES
Shadows of the Canyon • *Across the Years*
Beneath a Harvest Sky

HEIRS OF MONTANA
Land of My Heart • *The Coming Storm*
To Dream Anew • *The Hope Within*

WESTWARD CHRONICLES
A Shelter of Hope • *Hidden in a Whisper*
A Veiled Reflection

RIBBONS OF STEEL†
Distant Dreams

RIBBONS WEST†
Westward the Dream

SHANNON SAGA‡
City of Angels • *Angels Flight* • *Angel of Mercy*

YUKON QUEST
Treasures of the North • *Ashes and Ice*
Rivers of Gold

*with Judith Miller   †with Judith Pella   ‡with James Scott Bell
**with Allison Bottke and Dianne O'Brian

Chapter One

May 1917

"A yoona is dead."

Leah Barringer Kincaid looked into the face of Oopick and saw there was no exaggeration in her statement. "Dead?" The word stuck in her throat.

Ayoona's daughter-in-law nodded. "She went to sleep last night and . . ." Tears began to flow down the brown weathered cheeks of the Inupiat woman. "John stayed with her but told me to come let you know."

Leah shook her head. The news was unexpected; no doubt it had shocked John to have his mother suddenly taken from them. Ayoona was old to be sure, but she'd been so full of life, so capable just the day before. An emptiness settled over Leah. It wasn't that she didn't know where Ayoona would spend eternity—the old woman had believed in Jesus since attending a missionary school as a youngster and had often been a great source of encouragement when Leah's own faith

9

had seemed weak. But this loss, coupled with the burden and grief she carried for her missing husband and brother, had Leah feeling overwhelmed.

Last year her husband, Jayce Kincaid, and brother, Jacob Barringer, had journeyed north on a ship called *Regina*. The captain bore the world a grudge for the death of his wife. Still, he had an interest in the Arctic, though perhaps he had hopes of losing himself there. At best he seemed to presume the frozen north could make him forget his woes. Instead, his carelessness or forgetfulness had caused the ship to get caught in early winter ice floes, which took the ship hostage and locked them in tight. Whalers returning south for the season had shared of seeing the *Regina* trapped in ice and headed in a westerly current toward the Russian boundaries. But no one seemed to know exactly where the ship was now or if its crew and passengers had survived.

"I'll miss her so much," Leah said, forcing her thoughts back to Ayoona. "Just two days ago we were making plans to sew seal skins for a new *umiak*." The small skin boats were a tremendous asset to the Inupiat people, who sought much of their sustenance from the Bering Sea.

"We will sew the skins and remember her," Oopick said, wiping her tears. "We will tell stories of her life and be happy for her."

Leah hugged her friend close. Oopick was probably fifteen years her senior, but Leah loved her like a sister. "We will do just that. You let me know when to come, and we will sew the skins for Ayoona."

Just then one of Leah's twins began to cry. Leah released her hold on Oopick. "I'll come help with the body as soon as

Helaina returns to watch the children."

Oopick nodded. "I need to tell Emma and Bjorn."

Leah knew the missionaries would be devastated to learn of Ayoona's passing. The old woman was greatly loved by the people of the village, and her loss would be sorely felt for years to come. Oopick departed as Wills joined his sister, Merry, in crying for attention.

"Poor babies," Leah said, walking to the homemade crib her children shared. Both were soaking wet and in need of a warm bath and fresh diapers. Leah already had hot water on the stove and, despite her children's miserable howls, went in pursuit of the copper bathtub and towels.

She knew she was more fortunate than most in the area. The new house she and her husband had ordered from the States had arrived in pieces last year. When Jacob and Jayce failed to return from their summer mission to explore the Arctic coast and islands, Bjorn Kjellmann had organized men to build the house in Jayce's absence. The Swedish man of God knew no lack of enthusiasm for helping his fellowman, and because Leah and Jacob were much loved in the community, help was readily available to see Leah and her children properly housed for the winter.

It was Bjorn, in fact, who had helped them to figure a way to assemble the foundation on a system of stilt-like supports to keep the permafrost from melting and sinking the house. The house had settled some, but Bjorn assured Leah it would be fairly easy to remedy each year by adding or subtracting wedges under the house. All of this would hopefully keep the structure of the new home stable.

Once completed, their house brought the natives visiting

in throngs. Everyone wanted to experience the store-bought house. They laughed at the way it sat up off the ground. Their *innes* were built into the earth in order to provide insulation and protection from the wind. The fact that they flooded out each summer seemed insignificant; they were a nomadic people during the warm season anyway. It was the one thing Leah had never quite gotten used to in all her years on the Seward Peninsula. She longed for stability, consistency, and a sense of permanency. None of that could be had when a person constantly traveled.

Leah poured hot water into the tub, then added a measure of cold water until the temperature felt just right. With this accomplished, she threw a few more pieces of driftwood into the stove. Although it was finally May and spring breakup had begun, the air outside could be quite cold and could chill the house. She wanted nothing to threaten the health of her children and therefore kept the dwelling as warm as possible to afford them every benefit. The north was not kind to those who were weaker—children and the elderly often suffered the most.

Leah thought again of Ayoona. How strange it would be not to have her around to talk to. Ayoona had taught Leah so many things. Things that no doubt had kept her alive over the years.

With the water ready, Leah went to the twins' bedroom and noted that their tears had stopped. They were now quite caught up in playing with the sheet on their homemade mattress.

"Come, babies," Leah said softly. She opened her arms and smiled.

The twins eagerly pulled themselves up and balanced their walks by holding on to the railing of the crib. Leah could hardly wait until they could toddle on their own, yet she also feared that time. One baby would be hard enough to keep up with; she feared two would be nearly impossible.

She lifted her children in unison and made her way back to the kitchen, where the copper tub waited. Placing them on the table, Leah talked and cooed while undressing first one and then the other. The children seemed captivated by her voice, and it never failed to thrill Leah to realize they were her own flesh and blood. Of course, in the back of her mind she still felt haunted by the uncertainty about their parentage. Her husband was always good to assure her that such things didn't matter, but to Leah it was an ominous rain cloud that hung over her otherwise perfect party.

Looking at the twins, Leah couldn't imagine that anything so perfect might be the result of a hideous rape. There was simply too much joy and love to be had from these precious gifts from God. She sighed, unable to free herself from the memories of Jayce's brother Chase. The man had ruined her life in so many ways. . . . But despite his assault on her and his subsequent death, Leah fought to retain a hopeful future for her children. She couldn't let Chase's destruction perpetuate.

Leah pushed the memories of bad times aside and lifted her naked children. "Here we go. It's time for our bath." Her singsong voice suggested a great outing was upon them. And for the Kincaid twins, such a thing could be said. They loved their bath time, and Leah enjoyed it as well, finding a certain comfort in the morning ritual.

Placing each child in the water, she laughed as they

adjusted to their new surroundings and began to splash and play. Merry was far and away the more shy of the two, but she seemed to find her own measure of bravery here in the water. Wills, always the adventurer, sometimes stuck his face right down into the water only to pop back up as if surprised that he couldn't breathe in the liquid.

Leah let them play until the water began to cool off. She then took soap and quickly bathed each one. With the bath ritual drawing to a close, Leah wrapped the babies in warm towels that she'd kept on the back of the stove. It was just then that Helaina Beecham appeared.

"It's a glorious day," she announced. "I wouldn't be surprised to see the ice completely melt or drift out to sea."

Leah secured diapers on her babies, then began the arduous task of dressing them. "I hope you're right. The sooner the ice clears, the sooner help can be had for Jacob and Jayce."

Helaina pulled off a thick woolen hat and pushed back loose strands of blond hair. "I'd like to get to Nome and see if Stanley has sent any further word." She had been a good source of encouragement to Leah.

Helaina's brother had been faithfully helping the women get any available information on the *Regina*. Unfortunately, there hadn't been much the Washington, D.C., Pinkerton agent could offer. No one could travel north, and after a winter of waiting and praying, Helaina and Leah had reached the end of their patience.

"I would have suggested John could take you down, but we've just had bad news," Leah said, remembering her friend's death. "Ayoona passed away in the night."

Helaina's expression turned to one of disbelief. "I just

talked to her yesterday. She showed me how to clean and cook a goose."

"I know, but she's gone." Leah tried not to cry in front of the children. The twins weren't quite a year old, and anytime Leah cried, they were very sensitive to their mother and began to cry too. Leah often had to save her tears of despair for the dead of night when the household was asleep.

Helaina took a cup and poured herself some hot coffee. "I can't believe she's gone." Sitting down at the kitchen table, she shook her head, then took a long sip.

"Oopick was just here. I told her I would help prepare the body if you could watch the twins. If you don't have time, however, I could ask Sigrid. There's no school today, so she won't be busy teaching."

"Nonsense. I can watch them. Besides, Emma will probably want her sister with her. Won't they also help with the body?" She pushed her coffee aside as Leah got to her feet.

"I suppose so." Leah finished with the children, then handed Wills to Helaina. "Please hold on to him while I secure Merry. They seem to be everywhere at once these days."

"Come see Auntie Helaina," she coaxed, and Wills eagerly launched himself into Helaina's arms. She had become a special member of the family to Leah's twins. To Leah too.

It was hard to believe that this woman Leah had once hated had become so important to her now. Leah honestly loved Helaina. The woman had spent tireless hours helping to gather wood off the beaches, caring for Jacob's dogs, and working at the small store Leah ran from her old inne not twenty yards away.

Leah placed Meredith into a crudely constructed baby

chair, then scooted her to the table. Next was Wills' turn, but he was so intrigued with pulling Helaina's hair from its pins that he had nearly forgotten his hunger.

"Come along, son. You can charm the lady another time."

Helaina chuckled and reached again for her steaming mug. "I'd say he'll be charming all the ladies one day. He's quite the handsome young man."

Leah took a dish towel and tied her son in place. She'd learned the hard way that if she didn't secure the children in such a manner, they were only too happy to climb out.

"I have oatmeal on the stove for their breakfast. There's canned milk, too, and a precious little bit of sugar."

"I'll see to it," Helaina said, getting to her feet. She pulled off her coat and hung it on a peg by the door. "I think I'm finally warmed up enough to function."

"How did you sleep?" Leah watched her friend for any negative reaction. Helaina had just taken to sleeping in Leah and Jacob's old home the last few days.

"At first I was a bit unnerved. I kept thinking about that first summer I spent here, when you and Jayce were in Ketchikan. I hated it then. I was sure the house would cave in or that some animal would tunnel its way through the dirt and sod. But this time . . . well . . . it just made me feel closer to Jacob."

Leah felt sorry for Helaina. The woman had given up everything in the States, her home, her career helping Stanley catch criminals for the Pinkertons, even her social life—and all to pin her hopes on a man that might or might not return her affections. But Leah was almost certain he would return them, otherwise she would never have encouraged Helaina.

"I'm glad it had that effect," Leah said as she pulled on

her parka. "Soon enough it will flood out, but until then you might as well enjoy the privacy."

"I lived in it all summer, even when it was flooded," Helaina said, laughing. "The villagers thought I was crazy. I think I might have been at that, but the prospect of living in a tent in a land full of bears and other wildlife hardly appealed. I slept on the table."

Leah laughed. "Well, you won't need to do that this time. When the ground starts to thaw, just come back here. You know you're welcome."

"I do, but I also want to help you with the store. I have the inventory complete, and by tomorrow I should be able to finish the list of who owes how much."

Leah smiled. "I knew you'd be quite efficient. Jacob always admired that about you."

"Well, let's pray my efficiency will help get them home safely. As soon as we finish with Ayoona's funeral, I want to find a way to get to Nome. Even if I have to hike there by myself."

"You won't have to. I'll go before I send you out there blind to the trail." Leah headed for the door as Helaina pulled bowls down from the cupboard, and after a quick glance at her children, she walked to Ayoona's.

The day was beautiful, just as Helaina had said. The crystal blue sky was cloudless, and in the distance she could make out definite signs of spring.

"Lord, please let us find the men. Let us find Jacob and Jayce and the others. Please bring them home safely."

She couldn't count the times she'd prayed these same words over and over. She had never felt more helpless than when she'd realized last winter that she could do nothing to help her husband and brother. The winter had seemed to last forever, with one storm after another leaving them more and more isolated. With each blizzard, each stormy day, Leah thought of the men and wondered if they were enduring similar hardship.

Leah tried hard not to get discouraged, but it hurt to be without the people she loved most in all of the world. Jacob had been her mainstay through the years—especially when Jayce had refused her love long ago. But now that she and Jayce were married, Leah had quickly turned her focus on her husband. Jayce was the love of her life—her hope for the future—her heart's desire. If she lost him now, Leah wasn't sure what she'd do. If she lost them both ... well ... she couldn't even let her mind consider such a possibility.

Helaina had been an amazing tower of strength throughout the winter. When despair threatened and discouragement whispered in Leah's ear, it was Helaina and her faith in God that strengthened them both. Helaina hadn't always cared about what God wanted. After years of doing things on her own—relying on self-knowledge and preservation to see things through—Helaina had come to experience the same emptiness as others without God. Leah had known that the answer to her misery would be Jesus, but Leah also knew that until Helaina found such a thing for herself, it would do no good to force the issue.

So that was why it was a special joy to reflect on Helaina's love and consistent reading of the Bible. Many had been the night that Helaina had read from the Scriptures while winds raged outside and the twins howled inside. Leah and Helaina had discussed passages at length, sometimes even taking notes in order to ask Bjorn Kjellmann on a later date. He had laughed the first time they'd come to him with a list of questions, but after laboring over that same list and searching to give answers, Bjorn stopped laughing. He now said they were the iron sharpening iron—the students who caused the teacher to search deeper.

But Leah knew that book learning and heart understanding were two different things. She tried not to worry about the situation anymore than she needed to, but at times like this, she felt rather hopeless.

Her dear friend and mentor had gone home to be with the Lord.

Her brother was lost somewhere in the frozen Arctic.

And her husband might very well never return home.

Chapter Two

J acob Barringer looked out across the frozen waters of the Arctic. There was no real sign that spring breakup was upon them, but in his heart he felt certain it was coming. He could almost feel it in his bones. The winter was over—at least technically speaking.

He thought about all they'd gone through. He and the rest of the crew of the *Regina* had been fortunate to find the missing ammunition for the 30–30, as well as another rifle and pistol. A supply of medicines meant for the Canadian scientists they'd taken north had been located, and Dr. Ripley had been delighted. It had given them all hope for survival. Now that the winter was over, the men were anxious to get home. Tempers were flaring, and Jacob was worried about how they would endure much longer.

"What do you see?" Jayce Kincaid asked as he joined his brother-in-law.

"Nothing that wasn't there yesterday," Jacob admitted. "I know the thaw is coming, though. By my calculations it's got to be near the end of May. It won't take long for the ice to break free once things start warming up. I've seen mornings back home where we woke up with the ice and by evening it was gone. Once the ice is gone, the searchers will come."

"At least the ice had made the seal hunting easier."

"True. We've eaten pretty well thanks to that."

Jayce shook his head. "We've eaten well because you've taught us how to survive up here. Most of these men had no idea how to live in this cold, much less thrive. And with no help or encouragement from Captain Latimore . . . well, let's just say the responsibility has fallen hard on your shoulders."

"Yours too. The men look to you just as readily as they look to me. Once we landed on this island, you were the one who taught them how to build those snow-block houses."

"Only because I learned it from you," Jayce said with a laugh. He gazed out to the ocean and sobered. "I know they're out there, rescuers . . . Leah." He sighed heavily. "I know they are, but what I can't figure is if they know we're here."

Jacob nodded. "I'm hoping they'll remember the *Karluk* and figure the current might have taken us in the same direction. We'll be all right if they consider that. At least they'll close in on us."

"I pray you're right."

The next morning around five, Jacob awoke to storm clouds gathering on the horizon. The men went about camp, tying down the things they'd managed to secure from the

Regina. Jacob had helped direct the evacuation of the ship when the ice broke her apart. For weeks they had lived with nothing but several feet of ice between them and the Arctic waters. They were definitely blessed to have found land—even if it was desolate.

"Looks like a snow coming in," Jacob told one of the men. He pointed to a stack of cut driftwood. "Better get some of that inside. No telling how bad or how long this one's going to last."

"Latimore's missing," Jayce said as he came up behind Jacob.

"Missing?"

"No one's seen him since last night. When Bristol woke up this morning, he realized Latimore hadn't called him for his watch."

Jacob considered the situation for a moment. "Bristol was scheduled to take the four-o'clock watch, correct?"

Jayce nodded. "I looked around and found tracks that headed off toward the west along the beach. I'm thinking Latimore might have gone off that direction. Maybe he heard or saw something that caught his attention."

With continual daylight upon them, Jacob knew it should be easy enough to find the man if they spread out and searched. "We should be able to locate him if we split up. Gather the men, and we'll do what we can. He may have become confused or snow-blind."

Jayce quickly retrieved the men. They had long ago turned to Jacob as their leader, especially given Latimore's despondency toward life and his crew. "Look, it seems the captain disappeared last night. We don't know if he saw something that took him from his post or if he simply wandered away." Jacob didn't want to further demean the man, so he quickly continued. "There have been many bear tracks as you well know, so it wouldn't be wise to just assume Latimore is unharmed. Go in pairs, and take one of the firearms. If you haven't found anything in an hour," he said, gazing to the southwest, "return to camp. The skies are looking mean, and we'd best be settled back here before it hits."

"All it ever does up here is snow and be cold," nineteen-year-old Bristol grumbled. "I never knew you could have temperatures as cold as this place."

"Oh, stop complaining," Elmer Warrick, former first mate, commanded. "We haven't got time to list all of our problems."

Originally there had been fourteen men who'd abandoned the *Regina* when she sank. They'd lost four in accidents—accidents that had awakened the rest of the team to just how serious their station had become. Now with Latimore gone, that left nine men. They were a good bunch, as far as Jacob was concerned, but they were starting to get sick and irritable. It would only be a matter of time before they started feeling the desperation of their situation. Especially if help didn't come soon.

As the men paired up in teams, Jacob considered the lay of the land and each man's ability. Some were growing weak from the lack of a good diet, and Jacob didn't want to further risk anyone's life by making their trek too arduous. The snow was difficult to navigate at times, and unfortunately, many of these men were from southern states that saw very little cold or ice.

"Travis, you and Keith go north. Dr. Ripley and Elmer go west and follow the tracks Jayce found. Jayce, you and Bristol head east and Ben and Matt go northeast." Since they stood on the southern shore of the island and were able to see for some miles to the south, no one felt the need to head in that direction. Besides, the ice was far too unstable.

As the men gathered some supplies and split up, Jacob decided to head northwest, away from the shoreline. There was no telling if the tracks Jayce had found belonged to Latimore or to one of the other men. The captain could have gone any direction, for any reason. Jacob sighed. Latimore hadn't been much use to them since getting stuck in the floes, but he couldn't be forsaken—no matter the risk to the rest of them.

"What I wouldn't give for a few good dogs," Jacob muttered.

The landscape of their island offered some diversion. There were hills and cliffs where nesting birds had provided good meals for the team, but dangerous crevices and ice heaves were plentiful and difficult to navigate, and snow depths were often deceptive due to the drifts. It was truly an inhospitable wasteland. God forgive the leader of the *Karluk* expedition for calling it "the friendly Arctic." Vilhjalmur Stefansson was well known for declaring that the Arctic was merely misunderstood and that with proper training anyone could live quite easily in the frozen north. But Jacob knew better. Life up here was a matter of God's grace and common sense. Lose either one and you were doomed.

The glare from the constant sunlight was blinding. Jacob could only pray that the men were practicing wisdom and using their sun goggles. Jacob had shown each of them how to make the wooden glasses by carving tiny slits out of driftwood masks. They were crude but efficient, and the man who forgot to wear them quickly learned not to do it again. Several of the men had become snow-blind and suffered brutally; the pain caused by the condition was intense and would last for hours, even days. Now that their normal treatment of zinc sulphate solutions was nearly exhausted, the men were becoming far more cautious. No one wanted to endure such a fate.

Besides the lack of scenery, the monotony of their routine had nearly driven them all mad at one time or another. Bristol had a deck of cards that the men shared, but Dr. Ripley would have nothing to do with it, swearing they were the devil's tool of destruction. Dr. Ripley would therefore bury his face in one of three medical books he'd managed to keep with him after leaving the ship.

Travis, Ben, and Keith were quite good at singing and often entertained the group with their renditions of old folk songs and hymns. Travis, a meteorologist, kept records of their conditions, and Keith planned to keep similar botany records once the ground thawed.

Jacob often read from the Bible, sharing stories that the men knew from their childhood days in church. Besides botany, Keith was well versed in church history and the Bible, and Jacob had enjoyed dialoguing with the man from time to time. Ben and Matt also enjoyed such conversations, as did Travis. The others, however, avoided religious discussions.

Generally speaking, the men were a good lot. Jacob had feared there might be troublemakers in their group—men who would steal or kill in order to survive. He was glad to say that hadn't been the case so far.

Yet despite the men's good natures, Jayce was Jacob's mainstay. Together the two talked of home and of Leah. They remembered times spent in Ketchikan and of Karen's cooking and Adrik's stories. Their conversations sustained Jacob's hope of seeing home again.

He also often thought of Helaina Beecham. He wondered where she was and how she was doing. Had she gone back to work for her brother? A dangerous job such as bounty hunting should never have been allowed for women. Still, the world was changing.

Jacob thought of the war going on in Europe. He could only wonder if the war had extended to include America by now. So many people seemed to think it would happen that way. Still, it was possible the European countries had worked out their differences and had ended the war. That would be the best they could hope for, but somehow Jacob doubted it had happened. There had seemed no end in sight the summer before.

He trudged through the ice to crest one of the bigger hills and scanned the landscape in all directions. Using his binoculars, he spotted a great herd of seals on the ice. They were sunning themselves at the edge of a break—open water clearly available to them should a bear or man make an unwanted appearance. The water was a good sign. Perhaps the breakup would come sooner than Jacob anticipated.

There was no sign of Latimore, but the storm clouds were thickening and moving toward the island at an alarming rate. Jacob could feel that the temperatures had dropped significantly as the wind picked up and blew in the storm. He hurriedly scanned the rest of the land. There was nothing to suggest that a man had passed this way recently.

Making his way down the opposite side, Jacob tried to calculate the distance he and the men might cover in an hour. To press for more time would surely risk being out in the storm. He wondered if he'd be forced to leave Latimore to the elements rather than endanger the lives of everyone else.

The men, however, wouldn't consider this the loss of a leader. That had happened back in January when Latimore had sunk into a deep depression, isolating himself from most everyone. Jacob had taken it upon himself to hide the firearms from the captain for fear he might take his own life. With each small decision, the men began to think more and more of Jacob as their leader. Even the captain's first mate, Elmer Warrick, yielded all authority to Jacob. It wasn't exactly a responsibility Jacob had wanted, but having it thrust upon him out of necessity, he hadn't turned them away.

It had been clear that he and Jayce would be the only hope these men had. Most knew nothing about living in the Arctic; they had no training in hunting, neither were they very knowledgeable about survival off the ship. When fresh water ran desperately low, it was Jacob who taught them that good water could be had from the oldest parts of the ice floes, where ice could be chipped out and melted for a decent cup of water. With the fear of thirst defeated, the men then began to listen to Jacob in earnest for ways to survive the cold.

There Jayce had been equally helpful. They worked with the furs they'd managed to collect from their hunts, for prior to leaving the Canadian team at the Queen Elizabeth Islands, the crew had managed to shoot several bears, multiple caribou and seals, and a few fox. The furs came in handy as Jayce helped teach the men how to fashion warmer clothes for themselves. It was imperative they learned to keep their hands and feet warm and dry and their chest well insulated against the icy winds.

Jacob felt the wind blow hard against him and turned to observe the approaching storm once again. The mass was picking up speed, and the light was diminishing quickly as thick gray clouds descended. He checked his watch. They still had another twenty minutes before they'd agreed to return to camp. Jacob picked up his pace and decided to parallel camp just to the north. It would allow him quicker access to safety and give him the optimum time to search.

He crossed a frozen stream, hoping that the ice was still solid enough to hold him. Hours in the sun had weakened the foundation, however, and Jacob nearly fell through twice. He noted to go well downstream as he returned home, knowing that there he'd find a narrowing short enough to jump.

Time passed quickly, and soon the hour was up, but tracks that seemed fresh drew Jacob farther north and away from camp. Certainly they had to belong to the captain. Snow began to fall, and the wind blew hard against his back as Jacob topped another hill and strained against the pelting ice to see. He pulled his snow goggles up just long enough to put the binoculars to his eyes.

There, against the gray skies and snowy hills, was the unmistakable blue of Latimore's coat. Jacob called to him, but the man didn't hear. Hurrying, Jacob stumbled and slid most of the way down the hill. He jumped to his feet, sore but unhurt, and raced across the field to where Latimore seemed to wander in circles.

"Captain, are you all right?"

"I was not informed of the situation," he muttered. His face showed signs of frostbite and his lips were rather blue. "I can't seem to find the engineer."

"Sir, we have to get back to camp. There's a storm upon us. If we hurry, we might yet get back before the worst of it."

"You are not coming to the party, then?"

Jacob shook his head. Latimore had clearly lost his mind—at least temporarily. Not only that, but his eyes were nearly swollen shut from exposure. Jacob sighed. "Come, sir. The party is this way."

Latimore seemed momentarily appeased, but when Jacob pulled him along at a merciless pace, the man protested. "I cannot force the children to walk this quickly."

"The children will manage," Jacob replied, his gaze ever to the skies. If they kept this pace, they might make it back within half an hour. That would be just enough time, Jacob surmised. He absolutely couldn't allow the captain to slow for any reason.

"I haven't seen Regina. Is she here?"

The captain's mention of his wife surprised Jacob. "She's back at the camp, sir. She's waiting for you there," he lied, not knowing how else to ensure Latimore's cooperation.

This did the trick. "Then let us make haste. She is not one to be kept tapping her toes. She loves to dance, and the party will do much to raise her spirits."

The snow was blinding by the time they reached the camp. Had it not been for Jayce standing in the storm with one of their ship's lanterns, Jacob might have wandered out to sea. It was a danger he had often warned the men about. In the eternal darkness of Arctic winter, it was impossible to be certain where land began and ended without strict attention to detail. In an Arctic blizzard, it was just as difficult to gain your bearings.

"I see you found him," Jayce called above the winds. He reached out to take hold of Latimore's arm. "Let's just take him to our shelter."

"Have the others safely returned?" Jacob pushed Latimore while Jayce pulled.

"They have."

They reached the shelter of their makeshift house. The house had been built of pallets and wooden boxes from the ship's supplies. Around this they'd packed ice and snow, and it served them remarkably well. With the small camp stoves continually heating the shelter, they had survived sixty-below temperatures with only minor discomfort.

Jacob pulled off gear and helped Latimore to the stove. Keith and Ben got up to assist their captain, although it was easy to see they were disgusted with the man.

"He's confused and blind. I found him wandering in circles."

"I find the Atlantic abominable to navigate," Latimore stated as they helped him sit. Jayce brought several blankets and wrapped them around the man while Ben poured a cup of tea and handed it to Latimore. The man's hands shook so much that he couldn't hold the tin, so Ben gently held the cup to his lips.

Latimore drank, then eased back. "We shall never see

Scotland again." He sighed the words, then passed out and fell backward against Jayce.

"Will he live?" Ben asked.

Jacob shook his head. "Not if he doesn't want to."

Chapter Three

I'll take you to Nome."

John's statement startled Helaina. She'd been working to feed the dogs and hadn't even heard the native man approach. She straightened, ignoring the ache in her back. John's expression was emotionless, yet his eyes bore great pain. His mother's passing had not been an easy thing to bear.

"That's very kind of you. How soon can we leave?"

"Right now, if you can be ready."

"If you're sure. I don't want to . . . well . . . I know you're grieving."

"We are all grieving, but not just for my mother. I grieve for my friend Jacob. I grieve for Leah and her children. We must go and see what is to be done."

It was the moment Helaina and Leah had waited for all winter. "Let me get my things packed. I shouldn't need more than ten minutes."

"Meet me at the water."

Helaina nodded. The ice was gone and they would take the umiaks to Nome. It would be a blessing to the whole village, for she knew they would bring back ample supplies from her storehouse and that of any new shipments from Seattle and San Francisco. That was, if any of the ships had made it north yet.

She hurried back to the Barringer inne and gathered her things. The warm weather was already causing the ground to thaw, and it would be only a matter of weeks before the house started to flood. Still, she liked the place. Liked it because it reminded her of Jacob. She could see him here—smell his scent, hear his voice. Here she felt an unusual sense of peace that he would return to reclaim his home—and she hoped he might claim her as well.

Helaina hurried to pack a small bag of necessities for the trip, then threw everything else into her trunk and placed it up on the kitchen table. She would ask about having someone retrieve it and take it back to Leah's home. Maybe she'd just mention it to Leah when she told her good-bye.

Rushing for the Kincaid house, Helaina was glad to find that Leah was already waiting outside with the children. "John told me about the trip. I've packed you some food." Leah handed Helaina a gunnysack. "Hopefully the good weather will hold and you won't have to stop before reaching Nome."

"You're so thoughtful. I do appreciate your thinking of this," Helaina replied, slinging the sack over her shoulder. "I've packed up the rest of my things and left them on the table in my trunk. Could you have someone bring them here when you have time? I'd like to keep them from the water."

"Of course." Leah turned away from the toddling twins. "Please get word to me as soon as possible." The longing in her voice matched that in Helaina's heart.

Helaina reached out to touch her friend. "You know I will. No matter what. I'll let you know what's going on."

Leah nodded. "No matter what." The words were spoken with a kind of ominous resolve.

Helaina turned without another word and headed to the boats. John helped her in and tucked her things at the back with the rest of the supplies. Helaina knew the men wouldn't allow her to help row, so she settled in and tried to ready herself for whatever news she might encounter.

There's always the possibility, she rationalized, *that the men of the* Regina *managed to find help and get to land before too much trouble set in.* But in her heart she knew the chances were remote. Of course, the news could be that the revenue cutters had already gone in search of the men. After all, the ice had been gone several days now. This would be her prayer, Helaina decided. She wanted only to hear that a rescue ship was already en route and that everyone was certain of the *Regina*'s location.

She dozed off as the sun warmed the air. Her thoughts were of Jacob and her hope that he would be happy to see her in Alaska. She had prayed so often that he might still love her as Leah believed he did. There was no regret in her decision to come north, but Helaina knew that if Jacob refused her love, there would be no reason to stay. That thought saddened her more than she could bear, for then she would truly belong nowhere.

You'll always belong to me, a voice seemed to speak to her heart. She felt an immediate hope that grew every day as her knowledge of God grew.

Yes, she thought. *I belong to Jesus. I belong to God, and I will always have His love, even if Jacob has none to give me.*

In Nome Helaina learned that the war in Europe was not going well. American casualties were high, and no one had any idea of when the conflict might end. She worried about her brother, knowing that Stanley's patriot heart would cause him to want to sign up. His leg would keep him from being accepted—of that she was certain. After Chase Kincaid threw him from the back of a moving train, Stanley had never been the same. The leg had been shattered and other bones broken; Stanley had been lucky to survive. She shook her head slowly as she remembered it all. Had it not been for the Pinkertons' desperation to capture Chase Kincaid, she might never have met Jacob Barringer.

Helaina looked at the small building in front of her and tried to put worries of Stanley aside. Since it was Sunday and there would be no chance of receiving news or information from the army or other officials, she had decided to spend her time in church. The woman at the hotel had told her about a tiny church and of the love the people held for one another. It sounded like just the thing to lift Helaina's spirits.

"Are you lost?"

Helaina turned to find a determined older woman looking her square in the eye. "No. I was just planning to attend church."

"Well, you're in the right place." The woman offered a

huge smile, along with her outstretched hand. "I'm Mina Bachelder, and we're glad to have you. Are you new to Nome? I don't think I've seen you here before."

"I've been here on several occasions. In fact," Helaina leaned closer, so as not to make her next comment a public announcement, "I was the woman kidnapped when the deputies were shot and killed."

"Oh, mercy me. And here you are safe and sound. I guess I'd heard you went back to the States."

"I had, but . . . well . . . there was something and someone I needed to come back for."

Mina grinned and her whole expression lit up. "You should tell me all about it over dinner. I'm serving up a good caribou stew. Please join me."

Helaina nodded. "I'd like that."

After a wonderful church service, Mina led Helaina to her house on Second Street. "Will you be in Nome long?" she asked.

"No, probably not," Helaina said. "I came for information. My . . . well . . . a dear friend of mine has a husband and brother on the *Regina*." In church the pastor had asked the congregation to pray for the men of the *Regina*. It had blessed Helaina to hear the pastor offer up prayers for the men, comforting her in a way she couldn't explain.

Mina reached out to touch her arm. "So that's why you're here."

"Yes. I'm hopeful that the army or the Coast Guard can give me information as to whether any rescue ships have been sent north. I know it's early, but those men have endured a cold winter." She hated to even think of what kind of fate might have befallen Jacob and Jayce.

"Well, we've certainly been praying they've endured."

Helaina stopped in midstep. "They must have. They were good men—strong and knowledgeable. They wouldn't take chances."

"Seems they took a chance when they went north," Mina replied. "Here we are." She walked up a few steps and opened the door. "Just hang your coat on the hook. I'll get the dinner on."

Mina disappeared through yet another door while Helaina pulled off her fur parka. The house proved to be nice and warm. Apparently Mina had stoked up the fire before heading to church. Helaina closed the door behind her and observed the tiny living room. There was a colorful rag rug, several wooden chairs, and a horsehair couch that had seen a great amount of wear.

"Here's a cup of tea for you to sip on while I set the table. I hope you don't mind tea. I don't drink coffee."

Helaina smiled and took the offering. "Tea is just fine. I'm very fond of it." She sipped from the cup as she continued to study the room. A small fireplace had been trimmed with a simple wooden mantel. This in turn held pictures of people Helaina guessed to be Mina's family. She leaned closer for a better look.

Several of the pictures were obviously wedding photographs. Women who appeared a decade younger than Helaina peered out from white gowns and veils with sober expressions. They would have the viewer believe the day was nothing more special than any other—that having the photograph taken was a commonplace event that left the subjects fighting off moments of ennui. But Helaina knew better. This was the day most of them had waited for, prayed for. This was the beginning of a new life. A day so important that they had to commemorate it, no matter the cost, with a photograph.

Helaina thought momentarily of her late husband, Robert Beecham. The marriage seemed to have taken place a hundred years ago. She didn't dwell there long, however, as Jacob's image came to mind.

"I see you've found the children."

"Are all of these your children?" Helaina asked in surprise. There had to be at least a dozen different couples or families.

"Indeed. I bore my husband seventeen babies. Fifteen lived to see adulthood."

"Where are they now?"

Mina smoothed her colorful apron. "Some live right here. Some live down in the States. A couple made their way to other parts of the territory. They're all good to write—especially the girls. I have ten daughters, so they keep me well apprised of what's happening in the family."

"It's an impressive family to say the least."

"They're my blessing from God. And they all love the Lord as much as I do, so I can stand before Him on judgment day with a clear conscience."

Helaina heard the pride in the woman's voice. It was quite an accomplishment to raise such a large family in the wilds of Alaska, but an even greater feat to see them all come to a spiritual understanding of biblical truth. Helaina wondered what the woman's secret might be.

"How did you do it?"

Mina grinned. "Sit down with me and I'll tell you all about it."

Helaina did as she was instructed, listening to Mina offer a simple prayer for the meal, as well as for the men of the *Regina*. The sincerity of her words made Helaina feel the woman genuinely cared about the plight of those men.

"I always told my children," Mina began, "that whether or not they chose to believe in God—He was still God. He wouldn't make any special deals with them just because they were stubborn or confused. I told them that the good Lord had given them God-fearing parents for a reason, and that reason was to bring them up in the way they should go."

"And that caused them to believe?"

"That and the constant reminder that hell was a very real place where you would spend eternity in misery and absolute separation from all hope and love. My husband led devotions at breakfast and supper every day. We talked about the people in the Bible as though they were family. There wasn't a story my children didn't know, but their daddy was good to remind them that it wasn't enough to just know those lessons in their head. They needed to take them into their hearts and heed the message."

"Still, that's a big accomplishment to see fifteen children learn to trust God and believe in Him. I was late in coming to believe. It was very hard for me."

Mina looked at her sternly. "Were your people believers? Did your folks take you to church?"

"Oh, we attended church—but you must understand, I lived in New York. In our circle of friends, church was a place to be seen socially rather than for the sake of your soul."

"Goodness. I can't imagine that."

Helaina smiled. "Think of this: One of the churches I attended held row after row of highly polished mahogany pews. You earned the right to certain pews by nature of who you were associated with and how much money you gave the church. The closer to the front, the more important you were—the more you were valued."

"That's awful. Teaches a bad lesson."

"To be sure." Helaina sampled the stew. "Mmm, this is wonderful. Thank you so much for inviting me."

Mina handed her a platter with biscuits. "These are a couple of days old but should crumble up nice in the stew."

Helaina took one and followed Mina's example of tearing it up in her hands and mingling it with the caribou and vegetables. "How did you come to live here in Nome, Mina?"

"My husband brought us here when there was little more than natives around. It was long before the gold rush—such a difficult time." She tutted under her breath and focused on her food. "Nome has always had its problems, and those were grim days to be sure."

"Why did your husband want to live here?"

"We were missionaries, ministering to the people of this region. When my husband passed on, there must have been more than two hundred natives from Nome and the surrounding area at his funeral. They loved him."

"If his hospitality was equal to yours, then I can definitely see why," Helaina replied.

"The Lord calls us to hospitality. The Bible says you never know when you might be entertaining angels, so I try never to pass up a chance to invite a newcomer."

"Well, for me this was an unexpected treat. I'll remember it for some time to come."

"You'll come back and see me too, won't you? When you come to Nome, you're more than welcome to stay with me. You can leave that hotel and come here now if you like. I have a small room off the back that has a spare bed and its own stove. It'll keep you quite comfortable."

Helaina had never seen such generosity in New York. Life in Alaska was much different; people knew to look out for each other. To do otherwise might cause someone's death, and no one wanted that on their heads.

"I think it would be very nice to stay with you, Mina. If my time in Nome extends to several days, I will seek you out."

Mina nodded, satisfied that Helaina was telling the truth. "Eat up. I have a cobbler waiting for your attention."

The next day Helaina was still remembering the sumptuous meal with Mina when she came face-to-face with Cheslav Babinovich, a Russian man she'd met the previous year. "Why, Mr. Babinovich, is that you?" she asked the frightened-looking man.

"Ah, dear lady. It is I." He glanced over his shoulder. "Your name escapes me."

"Helaina Beecham. We met last year when you were seeking assistance. I introduced you to Dr. Cox."

"Ah, I do remember you." He rubbed the back of his hand against his thick black mustache. "I fear the despair of the last few months has left me greatly distressed. I am no good at remembering much other than the terror being experienced by my dear czar and his family."

"I've heard things in Russia are quite grim where the royal family is concerned. Someone mentioned the royals have been imprisoned."

"It is all true." He moaned and turned away. "I am desperate to assist them. I fear they will all be killed if I do not negotiate their release."

"Can you do that? Can you negotiate with their captors?"

"If I have enough money," he said, turning back to face her. "Money is the only thing that speaks in my poor country."

Helaina watched as several men approached. Babinovich ducked his head against his coat and turned toward the storefront window, as if making himself invisible to their scrutiny. When the men were gone, he once again faced Helaina. "One cannot be too careful. Spies are everywhere. They will hunt down all of us with royal ties and see us dead."

"Who will?"

"The new government in my country. The Bolsheviks. But I mustn't speak of it. There is too much danger." He lowered his voice. "I have jewels to sell. But for now, if word got back to our enemies that royal jewels were smuggled out of the country and sold to help the czar and his family—well, just let me say heads would roll."

Helaina frowned. "I wouldn't want to be a part of that."

"But you might be interested in purchasing some of my jewelry?" he asked hopefully. "You are such a good woman, you surely could not stand to see the children left in the hands of such vicious people. The czar's daughters are quite beautiful, and little Alexi is such a dear lad. They have no doubt been horribly misused."

Helaina frowned. The man's story was quite compelling. "I suppose I might buy a few pieces," she found herself saying.

Babinovich nearly forgot himself as he reached out for her. He stopped before actually taking hold of her. "Oh, Mrs. Beecham, you have made me most happy. I am sure we can save them now."

Helaina arranged for the man to meet her in the lobby of the hotel later that day, then turned her attention back to her destination. She needed to know what had been done for the *Regina* and her men.

———

Latimore rallied as Jacob spooned hot coffee, heavily laden with sweetened condensed milk, into his mouth. His eyes were less swollen, and it seemed to Jacob that perhaps he was regaining his vision.

"Captain, can you see me?"

Latimore squinted. "Just a bit." His voice was hoarse and his breathing labored.

"Good." Jacob set the cup aside. "You've been quite ill. It's been nearly a week."

"You should have let me die," the man said matter-of-factly.

"And what good would that have done your son?"

Latimore frowned and looked away. "I have no son."

"Saying it doesn't make it true. I could tell you that we were not lost in the Arctic, but rather had been found and were even now enjoying the luxuries of a Seattle hotel, but it wouldn't be our situation."

"I am of no use to the boy."

"Not like this. But there was a time when the Captain Latimore I knew would have been quite valuable to any child."

"That man is long gone."

"I don't believe that. I think you've merely buried him alive."

Latimore looked back at Jacob. He narrowed his eyes, then started to rub them. Jacob prevented the action. "That won't help, and in fact it could do more harm. Do you feel like eating some duck? We've cooked one and have a nice broth that might suit your stomach."

Latimore shook his head. "Why are you doing this? You would get along just as well—if not better—should you let me die."

Jacob leaned back and folded his arms against his chest. "I'm not in the habit of giving up on people. You have a great deal to live for, despite your loss. You must stop deceiving yourself and see this. God hasn't allowed you to live without reason. You have a job to do, but you are avoiding it. Running away from your son is not going to give you the peace you crave."

The last remnants of Latimore's strong walls began to crumble. "But when I look into his face . . . I see Regina."

Jacob nodded. "I'm sure you do. But perhaps that will eventually prove to be a blessing instead of a curse. You mustn't forsake your son, Latimore. He needs you. Regina is gone and she has no earthly need, except that you care for the child she gave you. You must draw on your strength and return to him. You must."

Latimore shook his head. "I don't think I can. I'm too far spent—too sick."

Jacob grinned. "I'm not giving up on you, Latimore, and I refuse to allow you to give up on yourself."

Chapter Four

Leah watched her twins with a proud heart as they toddled around, exploring the new growth of wild flowers just beginning to bloom. Most of the snow was gone, but that didn't mean the storms were behind them. She knew that snows could come suddenly and without warning. They were always on their guard for such surprises.

"Come along, Wills—Merry," she called and clapped her hands together. The twins immediately took note and waddled toward her in their awkward baby way. "We're going to see Sigrid," she said, lifting both children at once.

Wills kicked his legs immediately, wanting to get down, while Meredith snuggled her head against Leah's shoulder momentarily. Today the women were working on the sealskins for the umiak. Ayoona was to have led the group, but now they would work without her. Oopick promised, however, they would tell stories about the old woman and sew to her memory. The idea of such a gathering encouraged Leah's rather raw heart. She longed for the comfort of her loved ones—of Jayce and Jacob. She missed Ayoona's mothering and wisdom.

Sigrid had offered to watch the very small children so the mothers could work unhindered. Several of the Inupiat girls would help her as well. It would keep the mothers from constantly having to run after their little ones, and it would keep the children away from the oily skins.

"Good morning," Leah called as she entered the school. Sigrid was already busy playing with some of the children.

"Oh, hello, Leah. I see you've brought me two more friends." Sigrid got to her feet and came over to take Wills. He immediately grunted and pushed against her to be put down. "This one's ready to play."

"He's always ready to play," Leah said, laughing. She put Merry on the floor, but the baby didn't seem inclined to explore further. She clung to Leah's leg and hid her head. "Merry, on the other hand, is probably ready to be rocked to sleep."

Sigrid put Wills down and reached for Merry. The child went hesitantly but didn't cry as Wills darted off across the floor to play with the toys and other children. Sigrid cuddled Merry and cooed to her softly.

"Will you have enough help?" Leah asked. She saw that two of the older girls were here to assist but wondered if that would be enough.

"I have another couple of girls coming. They're quite excited to help. Emma has promised them each a special gift. I'm not even sure what it is, but the girls were quite excited."

Leah nodded. "I'm sure Emma will make it special. She has a way of doing that."

Sigrid grew sober. "Has there been any word from Helaina or John?"

"Not yet." Leah tried not to let her disappointment show. "It's only been a short time, however. I'm sure they'll be back as soon as they have news."

"I know they will. They won't have you wait too long if they have word."

Leah drew a deep breath and let it out slowly. "Waiting has never been something I have borne well." She frowned. "I suppose it's a lesson I'm still learning."

"Well, hopefully the wait won't last much longer."

Leah could see the sincere concern in Sigrid's eyes. "I pray you're right."

Leah left the children and walked slowly to the community building. Glancing beyond the building, her attention was drawn to the sea. Glints from the water sparkled hypnotically, beckoning her.

Forgetting the women for the moment, Leah walked to the edge of the water. She gazed longingly across the surface to where the sky met the sea.

"You're out there somewhere," she murmured. The aching loneliness nearly sent her to her knees. How could Jayce be so far away and yet so close—connected by the very water that touched her shores?

Leah knelt and touched the Bering Sea. Maybe somewhere her husband was doing the same. Sometimes the days went by so incredibly slowly that Leah thought she might lose her sanity. Other days she was so consumed with the children or other people she had little time to mull over her situation. But in truth, her heart was in a continual state of breaking. Every night she went to bed lonelier than the night before. And each day Leah awoke to the harsh reality of her situation all over again, and every day it hurt just as much as it had when she'd first realized Jayce and Jacob weren't coming home for a long, long time.

She hadn't yet allowed herself to believe they wouldn't come home at all, however. She couldn't. The pain of that thought could not even be comprehended. Leah feared the truth—feared that they might never know the truth, feared that the truth might not be what she wanted to hear. It was a terrible dichotomy. Pushing an errant strand of brown hair away from her face, Leah straightened.

"Father, please bring them home. I cannot bear this burden much longer. My children need their father and uncle. I need Jayce to return. I need Jacob." She wiped at the tears that came. "I trust you in all of this, but, God, I don't understand why this had to happen. Things had finally worked out. I was still troubled by what had happened with Chase, but now . . . now I just want Jayce back. Those old wounds have healed, but these new wounds never will unless they come home. Please, God—I can't make it through unless you help me."

The women were seated on the ground already wearing waterproof gear when Leah arrived. She pulled on her own protective garments and took a place between Oopick and her daughter-in-law Qavlunaq. Emma Kjellmann sat across from them, laughing at something one of the other women had said.

She looked up and smiled at Leah. "I'm so glad you came. I wasn't sure if the twins would be well enough. I heard they were teething."

"They are, but today they seemed quite fit. In fact, so fit that they were running circles around me." Leah picked up a needle and pulled the oily skin closer. They were sewing several large sealskins together to make the exterior wrapping for the umiak. Skin boats were the life of the village; they would use this large open boat for whaling.

Leah used her needle with confidence. They would have to be very careful with their stitches in order to make the boat watertight. Leah had participated so many times in this ritual that she was actually more skilled than some of the native women.

"We were just discussing village news," Emma continued.

Leah nodded knowingly. These gatherings were always a place where the women shared news of their families and friends.

"Mary was just telling us about her family in Teller. They have had several deaths among the children. It sounds like it might be diphtheria."

Leah couldn't suppress a shudder. "I pray it isn't." She caught Mary's worried expression. "We will pray for your loved ones."

Epidemics were feared everywhere, but perhaps more so in remote areas. It seemed the villages were always dealing with one health issue or another. Sickness swept through uninvited, stealing away whole families. Last Chance Creek hadn't seen the likes of such for a while, but everyone knew it was just a matter of time.

Emma changed the subject. "It looks to me that there will be a large amount of wild berries to pick this summer. The bushes and ground berries are blooming in abundance. I think we would all do well to make special plans for canning and drying."

The women nodded, and so the conversation continued. Leah found herself only halfway listening to the comments. She thought of the short summer and how few months there would be before the ice once again made northern travel difficult, if not impossible. Would there be enough time for a rescue of her men? Would the government even approach the matter with any degree of seriousness?

Pressing her leather thimble against the needle, Leah caught Emma's announcement that she was expecting. "The baby is due in November, as best I can tell." She smiled proudly. "We're praying God will see fit to let this one come to us."

"That's wonderful news," Leah said. She knew how hard it had been on Emma to miscarry during her previous pregnancy. "I have lots of little clothes to share with you. Some of them are yours from before."

Qavlunaq smiled shyly. "I'm having another baby too. We will have them together."

"Congratulations," Emma said. "The baby is due in November?"

"Yes, the same time as you."

Leah tried not to seem upset or unhappy as the revelry of the other women resounded in the large open room. She was quite happy for her friends to expand their families, but at the same time it only served to remind her of her own circumstances.

"I promised Leah we would speak of Ayoona and her days here in the village," Oopick declared. She looked to Leah and nodded.

"Ayoona was a good woman." The other women nodded, including Lopa, Ayoona's other daughter-in-law. Lopa was the second wife of Seal-eyed Sam, Ayoona's elder son. She was not nearly as sociable as Ooopick, but she'd come here today with her seventeen-year-old daughter, Mary, as Mary and her betrothed were the ones who would receive the boat as a wedding gift.

"Ayoona taught me to do many things better than my own mother taught me. She taught me to make better stitches for sewing the skins. She taught me about forgiving others their wrongs," Lopa shared.

Leah knew the truth of that. Ayoona had been a woman of faith, and she had given Leah much encouragement during lonely and difficult times. Just weeks earlier Ayoona had told Leah that she shouldn't worry and cry over her man.

"God will bring him home when the time is right, Lay-ya. You cannot be tellin' God what to do."

The memory made Leah smile. *No, I can't be tellin' God what to do, but I can certainly try to persuade Him.*

"When Ayoona was a girl, she ran faster than anyone in the village. Her mother always told her not to run so much. She was afraid it would make the spirits angry. Ayoona told her mother that the spirits could not catch her, even if they were angry." Oopick smiled and added, "Her running was a blessing later, when she surprised a bear. Ayoona told me she was just seventeen and she was picking berries for her mother. A bear was there picking berries too. She said they were both so surprised they started to run. But they ran the same way. The bear wasn't really chasing her—he just happened to go the same way."

Everyone laughed at the thought of the bear and Ayoona. Leah pictured the old woman running side by side with the animal. Leah had no doubts as to who would win, although bears could outrun most people—at least in short distances.

Another woman shared a story about Ayoona dancing some of the village story dances. Leah listened as one after another told their stories and shared their love for the old woman. Ayoona would be sorely missed in the village—of this there was no doubt. But maybe more important, Ayoona had left a legacy of love and knowledge. She had taught every woman present something about survival in the village. She had helped deliver most of the babies these women had birthed. Ayoona was more than just a part of the village—she was the village. In many ways she had sculpted and molded the village to reflect her loving heart.

Later that afternoon Leah worked quietly in her house while the twins were sleeping. The last thing she expected was to hear a ruckus in the yard. The dogs were barking madly, as if something or someone had come into their territory. Leah took up a rifle and slipped out the front door and around the side of the house. Jacob's dogs were yipping and whining as if their master were home. Leah felt her heart skip a beat as she picked up her pace.

She crossed the yard and went to where Jacob's inne

stood. There, much to her relief and surprise, were Helaina and John. They'd just returned.

"I was coming over as soon as we secured the dogs," Helaina said, embracing Leah. "John bought several new dogs while in Nome. They're good, solid animals. I think Jacob will like them."

Leah cocked her head. "You have news, don't you?"

Helaina smiled. "Well, some news. Not exactly the news we want, but it's good. There's a revenue cutter already searching in the north for the men. I got word while in Nome, and we headed home as soon as we were convinced we'd done everything we could to aid the cause."

"Do they have any idea where the *Regina* might have gone?"

"Just what we've sent them and what the sightings encourage," Helaina declared. She pulled her jacket away from her body and shook her head. "I need a bath."

"Come to my house—your things are there anyway. I've got lots of hot water. I'll get more on the stove."

Helaina glanced at John. "Do you have everything under control?"

"Sure. Go on." He was a man of few words, but he was clearly happy to dismiss the women. "I'll bring those things you wanted after I get the other items packed in the store."

"It's flooded in the inne," Leah said. "Maybe you should just bring them to my place."

John straightened. "We never did before. Not much sellin' goes on in the summer, anyway. Not when the hunting is good. We'll be moving up north pretty soon."

"You make a good point," Leah replied. "Just do it the way we always do."

"I've brought home some new material. There was a nice shipment brought in just before I left," Helaina announced as they walked toward Leah's house. "I think you'll really like what I have."

"What I'd like even better is to hear everything," Leah said as she pulled Helaina along. "What did you find out? Was there any news at all?"

"There was one other report. Apparently a couple of Russian fishermen spotted a camp in the distance on one of their islands. The Coast Guard services feel confident that it will prove to be the men of the *Regina*."

"Oh, I pray they find them soon. Summertime is so fleeting in the Arctic."

Helaina nodded and followed Leah into her house. "They've been out working their way north even before the ice was gone in Nome. They may have had to wait it out here and there, but they're trying to reach them."

Leah heard the excitement in Helaina's voice and felt hope surge anew. "I pray they hurry. I can't bear to think of what those men have endured."

"But they're smart. Smart and strong and they trust in the Lord. At least our men do."

Leah smiled at the way Helaina claimed Jacob as her own. She prayed her brother's love for this woman had not faded over time. "You're right. It's been hard at times to remember that God has always known where they are—even when I didn't." The thought offered comfort for the first time in a long while.

"The twins are asleep in their room, but I'll have your bath ready in your old room. Go ahead and start undressing. There are fresh towels and soap in the drawer." Leah turned to go, but Helaina stopped her.

"They're coming home, Leah. I just know it."

Leah felt her enthusiasm. "I know it too. I feel sure of it now. Even if I didn't before."

Chapter Five

On the eighth of June the village celebrated the first birthday of Leah's twins, and the children reveled in the attention. Wills went from person to person, never staying very long in any one place. He appeared to enjoy being the life of the party and laughed and clapped so much Leah was certain he would wear himself out. Even Merry was more outgoing than usual. She smiled shyly and accepted the gifts and food people offered.

There were several native dances offered to honor the twins. Both twins tried to mimic the steps, causing the adults to laugh at their efforts. Leah thought it all quite nice, but she couldn't help thinking about how much Jayce would enjoy the babies. She wondered if he was safe, if he had food to eat. Here they were stuffing themselves on all sorts of goodies, and Jayce and Jacob might well be starving.

When would Jayce come home? When could their lives move forward together?

Time was passing by, but Leah felt as though she were frozen in place. Only seeing the twins grow from babies to toddlers proved to her that the calendar had truly changed dates.

The day after the birthday celebration, a large number of the villagers packed up their tents and supplies and migrated to the north. Many birds and ducks had been sighted, and the promise of eggs and meat other than seal and dried salmon beckoned. Leah had gone on several of these bird-hunting excursions and had been amazed at the proficiency some women had with a bow and arrow. In fact, she remembered a time when Qavlunaq had been just a girl of eleven and had wanted to prove to her father that she was capable of hunting as well as her brothers. She accompanied her family as they hunted and managed to climb onto a ridge where she waited for the geese. As they flew by she took her bow and arrow and shot the largest of the birds. Her father had been quite proud of her that day. Leah still pictured the little girl grinning proudly and holding up her goose. Now that girl was a grown woman with a child of her own and another on the way.

Two days after the first group of villagers headed off, another group prepared to go. John and Oopick were among those who planned to leave. A part of Leah wanted to take the children and follow along for the sake of company and something to do, if nothing else. But the hope of Jayce and Jacob being rescued and returning to Last Chance kept her in place. After all, what if they came home to an empty village, with no one and nothing to celebrate their survival?

The day dawned bright and clear, but by nine o'clock a heavy sea fog rolled in without warning. One minute Leah could see across the open sea, and the next she couldn't see more than ten feet in front of her. She was used to these fogs but hated them nevertheless. They were terrifying out on the open trail. Once when she and Jacob were returning from Nome, a fog came in fast and thick. Jacob had been wise enough to hold up and wait out the fog despite his knowledge of the trail, but Leah would never forget the isolated feeling of not being able to see. She kept expecting someone to reach out through the fog and grab them. Jacob, sensing her fear, had told her stories of Colorado and their childhood. Stories Leah had forgotten.

"The fog is bad," Oopick said, entering Leah's house unannounced. The village was like a large extended family, and no place was considered closed to them.

"Will you still go today?" Leah asked, pouring Oopick a cup of tea.

"John says we can wait until tomorrow. He sees it as God telling him to take more time." The older woman smiled.

"I'm glad you'll be here at least another day," Leah admitted.

Oopick took the tea. "It's not too late. You can come with us. You could return early."

Leah weighed the suggestion. "No. I wouldn't want them to come back and not have me here to greet them."

Oopick lowered her gaze. "It could be months, Leah. Maybe until the ice comes again. You . . . well . . . ." She took a long drink from the cup as if to silence herself.

"Oopick, you speak the truth, and that's never wrong. I've thought of the possibility that they won't be found until late in the summer . . . maybe not even then." Leah had to force the words. "Still, I want to stay. There will be a few of the oldest people here, and they may need my help. Plus, Emma and her family will be here. I just feel like it's the right thing to do."

"What's the right thing to do?" Helaina questioned, coming from the back room.

"Staying here instead of going north with everyone else."

Helaina exchanged a look with Oopick. "I think she's right. We'll be fine."

"I have a lot of good seal meat thanks to John and Kimik, and soon the salmon will run in full. I'll venture out to catch as many of them as we can get from the river," Leah promised. "You'll see. I'll have the drying racks full before you even get back."

Oopick smiled. "You always work hard. I know you will do as you've said, but we'll see who brings home more fish."

Leah grinned. "That sounds like a challenge. I accept." She knew Oopick and the other women would gather far more fish, but it didn't matter. She liked the lighthearted banter; it helped to put her mind on other things. "Besides, it won't be long and you'll be back. Don't forget we'll have a lot of berry picking come next month."

"We'll have good pemmican," Oopick said, nodding.

"Jelly and jam too," Leah added. "I've ordered extra sugar for just such things."

"John will like that. He thinks that's a good treat. He likes to spread jelly on the salmon sometimes." Oopick laughed. "I tell him he better be careful or he'll turn into a white man."

Leah had never known a white man to put jelly on salmon,

but she laughed nevertheless. So did Helaina, who quickly added, "I've never tried that, but maybe I will. Sometimes even the best food gets old."

"John says we'll come back to check and see if you have news." Oopick finished her tea and handed Leah the cup as she turned to go. "He wants to know about Jacob. I want to know too."

Leah nodded. They all felt the misery of not knowing the men's fate. John had been worried enough to consider a trip north on his own; it hadn't been that long ago that he had said he might put together a search party. Leah had almost encouraged it, figuring that somehow—some way—she, too, would go on the search. But then reality set in, and Leah knew it wasn't wise for either of them to try such a thing. There was no way for them to be sure where the *Regina* had ended up, and they might only find themselves stranded in similar fashion. And, of course, there were the children.

Leah knew she could never leave them that long. It was one thing to make a trip to Nome—that was quite far enough when facing a separation from the children she loved. Considering that a search team could easily spend all summer looking for the missing ship, Leah knew the role of rescuer did not belong to her.

Helaina had agreed, encouraging Leah to trust the government to go after them. She had further stressed that should the ongoing war in Europe keep the government from searching, her brother, Stanley, would arrange a private search out of Seattle or San Francisco. Helaina's healthy bank account could afford such a venture. This comforted Leah to some extent.

The fog cleared around two o'clock, presenting a beautiful landscape that looked as if it had been freshly washed. Leah decided to leave her napping children with Helaina while she went to gather some herbs on the mushy tundra hillside not far from their home. To her surprise, she found a ship docked out in the deep water. There were already launches heading into shore. She held her breath and watched—hoping, praying that Jayce and Jacob might be among the men coming to Last Chance.

Shielding her eyes against the light, Leah studied the forms as they drew closer. No one looked familiar, and given the way some of the men were holding up bottles, Leah knew her husband and brother would not be among their numbers. These were whalers who unfortunately added to their business ventures by selling whiskey to any native who would buy it. Leah turned away in disgust. She hoped Emma's husband, Bjorn, would dissuade the remaining village men from giving in to the temptation. Furthermore, she hoped he would encourage the whalers to move on.

Leah lost track of time as she searched through the vegetation. There were a great many plants that were useful to the village's medicinal needs. Leah often found that natives who were Christians sought her out to help with particularly bad cases. Others, who held no use for the white man's faith, went to their shaman. Ayoona had once told Leah that such superstitions were difficult to let go of when you had been taught all of your life that they were true. She told Leah to think of how hard it would be for her and Jacob, should someone come declaring that Christianity was wrong—that everything they'd learned all of their lives was nothing more than a collection of stories perpetuated by a group of people who were ignorant to the truth.

This single statement, perhaps more than anything else, had taught Leah great patience and tolerance in living with the Inupiat. She often remembered Ayoona's words and knew that it would be quite impossible for her to accept any other beliefs as truth. Why should it not be equally as hard for the natives of Alaska? Emma and Bjorn had agreed with such thoughts and told Leah that living an example of Jesus' love was the best way to encourage the people to believe. When the natives saw the hope and joy that the whites had in life—especially in adversity—they would become curious and seek answers. This had proved true over and over.

Realizing that she needed to get back to the twins, Leah gathered her sacks and started back down the hill. She had no idea what the time was but figured it was probably late in the afternoon. With the summer in nearly continual sun, it was always hard to gauge the time.

Leah heard her stomach rumble and was glad to know that she'd left a stew simmering on the stove before heading to her gathering task. She hoped that it would be an appropriate time to set a supper table and enjoy her efforts.

Leah reached her small catalogue house, smiling as she imagined Jayce's reaction when he set eyes on the place for the first time. The house seemed quite out of place in the village. Except for Emma's house, everything else was built partially underground in Inupiat fashion. The Kincaid house was a pleasant enough sight, but it did stick out as a rather strange anomaly on the seacoast. She knew Jayce would like it, but even this would pale in light of seeing his children.

His children. The old thoughts trickled back to haunt her. *Are Wills and Merry truly Jayce's flesh and blood? Why can't I just let this go? Why can't I just be glad for what I have and stop worrying about the past?* She shuddered and pushed the memories aside. There was nothing positive to be gained by remembering those terrible things. There was nothing good to be had in asking questions for which she could not give conclusive answers.

Wills and Merry were Jayce's children. That was all there was to it. Leah would not think of it any other way.

A ruckus on the beach drew her attention even as Leah climbed the steps that led to her home. A sudden chill rushed through her body. She set the sacks down on the step and felt herself inexplicably drawn to the sounds of men fighting.

Reaching the community building, Leah could see that several of the natives were drunk. These were good men—she knew them well, but liquor had clouded their senses. They were angrily raging at each other, and one man was waving a gun. She knew this wouldn't end well; someone would no doubt get hurt. The whalers with their liquor appeared to be nowhere in sight.

"Put down the rifle," John commanded as he stepped toward the man.

"He stole my axe," the man declared.

"He tried to take my wife," a man named Charlie replied. "I'm going to give his axe back—right in his gut."

"I didn't want your ugly woman," the man shouted in Inupiat.

Leah felt someone at her side and turned to find Oopick. They could only stand and watch the situation play out. Some

of the other native men joined in commenting on the situation, some taking Charlie's side, others taking the side of the
armed man.

"You got to put the rifle down, Daniel," John demanded.
"Somebody's gonna get hurt."

Then, as if John's words were prophetic, the rifle went off
with a loud cracking sound. Everyone fell silent as Charlie
grabbed his stomach and sank to his knees. He looked up,
then collapsed on the sand.

Leah put her hand to her mouth. To witness this awful
affair, a situation that might never have come about but for
the whiskey, was more than she could fathom.

"That's enough. Give me the rifle."

"You're gonna kill me." Daniel's eyes were wild with fear.

John shook his head. "No. I'm gonna take you and hold
you until the *Bear* shows up. When those government officials
come, then I'll turn you over to them."

Leah shook her head. There was no telling how long it
would be before the revenue cutter returned. Charlie's family
would return to the village for revenge. This could be counted
on.

"I won't go," the man said, leveling the rifle again. Before
anyone could do anything the man began backing away. "I
won't go."

John approached him, matching each of the man's steps in
equal pacing. "Come on, Daniel. You know it's the way."

"I can't. I won't." He backed up another step and stopped.
"You go on now, John, or I'll ... well ... I'll have to shoot
you."

John shook his head. "Don't do it, Daniel. They'll see you dead if you do."

"They'll see me dead anyway."

John reached for the barrel but had no time to push it away before the gun fired. Leah screamed and Oopick went running. The bullet hit John in the stomach. The big man didn't fall immediately; instead, he seemed to contemplate the situation as several men rushed Daniel and wrestled him to the ground. Oopick reached her husband's side just as his body seemed to register what had happened.

Leah was just paces behind Oopick. She'd thought at first that maybe John hadn't been struck, but when he fell to the ground she screamed, "No!"

Oopick knelt beside her husband, pulling at his clothes to see how bad the wound was and exactly where it was located. Leah helped her, forgetting the others around them.

The wound, located just six inches in from John's left side, bled profusely. Leah pulled off her *kuspuk* and pressed the soft cotton cloth against John's abdomen. "We need to get him home," she said, looking up. "Is anybody sober enough to help?" Her tone held great anger.

"We can help," several men announced in unison. They came forward to await instruction.

"We need to be careful with him," Leah commanded. "One of you will need to hold this cloth to the wound while the others carry him. Can you do that?"

The men nodded and Leah stood. Oopick was sobbing uncontrollably, reluctant to leave her husband's side. Kimik, her son, appeared and helped the men lift his father as Leah took hold of Oopick.

"Come on. There will be time for tears later," Leah encouraged. "Right now John needs us both." Oopick looked into Leah's eyes as if trying to comprehend her words.

Leah knew the next few moments would be critical. "Oopick, John needs us to keep him alive. Come along—we have work to do."

Chapter Six

T he ice is melted enough," first mate Elmer Warrick declared. "I see no reason for us to sit here and wait for a rescue that might never come."

Jacob shook his head. "It's very risky to consider heading out, not having any idea of where we are."

"We have a good idea that we're close to the Russian Territories," Dr. Ripley replied. "Not only that, but as the crew's physician, I have to interject my opinion on the matter. We all have scurvy in various stages. Our diet is so imbalanced that most of us are dying of malnutrition. Not to mention that the captain has developed trouble with his heart and Bristol is sporting three toes that we're going to have to remove tonight or see him dead in a week."

"We're all dying?" Matt questioned. He cast a quick glance at Jacob, as if to ascertain the doctor's truthfulness.

Ripley shrugged. "If not exactly, then we soon are to be.

Our bodies need a balance of vegetables and fruits. Foods that are obviously missing from our diet. Exposure to the elements is another issue entirely."

"But to head out without any idea of where we're going," Jacob began, "is risking death as much, if not more, than staying here."

"I agree with Jacob," Jayce said, looking to each of the men. "We have shelter here and enough food for the time being. I propose a compromise: Rather than just sit here indefinitely, what if we agree to remain here until July tenth? That will still give us plenty of time to head out and risk the open water."

The men considered this for a moment while Jacob posed a question. "Dr. Ripley, since you are concerned about the issues of our health, would this be an acceptable compromise to your way of thinking?"

Ripley rubbed his bearded chin. "That's not much more than a month. I suppose it would be acceptable. Although I will say that every day we wait, we grow weaker from our lack of proper nutrition."

"I agree," Jacob said, nodding. "Captain Latimore is a very sick man, even now. I know Ben and Travis are suffering a great deal as well." Those two hadn't been themselves since developing a bronchial infection two months back. "It's not my desire to keep any of us here a moment longer than needed. You must understand me on this point, if nothing else. I desire to be home as much as anyone here. I won't keep us here any longer than necessary. You have my word on this."

The men met his earnest gaze and one by one nodded in agreement of his words. Jacob knew their longing for home was strong—as was his own. He wanted nothing more than to wake up in his own bed and be among friends and family. The crew needed to see that he was just as connected to this goal as they were.

"Very well. We shall stay here until July tenth. If rescue hasn't come by that time," Jacob announced, "we will set out on our own."

He walked away from the group, feeling a mixed sense of frustration and relief. He was glad that Jayce had suggested the compromise but worried about what would happen if no one found them by the tenth of July.

"I hope you didn't mind my suggestion back there." Jayce came alongside Jacob and matched his stride. "I wasn't trying to usurp your authority."

"I'm glad you thought of it, Jayce. Someone had to come up with something to calm them down." Jacob stopped and looked back at the waters of the Bering. There was still ice here and there. A great many floes dotted the otherwise tranquil waters.

"They just don't know what they're asking for. I've been out there in an umiak when the village was hunting whale. It isn't easy even when you have healthy, experienced men who know the lay of the land and the currents. These are men whose bodies have been compromised by the elements and lack of proper food. They are weak, and their minds are not as clear as they need to be." Jacob turned back to Jayce. "None of our minds are working as well as they should. I found myself struggling with a column of figures this morning that normally would have been easy to add."

"I know what you're saying is true, but we can't give up

hope." Jayce pointed out across the water. "There are a lot of seals with pups out there. The fishing has been decent, and now that we've located the area where the birds are building nests, we can have eggs. All of these things will keep us alive and well fed, even if they don't offer the balance the good doctor wishes us to have."

Jacob shook his head. "My teeth are loose. My gums are spongy."

"Mine too," Jayce admitted. "So we have scurvy. It's to be expected."

"It'll kill us if we don't find better food or someone to rescue us."

Jayce shrugged. "We can't sit around worrying about it. Someday something is going to kill us. If we just dwell on it, we'll only manage to hurry it along. Frankly, I think we've come through Arctic winter in good order. I honestly believe help is on the way. We're going to make it."

"I can only hope and pray that we've gotten through the worst of the weather," Jacob muttered. "I know for sure we can't go through another winter unless we prepare."

"We aren't going to need to go through another winter," Jayce declared. "You agreed to the compromise. If rescue hasn't come by the tenth, then we'll head out."

Jacob tried to imagine making it back to Alaska. "Jayce, do you hear what you're saying? Do you understand the dangers and the near impossibility of such a trip with these sick men?"

Jayce grinned. "But you taught me that we serve a God of impossibilities. Are you suddenly changing your mind?"

Jacob sighed. He felt wearier than he'd ever been in his

life. "I don't know what I'm doing. I'm tired, and like I said, I'm not thinking clear. I think heading out will be death, but I can't blame them for wanting to get home."

"We all want to get home, but we need to make sensible plans," Jayce said, matching Jacob's stride. "We can do this, but as you've said over and over, we need to work as a team. If you desert us now, the team will fall apart."

"But what happens if no one comes for us by the tenth?" Jacob looked at Jayce without stopping, then just as quickly turned his attention back on the hill they were climbing. "Those men will expect me to produce a miracle. A miracle I simply do not have."

"Since when have you ever been in the miracle business?" Jayce asked sarcastically. "You aren't God, Jacob. Stop trying to be Him."

This caused Jacob to pause. He felt his anger rise as his hands automatically balled into fists. He wanted to punch Jayce, but just as quickly he calmed, knowing that Jayce had done nothing wrong. He'd spoken the truth. Jacob squared his shoulders and walked a few more steps to the ridge. "If no one comes, we will load up the boats and head out. But to where? To what? How will we make our way if the storms come? You can't ride out a late-season blizzard in an umiak."

"I don't have all of your answers, but we can pray and trust that God will send us what we need. If not a rescue ship, then surely Latimore can be of help. He's sailed the waters of the Bering before."

"If Latimore survives he might be able to offer some insight, but by his own admission, he has never been in this area. We may be in the Chukchi or even East Siberian Seas.

There's no real way for us to know."

At the top of the hill, Jacob sat down on a rocky outcropping. "I keep looking for a sign—something to tell me where we are. Are we on Wrangell Island or Skeleton Island or something else entirely? We found signs of that one camp, but we don't know that it had anything to do with the men of the *Karluk*. I was under the impression that some kind of marker had been left behind."

Jayce eased onto the rock with a bit of a moan. Jacob had forgotten that Jayce had twisted his back just days earlier as they wrestled a seal onto the shore. He seemed to still be quite sore, and that only made Jacob feel more guilty for his rapid ascent to the top of the ridge.

"How's the back?"

"It's better. Truly." Jayce added the latter as Jacob cast him a look of doubt. "I think a nice hot bath would help." He grinned. "Maybe a Turkish bath with steam and eucalyptus branches."

"And a soft bed," Jacob added.

"And Leah to give me backrubs." Jayce picked up a rock and gave it a toss. "I miss her more than anything else. I can't help but wonder what the little ones are doing now."

"They aren't so little is my guess," Jacob countered. "They're a year old. I thought of that the other day. If we've managed to keep proper records, then they've had their first birthday."

"I know. I realized that too," Jayce's voice was filled with longing.

"I've been doing a lot of thinking. When we get back . . . I'm leaving Alaska."

"What?" Jayce shook his head. "What are you talking about? You told me Alaska was in your blood—that you'd never leave."

"Helaina Beecham's in my blood too," he answered softly. He had her face emblazoned on his memory. "She's all I think about—she's all I really care about."

"But leave Alaska?"

Jacob leaned his arms against his knees. "She said Alaska was too hard for her. That life there was too isolated. How could I go seeking her as a wife, knowing that she'd only be miserable there?"

"But to give up your life for the love of a woman—that's kind of dangerous. You know it could spell trouble in the years to come. When things are hard, you'll blame her. You might even end up pining away for what might have been and come to resent her for taking you from all that you knew."

"I could never feel that way about her. Could you feel that way about Leah?"

Jayce sighed. "That's a bad question to ask me—or maybe I should say a good question. I'm the one who avoided a relationship with her not only because of her age, but because I figured she'd leave Alaska and I didn't want to. Even the summer before we married she was talking of going to Seattle to hunt for a husband. That put me at odds again. Would she really leave Alaska? Would she ever come back? I knew I would never have planned to be at odds with her if we married and she suddenly wanted to leave the Territory. Neither would you set out to feel that way toward Helaina, but it could come later in life. You have to be realistic about this and not just think about it with stars in your eyes and your heart all aflutter. You're talking about a life change that you would never consider for any other reason."

"But I love her," Jacob said softly, and in his heart he could only think of his need—of the emptiness without her in his life. "I was so happy when she came to believe in Jesus. Her anger and misery over the past was like a burden that weighed her down. She blamed herself for her family dying—for her husband's death. She carried that inside and it nearly killed her. She wanted only to be free, but she honestly believed it was her punishment—her grief to bear for eternity."

"Sometimes we torture ourselves with things like that," Jayce agreed. He shifted ever so slowly, and Jacob worried that perhaps his friend was in more pain that he'd let on. "Sometimes we choose to take on the responsibility of something when God never expects or wants us to."

"You mean like my leaving Alaska for Helaina?"

Jayce shrugged. "I mean only that you should be certain that it's the Lord's leading and not your loneliness. Once you make a decision, you will have a price to pay no matter what."

"I have prayed about it. I continue to pray. I've told God that if I get out of this alive, I'll do whatever I can to win her over."

"You told God, huh?" Jayce grinned. "What happened to asking Him what He wanted for your life? You used to tell me that was the most important thing for a man to do."

Jacob blew out a loud breath. "I know, and I'm not saying that I haven't *asked*. It's just that ... well ... the Bible also talks in Proverbs about making your plans and trusting God to direct you. I have to believe that the plans I'm making are

His direction. They seem right. They feel right."

"I'm not saying they aren't right," Jayce said, stretching to rub the small of his back. "I'm just cautioning you. Take it slow and really think things through. Otherwise you may be sorry. Sorry in a way that can't be fixed in a day or two."

Jacob thought a great deal about Jayce's words long after they'd returned to camp. He knew his friend was only concerned with his well-being. He didn't want to keep Jacob in Alaska for his own purposes or desires. He cared about Jacob like a brother and wanted him to make the right decision.

"But what is the right decision?" he murmured, glad to be alone in the shelter. He yawned and leaned back onto his pallet. With the worst of winter weather having eased, they had moved camp and set up new dwellings. The room around him had only recently been created using some of the boxes and tent canvas that they'd brought with them from the *Regina*. The doctor had thought this good for the health of everyone. Jacob had thought it good to keep them occupied.

Now he wrestled with what to do and how to do it. Jayce had offered wise counsel. Jacob felt that a lack of good food and decent living accommodations had left him addlepated at times. Could he even make the right decision?

The decision had to include Helaina, he told himself. If she wasn't a part of the matter—then his life wouldn't be the same.

But why would you want her if the Lord doesn't also want her for you?

The thought came unbidden, and no matter how hard Jacob tried, it wouldn't leave his mind. What if Helaina wasn't the right woman for him? Would he really want to impose her with a life of misery if he weren't the man for her?

Jacob fell asleep with these troubled thoughts. He pulled a seal fur around his body and over his head to block out the light. Somehow—some way—he knew God would direct his steps. He only hoped the path led him back to Helaina.

———

Jayce prayed for Jacob long into the night. Except there was no night. Not these days. The light in the sky at one in the morning might as well have been one in the afternoon. Jayce had been unable to sleep and had decided a short walk might help. But it hadn't.

"Couldn't sleep?"

Jayce looked up to find Keith Yackey. As was often the case, a Bible was in his hands. One of the rifles hung casually over his shoulder. It appeared to be his time at watch.

"I needed to pray. For a friend."

Keith nodded. "I'd love to join you. I can guard camp, watch for ships, and pray all at the same time. God will still listen even if I don't close my eyes."

Jayce chuckled. "I can be sure of that. I've prayed a great deal while pacing or driving dogs. I didn't close my eyes then either."

"I've been memorizing some Scripture," Keith told him. "I figured to go back to civilization with a big portion of the Bible memorized."

"And is it working?" Jayce asked.

"I've got most of the New Testament done. I'm working on Isaiah now."

"That's impressive." Jayce glanced back at the shelter. "I

have a friend who has a difficult decision to make. A life-changing decision. He trusts God, but this is a matter of the heart."

"Which always complicates matters," Keith added.

"Have you ever been in love?"

Keith laughed. "I still am. I have a wonderful wife and three beautiful children."

"You must miss them very much. I know I miss my wife and the twins."

"I knew you had twins. I heard Jacob talk about them. You're married to his sister, right?"

Keith's knowledge of his situation only served to make Jayce feel worse about not having gotten to know the man better. "Yes. Leah is Jacob's sister. She's an amazing woman."

"She'd have to be to live in Alaska."

"Where is your family?"

"California."

Jayce smiled. "Where it's always nice and warm."

"Well, most of the time," Keith admitted. "We have our storms and our problems, but nothing like this."

"Will your wife despair over what's happened?" Jayce asked cautiously. "Will she believe you to be lost—dead?" He forced the final word.

"Janessa? Never. She's not one to give up easily. That's one of the things I love about her. She has great faith and hope." Keith opened his Bible and started to say something more but was quickly hushed.

"You dirty rotten . . ." The sound of men fighting spilled into the peaceful moments Jayce had been enjoying with Keith.

Both men turned to look toward one of the other shelters. Bristol and Elmer were arguing about something. Then without warning Elmer raised a pistol and fired it over Bristol's head. Things had taken a deadly turn.

"What's going on?" Jacob asked as he came outside.

"I don't know," Jayce answered. Keith was already heading off to see what was going on. "It just started. Elmer fired the pistol at Bristol, but just over his head."

"I heard it. I thought maybe the war had come to us."

Another shot sounded. Jayce narrowed his eyes as Jacob checked his own revolver to make sure it was loaded. "Come on. We'd better see what this is all about."

Chapter Seven

Elmer! Bristol! What's the problem?" Jacob called as he approached. He didn't want to startle the men and have them turn on him, so he slowed his pace and tried again. "Elmer, put down the gun and tell me what's wrong."

"He said I was stealing. Called me a thief."

"You are a thief!" Bristol countered. He could barely stand due to his bad foot. "I saw you get into the food locker. You were taking what didn't belong to you."

"Food belongs to all of us. I went out on the last hunt and brought down the biggest seal. That ought to count for something."

"There's no call for using a weapon against a man. Not here. We're too few in number, and we need every man just to survive." Jacob kept a tight grip on his revolver. "Put the gun down, Elmer, and let's talk about this like civilized men."

"This ain't a civilized place," Elmer replied. "Neither is

he a civilized man. I don't see how losing my weapon will help the matter."

The other men had gathered by this time. Dr. Ripley rubbed his eyes. "I thought we were under attack. Are you men absolutely certain you wish to give me more work to do—under the circumstance?" He turned to Elmer. "Good grief, man. Have you actually lost your senses?"

"He accused me of stealing, and I ain't lost my senses."

Ripley shook his head. "Well, at least have the decency to shoot off those three bad toes if you have to shoot him at all. That way maybe I won't have to perform two surgeries." Bristol frowned, looking momentarily confused, but Elmer merely steadied his aim.

"Just put the gun down and we can talk about what happened," Jacob interjected.

"What happened," Bristol said in a heated manner, "is that he thought we were all asleep and went to help himself to an extra portion of food. He's a thief."

"Am not. I was just hungry!"

"Enough!"

Everyone turned to find Captain Latimore struggling to make his way to the two men. He pushed past Jacob and Keith and went directly to Elmer. "Give me that weapon."

"Uhh . . . Captain, I . . ."

"Hand it over now." Latimore stared at him hard. "We will discuss this in my quarters, but we will not be armed to do so."

To Jacob's surprise, Elmer handed the pistol over. Latimore turned to Bristol. "Come with me now." The younger man nodded, looking almost sheepish. He limped toward the captain.

Latimore headed back to his tent with the two men following behind. Jacob exchanged a glance with the captain as he passed. It was evident the episode had cost him every bit of strength. However, there was a look to his countenance that suggested he had regained the will not only to live but to take back his command.

After the men had disappeared, Jacob turned to Jayce. "It's good to see Latimore take the matter in hand."

"Yes. It's obvious the men have needed him."

Keith nodded. "He's a good man. A fine captain. I was sorry to see him so grief stricken, but perhaps now things will be righted." He walked away to join the other crew members.

Jayce turned to Jacob. "He's right, you know. If Latimore is able to rally his men, we may see positive spirits restored."

"I hope you're right." Jacob yawned. "I suppose for now we should head back to bed. We've had enough excitement for one night." He watched Keith pass the rifle to Travis. "They're good men—the demands of survival have been too much for them."

"God will see them through. Just as He'll see us through, Jacob. You know it's true. Rest in it."

———

Eight hours later, Jacob sat across from Latimore. The captain looked better than Jacob had seen him since the *Regina* went down.

"The problem is that the men do not have enough to keep themselves busy with. Do you have suggestions, Jacob?"

"I do, but you may be no happier to hear about it than they will be."

Latimore eased back against a pile of furs. "You'll have to excuse me; I still have great weakness."

"Please feel free to rest. We can discuss this another time."

"No. I think we should talk now. If Elmer were kept busy, I don't think he would be so fearful about starvation. You see, as a boy he was quite impoverished. He went hungry most of the time. It's haunted him into his adult years. He's not really a bad person, but his fears are causing him to make bad choices."

"I can understand that, but the men are angry about it. They feel he's cheated them of food that should rightfully be shared. Starvation is something we all fear."

"I am not making excuses for Warrick, merely pointing out the truth of the matter. I have confined the man to my presence when he's not busy with required duties. Which brings me back to that situation. My men are used to hard work. They need to have a purpose."

"We need to lay up food," Jacob said. "Between you and me, there is always the possibility that help will not come. A compromise was struck that we would leave the island on July tenth if rescue has not reached us. Still, whether we wait it out here on the island or take the umiaks and try to make our way back to Alaska, we will need food. The men don't seem to understand this or respect it. Well, perhaps I should say a few of the men do not see the merit. Some are quite cooperative."

"I will speak to them. Hunting and butchering are not their best skills, but they must do this for the sake of their own survival. Perhaps, too, if they see this as a goal toward leaving the island, they will be encouraged to help."

Jacob could see the wisdom in the captain's words. "We could also let them know that rescue may come in the form of the Russians or Inupiats. They will be much easier to deal with if we have something to barter in return—such as dried meat."

"That is a good point. I will mention it as well."

Jacob looked hesitantly over his shoulder before leaning toward the captain. "I cannot in good conscience say that I wholeheartedly agree with the plan to leave the island on our own if help fails to reach us. I did agree to the compromise, but it was very much against my better judgment."

Latimore considered this for a moment. "I know I've been a burden to you, Jacob, but you've always proven yourself to be a man of sound reasoning. I trust you to know best in matters of this Arctic survival. That said, how can we hope to exist another year in this environment? The winter has been cruel."

"You're a man of the sea," Jacob interjected. "You know the dangers out there in a large ship like the *Regina*. Imagine trying to survive a storm in one of the skin boats. We would perish for certain. The men are weak—most are suffering more than one affliction. Trying to navigate our way home would be difficult at best and deadly at worst."

"What would you want from me in the matter?"

Jacob thought for a moment. "I suppose I would like for you to override the decision regarding the compromise. You weren't there to put in your vote and you are the captain of this expedition. Now that you are recovering, the men will again look to you for decisions. You could explain that you've been apprised of the matter, but believe it lacks ... well ... sound reasoning, I suppose."

Latimore nodded and rubbed his bearded chin. The white, which had once dotted his hair and beard, now appeared quite prominent. "Let me think on the matter. It could be that it will resolve itself. If the time grows near and there is no sign of rescue, I will speak to the men."

"I hope so." Jacob knew he didn't sound entirely convinced.

Latimore looked at him for a moment, then cleared his throat. "About the rescue, Jacob."

"What of it?"

"Do you believe it will come?"

Jacob thought back to the time years earlier when the *Karluk* had disappeared. Everyone presumed they were lost forever. No one expected the men to actually make land and survive the winter. There were other ships that had gone missing as well. Ships that had never turned up. But then he thought of Leah. Leah would never let them go without a fight. She would believe the very best until proof told her otherwise.

"I believe there are people looking for us even now," Jacob admitted, wanting to be optimistic. "My sister is a determined woman. She will use whatever means available to seek our rescue. She won't give up—no matter how bleak it might seem."

"But you are concerned. I see it in your eyes and hear it in your speech."

"We don't know where we are. The searchers don't know either. They will have to cover a large territory in a short amount of time. The ice will freeze this area over in a matter of months—it might be even better gauged in weeks. Arctic summer forever holds a whisper of winter."

"I can imagine that to be true. Still, you speak greatly of the powerful effects of prayer. I presume you have been praying about our rescue as fervently as you prayed for my recovery." He smiled at Jacob's raised brow. "I heard you pray over me when I was in a barely conscious state. God has surely heard those prayers—why not the prayers for rescue?"

Jacob felt rightfully taken to task. "You are right. I have been rather faithless. It just seems the closer the time comes to what might be our salvation, the more despair I feel."

Latimore nodded knowingly. "It's rather like when I take to sea. If we pass far from land and spend many weeks isolated from our loved ones, I sometimes feel a sense of anticipation—even despair. There is always the lingering question of whether or not we'll make it back again. I suppose my despair has been greater on this trip than any other."

"But you had other circumstances to consider as well. Losing your wife, leaving your home and child—those are strong influences for any man."

Latimore shifted and crossed his arms against his chest. "I still find it difficult to imagine my life without Regina."

There was such a sorrow in his voice that Jacob thought he ought to change their focus of conversation. He'd opened his mouth to speak when Latimore interrupted. "Have you ever been in love?"

Jacob felt a dagger of pain pierce his heart. "Yes. I am in love."

Latimore smiled. "But you haven't yet wed?"

"No, the timing wasn't right." Jacob shook his head. "No, it was more that the place wasn't right. She hated Alaska."

"Hate is a powerful thing, but so too is love." The captain sighed. "Regina hated my being a sea captain. She said it took me away from her too often. That's why she sometimes traveled with me. She was miserable on my ship but happy to be in my company."

Jacob realized they shared more in common than either had suspected. He dared to ask, "Do you regret not having given up the sea for her?"

Latimore's eyes narrowed. "I regret that she died. I regret that she could not safely give birth to the baby she so loved. I regret that we didn't have more time. So I suppose in many ways, I regret not having given up the sea."

"Could you have been a good husband—a happy man—if you'd given up the life you loved for her?"

Latimore chuckled. "So long as she was in my life, I would have found a way to be happy. Sometimes love requires sacrifice. Often we're too blind to see that we can lose something seemingly important in order to gain something infinitely more valuable."

"'He that findeth his life shall lose it: and he that loseth his life for my sake shall find it,'" Jacob quoted.

"What's that?" Latimore leaned up as if the conversation had suddenly become quite important.

"It's a verse from the book of Matthew. The whole chapter is full of so many good things. Jesus is sending out His disciples and He tells them what to do and not do. He instructs them to be on their guard. He warns them of persecution when people hear the Gospel preached. He tells them not to be afraid of those who can only kill the body, but rather to fear God, who can destroy both body and soul. It also shows that Jesus knew His ministry would divide people."

"How so?"

"In the passage I was quoting, Jesus also says that if you love your father or mother, son or daughter more than Him, you aren't worthy of Him. He wants us first and foremost. It isn't that we can't have the other people in our lives, but we cannot put them first."

"As I did with Regina," Latimore said regretfully. "Perhaps that is why He took her. He is a jealous God, is He not?"

Jacob reached out and put his hand atop Latimore's. "I do not believe God is as cruel as that. He is a just and loving God also. People die, Captain. They are born and they die, and that is how it is in this fallen world of ours. I do not believe God would sneak in and steal your Regina away because of your love for her. But I do know that God wants our loyalty, our faithfulness. He wants us to seek Him above all others—first . . . always." The words comforted Jacob even though he had hoped to comfort Latimore.

He continued. "Sometimes we are called to lose the things we hold most dear. Obedience is sometimes painful."

Latimore nodded. "Indeed. It is no different than the child who must choose between following his own path or that of his father's instruction. One path may seem easier, quicker—but experience might tell him that the more difficult path will be better, safer, more fulfilling."

Jacob took the words deep into his heart. What path was God sending him on where Helaina was concerned?

"It seems you are contemplating weighty matters," Latimore said before falling back against the cushion of furs.

"Perhaps too weighty for me to impart any wisdom that would be of use."

"You've already helped me more than you realize," Jacob replied. "I'm glad to have you back. I'll pray for your continued recovery. The world needs more men like you."

"Perhaps not so much the world," Latimore replied, closing his eyes, "as one little boy."

Chapter Eight

John hovered near death for days. Leah and Oopick worked together to help his body mend, but he'd lost a lot of blood. Fever and infection had been their biggest concern, and both had come with a vengeance. Leah knew their herbal remedies were good ones and that her own training was useful, but still she wished they had a doctor and a hospital.

"If John were stronger, I'd suggest having Kimik take him to Nome," Leah said, looking up to meet Oopick's and Kimik's fretful gaze. "But the trip would kill him. I feel certain of it."

"I think we should get the shaman," Kimik declared. His defiance toward God had been building since the shooting. "My father deserves to have the care he's always known."

"Kimik," his mother began, "you know your father no longer believes the old ways. I cannot go against his wishes, even if he cannot speak them now."

"Your father believes in God's ability to help him," Leah

offered. "God would not want you to yield to superstition. Put your faith in God, Kimik."

"God didn't keep my father from getting shot."

"Neither did God shoot your father," Leah countered. "Whiskey caused another man to do that. If you want to do something positive for your father and this village, then convince the men to keep whiskey out. It's not supposed to be here—so why not make a stand to enforce the law?"

"She's right, my son." Oopick put her hand on Kimik's shoulder. "Your father would not want you to lose faith in God. He believes that God is powerful. He believes God loves us all."

"Letting him get shot isn't very loving. Why would God let this happen? Why would He not protect someone who loves Him?" Kimik sounded like a frightened boy instead of a grown man.

Leah felt sorry for her friend, knowing how hard it was to keep faith in the face of adversity. Hadn't she asked these same questions regarding Jacob and Jayce's disappearance?

"Kimik, who are we to question God? He does not think like we think. Your grandmother would tell you to clear the mud out of your ears and listen to what God tells you. He will not forget you. He has not forgotten your father."

Leah saw tears come to Kimik's eyes, and she longed to comfort him.

"I hate this," Kimik finally said. Anguish was replaced with anger. "God is not fair. He is not merciful. If He were, my father would not be dying." He stormed from Leah's house.

"I am sorry for Kimik's words," Oopick said. She reached for a rag and began to wipe her husband's brow. "He felt such sorrow over Ayoona's passing. I think he's afraid that same sorrow will come if his father passes."

Leah mixed a bowl of herbs that she would use as a cleanser for the wound. "I think it's fear that overwhelms him right now. Fear often makes me angry." She pulled back the poultice they'd put on a few hours earlier and surveyed the wound. "It looks better." And it did. Much of the inflammation was gone, and the swelling had lessened. "Let's clean and dress this side, then see how it looks on the back side."

The bullet had gone completely through John's abdomen. Leah could only pray that it hadn't caused problems with his internal organs, for there was no possible way she could perform the surgery necessary to heal that kind of injury.

Once the wound was redressed, Leah looked at the clock. "I'm going to get some rest. You should too." Earlier she'd set up a small bed for Oopick right alongside John. "I also want to see the children."

Oopick nodded. "I will rest. I will call for you if something happens. You have been a good friend to John—to me."

Leah smiled and went to embrace the older woman. "I love you both so much. You are like family to me. I couldn't bear to lose either one of you."

Oopick's brown-black eyes swelled with tears. "You are my family too."

Leah wiped her eyes and stretched as she left the dark quiet of the room she'd given to Oopick and John. Helaina was there to greet her, as were the twins.

"Ah, there's Mama," Helaina said, pointing Wills in the right direction.

Merry had already spotted her mother and came running. Wills joined her just in case there was something of interest. Leah dropped to her knees and embraced them both.

"How is he? I saw Kimik storm out and feared the worst."

Leah met Helaina's concerned gaze. "John's actually doing better—at least in my estimation. The wound seems less infected. The fever is nearly gone. I see those things as positive signs of healing."

"Has he regained consciousness?"

"Only for very brief moments. Oopick wanted to keep him sedated as much as possible so that the wound would heal. We're worried about how much damage that bullet did internally. There's a possibility it managed to miss the most vital spots, but on the other hand, it could have injured a great deal and we'll never know it until it is too late."

"I'm sorry. I know this must be very frustrating to you." Helaina began to pick up around the room.

"You have been a great help to me," Leah said. Merry toddled off to play with her doll, and Wills seemed oblivious to everything but the new puppy Leah had allowed them to have. She thought it would be wise for the twins to have a guardian—especially for those times she couldn't be everywhere at once. Champion—so named because she hoped he would take that role on behalf of the twins—was nearly the same size as Wills. Champ seemed delighted to be the boy's playmate; the two were already inseparable. Merry was afraid of the dog at first, but even she was warming to their new companion.

"As I bathed them last night, I thought about how it would be to have my own children. I imagined a home of my own and . . ." Helaina fell silent and turned away to pick up a towel that had somehow fallen to the ground.

"That day will come, Helaina. I'm sure of it. You'll have a family all your own."

"If that's what God has for me." Helaina turned and shook her head. "But what if it's not? What if Jacob—"

"Don't say it," Leah said, holding up her hand. "I couldn't bear to hear it right now."

Helaina gave her an odd look. "I wasn't going to say what you think. I was merely suggesting that it's possible Jacob will return and have no feelings for me."

Leah let out a sigh of relief. "I'm sorry. I'm just so tired of the unknown. So many people asked me over the winter and now into the summer, 'What will you do if they don't come back? What will you do if they're found dead?' I just couldn't stand the thought of hearing it again."

Helaina came and put her arm around Leah. "I know, but that's one question I will not ask. They are coming home. I know they will."

"I just can't stand the waiting. And now the only person who might have taken me to them is lying wounded in my spare room. It's just more than I can bear." Leah felt tears slide down her cheeks. "I feel as bad as Kimik. He was questioning why God would let this happen to his father, and I feel no different. I know God must be so disappointed in me. Where's my faith? Where's the peace that passeth understanding?"

"Leah, we all have our times of doubting and discouragement."

Leah pulled away. "But I know better. God has proven himself to me over and over. It seems I never learn. Why can't

I just understand and accept that whatever happens, happens. That He has been in control all along and that I need not fear the future."

Helaina drew a deep breath and sighed. "I keep reminding myself the same thing. But, Leah, even Jesus, knowing what His purpose was in coming to earth, asked to be let out of it."

Leah thought about that for a moment. "That's true. He even knew what the outcome would be—and still He died for me."

"And rose again," Helaina replied. "I know you're discouraged, Leah. I am too. I know it may seem I'm being strong and accepting, but it's been so hard. I believe they'll come home safe and sound. I don't know why I believe it, but I've never been more confident of anything. What I don't know is what Jacob's heart will feel for me once he gets here."

"I know he loves you," Leah offered.

"Maybe. But adversity sometimes changes people."

Wills ploughed into Leah's legs and laughed as though it were a special game. Champ was right at his side. She looked at her son and saw the startling reflection of his father's face staring back up at her. "That's what I'm afraid of," she whispered. She lifted Wills into her arms, and for once he didn't try to flee. Instead he took hold of her face, almost as though demanding she see him for who he was. Champ whined for a moment, then went to check on Merry.

"I sometimes get so afraid that they aren't his children. I try not to think that way, and most days I'm all right. But I keep wondering what if he's decided that they aren't his? What if all this time he's been pondering the situation and has decided that the twins are from Chase?"

"You can't dwell on that. You know this. We've talked about it over and over. Leah, it doesn't matter. They're your children first and foremost. Your flesh and blood. You cannot worry about anything more. Jayce loves you and he loves the twins. He won't deny them—not even after this long separation."

Leah gently touched Wills' hair. "But he hasn't been here to watch them grow—to love them and know them. He hasn't endured their tearful nights or sicknesses, nor enjoyed their sweetness." Wills let go of her face and snuggled against her in uncharacteristic fashion. He seemed to sense her need for comfort.

"You worry about whether or not Jacob will love you, but I have the same worries," Leah admitted. "What Jayce has endured may have changed him. I have to accept that possibility."

"That's nonsense. Has it changed your heart toward him?" Helaina asked, putting her hands on her hips like a scolding mother. She cocked her head to one side. "Leah Kincaid, you know better. This is just the devil trying to get the better of you."

"I suppose you're right. I'm so tired right now it makes no sense to even try to have a proper conversation." She looked up and smiled. "I'm sorry to be so gloomy. Is there anything to eat? I need to sleep, but I also need food. I feel as though I haven't eaten in weeks."

Helaina laughed. "I have a nice caribou steak for you. With that are some fried potatoes."

"Potatoes?" Leah's mouth watered. They hadn't seen potatoes in so long.

"Whiskey wasn't the only thing the whaler brought us. I

secured these for us. The natives might not miss such things, but I do on occasion."

Leah ate while Helaina prepared her tea. Once the cup was in front of her, Leah knew she wouldn't last much longer. She took a long drink of the warm liquid. "Thank you for all of this. I suppose I should go rest now."

"You do that. I'll save this for you," Helaina said, picking up Leah's plate. "Your appetite will be stronger once you get some sleep."

Leah nodded and got to her feet. "Call me if anything happens with John."

"You know I will."

Helaina watched Leah head off to rest. She admired Leah like no other woman. She could easily remember their first encounter and Leah's kindness. Later, however, Leah had wanted nothing to do with her. She'd resented Helaina's interest in her brother and blamed Helaina for all of them having to risk their lives in the wilds.

Helaina felt they were only right to blame her. She had known their forgiveness and God's, but she wasn't sure she'd fully accepted that release. So much had changed in her life these past years, and now the one question that continued to haunt her was the one thing she couldn't answer. Not until Jacob came home.

"Either he loves me or he doesn't," she told herself. "If he loves me, then all is well. And if he doesn't . . ." She felt a wave of despair wash over her. "If he doesn't . . . then . . ." She thought of her words to Leah and smiled. She had to take such negative thoughts captive. "If he doesn't love me still, then I shall make him fall in love with me all over again."

Chapter Nine

July brought beautiful sunny days and a healing in John that gave new hope to Leah. With John on the mend, Oopick insisted they move out of Leah's home. Kimik set up a tent at the beach for them. He seemed less angry with God, but Leah worried that a barrier remained between him and the God of his father. Kimik's wife, Qavlunaq, helped Oopick, freeing Leah to focus her attention on her family. Unfortunately, that caused her to feel an overwhelming sense of grief as the days continued to pass without word from Jayce or Jacob.

July also brought a letter from Karen and Adrik. They were coming with their children to be with Leah for as long as needed. They had been so upset to learn of the *Regina's* disappearance the year before. Adrik, Karen wrote in her letter, had nearly loaded up a sled and team to reach Leah across the interior.

"'He still thinks himself a young man,'" Leah read aloud from the letter. "'Of course, our rather rowdy boys are good at reminding him he is not.'" She grinned. "I know how that goes. Wills and Merry leave me exhausted most days."

Helaina motioned to the letter. "Does it say when they intend to leave or arrive?"

Leah read on. "She says they'll leave at the end of June. That means they should be here soon. No telling what kind of storms or fogs might have slowed them down, but even so, it's already the eighth."

Helaina got to her feet. "I'll pack my things and move back to the old place. The flooding isn't that bad, and I could always use one of the tents. That way you'll have the extra room for them."

"I hate to have you go. We can surely just fit everyone in."

"No, I think it's better. I go there to take care of the dogs anyway. Besides, I like it there."

Leah laughed. "Good thing, too, since you may call it home for a good long while."

Helaina paused at the door. "I'd love nothing more."

————

The salmon run proved to be abundant. Leah spent her free time catching as many salmon as possible and drying them for winter. Each evening they enjoyed fresh salmon for supper and even managed to have a few early bog blueberries.

Leah kept as busy as possible, knowing that this would help the time to pass more quickly. She read the Bible every day, washed and mended, played with her children, and helped with the dogs. She hunted for eggs and berries and caught salmon to provide for their needs, and she managed to work with Helaina to see the store had the supplies necessary for winter.

There was a great deal to do, but while this occupied her hands, Leah had to force her mind to be otherwise engaged. It was so easy to dwell on what she didn't have instead of focusing on what the Lord had given.

Karen and Adrik arrived four days after their letter. With their baggage and crates sitting on the beach, Leah offered them a quick tour of the village on her way home.

"It's a very small village, as you can see for yourself, but the people are very efficient. Some of the people have moved off to Teller or around Nome, but those who have stayed are just like family."

Wills seemed in awe of Karen and Adrik's boys. He didn't run ahead in his characteristic manner but rather kept pace with the older boys, laughing and babbling as if he were giving the tour in his own way.

Leah looked at Karen's children and shook her head. "I can't believe how you've grown. Why, you're nearly grown men."

"I'll be thirteen on August eighth," Oliver declared proudly.

Christopher frowned. "My birthday doesn't come 'til December."

Leah laughed. "We'll have to celebrate enough for both of you. I doubt you'll be here on your birthday, so maybe we can pick a day and celebrate ahead of time."

Christopher perked up and looked to his dad. "Could we?"

Adrik seemed to consider the matter seriously for a moment. "Well, I don't know."

"Please, Papa. Please!"

Adrik finally couldn't keep the stern look in place. Laughing, he answered, "I don't see any reason why not. I'm always game for a party."

Merry seemed quite happy in Karen's arms. "She's so beautiful. Wills too. You must be so proud of them."

Leah nodded. "They are truly a blessing."

"A blessing out of sorrow," Karen murmured. "How like God to give such a special healing."

Leah considered Karen's words. She was still haunted by the question of their parentage and whether or not Jayce would love them, but she often forgot how much they had helped her to focus on the future. Of course, they were also bittersweet reminders of the past.

"I can't believe how big they are. I wish I could have seen them sooner."

They came to stop in front of her home. "This is it," Leah said.

"This is quite the house, Leah. You say you ordered it from a catalogue?" Adrik asked.

"Yes. All the parts and pieces came on a ship. It was quite an ordeal putting it together." She leaned toward the man. "We had an amazing number of pieces left over and have no idea where they go."

Adrik let out a powerful guffaw. "Well, it seems to be holding up well enough. I especially like the way you've built it up on pilings."

"Jayce learned about it from some men who had experience with houses in Boston, of all places. Apparently they've reclaimed some of the land closest to the ocean, and to build on it, they've put the houses on pilings. It's more complicated than that, but it caused Jayce to start thinking, and this is what he planned."

"But he wasn't here to build it?" Karen questioned.

"No, but he had left drawings. John and some of the others worked together and figured it all out. Anyone who says the native people are ignorant can't possibly have spent any time with them."

"I certainly agree with that." Adrik had not only spent a good deal of his life around the Tlingit people of southeast Alaska, he was part Tlingit.

"The house has been harder to keep warm, of course," Leah continued. "The people build into the ground around here for a reason. When the winds come up, we get a good chill. I think we'll have to insulate better, but I like not living underground. It was the one thing I could never quite get used to. I always felt buried alive."

"When will the villagers come back?" Karen asked. She put Merry down to play with the others.

"I've heard that the hunting has been good. Some have come back to set up drying racks and such. Others will wait until August. The berries around here look like they'll be abundant, so many will want to be sure and get in on that. The village people are so good about helping each other. Like with us—Helaina and I can't very well hunt seal for ourselves, and that is a staple of our diet out here, as well as a mainstay for clothing, oil, and such. John and his family have always been good to supply us with our share. Same with the whaling.

The men will bring me my portion. They know they can count on me to trade store goods that the ships have brought me. We have a good system here."

"It definitely seems that way. Nevertheless, the boys and I will do our best to help out while we're here," Adrik said, looking around.

"How long can you stay?"

"As long as you need us," Karen said softly. "If things . . . well, if the worst should happen . . ." Her voice trailed off. She lifted her eyes to meet Leah's gaze. "You always have a home with us. You know that, don't you?"

Leah nodded and offered a weak smile. "I know that." She wanted to maintain her composure, but just having family with her once again made Leah feel weepy.

"Where are your trees?" Christopher asked.

Leah immediately turned her attention to the boy. "They all blew away. At least that's the story I've heard the natives tell. The winds from the sea blew so hard that they blew all the trees to the east."

The boy shook his head and looked at the open landscape with disapproval. "It doesn't look very pretty this way. I'd miss not having trees."

Leah surveyed the treeless landscape. "I do miss them from time to time. I remember living with you in Ketchikan and the tall firs and pines. Oh, the aroma was heavenly. I'll never forget the long walks in the forest. I always felt so protected there."

Wills and Champ wandered over. "Eat, Mama," Wills said, pulling on Leah's skirt.

Leah nodded. "I would imagine everyone is starved.

Helaina has been cooking for us, and lunch is likely ready. Why don't we go inside?"

Christopher helped carry Merry, while Leah took Wills by the hand. Champ seemed excited and happy just to be included and bobbed along at Leah's heels. Inside, the delicious aroma of salmon and vegetables filled the air.

"Oh, I nearly forgot," Karen said as they gathered around the table. "We brought several crates for you."

"For me?" Leah's surprise was evident. "You certainly didn't need to do that."

"We wanted to. We didn't want to just show up empty-handed, but we also had gifts we wanted to bring just for the fun of it—including some new books for you."

"Books? How wonderful." Leah had seen very little in the way of new reading materials since the twins were born. Not that they would be very fond of letting her read. Leah struggled just to find quiet moments when she could read her Bible.

"The boys and I will go down after lunch and bring them up," Adrik said, rubbing Oliver's head in a good-natured manner. "You should just see how strong these boys of mine are. They can be good help."

"I'm sure." Leah helped Helaina finish setting the food on the table.

"I've already eaten," Helaina announced. "I'm going to head over to the store and tidy up."

Leah looked at her oddly. "No, stay with us. You're practically family."

Helaina shook her head, and Leah noted the sorrow in her eyes as she whispered, "Practically isn't good enough." She hurried from the room before anyone else could question her.

"What was that all about?" Karen asked as Leah took her seat between the twins.

"She's in love with Jacob. She gave up everything and came back here, hoping that he would return that love—which I'm confident he'll do. However, she's feeling quite uncomfortable right now. She knows you will remember her past and what she did to Jayce and the trouble she caused."

Karen helped mash some vegetables for Merry while Leah did the same for Wills. "But that's all in the past. Surely Helaina knows we won't hold the past against her. Not when she's sought forgiveness."

"Eat. Eat," Wills declared.

"I think she's reminded of the shame," Leah said, handing Wills a cracker to still his ranting.

"Maybe we should bless the meal," Adrik said, joining hands with his sons. Leah and Karen did likewise with the twins. Adrik prayed thanksgiving for the food, for their safe journey, and then asked God's hand to be on the missing men of the *Regina*.

"Amen," they murmured in unison after Adrik ended his prayer.

Before Leah could say anything, he picked up their conversation as though it had never been interrupted. "We all have things in our past that we're ashamed of. Helaina is no different. I'll talk to her after we've eaten. Maybe she just needs to know we don't hold her a grudge."

––––––

"Oh, these fabrics are wonderful!" Leah held up a bolt of blue flannel. "This will make nice warm shirts."

"I thought the same when I saw it," Karen replied. "And look at this. Sturdy canvas. You could make all sorts of things with this."

Leah noted the dark-colored cloth. "To be certain."

"I brought you some of my preserves and jellies," Karen said, reaching into one of the other crates. She pulled some straw packing out and with it came a jar of dark liquid. "I even made some syrup for flapjacks."

"I still have the sourdough starter you gave me," Leah said proudly. "It's amazing to be making bread and pancakes from starter over twelve years old."

"It's older than that now—at least the original piece was. I brought it down with me from the Yukon." Karen pulled one jar after another from the crate. "I think they may have all survived. Adrik was so meticulous in caring for this crate. He wouldn't let anyone else touch it."

"This is certainly generous of you. It feels like Christmas."

"Well, it's not over yet." Karen pulled off the pried top of another crate. "I made a few things for your new house." She took out a large, thick quilt. The squares were done in shades of blue, yellow, and white. It was quite bright and lovely—like an Arctic summer day.

"Oh, it's . . . it's beautiful." Leah touched the corner in amazement. "I've never seen anything so pretty."

"There's no sense in not having pretty things. A gal needs them now and then. So what if you have to put a fur underneath it to keep warm enough? Better yet, just snuggle up closer to Jayce when he gets home." Karen's blue eyes seemed to twinkle in amusement. For a woman who'd just turned fifty in May, she was amazingly young at heart.

"I also made clothes for the children," Karen said as she reached into the box again. "I knew you would make plenty, but it was just so much fun. It'd been ages since I'd had any reason to make such tiny things."

"Maybe Ashlie will marry soon and you'll have grand-children."

"That's always possible. She's having a wonderful time in Washington. She thinks she might like to become a nurse. Wouldn't that be grand? To have her return to the territory and help sick folks?"

"What if she doesn't want to return? Does she still talk about roaming the world?" Leah inspected the little dress Karen had just handed her. "Your stitching is always so per-fect."

"Ashlie loves the city. She's told me that many times. But she also talks about the things she misses most about home. I know there's a part of her heart that still belongs in Alaska."

"Are there any romantic possibilities?"

Karen handed Leah another outfit, this one for Wills. "She's attending a school for young ladies, so there aren't any young men on a regular basis with which to have conversa-tions or outings. However, church seems to be another story. There are a great many young men there who have been quite intrigued with her. They have a regular Sunday school class for her age group, and apparently there are far more boys than girls."

"It wouldn't be so bad to meet the man of your dreams in church," Leah said with a smile.

"Not at all." Karen winked. "Maybe even better than

meeting him in the wilds of the Yukon."

"Or Alaska," Leah countered.

———

"You sure hurried off at lunch," Adrik said, coming upon Helaina as she worked with the dogs. She'd donned an old pair of Jacob's work clothes and tucked all her hair up under a cap.

She wasn't surprised to find him there, but apprehension filled her. "I thought you all deserved time alone. I know it's been a while since you had time to visit."

Adrik leaned against the birthing shed and studied her for a moment. His gaze made Helaina uncomfortable. "I'm keeping Jacob's dogs." She offered the information as if he'd asked.

"Leah tells me you're very good with the animals. That Jacob trained you the summer she and Jayce came to stay with us."

"Yes. I had to earn my keep," she said with a small smile. "I don't mind at all, however. I love the dogs."

"Love Jacob, too, as I hear it."

This startled her. "I . . . uh . . ." She turned away, hoping she wouldn't say something stupid.

"It's all right. I think it's great. Leah tells me that Jacob is in love with you as well."

"She doesn't know that's true anymore," Helaina said, lifting a can of fish entrails. The foul smell was something she'd never quite gotten used to, but every time she had to deal with it, she reminded herself that she was doing it for the man she loved.

"Jacob isn't a fickle man. If he's given his heart to you, you can rest assured that he won't be changing his mind."

Helaina put down the can and straightened. Turning, she braved a glance at Adrik's face. She found only compassion there. "I know you must think me a horrible person, Mr. Ivankov."

"Call me Adrik. And, no, I don't think you a horrible person."

"I caused your family so much trouble. For that I'm sorry."

He smiled and moved toward her. "You're forgiven, even if you don't believe it."

"I believe God forgives, but I know it's hard for others. Especially when great pain was inflicted. So many suffered because of me. Lives were threatened, and . . ." She fell silent, thinking of Leah's rape.

Adrik surprised her by taking hold of her hands. "It might be hard to forget the past, especially for some. But when Jesus lives in your heart, you need to forgive and forget. The Bible says God forgets, even for His own sake. If it's good enough for God, it's good enough for me."

Helaina bit her lower lip to keep it from quivering. She felt like collapsing in Adrik's fatherly arms and crying like a baby.

"You don't have to worry about whether we can accept you as Jacob's wife," Adrik said softly. "Truth is, Jacob is a wise man, and if he loves you, that's good enough for me."

"But that's just it," Helaina said, tears spilling down her face. "*If* he loves me. He's been gone for a long time. The last time he saw me he didn't make any promises or pledges. He didn't speak wonderful words of love. How could he love me? He let me go."

"He let you go *because* he loved you. What good would it have done either of you to have him declare his love and press for your love in return, when he knew you couldn't stay here in Alaska?"

Helaina studied his face for a moment. He seemed to know everything—no doubt Leah had been open with her family about Helaina's presence in her life. It only took Adrik's letting go of her hands and opening his arms to her to finish breaking Helaina's pretense of strength. She fell into his arms and sobbed.

"I just want him back. Even if he doesn't love me. I just want him back."

Chapter Ten

I t's already August." Ben Kauffman wasn't one given to
elaborate shows of emotion, but the anger was evident in
his voice.

"We did as you asked, Captain," Travis added. "But we
have to make plans now to leave this island and get back to
civilization."

The other men quickly agreed. Jacob knew they wouldn't
be satisfied to remain on the island, yet the idea of heading
into the open waters was daunting. No one wanted to be home
more than Jacob, but he wanted to get there alive.

The captain rubbed his bearded chin. "Look, men, I know
how you feel. I, too, long to be with my family and loved ones.
I would like a more palatable fare for my meals and a bed of
down instead of fur. However, we have to be sensible about
this matter."

"Indeed we do," Dr. Ripley said, taking a step forward.

"Sir, I respect your command, but as you know, we already have two sick men. One is injured and in desperate need of more attention than I can give him here. The other has some kind of sickness that I do not even understand. I seriously doubt either one will live much longer. Not to mention we're all sick from lack of proper diet. There's not a man here who isn't suffering from scurvy."

"And well I know it, Dr. Ripley. However, would you put weakened men into boats and send them out on the water without hope of reaching their destination? Should we desert the sick men—leave them here to die?"

"Why do you speak without hope when referencing our attempt to leave by boat?" Ripley countered.

"Because I see very little hope for us if we head out wandering around the ocean. First of all, as weak as the men are, they'll be no match for the strong currents that flow in this area. Second, we won't stand a chance if a storm should come our way, which of course we can count on experiencing. These northern waters are always volatile."

"Better to take our chances and leave this accursed island before winter sets in than to suffer another year here," Ben muttered.

Jacob felt it important to back the captain's position. "We have two small umiaks, but none of you are familiar with the use of such boats. We used them to haul goods over the ice and little else. I'm very familiar with the umiaks, and yet I wouldn't begin to feel comfortable taking them out on the water with the purpose of trying to navigate the Arctic Ocean or the seas that might take us home."

"Then stay here," Travis said flatly.

"Men, we need to work together," Captain Latimore said sternly. "What we need is more driftwood for our warmth and cooking. We also need to work on sewing those skins. We need to ensure that we have proper warmth against the chilling nights. Even if we can work out a way to take the boats and leave the island, we will need to be prepared."

The men grumbled but said nothing that could really be heard. One by one they wandered away to go about their duties, but Jacob could tell it would only be a matter of time before they mutinied, and then what?

"I'm sorry about the trouble, Captain," Jacob said as the last of the men left them. "I know this is hard on the men. I wish I had a simple solution. I had hoped we would be rescued by now."

The captain picked at his well-worn jacket. "The men are right to feel a sense of desperation. They sense the change of weather. They know what's coming."

Jacob nodded. Just then Jayce came into view. He'd been off hunting and carried several ducks. They'd make a good meal to be sure.

"Captain, if you feel confident that we can navigate the ocean, I'm willing to reconsider the matter," Jacob said turning his attention back to Latimore.

"I will think on the matter and speak with the men. I see value in looking at all sides of this issue."

"As do I," Jacob replied, though he was uncertain whether he'd go along if the men decided to leave the island.

Jayce crossed the distance and held up his catch. "They're nice and fat," he said, tossing them down on the ground.

"It'll be a good change. Maybe duck has better nutritional

value than seal," Jacob said with a shrug.

"When I was atop the hill I saw you had the men gathered," Jayce said, pulling the shotgun from his shoulder. "What was that all about? Nutritional values?"

"The men are restless." Jacob lowered his voice lest they be overheard by anyone other than Latimore. "I fear it will be mutiny if we can't find some way to give them hope."

"How are Bristol and Elmer?" Jayce questioned.

Bristol had been gravely ill after a wound he suffered while skinning a seal had become infected. Now the doctor was certain he would die. Elmer's ailment left the doctor with the same conclusion, although he had no real understanding of the disease that was slowly killing the man.

"Bristol isn't good. The doctor says he's gone septic. It's just a matter of time. He's been unconscious all day. Elmer isn't much better. He's in hideous pain. His abdomen is distended and feels warm to the touch. Dr. Ripley gave him a good dose of cocaine in hopes of easing the misery, but I don't see that it's helped much."

"Pity. The poor men have nothing to comfort them. They must surely realize the situation." Jayce looked toward the dwelling where the sick were being kept. Latimore readily shared the shelter with the sick, but the other men had crowded into one place to avoid having to face anyone's mortality.

"I guess I'd best get to work fixing these ducks," Jayce said, tossing the shotgun to Jayce. "There's still plenty of daylight for more hunting."

Jayce nodded. "I think some time alone would do me good. Maybe God will give me some answers."

He moved out across the land, following the shore to the east. Sometimes things just didn't make sense. He truly believed that all things happened for a reason—that God didn't just allow His children to go through situations for no reason. Of course, Jacob also believed that some things just happened because life was . . . well . . . life. There was no way to keep the natural course of living from happening. Jacob had known there was a risk when he took this expedition north. There were enough horror stories to keep any sane man from making such a choice.

"But maybe I'm not all together sane," he mused aloud. Surely a sane man wouldn't have let the woman he loved get away.

Jacob had been considering what he needed to do once he returned to Last Chance. The plans rolled through his mind once again. He would need to sell the dogs. Jacob couldn't imagine a life without the dogs; the past year had been incredibly lonely without his favorite companions. But at least he didn't have to worry about them. No doubt John would take most of them and would see that the animals were well cared for.

Jacob stopped and looked out across the island he'd called home for all these long months. It wasn't such a horrible experience. In fact, it had proven to him that he could endure most anything. And in his mind, that included leaving Alaska forever.

"If that's the price for Helaina's love," he said with a sigh, "then it will be worth the sacrifice."

_____

They were starting to have a few hours of actual darkness, for which Jacob was grateful. He drifted into a fitful sleep that night, praying and pleading for God's intervention on their behalf.

Send us a rescue ship, Lord, he prayed. *Send someone soon to take us home.*

It seemed he'd barely closed his eyes when something caused Jacob to bolt upright. He wasn't sure what had awakened him. Nothing seemed amiss. Jayce slept not far from him, his even breathing evidence that he was alive and well.

Jacob strained his ear to hear anything else. One of the men would be on guard duty watching for ships and protecting the camp against animal attacks—especially bear, although without the vast stretches of ice for the bears to utilize, there were fewer and fewer on the island. Still, they couldn't let down their guard. A polar bear could swim over fifty miles without resting. John had told him this—had experienced it himself when a bear followed after him once. John had only had his small kayak, and the bear seemed determined to do him in. John had finally harpooned the bear and brought him home for food.

Jacob listened again for any sound that might indicate a problem. Then it dawned on him: Perhaps one of the sick men had died in the night and Latimore had found it necessary to draw the man out of the shelter. Whatever it was, something wasn't right. Jacob pulled on his boots. He needed to see what was going on in camp. Maybe it was nothing—but on the other hand, maybe it was a problem that couldn't wait until morning.

"What's wrong?" Jayce asked groggily.

"I don't know. I just have a strange feeling. It woke me from a dead sleep."

Jayce sat up, yawning. "Wait for me and I'll come with you." He threw off his fur covering and reached for his own boots. "Did you hear something?"

"I don't know. I was sound asleep, but something woke me up. I can't say that I heard anything at all, but I just feel like something is happening." He crawled to the opening of their shelter, with Jayce right behind him.

Outside, it was already getting light. Streaks of a sun on the southeast horizon showed the promise of a beautiful day. The camp was quiet. . . . Maybe too quiet. Jacob looked for the sentry but found none.

"Who was supposed to be on guard duty?"

Jayce suppressed another yawn. "I think it was Matthew."

"I don't see him anywhere." Jacob walked a few steps across the way, careful to avoid a stretched-out seal hide.

Jacob scanned the beach in both directions, but the man in question was nowhere in sight. Then it occurred to Jacob that something else was missing. "Where's the other umiak?"

"What?" Jayce looked at him oddly. "The other umiak?"

"Yeah. Look for yourself. There's the one we used to help make the shelter for Latimore and the sick men. Where's the other one?"

"Well, it was on the beach, last I knew." Jayce followed Jacob to where the boat had once been. There were clear markings to indicate it had been dragged toward the water.

"They've gone." Jacob felt a sickening sensation settle over him.

"Surely they wouldn't just load up and leave us here,"

Jayce said. "The captain wouldn't let them do that."

"The captain probably had nothing to say about the matter. He was on our side, remember? My guess is that he's still sleeping with the sick men." Jacob walked toward the shelter where the others would have been. One look inside confirmed his worse fears. "They're gone."

"Guess we should wake up Latimore and let him know what's happened."

Jacob straightened and shook his head. "Might as well let him sleep. There's nothing we can do at this point." Dread washed over him in waves. Dread for the men who'd gone, as well as for those left behind.

"They're completely ignorant of what they're facing," Jacob murmured as he went back to bed. "They won't make it."

"Dr. Ripley no doubt encouraged it. Those men were good about following Latimore unless Ripley got them stirred up."

"I'm sure Ripley had something to do with it, but the men were already eager to go. I'm sure it was a mutual decision. Just as I'm sure it will be a mutual disaster."

Three hours later, Latimore met Jacob and Jayce at the campfire. Jacob was working on sewing fur coverings for his well-worn boots.

"It's just as you said," Latimore confirmed. "I looked through the tent and everything of personal value is gone."

"They also took all of their furs and a good portion of the meat stores," Jayce said, looking up to meet the captain's grim expression. "They're thinking to make it back to the mainland, but I don't see that happening. They're too in-experienced."

"Indeed. For many it was their first time working on board a ship. They had little real knowledge of the sea. There's not a man among them who could navigate by the stars. Only Elmer was good at that, and he's here with us." Latimore eased onto a makeshift seat while Jayce poured him a cup of tea.

"They left us a few supplies. Probably knew it would be murder to do otherwise."

Latimore took the cup. "I'm sure they meant us no harm. I pray they make it to safety."

Jacob stretched out his feet. "I wouldn't give them much hope. It would take God's direct intervention, as far as I'm concerned. I would believe we would have a better chance walking out over the ice this winter to Siberia than trying to navigate the waters ourselves."

"I'm going to take some of the seal broth to Elmer and Bristol," Jayce announced. He lifted a tin can from the edge of the fire and got to his feet.

Once he was gone, Jacob's anger replaced his shock. "Those men considered no one but themselves. Their com-rades lie sick—even dying—and they desert them."

"Jacob, everyone has their breaking point." Latimore shook his head. "Those men would not have acted as they did had they any hope of rescue or enduring the days to come. I'm also very certain Dr. Ripley influenced them. The man has given me no end of grief in trying to persuade me to change my mind about leaving. I place this event at his feet."

"Jacob, Captain, you'd better come. Bristol passed on in the night, and I don't think Elmer will be long in following."

He was right. An hour later they were faced with the task of burying two men. Jacob knew the permanently frozen ground would make burial difficult. They finally devised a place by scooping out the earth as best they could, then piling rocks atop the two dead men. It hardly seemed a fitting end.

Jacob's rage burned. He didn't know which made him angrier—the fact that the other men had deserted them or that he hadn't been able to prevent it from happening. *There should have been some way for me to stop it. Some way to persuade them from leaving. Now they'll die. They'll all die.* He shuddered at the thought of the men forever lost to the icy depths of the Arctic Ocean.

Jayce opened the Bible and began to read aloud, but Jacob hardly heard the words. *How dare they leave us to this?* The isolation of their circumstances seemed to overwhelm Jacob all at once. Somehow with nearly a dozen men on the island things hadn't seemed so bad. With just the three of them, however, Jacob felt as though they were the last men on earth.

"Jacob, would you like to pray?" Jayce asked.

The words startled Jacob. "Pray? I've been praying. I've prayed without ceasing since we were marooned on this island. Pray?" He'd had enough and walked away. If he didn't get away by himself, there was no telling what he might say. He certainly didn't want to take out his anger on Jayce or Latimore.

He stalked up the hillside as he'd done a thousand times before. Often he'd gone to the top to seek solace, other times he'd gone for information. The perch had generally afforded him a clear view for as far as he could see to the east and south, as well as a good portion of the west. Only this time he had no interest in the view.

"Wait, Jacob." Jayce followed after him.

"It would be best to just leave me to myself, Jayce. I'm not good company."

"Maybe not, but I think you need a friend. Even if it's just a silent one."

Jacob stopped. "I don't see how decent men could make the choice those men made last night. They would have to know we stood a better chance together than apart."

"They made a mistake. Dr. Ripley influenced the younger men. It's sad and may very well end tragically for them, but I don't believe they meant us harm. Just as Latimore said, we knew them to be good men overall."

Jacob let out a growl. "Being good men hasn't fixed our circumstances. I don't know what God wants from me here. I trust Him to bring us through. I believe in His power to provide, despite our failing health. I just don't know what more He wants from us."

Jayce nodded. "I know exactly what you mean. I've asked Him that very thing over and over. I don't know why I should have to spend a year away from my wife and children. Children whom I don't even know—who don't know me."

Jacob softened at this and the anger left his voice. "I know. I'm sorry."

"We've both endured a great deal, but we've known God was with us every step of the way. It's not like I understand the circumstances of our situation, but the alternative is not an option for me. I can't turn from God, even in this."

"Nor I." Jacob's voice was filled with resignation. "I've never even contemplated that, but in my anger I've known a sense of separation from God that troubles me deeply. I don't want to be filled with rage—it serves no purpose. Still, I don't understand why this situation goes on and on."

"I don't either, Jacob. But I do know that we must continue to trust the Lord."

"I know that as well. It's just hard to face the possibility of another winter here—apart from Leah and Helaina. It's hard to contemplate whether we'll be strong enough to survive."

"Jacob! Jayce!" Latimore called to them.

Jacob put his hand to his eyes and squinted against the brilliant sun. "What is it, Captain?" The concern about predatory animals caused Jacob to give a quick glance over his shoulder.

"A ship!" Latimore called again. "There's a ship on the horizon!"

Chapter Eleven

L eah slung her rifle over one shoulder and hoisted two large buckets of blueberries. The day was unseasonably warm, but the sun felt good against her skin. Lifting her face to the sky, Leah breathed in the heady aroma of sea air and spongy tundra. She loved her life here, but the longing would not leave her where Jayce was concerned.

"It's already August," she whispered. "Already August and they've still not returned." The likelihood that they'd be found yet that summer was fading quickly. Soon the ocean would start churning with ice and the temperature would drop. Ships seldom went very far north after October. Some captains refused to venture to the Bering after mid-September.

Karen and Adrik had suggested that if the men were not found, Leah and the children should come back with them to Seward. If that didn't appeal, Leah could take up residence in their cabin at Ketchikan. After all, she was familiar with the area and people. It might offer her comfort.

But nothing offered her comfort these days.

Leah was no fool. She knew the odds of finding the men before summer's end was lessening with each passing day. Winter would soon be upon them, and she had to face the facts.

She headed down the hill with the buckets in tow. At the base, a small wagon awaited her. Leo and Addy, Jacob's two favorite dogs, were at the helm. Leah put the buckets in the wagon, then went to the dogs. She took a moment to pet them. They missed Jacob as much as she did. For weeks after he'd left home, they'd done nothing but howl and whine.

Straightening, Leah sighed and released the wagon's brake. She was some three miles from home, but the dogs would make short order of the distance. The buckets had packed easily into the small wagon, leaving room for Leah if she chose. She decided against it, however, knowing the walk would do her good.

On their way, Leah made up her mind. If the men had not returned by the time Adrik and Karen felt it necessary to head back to Seward, Leah and the children would go with them. The twins would have better access to a doctor should they grow ill, and Jayce and Jacob would know to look for her there. It just made sense.

Up ahead on the trail, Leah saw Adrik hiking toward her. It seemed perfect timing to announce her decision. "What are you doing out here?" she called.

"Looking for you. Karen was worried and the twins were asking for you."

Leah laughed. "They're always asking for me." She drew up even with Adrik and slowed a bit, knowing there was no sense in delaying her announcement. "I made up my mind to return with you and Karen and the boys if the men haven't returned by the time you head out."

"I think that's for the best," Adrik replied, his voice low and gentle. "I know it isn't easy to consider them not coming home."

"I have to be realistic about the matter." Leah looked up and met his gaze. "They may never come home. I've not been willing to truly consider that matter until now. Helaina has always been so strong—so sure that they're returning, but . . ." Her voice trailed off as she remembered her father leaving for the Yukon gold fields. He had promised to return as well. Then Jacob had headed north, and had they not gone after him, Leah would probably have never seen him again.

"But the summer is fading and winter's chill is in the air," Adrik said.

He had always been a very eloquent man, despite his back-woods upbringing. Leah smiled. "Yes. I know that I have to be sensible. The twins must be safe and have the things they need. The winters are harsh here and without a man to help care for us, it will be even worse. So many times we've faced famine and death. Disease runs amuck and epidemics aren't at all unusual."

"You can face those things in Ketchikan or Seward as well," Adrik interjected. "Although I will say famine has never been an issue. That land is so plentiful with meat and other vegetation."

"And the harbors don't freeze," Leah added. "We could

always get a shipment of needed goods, even in the dead of winter."

"True enough. Well, you know how we feel on the matter. We want to make you comfortable and Karen loves those babies as if they were her own grandchildren. I guess in many ways, they are exactly that."

"Yes, they are. I've always seen you and Karen as a second set of parents. God provided abundantly for me in my loss. Karen has been a mother to me in every way, and you . . ." She paused and drew a deep breath. "You've always been a father, offering security and strength. A kind of strength that I could not find in other people—with the possible exception of Jacob and now Jayce."

"I've always cared deeply for you and Jacob. You know that. I promise you, Leah, I will see you and the children amply provided for. I know Karen will enjoy your company, but even more than that, she'll be glad to know of your safety under her roof." He gave a chuckle. "You know my wife. She thinks she's the only one in the world who can care for her loved ones. It makes her positively impossible at times when she considers Ashlie living so far away."

"I'm sure it does, but Karen waited so long for a family of her own. I know how that feels. You tend to want to hold on to your children and never let go. It isn't easy. The twins are barely a year old, and yet I cringe with fear at the thought of them wandering out of sight. I can make myself ill if I dwell on all the risks at hand."

"Life is a risk, Leah. But the alternative is to die. Still, we need not fear either one. God is our strength, our help. He

won't let us down. Even when it seems He's forgotten us—
He's still there."

"Like now." Leah halted the dogs. "I try to have a strong
faith, but honestly, I think God must find me terribly disap-
pointing."

Adrik smiled. "I have said the same thing on many occasions. Darling, there is no easy walk on this earth. Oh, some
folks seem to have a better way—a gentle existence—but they
all face loss in some way. Faith wouldn't be faith if it came
easy. Abraham had to stand over Isaac with a knife before his
faith was fully born. Abraham learned a big lesson that day.
He learned that he could trust God even when the situations
around him made no sense. He learned to have faith that even
when God was calling him to a frightening new place, he could
rest in God's perfect faithfulness."

"I want to rest there too," Leah admitted. "I suppose
that's why I decided to go back with you. I'm not doing it
because I've given up hope. But rather, it seems the best choice
given the circumstance."

"I agree. I want to know that you and the children will be
safe. The people here are good to you, but the long winter is
going to be difficult to endure."

They walked a ways in silence before Adrik posed another
question. "What of Mrs. Beecham?"

"I hadn't really considered the matter much," Leah said,
shaking her head. "I doubt she'll leave. But then, she doesn't
have children to worry over. She can stay in my house if she
chooses to remain here."

"Or she can come with us. We wouldn't deny her a place

to stay. It would be a squeeze, but there's always room for one more."

Leah was deeply touched by Adrik's generosity. "I'll talk to her and let you know. I know she's been waiting for me to make up my mind. I guess now that I have ... well ... she'll have to make up hers as well."

———

With August, the long hours of summer light began to fade. Helaina wondered how she would ever bear the long dark winter if Jacob didn't return. She had prayed for his return and thought of it—dreamed it so realistically that she had to stop upon awakening in the morning to rethink what was real and what was her imagination.

Now summer was nearly over and the ships were heading south again. There'd been no word from any revenue cutter or the Coast Guard service. She longed to know the truth, even if the truth was painful and sad. Still, there was no word. Stanley wrote to tell her that no effort was being spared to locate the men, but still her heart was heavy.

Helaina heard Leah humming softly in the children's room. She was putting her babies to bed and offering them whatever comfort and peace she could. Leah had decided to go back to Seward with Karen and her family, but Helaina felt bound to Last Chance. When Jacob came home, she wanted to be here to greet him. She had to be here.

"Well, I think they're finally asleep," Leah said as she came from the children's room. She stretched and rubbed the small of her back. "I need to get outside and work on that sealskin.

Seems the work is never done." She reached to pick up several toys that were on the table.

"I'll go take care of the dogs," Helaina volunteered. She got to her feet and dusted off the front of the lightweight kuspuk she wore over bibless denim overalls.

Leah paused at the door. "Do you really plan to stay?"

Helaina nodded. "I can't go. I need to feel close to him, even if it's just to care for his animals."

"It may take a long time before they come home."

"I know," Helaina said, meeting Leah's gaze. In the air hung the unspoken phrase, *If they ever come home.*

Leah shrugged, as if realizing it would do little good to try and talk Helaina out of anything once her mind was made up. "I'll be just outside if you need me."

Helaina made her way to where the dogs were staked and housed. They began to yip and howl at her appearance. They had come to accept her as their mistress and tried hard to please her. All through the winter they had performed for her as well as they had for Leah. They seemed to understand her love for them was somehow bound to their missing master.

"Hey there, Toby," she called, reaching to rub her hands over the blond-brown fur of the first dog. "How are you?" He whined in reply.

She gave attention to the first row of dogs, then gathered food from the locker and began to feed them. The other rows of dogs put up a huge fuss, believing themselves somehow slighted.

"I'm coming, fellas," she called.

She made the rounds and saw that all were fed, watered, and given due attention. There were three new batches of puppies, and Helaina checked on each of the new mothers, scandalously giving them each a nice chunk of seal liver from a new catch. Leah had told her that Jacob liked to do this for the nursing females to enrich their milk supply. Helaina could see no reason to do otherwise.

Working to clean up the grounds around the pens, Helaina was surprised when she looked up to find Leah standing not six feet away. She laughed. "I didn't hear you come up. I guess my mind was elsewhere."

Leah looked pale, almost as if she'd had bad news. A sense of dread washed over Helaina as she stopped her actions. "What is it? What have you heard?"

"Sigrid just came to the house. There's a cutter in the harbor. Word has come that it's the ship that went searching for the men of the *Regina*."

Helaina swallowed hard. "What of the men?"

"I don't know. There's a launch coming ashore. Sigrid's offered to stay with the twins. Will you come with me?"

"You know I will!" Helaina tossed down the shovel. "Let me wash my hands." She hurried to where a pail of water sat perched atop an overturned washtub. Without a word Helaina washed and then dried her hands, while shaking so hard she could hardly hold the towel.

"If they didn't find them . . ." Leah began, then halted.

"We can't worry about ifs right now. Let's go see what the truth of the matter might be. Then we can make our plans."

They hurried to the beach where a crowd of people had already gathered. Many of the villagers had returned from hunting, and there were a variety of things happening. One group had managed to bring in a whale, but without the icy shores to help slide the mammoth creature along, they were forced to pull the beast ashore by using dogs and manpower. No doubt most of the people assembled were there for the purpose of helping with the whale kill rather than to greet the cutter.

Leah pulled away from Helaina and put her hand to her forehead to shield her eyes from the setting sun. It was hard to see who the men in the launch might be, but when Helaina heard Leah gasp, she knew Leah had spotted someone.

"Who is it?" Helaina asked, but already Leah was running for the beach.

She watched from afar as Leah splashed into the water. She could hear the people shouting, but it all seemed again like one of her dreams. Moving very slowly, Helaina began to walk again toward the gathering. A man was climbing out of the launch—jumping into the knee-deep waters of the Bering Sea. He waded through until he reached Leah's outstretched arms. It was Jayce.

Helaina felt her breath catch as the couple embraced. She backed up several steps until she was hidden from view by the head of the newly caught whale. Helaina preferred to remain out of sight until she could calm her overwhelmed nerves.

Lord, what will I do if Jacob hasn't come back as well? How will I live if he's returned but no longer cares for me?

She peeked around to see that Jayce had lifted Leah and was carrying her to shore. It was the stuff of fairy tales and beautiful love stories. It was the happy ending that Leah so richly deserved. Helaina stepped out and moved toward the crowd of people. She had to know that Jacob was safe, if nothing else.

And then she saw him. The launch settled on the shore, and the men disembarked. Jacob was there, along with several other men. This was her moment of truth. This moment would determine her future.

Helaina eased her way through the crowd just as Jayce put Leah on the ground. Jacob immediately embraced his sister. Helaina fought to keep from crying, wishing he were holding her instead. *Please love me. Please still care.*

She stepped forward, inching her way toward the trio. Drawing a deep breath, she straightened her shoulders.

Just then Jacob looked up. Shock registered on his face as his gaze met hers. He immediately left his sister and crossed the distance to where Helaina now stood. For several moments neither one said a word. He looked at her so intently that Helaina felt as though he were memorizing every feature of her face.

"It took you long enough to get here," she finally managed to say. She gave him a smile as her joy threatened to bubble over.

"If I'd known you were here waiting, I would have come sooner," he said. Then without warning he pulled her hard against him and kissed her soundly on the lips.

The despair, frustration, and agony of the last year's wait faded from Helaina along with all reasonable ability to think. She felt the warmth of his hands on her face, and he deepened his kiss. When he finally pulled away, she could only look at him in wonder.

"I can't believe you're here," they murmured in unison, then laughed.

"When did you come back?" Jacob asked, his hands moving to gently touch her shoulders.

"Last year this time. I sold everything I owned and returned to Last Chance."

"Just like that?" he mused. "You traded your life there to be here?"

She shook her head. "No. I traded it all to be with you." She waited anxiously to see how he might respond. For a moment he said nothing, then he dropped his hold on her and took a step back.

"Are you sure about this?"

Helaina put her hands on her hips. "I've had a whole year to think it over." Her tone was rather indignant, but he deserved it after what he'd put her through.

Just then Bjorn and Emma joined the revelry. "Jacob!" they exclaimed before Bjorn pulled him into a hearty bear hug.

"We're so glad you've returned. Praise God for His provision!"

Emma nodded and added her own embrace. "*Ja,* Jacob, we have prayed every day for you."

"And well I know it," Jacob answered, casting a glance over their shoulders to Helaina. "Because God has just answered all of my prayers."

Chapter Twelve

The village used the men's return as a wonderful excuse to celebrate. Before long there was food and drink, as well as singing and dancing. Leah woke the twins, who, although irritable at first, adapted rather easily to the revelry. They seemed particularly interested in their papa, who happily tossed them up and down in the air and got on the floor to play. Gone was any worry that they might reject him. To Leah's amazement, they warmed to Jayce immediately.

Jacob and Helaina seemed completely engrossed with one another, although since the homecoming they had not had a moment to themselves. But Leah knew her brother. He would find a way to get Helaina alone. And if he didn't, Helaina would. It was clear that Jacob's feelings for Helaina were as strong as ever. Leah couldn't help but notice the way her brother's gaze never left Helaina, no matter where she was in the room. Leah felt the same way about her husband. She watched him so intently most of the evening, she was certain he felt her gaze boring right through him. If he minded, he never said as much.

It was so hard to believe they were really home. What had seemed like a never-ending nightmare had come to a conclusion with so little warning, that the matter seemed . . . well . . . almost common. Sailors returning home from the sea. Nothing more.

Leah longed for time alone with Jayce. She wanted to hear his stories and know what he'd gone through. She wanted to know the bad as well as the good, for it was an entire year of his life that she didn't share. She knew there would be time enough for them to be alone, but selfishly she wanted to put the children to bed and find a quiet place to curl up in Jayce's arms. She could only wonder if he felt the same. He seemed so content just to play with the children. Had he lost his passion for her? Had the experience left him with a changed heart?

"I can't believe how big they are," Jayce declared as he lifted Merry and came to sit beside his wife.

Leah watched their daughter tug at Jayce's beard, laughing and babbling all the while. Despite her shy nature, Merry seemed to take easily to her father, even though she scarcely knew him. Wills was no different. He rammed up against Jayce as though they were old buddies and shouted over and over, "Play."

"They were just little bundles when I left," he said, gently stroking Meredith's brown curls.

"It's been a long year," Leah murmured. She met Jayce's eyes and knew he understood.

"Yes. Much too long."

"If I can have everyone's attention," Bjorn announced, "I would like to offer a word of thanksgiving for the return of Jacob and Jayce and Captain Latimore. I would also like to pray for the men who struck out on their own. There's been no sign of them, and Jacob has asked that we remember them. We will pray, too, for a quick end to the war. As you know, American lives are being spent on the battlefields of Europe, and surely only God can bring a quick end to such hideous events. Let's pray."

As he began, Leah felt strangeness in the moment. It was almost as if she were dreaming the entire thing. She knew Jayce and Jacob had truly come home, but there was something that felt most awkward in their reappearance. She couldn't put her finger on it, but maybe it was something that always came with long separations. She knew when Jayce had first come back into her life years earlier that there had been an uneasiness, but she'd attributed most of that to her anger.

She wondered if the wives of soldiers felt the same way. They, too, had to wait and see if their loved ones would ever return alive. They no doubt spent endless hours of worry and anticipation without word or understanding. As the days and months drifted by, there were likely some who even faced the reality that the odds were against them. Perhaps that was the key to knowing her heart in this. There was a part of her that had accepted the possibility of her husband's and brother's death. Maybe she'd even lost hope that they would actually come back alive, and now that they had, she felt almost like a traitor for having given up. After all, she'd told Adrik earlier in the day that she would leave Last Chance and go back with him and Karen to Seward. Perhaps that was her way of declaring the matter to be a lost cause. Guilt washed over her.

Helaina never gave up hope. Why was I so easily discouraged?

Bjorn concluded his prayer and asked Captain Latimore to say a few words. The man stepped forward. Though somewhat weak and much thinner, his countenance bore a strength that reminded Leah of the first time she'd met him.

"You honor me with your kindness," he began. "I am so pleased to be here—thankful for the rescue and return to civilization. And this is a wondrous civilization compared to the place I spent the last few months." The villagers laughed as he continued. "I never thought to be so grateful for simple things like real chairs and tables—and I'm especially looking forward to a real bed."

"So am I," Jayce said in husky whisper.

Leah felt her cheeks grow hot and knew better than to meet her husband's gaze.

"I have to say," Latimore continued, "that none of us would have survived had it not been for Jacob Barringer." The people cheered at this and Latimore motioned to Jacob. "This man, along with Jayce Kincaid, took charge and led the expedition when we were at our worst—when I was at my worst. They were able to show the rest of us how to survive the bitter Arctic cold, and for that I will be eternally grateful. Jacob, why don't you share our story with the people?"

Jacob, looking older than Leah remembered, stepped forward. "My friends, your love and training over the last twelve years saved my life out on the Arctic ice. I remembered the wisdom and traditions passed down among the Inupiat and put them into practice. Clearly the praise cannot be Jayce's or mine alone. The Real People have played their part as well. You should be proud of yourselves and the gift you gave. It is in keeping with God's direction for each of us—that we should help one another and bear one another's burdens." He paused for a moment, as if uncertain how much to say.

"We faced a difficult time. Lives were lost. Our ship was locked in ice and then destroyed. We had ample time to get our gear off the ship, but leaving its safety for nothing more than an ice floe was difficult. We were fortunate to find our way to land—a small island not far from the Russian shores. There we set up camp and began to hunt. Through it all, God was our mainstay. I can't say that I understand the time spent trapped on that island, but I do know that even in this, God had a plan. I can't say I was always strong and faithful, but I can say that God was."

Leah saw many of the people nodding. John had even managed to come for the revelry and smiled up at Jacob with pride. Oopick, too, seemed quite pleased with Jacob's words.

"I'll be happy to share further stories with you in the future, but the hour is late and I know you're tired. Thank you for the prayers and for not forgetting us."

Cheers went up as Jacob concluded and walked off the small platform. Bjorn once again took his place on the makeshift stage. "Jayce, would you like to say a few words as well?"

Jayce shook his head. "Maybe another time." He looked down at his sleeping daughter and the content expression on his face warmed Leah's heart. He loved Merry and Wills. There was no doubt about it. Fears of how he might accept or reject them faded from Leah's mind.

"He looks good," Adrik said as he and Karen came up

beside Leah. "A little thin, but no doubt you women will rectify that."

Leah nodded. "I was just thinking about that." She smiled and tried to suppress a yawn. "How much longer can you stay with us?"

"Well, we figured to talk to you about that," Adrik said with a hint of mischief in his expression. "We have something to propose when we return to your home."

"I think Jacob has something to propose as well," Jayce said, grinning. He motioned to where Jacob and Helaina stood amidst well-wishers.

"If Helaina doesn't propose it first," Leah countered.

The party gradually broke up with promises to share supper together again the next night. There was great talk about working to finish the butchering of the whale, but Leah knew that wouldn't involve her. She walked alongside Jayce, carrying Wills. He slept soundly against her shoulder, having finally played himself into an exhausted state. Leah hoped they would both sleep through the night and give her some much-needed time alone with Jayce.

After putting the babies to bed, Helaina appeared at the door with suitcase in hand. "Where are you going?" Leah asked.

"I couldn't very well stay in Jacob's house." She shifted the case. "It would hardly be proper."

"You know you're welcome here," Jayce interjected. "I can't repay all you've done for my family. Leah tells me she wouldn't have made it through without you."

"Leah exaggerates," Helaina said with a grin. "She helped keep me sane. I might surely have gone mad without her company. We bore the burden together."

Jayce pulled Leah close. "I'm glad you did. We share a strange past, we three, but God has taken it and made it something quite extraordinary."

"Indeed," Helaina replied. "I just stopped by so you might tell Jacob . . ."

Just then Jacob entered the house. He took one look at Helaina and frowned. "Tell Jacob what? Where are you going?"

"Sigrid has offered to share her room with me at the Kjellmann's. They are also taking in the captain, and Emma said one more person wouldn't be a problem. I figure Leah and Jayce already have enough people, what with Karen and Adrik's family."

"Where have you been staying?" he asked.

Helaina blushed. "Well . . . if you must know, I was staying at your place. It's no longer proper for me to do so, given that you're back."

"You could always make it proper," Adrik teased as he came from the back room. Karen was right beside him and elbowed him hard. "Ow! What was that for?"

"For not minding your own business," Karen said sweetly. She smiled at Jacob and the others, then turned to Leah. "We just wanted to tell you good night. I'm hoping we'll have time to talk with you all tomorrow. Adrik has something to ask you."

"I'll be here," Jacob answered.

"Us too," Jayce threw in.

Adrik nodded. "Good. I think you'll like what I have to say. Good night, then." He turned and pulled Karen along with him to their room. Leah heard Karen giggle as Adrik whispered something in her ear. After all this time they still acted like a couple of newlyweds.

"Well, I need to be going," Helaina said, appearing uncomfortable.

"Give me that," Jacob said, reaching for the suitcase. "The least I can do is walk you over to the Kjellmanns'."

Helaina nodded, and Leah could see the hint of a smile on her lips. Things were working out. She knew from the way Jacob acted that he was still in love with Helaina. It delighted Leah in a way she hadn't expected. She was happy for both of them.

"Well, I'll expect you both for breakfast," Leah declared.

"A very late breakfast," Jayce said, yawning. "At least I hope it will be a late one."

Jacob laughed. "Me too."

When they were gone, Jayce turned to Leah. "How I've missed you. Even the smell of you." He took her in his arms and buried his face in her hair.

Leah wrapped her arms around Jayce's neck. "I despaired of ever seeing you again. I wasn't strong or brave. I hope you're not terribly disappointed in me."

He pulled back and looked at her oddly. "You aren't serious, are you?"

Leah shrugged. "Well, Helaina was so certain of your return. She kept such hope, while I felt more and more discouraged. Some days I felt confident that you would find your way back to me. Other times, however ..." She shook her head. "There were some bleak times."

"I know—for me as well. I tried not to let on to Jacob,

but I feared we would all die of some hideous and painful malady and the last thought I would have would be of regret. Regret that I ever left your side. I was a fool, Leah. Please forgive me." He stroked her jaw with his thumb, sending a shivering sensation down her spine. How she loved this man.

"You were only following a dream." She was barely able to speak. "There's nothing to forgive."

"I'm done with dreams. I want the honest truth of what my life has become. I want a future with my wife and children. I want to make a home with you." He lowered his mouth to hers. "Now and always," he whispered against her lips. "Now and always."

Jacob slowed his pace, hoping Helaina would take the hint. "I wanted to tell you something," he began, "now that we have a moment to ourselves."

Helaina looked up, but the darkness made it difficult to see her expression. "Then tell me."

He stopped and put the case on the ground. "Come here." She moved closer and he reached out to touch her face. "I still can't believe you're really here. You were all I could think about while we were gone. I knew when you left that it was a mistake, but I couldn't bring myself to beg you to stay. I knew that if you hated Alaska, you would always be miserable, even if you loved me."

Jacob buried his fingers in her carefully pinned blond hair. He knew he was making a mess of things, but he wanted this moment to last—to go on and on. There was a sense of desperation in his heart.

"I want you to know that I made a decision to leave Alaska."

"What?"

He sighed. "I can't bear to think of life without you. I'm willing to give up Alaska if it means having you at my side for the rest of our lives."

She laughed lightly. "Oh, Jacob. We are a pair. I sold everything I owned in New York and Washington, D.C. I sold the estates, the apartment, the furnishings. I even gave away and sold off most of my clothes to the secondhand stores. I kept very little because none of it mattered without you. I missed Alaska the minute I went away. I kept thinking about the beauty and the people. I realized I was no longer content in a noisy city where no one knew anyone, nor cared to."

"Then you'd make your life here—with me?"

"Of course." She reached up to place her hand against his cheek. "Jacob, I've loved you for a long time. I've loved you for so long now, I can't even really say when it began, but I suspect it was when you nearly ran me over on the streets of Nome. I came back last year so that I might be here when you came home. I wanted to see you and find out if there was a chance that you could possibly love me ... as much ... as I love you."

She started to cry, which took Jacob by surprise. Helaina Beecham was such a strong woman that he'd seldom ever seen her give such a display of emotion. He gently brushed away her tears with his fingers as she continued.

"When we learned that you were ... lost ... I thought I would die." She drew a ragged breath. "I went crazy trying to get news. It seemed the *Regina* and her whereabouts was of far less importance than other issues, like the war in Europe. Stanley tried to help me, but no one had any answers, and of course, no one would do anything until warmer weather.

"But I never gave up hope that we would see you again. Somehow I just knew you would make it—you would come home. What I didn't know . . . what I doubted in my heart . . . was whether you might love me."

Jacob pulled her against him and held her tight. "I love you, Helaina. I will always love you. Never doubt it, and never be afraid that you will lose my affection."

She held on to him as though he were her salvation. Jacob loved the feel of her in his arms; they fit each other perfectly. He'd only dared to dream of this during those long months in the north. He'd prayed and hoped against all reason that he might be able to find her again, and in answer . . . here she was.

"Marry me, Helaina," he whispered.

"Of course." She composed herself and pulled away. "When?"

"Now."

She laughed, and it filled the silence of the night like music. "Now?"

"Why not? I'm sure everyone is still awake. We've only been here for a few moments. Let's just go and get Bjorn and Emma and get married."

"What of Leah and Jayce? What of Adrik and Karen?"

"We'll get married at Leah's house. That way the babies can sleep."

She sighed. "I'm glad you've thought this all out. I'm too tired to make reasonable decisions."

Now it was his turn to laugh. He grabbed the case and reached out to pull Helaina along with him. "Are you saying that marrying me isn't a reasonable decision?"

"Well, not exactly. I think the decision is reasonable, but . . . I'm not sure the procedure is such."

Jacob knocked on his sister's door. "You stay here and tell them what we're doing. I'll go get Bjorn and Emma."

Helaina took her suitcase and nodded. Jayce opened the door as Jacob turned to go. "What's wrong?" he questioned.

"Nothing's wrong," Jacob called out. "We're just going to get married at your house—right now."

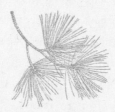

Chapter Thirteen

Leah helped Helaina get ready for her wedding by arranging her long blond hair. "I wish you'd wait and let us give you a more proper wedding."

Helaina laughed. "This is as proper a wedding as I desire. You forget—I've been married before. I had the most lavish wedding money could buy. My father bought out every white rose for two hundred miles around. There must have been hundreds of them."

"I can't imagine," Leah said, trying to mentally picture such a thing. "What about your gown?"

"That was a special creation by the finest designer of the day. I spent months going for my fittings. It had a beautiful bodice with an ivory overlay that went to my neck. The sleeves were long and fitted and the train stretched out some twenty feet. It was truly magnificent. I wore it several times in our first year of marriage, but after that it was packed away, and after Robert died, I later gave it to a distant cousin who thought she'd like to have it for her own wedding."

"You must have been a vision," Leah said, thinking back to her own simple wedding.

"I'm sure you were a vision on your wedding day too," Helaina declared, seeming to read her mind. "I will always regret not being there."

"I wish you would have been there too. Those days were so hard—so bleak. Still, after waiting all those years, I can't complain. Jayce was the prize, after all."

"Just as Jacob is all I really want. The ceremony is not nearly so important." She turned as Leah applied the final pins. "What is important is to have all of you here. Leah, I'm so glad we're friends. I never really had a friend like you. Most women were jealous of my wealth or standing. New York is a very difficult place with its hierarchies and rules. You might find peers at your own level of society, but should they somehow be lowered in status or advanced, your relationships are forever changed. It just comes with the territory."

"I can't imagine. I couldn't live like that. I mean, if I suddenly found myself elevated to a new level, I couldn't just turn my back on those I loved."

"With family, of course, you would not be expected to, but friends would be another story. Unlike in England, where having a poor but titled friend is still worthy of your attention, Americans are snobs when it comes to such matters. It was one of the reasons I refused to get too close to anyone. It was also the reason it was so very hard on me when my parents and Robert died. I had no one in whom I could confide, except

Stanley, and he was far away and often too busy. Those were hard times."

"Well, you won't have to endure them again," Leah said handing her the mirror. "Now we will be sisters, as well as friends. No social standing or financial fiascos will separate us."

Helaina took the mirror, but instead of looking at her reflection, she met Leah's eyes. "I know that with confidence, and it blesses me as nothing else could. When I think of the past and all we've endured together, the things you did for me—risking your life with Chase and ... everything else. I might not have come to believe in God had it not been for you."

Leah shook her head. "The past needs to stay in the past. I know I'm a poor one to talk, given my inability to do exactly that, but I am trying. You would have found your way to God with or without me, but the Lord knew I needed to be humbled and taught mercy. I wasn't very kind to you back then, but your forgiveness has blessed me like a warm fire after days on the icy trail. I will always be here for you."

Helaina nodded. "And I will be here for you. No matter what."

"What's this?" Jayce called from the doorway. "You two seem mighty serious about something."

"We were just having a bit of girl talk," Leah said, smiling. "Don't you think our bride is beautiful?"

"She is lovely," Jayce said, surveying Helaina as she stood.

"Thank you." Helaina looked at her reflection momentarily, then passed the mirror back to Leah. "Jayce, I hope you know that I ... well ... I ..." She seemed to fail for words.

Leah knew Helaina wanted to make sure things were at peace between all of them. "I think Helaina wants to go to her wedding knowing that the past is forgiven and that we are all friends."

Jayce put his arm around Leah's shoulders. "The past is gone. Of course we are all friends. My time out in the Arctic taught me much, not the least of which was to let go of my past. The burdens I carried for years seemed unimportant in the face of that adversity. I hold nothing against you, Helaina, and I pray you hold nothing against me."

Helaina came to Jayce, tears in her eyes. "I don't deserve such mercy, but I am grateful for it. You, Leah, and Jacob have done so much to teach me about being merciful even when someone deserves otherwise. It's been hard for me, but I've finally been able to come to terms with my parents' deaths—and Robert's death as well. It hasn't happened overnight, but as I've sought God's heart in the Bible, I've realized that He offers forgiveness for all, and I must strive to do likewise. I must also learn to put guilt aside as God forgives and covers my mistakes with His love. Guilt has eaten away at my heart for so many years. Jacob was able to see that and admonished me to do something more productive with my time." She gave them a rather coy smile. "I guess Jacob will be that 'something more productive.'"

They laughed together.

"I'm back!" Jacob called from the front door.

Helaina bit her lower lip and threw a quick glance over her shoulder as if she'd forgotten something. Leah reached out to calm her. "You look perfect. Remember this moment fondly."

Helaina nodded. Jayce extended his arm to her. "Shall we?

WHISPERS of WINTER

If we don't get out there soon, he'll just start bellowing again and wake up the children."

Helaina smiled and took hold of Jayce as though she needed the extra support. "I'm ready."

Leah watched them walk through the door. Jacob would finally be married. He would finally have a family of his own. She wiped a tear from her eye and drew a deep breath. Their lives were changing again, but this time it was something very good.

In the living room Jacob waited with Adrik, Karen, Sigrid, and Bjorn. "Emma stayed home with the children. She knew Sigrid would be beside herself if she missed out on seeing Helaina married," Bjorn said.

"Well, we've gotten to know each other very well this last year. As the only single, white women in the village, we had a great deal in common," Sigrid offered as an excuse.

Bjorn yawned. "Ja. They have talking in common for sure."

Leah grinned. Her husband was home, her brother was marrying the woman he'd loved for a long time, and her family was safe and sound. What more could she want?

Bjorn began the service by reading from Genesis. "God doesn't want man to be alone—He said it wasn't good." Leah always enjoyed his thick Swedish accent. "And it's not good. To be alone is a terrible thing—especially here in the north. Solomon, too, talked of two being better than one. They share warmth and a helping hand. When two people come together to marry, they share those things as well as love and hopefully a belief in God's saving grace."

Helaina looked at Jacob as though he hung the moon and

the stars. Leah looked to Jayce, who was waiting to officially hand Helaina over to Jacob, already missing his absence at her side.

"Helaina, do you love the Lord and have you taken Jesus as your Savior?"

"I have."

He smiled and turned to Jacob. "And Jacob, do you love the Lord and have you taken Jesus as your Savior?"

"Yes, sir." The catch in Jacob's voice made him sound like a teenager again instead of a man in his thirties.

"Who gives this woman?"

"We do," Jayce replied. "I and her other friends."

Bjorn nodded and Jayce extended Helaina's arm to Jacob. "Take good care of her," he admonished in a fatherly way.

Jacob nodded with a grin. "You know I will. I've waited a lifetime for her."

Jayce stepped back to join Leah. He slipped his arm around her waist and pulled her close. Leah smiled up at him, sensing his happiness.

The ceremony was short and simple. They exchanged their promises of love and support, then Jacob surprised them all by producing a small gold band. Leah recognized it as having been their mother's. Jacob had tried to give it to her on one occasion, but Leah knew that their mother had wanted him to save it for his bride.

As he slipped the ring on Helaina's finger, Leah couldn't help but sniff back tears. Their mother would be so proud. Their papa too. Leah liked to believe they were watching from heaven and knew they would surely approve of this union.

"You may kiss your bride, Jacob. You are man and wife," Bjorn announced.

Jacob pulled Helaina into his arms and gave her a brief but sufficient kiss. Cheers broke out among those in the room as Leah's gaze settled on her brother. They had always been so very close. They had taken care of each other when no one else was there for them. They had endured great difficulty in just getting to Alaska, but also in living there. The land was hard and difficult, but the rewards had been so great. Leah couldn't help but wonder what the future held now. Would they all go their separate ways? Would God see fit to keep them all together?

"I want to congratulate you both," Adrik said, coming to give Jacob a bear hug. He turned to Helaina. "Do I get to kiss the bride?"

She nodded and seemed delighted to be embraced into the family in this way. Karen, too, came and offered her a kiss and a blessing. "May God richly bless your marriage. May you always remember Him first in all that you do, and may your love endure the tests of time."

"Thank you," Helaina said, embracing Karen. "I feel so very blessed."

Leah came forward and hugged Helaina. "You are truly my sister now. I've always wanted a sister."

Helaina laughed and tightened her embrace. "I have, too, and now God has answered that prayer as well."

Jayce swept Helaina into a hug as Leah turned to her brother. They just looked at each other for a moment, and in Jacob's eyes, Leah saw the passage of two decades of time. Jacob sensed it as well.

"When we first came north, I cursed it," he admitted. "I saw very little good here. You know that."

"I do. I felt the same way," Leah admitted.

"But now I see so clearly the hand of God in all the choices—good and bad. It amazes me how God could take even my rebellious choices and work them together for good."

"I know. I was thinking much the same. You were always there for me."

Jacob held her close for a moment. "I love you, Leah. No man could ask for a better sister."

Leah stepped back as he released her. "And no woman could ask for a better brother."

Helaina looked down at her finger and could scarcely believe she was finally married. Her dreams of having Jacob for a husband had come true. She thought only momentarily of Robert and of the beautiful diamond and sapphire ring he had given her on their wedding day. *He would be happy for me,* she thought. *He would tell me it was about time I stopped grieving him and moved forward with my life.*

She smiled to herself as she compared her old life to the new one. Things would never be the same—but then again, she didn't want them to be.

"Well, you can party all night if you want to," Jayce finally announced, "but Leah and I are going to take our leave. I haven't seen this woman in over a year, and ... well ... let's leave it at that."

Adrik laughed and pulled Karen toward their room. "We'll

WHISPERS of WINTER

say good night as well. It'll be good to see you all at breakfast."

"Late breakfast," Jacob called back as he pulled Helaina close. He stunned her by lifting her in his arms. "A very, very late breakfast."

They all laughed at this, but no one protested the idea. Helaina felt rather embarrassed by Jacob's grandiose gesture, but at the same time she relished it and snuggled down in his arms. She sighed contentedly.

"I feel the same way," Jacob said as he carried her to their inne.

"I'm just amazed that it's finally happened. I'm so happy ... so blessed," she whispered. "I love you so very much, Jacob."

"And I love you, Mrs. Barringer."

———

The next morning Helaina awoke with a start. For just a moment she couldn't remember where she was, and when she found Jacob sleeping beside her, it startled her even more. Then the memories of the night before flooded her mind. She moved closer to Jacob for warmth and smiled as his arms closed around her and pulled her near.

"Good morning," he said, his voice low. "How did you sleep?"

"Like a dream. In fact, I woke up thinking maybe I had dreamed it all. I'm glad to know that this is very much real."

He laughed. "I hope all of your dreams are just as sweet." He kissed her passionately and Helaina forgot about dreams and nightmares. Suddenly there was only Jacob. And Jacob was truly enough.

When they showed up an hour later for breakfast at Jayce and Leah's, they found themselves the objects of teasing.

"It's nearly lunchtime," Adrik said, looking at his pocket watch.

"It's been light for hours," Karen agreed.

"It's always light for hours during Alaskan summer," Jacob replied, not willing to let them get the better of him.

Leah brought their plates from the back of the stove. "We've been keeping this warm for you. Pay them no attention. They're old married folk who've grown quite bored with one another." She laughed as she gave Adrik and Karen a wink.

"My mama and papa aren't old," Christopher protested.

Leah gave his cheek a rub. "No, they really aren't. I was just teasing them."

Oliver had long since eaten his breakfast and was ready for adventure. "Kimik said we could hunt with him today. Can we?" he asked as Christopher nodded hopefully.

"I don't see why not," Adrik replied. "It seems like it will be a great time for you boys. Just make sure you do everything he says, and stay right with the party. This place isn't like home. You don't know the trails, and fog could come in and you'd be lost."

"We'll stay with him, I promise. I'll keep a good eye on Christopher too."

"But you're not my pa," the boy reminded his brother. "So you can't tell me what to do."

"Kimik isn't your pa either," Adrik countered, "but if you

aren't willing to take instruction and correction from him, you'd best stay here with me."

Christopher grew very serious. "I promise I'll be good. I'll do what he tells me to do."

"All right, then. You boys head on over. I'm sure Kimik is more than ready to leave."

Leah put the twins on the floor to play as she began to clear away the breakfast dishes. Helaina dug into the food Leah had given her and thought nothing had ever tasted so good. She felt ravenous as she bit into the caribou sausage.

"I hope you're up for a bit of discussion," Adrik began. "There's something I've been wanting to talk to all four of you about."

"If it's one of Adrik's plans," Jacob said, leaning back with coffee cup in hand, "we'd better hold on to our seats."

Adrik exchanged a quick glance with Karen and laughed. "You're right on that count. I suppose my ideas can be a bit bold at times."

"Why don't you tell us what you have in mind?" Leah prompted.

Adrik folded his hands together and looked at each of them before he spoke. "I'd like you all to consider coming back with us."

"To Ketchikan?" Leah questioned.

"No, to Seward. Well, to Ship Creek, really—though they're starting to call it Anchorage now."

Helaina felt Jacob's interest even before he spoke. "For what purpose?"

"Well, that's what I want to talk to all of you about. Are you game to listen?"

Chapter Fourteen

T he situation is this," Adrik continued. "The railroad is going in all the way to Fairbanks, and the place is hopping with activity. I've been hired by the railroad to hunt and bring in game for the men to eat. It's a whole lot cheaper to hire me than to bring food up from the States, after all. The only problem is, I'm just one man and, frankly, the number of workers is growing every day. They estimate some four thousand workers now. I don't think the territory will stay unsettled for long."

Jacob shrugged. "We've seen people come and go with the gold strikes. Alaska requires a special kind of person to stay."

"Jacob's right. It's going to take more than a few thousand men to settle this place and make the world take notice," Jayce said.

"But it's a start. The railroad adds a sense of settlement and permanency that will draw people to come and stay."

"So you're proposing we work for the railroad?" Jacob asked.

"No, I'm proposing we work for ourselves," Adrik replied. "Look, we can team up—maybe even add another couple of men I trust and form our own corporation of sorts. You wouldn't believe the number of times I've been hired just to lead city folks out hunting wild game. Most want the thrill of bear or moose, some just want to enjoy whatever comes their way, so that's an entire different aspect to how we can make a living. Initially, we could contract with the railroad to provide a particular amount of meat per week and split the funds between us."

Jacob rubbed his chin thoughtfully. "Where would we live?"

"The Ship Creek area. That's a good place to headquarter. The railroad from Seward has just connected to that place and is headed on out to Palmer and Wasilla. If things continue this way, we might see completion in another couple of years. Of course, we have to get through those mountains up north, and that will be no easy feat."

"And do you plan to move north with the railroad?" Jacob asked Adrik.

Adrik looked to Karen and shrugged. "We're trying to be open to where the Lord would take us. We've found there's plenty of work to do in the area, but we also miss our home in Ketchikan. We'll just have to see where the Lord wants us."

"Not only that," Karen began, "Seward is a year-round harbor. We can get a steady supply of goods whenever we need them. Well, at least a decent supply," she added with a smile. "There are good doctors, plans for a hospital in Ship Creek, as well as a power plant and electricity."

"That would be incredible," Leah said, shaking her head. "I remember how wonderful it was when we were in Seattle."

"Not only that, but they're laying water pipes that will bring water right into the house," Adrik added.

"It's like we said," Karen continued. "The area offers many benefits that can't be had in the more isolated parts of Alaska. And there would be no winter isolation due to ship traffic being halting because of frozen harbors."

"That would definitely be a benefit," Leah admitted. She hated to say it, but having children gave her a much different perspective on where to live. "Still, I'm happy to live wherever Jayce wants to be. I know he'll provide for us and that we'll be well protected in his care. So long as my family is with me or close by, I'll be content."

She looked to Jayce and could see he was strongly considering the possibility. "I believe it's definitely something to think about," he said.

Jacob looked to Helaina. "What about you? What do you think of this wild scheme of Adrik's?"

"I feel the same as Leah. I had to wait all this time to get you. I don't really care where we live so long as we aren't long separated."

"That's a good point. How long are these hunting expeditions?" Jacob questioned.

Adrik shrugged. "Depends on how plentiful the game is and how far out we have to go to get to the animals. We would rotate being gone, however. A team of men would go out and hunt, while another team would stay at home and deal with the meat, the hides, and the railroad officials. There's also some good money to be made in fur trading, so seeing those hides prepared will be another big job."

"We could help with that," Leah threw in. "I've done plenty of tanning."

"I'm not sure I'd want you to help, Leah," Adrik said, shaking his head. "I suppose it would all depend on where we set up our work site. The men in the area can be a little rough—especially those from the States recruited to bring their railroad work experience to the frozen north. Don't get me wrong—it's a good place to live and most folks are perfectly well-mannered. But it's a man's world."

Leah nodded, understanding Adrik's words completely. He had no problem with a woman helping her family to exist, but he wanted to see her safe from harm.

Jayce looked to Jacob and shrugged. "What do you think, Jacob?"

"Couldn't be worse than living in the Arctic for a year." His smile broadened. "I say let's give it a try. We might find we really like the area. If nothing else, we'll have had a hand in civilizing the territory. We can someday tell our children we helped bring the railroad to Alaska."

"I agree. I think we should give it a chance."

Adrik slapped the table. "That's great news, boys."

Leah felt a strange sense of excitement mingled with regret wash over her. They were going to leave Last Chance—maybe for good. She'd miss her friends dearly, but she'd have Karen and the boys back in her life. She'd missed them all more than she could even begin to say.

Jayce turned to her and gently lifted her face to meet his. "Are you sure this is all right with you?"

She thought for a moment. "It's not without regret, but I'm happy to go wherever you lead." She threw a glance at Jacob and Adrik. "I think it will be a blessing for all of us."

"I just want you to make certain that you'll be happy."

She laughed and shook her head. "We both know there are no guarantees for that. I very much like the idea of having better things for the children, but even if you desired to stay here, I wouldn't protest. I'm just glad to have you back. I promised God if He would just send you home, I'd do my best to never be quarrelsome again."

Jayce touched her cheek. "I want you to be happy. That matters a great deal to me."

"I think it will be a good experiment," Jacob interjected. "It's not like we can't return here should things not work out. I can't really say why, but it just seems like the Lord is leading us to Anchorage. And since it's already August, we need to make up our minds and secure ship passage."

"That's true enough. We had already booked our return for the twenty-sixth," Adrik told them. "I don't know if there will be enough room for all of us, but I'd bet there will be."

Leah realized the twenty-sixth was only a few days away. It wouldn't give them much time for packing. Then again, she didn't really know what they'd need. Would they have a house or share one with Adrik and Karen? Would they need to bring all of their things, or should they wait until they had a better idea of how long they'd stay?

"We'd have to move fast to be able to head back with you," Jacob said. "We'd need to be packed by the day after tomorrow and secure Kimik and some of the others to take us to Nome."

Two days. That was all they'd have. Today and the next day. Leah shook her head. It was hard to imagine that she'd pack up their lives and leave in two days. "We could take a later ship," she said without thinking.

"You could, but I think it's better to come with us if there's room," Adrik replied. "We can help with the bulk of things you want to bring. I can get people in Seward to help us get the stuff north. Once I explain, the railroad will probably transport us for free. It would just work well for us to all go together."

"I agree," Karen added, "and I could help with the babies."

"Let's commit this to prayer. I feel good about it—very good about it—but I want to make sure it's the direction God has for us," Jacob said.

Jayce nodded thoughtfully. "I agree. God's pacing is never frantic and ill-thought. I suggest we begin our packing and make arrangements but all the while pray fervently about the matter."

———

Leah looked out over the landscape, turning as she stood in one place to take in the view in all directions. It would be strange to leave this place, but the adventure of a new start— a new life in Ship Creek—excited her. It seemed that all was in keeping with God's plans. John and Oopick's reaction was positive, and they promised to buy as many dogs as Jacob wanted to leave behind. They also offered to take over the inne and see to it that things remained in good repair.

Sigrid had offered to stay at Leah and Jacob's house and keep it for them until they decided if they wanted to sell it or move back. That comforted Leah greatly. It was good to know they weren't breaking all of their ties to Last Chance Creek.

"Are you all right?"

Leah turned to find her brother stalking up the hill toward her. "I was just thinking about our leaving. Jayce feels God's hand in the matter—as I know you do."

"But you don't?"

"I didn't say that." Leah looked at Jacob. He seemed so much older than he had a year ago. "I still haven't heard from you about this last year. I've not had a single moment to just sit down with you and ask about the way things went."

It was Jacob's turn to stare off into the distance. He frowned momentarily. "At first I felt we were more than capable of making it all work together for good. I didn't like the idea that God had allowed it, but I felt it wouldn't be the end of us.

"There were days, however . . ." His voice grew soft, barely audible. "I really started to despair at the end. The men were so angry. They couldn't understand why we wouldn't allow them to just set off for home. They couldn't see the dangers. They'd never been out at sea in an umiak and didn't know the risks. I fear them all dead now."

Leah put her hand firmly on Jacob's arm. "You are not in the wrong. Your admonitions to stay were sound. *They* chose to throw off the counsel of their authority."

"They didn't see our authority as valid. They felt we were just men like themselves and that our knowledge didn't give us the right to make their choices."

"People often see their authority figures in that way,"

Leah said. She pushed back the hood of her kuspuk. "Especially when it comes to God."

"You're right on that account. But, Leah, those were good men. I talked many nights with each one. They were homesick and longing to have their families once again at their side. Unfortunately, it caused them to make bad decisions, and I fear they'll never see civilization again, much less their families."

"If they are dead, you cannot change it by mourning what might have been," Leah said, squeezing his arm. "I've no doubt you offered sound counsel and wisdom. I believe most sincerely that you offered friendship and kindness."

He turned to her and placed his hand atop hers. "We've been through a lot in this country—you and me."

Leah saw that the sorrow had left him at least momentarily. She smiled. "Yes, we have. We've seen a great many things, good and bad."

"But the blessings have been greater than the problems."

"Yes. I wasn't honestly sure I would ever be able to say that," Leah began, "but the Lord has worked on my heart this last year. Maybe I wasn't very willing to listen to my authority either." She moved a pace away and turned to look out across the vast expanse of water.

"There were days," she said, the longing clear in her voice, "that I would stand here and stare out at the ice. I knew you were both out there. I felt you must surely be alive, because I just didn't feel like you were dead. But feeling a thing and making it so ... well, those are two different things. I lost hope. I began to fear the worst. Helaina told me over and over that you were alive—that you'd both return. I wanted to have her faith, because mine seemed so insufficient."

"I know what you mean. I listen to her talk about how she waited here, knowing I'd come home, and it both humbles and embarrasses me. Why couldn't I have stood the test of time? I've been saved a whole lot longer than she has."

Leah laughed. Jacob always had a way of bringing a matter right down to the point. "That's the pride in both of us, I guess. We rose to the occasion and proclaimed our trust in God, then sat alone, miserable for fear that our trust had been misplaced. Then when we see that others were stronger and more inspired to believe the truth, we feel regret and frustration. And it's all because our pride is wounded. We were so confident that we would be strong. We were so confident that we could take on any trial God sent our way."

"You know the Bible talks about how we don't wrestle against flesh and blood—"

"'But against principalities, against powers, against rulers of the darkness of this world, against wickedness in high places,'" Leah finished the verse from Ephesians 6. "I cherished that passage during your absence. I felt I was trying so hard to be all things to all people. I didn't want people to see how sad or lonely I was. I didn't even want to share that with Helaina."

"I know. I felt the same way about sharing it with Jayce." He reached out and took hold of Leah's hand. "We're so alike. I guess only having each other for so long made us that way. I hope you know you will always hold a special place in my heart. I know a lot of men have no lasting relationship with their siblings. Jayce is a good example. He hasn't heard from them in years, save Chase."

Leah frowned at the thought of Jayce's twin.

Jacob immediately recognized the mistake. "I'm sorry. I shouldn't have mentioned him."

"No, it's really all right. I'm trying hard to put him behind me. I feel bad because I can't even comfort Jayce on the loss of his brother. I never want to hear about what happened out there—not that Jayce has ever really offered me any more details than what he shared when he returned. Chase was attacked by a bear—maybe the same one I shot earlier in the day. His death was as ordained by God as a thing could be."

Jacob hugged her close. "I want things to be better for you. I felt so guilty about not being able to save you from him."

Leah pulled back. "Don't feel guilty. I've borne enough guilt for both of us."

"But you were completely innocent of everything. Even Helaina could take partial blame for what happened, but not you."

"No one is to blame but Chase." Leah forced the name from her lips. "He made bad choices. He made them all of his life. He cared more about himself and his own pleasure than anyone else. He did the things he did to gratify himself and to punish Jayce for the good life he had known."

"Still, I wish I could have saved you from it."

Leah hoped her next words would free Jacob from any further guilt. "Jacob, I never thought I could say this, but I wouldn't trade my children for anything. Not even if they are the result of what Chase did."

Jacob looked at her oddly for a moment. "Truly?"

"Truly. They are my heart. Even if they were born out of

the rape, it isn't their fault. They did nothing wrong and shouldn't be punished because of someone else's sin. Not even for the sins of their father—if Chase truly played that part. I can't say I never struggle with this," she admitted, "but my struggles are not over whether or not Chase's actions caused my pregnancy, but more as to whether Jayce can accept the babies I love as his own. Or whether he will come to hate them, should we have other children that we know are his."

"I'd never considered such a matter, but I can tell you it would make no difference to me if the same had happened to Helaina. I would love any child of hers—because it was a part of her. I'm sure Jayce feels the same way. I know he regretted the separation. He talked of you and the babies often."

"I think this new start will be good for all of us. It will be a lot of work, but I think it will also benefit us greatly."

"I do too. It's rather like taking off for a whole different kind of goldfield, eh?"

Leah thought back to when their father had first dragged them to Alaska. She also remembered the trek north to find Jacob when he left Dyea and headed to the Yukon. "It is very much like those adventures, but it holds a greater promise than gold. It holds the promise of love."

Chapter Fifteen

December 1917

The Christmas holidays were rapidly approaching, much to Leah's amazement. It seemed they had just arrived in the Ship Creek area only days before instead of months. The cabin she now shared with Jayce had only been finished a few weeks earlier. Leah felt very privileged; most folks were still living in tents, and she remembered only too well what that was like from her time in the Yukon. The cabin was much better.

To her specifications, there was one large common room with two smaller rooms off the back of this. The latter were bedrooms, one for Leah and Jayce and the other one for the twins. The twins' room held a low rope bed that could accommodate both children. A small steamer trunk served as their clothes chest, and another trunk rounded out the furnishings as a makeshift toy box. Adrik promised a much nicer one as a Christmas gift, but the twins didn't seem to mind the current arrangement.

Leah and Jayce's room wasn't much larger than the children's room. There was a more substantial bed that had been designed by Adrik. The peeled-log frame offered a sturdy foundation, while the feather-stuffed mattress provided a comfortable night's sleep. A large wooden dresser stood in one corner of the room, also compliments of Adrik. The house was a tight fit, but the snugness only added to the hominess.

Leah loved having the privacy it afforded as well. When they'd first arrived at the house Adrik had built for his wife and sons, it was clear that things would be quite crowded for a time. The land was plentiful, but the buildings were not. It took time to fell trees and put together structures. But the people were just as eager to help each other here as they had been in Last Chance. One day a group of men from the railroad and church had gathered and cut trees and notched logs for two small houses. They accomplished an incredible amount of work in the all-day extravaganza, and only later did Leah learn that all three men in her family had offered the men pay, but they'd have none of it. Their act of kindness touched her deeply.

Another obvious difference in Leah's life was the development of the twins. They were rapidly changing in appearance and, where they had once looked very much like each other, now they were showing definite male and female qualities. Merry's face seemed more delicate, her lips fuller, and the lashes that edged her eyes were longer and thicker than her brother's. Wills developed a set to his face that reminded Leah of Jayce. He would often knit his brow together while considering some toy or other object of fascination. His nose appeared a little fuller, while his lips seemed thinner than Meredith's.

There were also changes of personality. Merry, while still shy, had taken on a personality that reflected Leah's quiet nature. Whenever Wills got into trouble, Merry was always there to smooth things over. When Leah was upset, Merry would often pat her mother's leg as if to console her while gazing sympathetically and babbling incoherent words of encouragement.

Wills' personality, on the other hand, reminded Leah so much of Jayce. His eyes were much darker blue than Merry's glacier blue. He was fiercely independent and fearless. Even now as Leah watched them play, she worried incessantly about Wills getting too close to the stove. He seemed to have no concern about whether it would cause him harm or good. Wills saw everything as an adventure. Why should the stove be any different?

A knock on her door took Leah out of her reflective thoughts. "Wills, you stay away from the stove. That's hot. It will hurt you." Wills looked up, as if trying to ascertain the validity of his mother's words.

Leah opened the door to find Karen and Helaina. Both held numerous evergreen boughs in their arms. "What a surprise. Looks like you two have been busy." She stepped back to admit them in from the cold.

"It's snowed another six inches," Karen said. She shook the branches, then handed them to Leah. "We were gathering these to decorate for Christmas and thought you might like some too. With the babies toddling around, I wasn't sure you'd have time to gather any for yourself."

"That was very thoughtful." Leah pressed her nose into the bundle. "Mmm, they smell so good."

"I can't believe Christmas is nearly here," Helaina declared. She put her branches on the nearby table and leaned down to see what Wills was playing with. "What is that, Wills?"

He held the toy up and grinned. "Doggy nice."

Helaina nodded. "It's a very nice doggy indeed."

"Baby!" Merry declared, holding out her doll from the other side of the room.

"Merry, what a pretty baby. Come show me." Helaina continued to play with the children for a moment while Leah tried to decide where would be best to store the boughs. "If I don't put them up, the children will surely destroy them."

"Oh, I wanted to tell you," Karen began, "I had three letters arrive today with the post. One was from Grace, another from Miranda, and the final one was from Ashlie."

Leah loved to hear news—especially from loved ones far away. "I wish I could hear something from Last Chance. I probably won't know how anyone is doing until spring, however. You know how impossible it is to send mail across the interior."

"Yes. There were so many times I would have loved to have sent you letters and packages during the long winter."

"Me too," Leah said, easily remembering the isolation. "So how is Grace?" Grace had once been Karen's charge when they both lived in Chicago. Karen had loved being a governess to the wealthy girl. They'd both come north to Alaska when Grace had been determined to escape an arranged marriage. Then while in Alaska, Grace and Karen had both found true love and married. Karen had stayed, but Grace had gone to San Francisco to live with her husband and his family.

"They're all very well. Grace is worried because her son talks continually about joining the army to fight in Europe. Grace is heartsick over the thought that he might sneak off in the night and do something rash."

"Hasn't Peter tried to reason with him?"

"What's a father to do?" Karen shook her head. "I'm sure Peter and Grace have both done their best to convince him to remain at home, but you know how headstrong children can be. Andrew is almost eighteen, and he's confident he knows more than his parents. At least to hear Grace tell it."

"I'm sure," Leah said with a nod. "What about the other children?"

"Well, let's see. Jeremiah is fifteen and very much in love with the sea, just like his father. Belynn is twelve, and Grace says she plans to be married with six children by the time she's twenty."

Leah laughed and tried to imagine what life would be like for the twelve-year-old Belynn. Why, there were automobiles and airplanes, not to mention all kinds of machinery that helped with the everyday chores of life. Leah's children might never know such luxury if they remained in the wilds. "And what about Miranda? Where will she and Teddy spend this Christmas?"

"Well, Teddy wanted to explore some islands off the coast of South America. They were actually in San Francisco with Peter and Grace when Miranda posted this letter, but she said they were southbound. It seems Teddy would like to write a book dealing with the flora and fauna of that area."

Leah nodded, remembering quite well that Teddy Davenport had a passion for botany that was only preceded by his love for Miranda. "And what did Miranda's brother think of that?"

"Peter was very happy to assist them. They will journey south on one of his ships, in fact. The Colton Shipping Company is quite expanded from what it used to be."

"It's too bad Peter's mother and father didn't live to see what a successful businessman Peter has become. I'm sure they would have been proud," Leah said thoughtfully. "So you've saved the best for last. What does Ashlie have to say? Oh, where are my manners? I have some hot tea. Would either of you care for a cup?"

Helaina straightened and rubbed the small of her back through the thick parka. "I'd love some. I'm still a little chilled."

"Me too. Tea sounds perfect." Karen pulled her coat off and went to hang it by the door. "I hope I haven't dripped water all over your floor."

"It needed washing anyway. It's very dirty you know," Leah said, glancing down at the hard-packed dirt with a grin.

Karen chuckled. "You'll have floors before you know it. Adrik has been very concerned that you should be living without them, you know."

"We're fine. We've certainly had to deal with worse." Leah poured her guests tea and brought the steaming mugs to the table. "You'll have to forgive the cups, my good china is otherwise engaged."

"Engaged where?" Helaina asked with a smile.

Leah shrugged and gave a girlish giggle. "I'm sure I don't

know since I haven't any good china. But wherever it is, I'm sure it's otherwise engaged."

"You'll remember I had some very pretty china when I first settled in Ketchikan with Adrik. He couldn't even get his fingers around the cup handle. It was most amusing. What wasn't as humorous was his penchant for dropping them. They were just too delicate and would slip right through his fingers. Mugs turned out to be much better for us."

"I suppose that's why I've never worried about china," Leah said, shrugging. "I'm sure you must miss such things, however." She looked to Helaina, remembering the grandeur her life had once known.

"There are times," Helaina admitted, "when I miss some of the finery. But I love it here, and it's senseless to have things that serve little or no purpose. Mugs are fine by me. What I miss is the convenience of things. Hot baths, large selections of scented soaps and such. It's that kind of thing I miss."

"I can remember Seattle well enough to know exactly how pleasant it was to have a bath anytime I wanted one," Leah agreed. Seattle spurred on memories of Ashlie. "All right, tell us about your daughter."

Helaina nodded enthusiastically. "Yes, please do. Is she happy? How's school going?"

"She is happy," Karen said with a bit of regret in her tone. "It's not that I wouldn't wish her so, but there's that part of me that wouldn't mind if she were unhappy enough to return home to me. I miss her so much."

"I know you do," Leah said, putting her hand on Karen's arm. "I hope we might ease some of that longing by keeping you too preoccupied to miss her overly much."

"It has been a pleasant diversion to have you so close—both of you. The boys are poor companions at times; I'm convinced that neither of them needs me. They want to be off hunting or exploring the minute their studies are concluded. They are not exactly conversationalists." The three ladies laughed at this statement.

"Does Ashlie have plans to come home anytime soon?" Leah asked.

"No. She's busy with church activities and, of course, her studies. Cousin Myrtle has definitely enjoyed her company as well. Ashlie tells in her letter that they attend many plays and parties. Ashlie has brought new life to my cousin, and for that I'm grateful. Myrtle was never blessed with children of her own, and having Ashlie has given her a great deal of pleasure. I'd beg Ashlie to return to us, but I know it would break Myrtle's heart. Not to mention Ashlie, who would like to attend college. She's been quite smitten with school and learning."

There was a sad resignation in Karen's voice that Leah couldn't ignore. "It has been with no small amount of sacrifice on your part that Ashlie has enjoyed another kind of life. The world in Seattle is so very different from the one we know here."

"I know that's true. It was no easy feat to adjust to life in Alaska. When I came north with Grace, it was exciting to try something new, but where life in the south might allow for mere existence, Alaska demands much more. There is no mere 'getting by' up here. You will die if you don't put a definite effort into survival."

"That's true," Leah said, nodding, "but Ashlie knows

about survival. She was born and raised here, and she's nobody's fool. Let her enjoy her time and see what life has to hold. She's in good hands, and obviously she's benefiting your cousin as well."

Karen nodded. "To be sure. Still, she's almost eighteen. I've already noted comments in her letters that mention young men who would like to be her suitor. So far she's kept them all at arm's length. She tells me she's not been overly impressed with any of them. But I don't try to fool myself. The day will come when that one man . . . that perfect man . . . will sweep her away."

"Just like it happened to each of us," Leah said with a smile. "Would you want anything less for her?"

Karen shook her head. "Of course not. I just . . . well . . . I worry that she'll never come back to Alaska after that."

"She'll always come to wherever you are," Leah encouraged. She gave Karen's arm a squeeze and raised her gaze to see that the twins were still happily occupied with their toys. "So did any of the letters offer news of the war in Europe?"

"Only to say that things were continuing to drag on. It's so sad. So many have died," Karen spoke more quietly. It was almost as if she didn't want the twins to overhear the bad news. "Things definitely do not look good for the Russian people. They've taken the czar and his family captive, and no one knows what will happen to them. And King George of England, who happens to be a relative—I believe a cousin perhaps to either the czar or his wife—refused to let the family come to England for asylum."

Leah shook her head. "How awful to reject your own family. What kind of man does that when he knows it will no doubt bode poorly for the czar? I read in one of the old papers that the new government is not inclined to be sympathetic toward royalty."

"I met a man who was closely affiliated with the czar and czarina," Helaina joined in. "He was here seeking to find a place to hide the family should they be able to sneak out of Russia. He believes they will face death."

"And still the King of England will not allow them refuge?" Leah questioned.

"Ashlie said in her letter that it seemed the government of England advised the king that it would be best to stay out of the situation. Apparently they feel there is little to be gained, and perhaps it would damage relationships with the new government and cause them to turn from the side of those fighting the Germans."

"That's so sad," Leah said, shaking her head. "I hate war. I can't imagine what the soldiers must have to endure. Just as bad, I can't fathom what their families must have to bear here at home. The news is so long in coming and then you can only wonder at the accuracy."

"The news is coming regularly in the States," Karen said, staring at her mug. "But it seems the news is always bad."

"Well, I for one have had enough sad talk," Helaina said, putting her mug on the table. "I have some good news that I'd like to share. I was going to wait until later, but I want you both to be the first to know." Leah and Karen both met her gaze. Helaina grinned. "I'm going to have a baby."

Leah could hardly believe the words. Her brother was finally going to be a father. "Helaina, that's wonderful!" She reached over to embrace her sister-in-law. "What did Jacob say? Oh, I can imagine he's beside himself."

"He doesn't know yet," she admitted. "I've been waiting to be certain and now I am." She gave a little shudder of excitement. "I can hardly believe it's happening."

"When is the baby due to arrive?" Karen asked.

"By my best calculations, it will be in May."

"A wedding night baby," Leah said after a quick mental calculation.

Helaina blushed. "That's the way I see it as well."

Karen laughed. "Jacob was never one for delaying things that he wanted done. That boy ... well, hardly that ... he's wanted a wife and family for so long, he probably figured to just accomplish it all at once."

Leah sat back in her chair. "When will you tell him?"

"Tonight, if possible. I knew they'd be busy today, and I just wanted to wait until there was plenty of time to enjoy the moment. Tonight will be soon enough."

"I won't say a word to him," Leah promised.

"Neither will I," Karen agreed.

Helaina put her hand to her stomach and shook her head. "I can hardly believe this is happening to me. I'm so happy I could cry."

"Well, don't do that, or Jacob will know that something's going on." Leah got to her feet. "I think it's time for the twins to go take their nap." She motioned to where Merry now sat groggily leaning against the log wall, while Wills yawned from where he sat on the rug.

"I need to get home to finish supper." Karen got to her feet. "Tomorrow we can make plans for our Christmas cele-bration. This is going to be such a merry occasion." She drew on her parka. "May will be a perfect month for a new baby."

"I was thinking the same thing," Leah said as she lifted Wills.

"Around here things will be warm and beautiful. Last year there were flowers and nice warm days where it was a pleasure to be outside in the sun. You can never tell about Alaska weather, but chances are good that it will be a very nice time to bring a new life into the world."

Helaina smiled. "It comforts me just to know you'll both be here. You will stay with me, won't you? I mean when the time comes?"

"Of course we will." Leah heard the apprehension in her voice. "You would be hard-pressed to be rid of us."

"That's right," Karen added. "I have helped with many births, as has Leah. We certainly wouldn't want to miss this most important occasion. We'll be there for you."

Jayce surprised Leah by showing up an hour later for lunch. "I hope you have something to eat. I'm starved," he said as he bounded into the house. He was covered with snow from head to foot. "I think logging is much harder than just hunting for a living."

Leah looked at him and shook her head. "Could you please leave some of winter outside?"

Jayce glanced down and shrugged. "It just seems to follow me wherever I go. I'll do what I can."

He came back in a few minutes later, parka in hand. He'd dusted himself off and had given the parka a good shake. Leah smiled over her shoulder at him. "You look better now. I'm warming up some of the stew from last night. I hope that's good enough for now. I promise to have thick moose steak for you this evening."

"Sounds good. We've been cutting logs to deliver to the railroad later this afternoon, and then Adrik says we won't go out again for quite a while. Winter weather has shut down most every aspect of the rail line. The officials are still intent on building up supplies and getting new houses up for some of their men, however."

"I don't understand why they can't continue to put in tracks during the winter. It's not that cold right now."

"The ground is frozen, though, and there's not a good way of telling how firm the ground will be come spring thaw. If we lay tracks in an area not knowing it needs to be reinforced or elevated, we could have a swamp train. It will probably save a good deal of money to just wait until May. Even if they have to rehire a new crew. I heard most of the men are heading back down to the States."

"If they're not used to Alaska winter, then I can't blame them. It's probably best they go." Leah stirred the contents of the black iron pot. "Oh, I have good news." She put the spoon down and came to where Jayce had planted himself at the table.

To her surprise, Jayce pulled her onto his lap and snuggled his bearded face against her neck. "Hmm, this is a wonderful way to warm up."

"Did you hear me? I have some wonderful news to tell you."

"Hmmm, I heard."

"I don't think you're even listening to me." She playfully

pushed him away, but Jayce only tightened his hold.

He looked up at her and grinned. "What is it that's so important?"

"Well, you have to promise you won't say a word about it, until the right time, of course."

He frowned and let her ease away. "Well, I suppose I can promise that much. Now tell me."

"Helaina and Jacob are going to have a baby. But Helaina hasn't told Jacob yet."

A broad smile broke across Jayce's face. "That is good news. I know Jacob will be excited."

"It's the best news of all. I'm so happy for them."

Jayce pulled her back to him and cradled her tenderly. "Life is so different with a wife and children. Jacob will feel himself become complete. There's nothing like looking into the face of your children and knowing that a part of you will go on, even after you're dead and gone."

An image of Chase flashed through her mind. Leah pushed the thought aside, but Jayce noted the difference in her. "What's wrong?"

She covered her reaction quickly. "The stew. It's going to burn." She got up quickly and walked to the stove. *Dear Lord, how long will it be before the old thoughts stop tormenting me?* She sighed. They came fewer and farther between, so that was good. Nevertheless, Leah couldn't help but wonder what it would take to finally lay all of her demons to rest. There had to be an answer. There just had to be a way.

Chapter Sixteen

J acob loaded the last of the peeled logs onto the wagon. "This is it."

Adrik nodded and made note in his ledger. "Not sure what they plan for all these logs, but at least they'll have a stack to work with. There are plans to expand the lumber mill, and that will prove beneficial for everyone."

"Do you think they'll start working on the railroad again before spring thaw?"

Adrik shook his head. "They'd be foolhardy to try. There are so many issues at hand. Money is always the biggest, right along with conditions. The war is another. I'm not sure how things will come out in the wash."

Jacob grinned. "You sound like Karen now. I remember her using that phrase."

Adrik leaned closer and closed the green ledger. "I have some news. I'm just about beside myself to share it with someone."

"I'm your man," Jacob said, glancing around. "You look as though it might be an issue of national security."

"Nah, just Ivankov security. I've made arrangements for Ashlie to come home for Christmas. Remember Karen's nephew Timothy?"

"Of course."

"Well, he'll accompany Ashlie. They should arrive any day."

"Karen will definitely love you for that." Jacob could only imagine her happiness.

"I've been working on it for some time. I tried to get Myrtle to come too, but she didn't feel up to making such a long trip. She'll spend the holidays with some of Karen's other family members, so she won't be alone."

"Timothy was a great help to us in Seattle," Jacob remembered. "I'll be glad to hear from him—his take on the war and such. I have to say I've had some twinges of guilt when I think of the men going off to fight. Maybe if I didn't have a wife, I'd be more inclined to give it serious consideration."

"Well, they're only requiring younger men to register— under thirty-one, I think I heard."

Jacob leaned against the cart. "I know. Still, I think about the liberty and freedom I've enjoyed all these years, and it makes me think I should do something more."

"You can always pray," Adrik suggested. "Folks need a whole lot more of that than they know."

"True enough. You about ready to head out?" Jacob asked. "Temperature's dropped so much I'm actually starting to feel it. The horses are anxious too. I'm ready to be done with this." Leo and Addy gave impatient whines. "Guess they're ready too." The two Huskies cocked their heads in unison as if knowing their master was speaking of them.

"I'll just check the area for tools," Adrik said, throwing a saw onto the wagon. "Remember to keep quiet about Ashlie," he called over his shoulder.

"You know I will. I think it's mighty thoughtful of you, Adrik. Most men wouldn't be half as considerate of their wife as you have been." Jacob climbed onto the wagon.

"Karen's a special lady. She has her ornery side, but her loving nature makes it worth living with those few times when she plays prankster."

"Like the time she kept sewing your trousers smaller and smaller?" Jacob fondly remembered the event. Adrik had refused to throw away a particularly ugly and well-worn pair of pants. To encourage her husband to part with the pants, Karen took up the seams a little every few days. At first Adrik thought he'd added a few pounds, but nothing he did helped. In fact, the pants just got tighter and tighter.

"I'd almost forgot about that," Adrik admitted with a grin. "Almost, but not quite. She's ornery. There's just no tellin' what she'll do from one minute to the next. What I do know is that she'll be as happy as she's ever been to see Ashlie come home."

Adrik took his place behind the team and picked up the reins and snapped them once. "Let's go."

Leo and Addy, longtime favorites of Jacob's, led the way. Adrik had fixed runners in place of the wheels so that the wagon could move easily over the snow, carrying the maximum amount of weight. With fewer men on the railroad's payroll, hunting had lessened to a minimum. They seldom had to go out more than once a week to keep everyone in their area well provided for. Jacob didn't mind the change of work. Trading the constant smell of death for the heady scent of spruce and earth made the hard work worthwhile. It also paid a bit better, although the railroad was not known for paying anyone very well.

Jacob thought about the days to come. He was excited to have secured a beautiful wedding ring for Helaina. He planned to give it to her Christmas morning when they were alone. Sometimes it was nice to have a lot of family around, but he also craved privacy with his wife. Helaina wouldn't be expecting his gift—of this he was confident. After all, he'd given her his mother's gold band when they'd married in Last Chance. But the simplicity of that gold band, and the fact that Jacob hadn't picked it out special for Helaina, had left him unable to think of much else. When the opportunity presented itself, Jacob had purchased the new ring with great enthusiasm. It would look perfect with the gold band and offer Helaina the best of all his love.

"You're mighty quiet over there," Adrik said as he maneuvered the wagon down the slippery roadway.

"I'm tired," Jacob said, pulling up his collar. "Tired and cold. I'm glad we'll have some time away from the railroad. The break will do us all good. It's hard to go from being your own boss to having to meet somebody else's demands."

"You talking about being married or working for the railroad?" Adrik teased.

Jacob laughed. "The railroad. I still like being married."

"Well, so do I. At least as long as I remember who's boss."

"I've been doing a lot of thinking about jobs and what I

can do once the railroad moves on."

"What'd you have in mind?"

"Actually, I've been praying on that. I've thought about opening a store. I enjoyed trading with folks back in Last Chance, and it seems it would be a responsible business to start up here. Most of the places here are crude at best. I'm thinking maybe I could talk to Peter Colton and see about getting some regular shipments into Seward."

"And move down there?"

"Not necessarily. Maybe have a warehouse there if need be. Ship Creek seems to be growing enough to support more business. If the train proves successful, it would be easy enough to bring goods up from Seward. Guess I'll see just how much I like it once I've wintered here. It can't be as hard or isolated as life in Last Chance."

"Well, I'll give you that." Adrik scratched his gloved fingers against his bearded face. "A store would be a great pursuit. A lot of work, though. You sure you want that kind of work—what with having a new wife and all?"

"Helaina tells me all the time that she would love to work with me at something. Hunting isn't a good thing to drag her around doing, so I just keep thinking about the store."

"So you both plan to stay here in Alaska?" Adrik asked. He glanced at Jacob as if to read his expression. "Seriously."

"We both love it here. It's so unspoiled, and while it doesn't provide the comforts of big city life, you're also away from the burdens. You know, Helaina told me just the other night that she's never felt safer any place in the world. In New York, they worry about locking up their doors for fear of someone coming in and stealing their possessions."

"I couldn't live like that," Adrik said, shaking his head. "It's a sorry state of affairs when you have to look with suspicion at everyone who passes your way. Seems almost that you create a sort of prison for yourself and your things."

Adrik seemed to relax as the trail opened into a level snow-covered valley. He gave the horses a signal and let them move out at full speed before Jacob picked the conversation back up.

"I agree. For all the time I've been in Alaska, we never had enough to worry much about locking things up," Jacob admitted. "Folks knew they could take refuge at empty cabins on the trail—the owners would even leave enough fuel for a fire."

"That's the law of the north. Folks know not to run off without leaving some manner of provision for the next fellow."

Jacob knew that law well. "Even while running the store in Last Chance, we never worried about keeping track of things too closely. Leah kept records and such, but many was the time when people just came over and helped themselves. They always made it right later on."

Adrik nodded. "I would expect as much. Still, you have thievery up here as well. Remember how bad it was during the gold rush?"

"Oh sure," Jacob agreed. "People are always wanting something for nothing, but the weaker ones went south after they tried their hand at gold and other means of getting rich quick. It's discontentment that leads people into foolishness. I'm a content man, so I care little about chasing after things that might or might not make me happy."

The valley began to close up again, but the trail was wide

and well-traveled, and Jacob knew the horses would have little trouble taking them right back to their base camp. The sounds of civilization broke through the silence. Jacob found it amazing that the little townsite was already planning for the day when electricity would ease their long winter darkness with streetlamps and well-lit homes.

"Look, I'll go ahead and drop this off at the lumberyard. Why don't you head on home?" Adrik suggested.

Before Jacob could answer, a man called to Adrik as he made his way up the trail. He waved and hailed them. "Adrik, there's word about your relatives. They've made it to Seward."

"That's great news, Morris. Thanks for coming to find me."

Morris chuckled. "Thanks for being on your way back. I feared I was in for quite a hike. Guess I got lucky. What else have you to do?"

"This is the last load of logs," Adrik replied. "I'm especially glad now that you've told me what I've been waiting to hear." He turned to Jacob. "Look, I'm gonna need some help from both of you. I want to go down to Seward and help Timothy and Ashlie make the trip here."

"I'll finish with this delivery," Jacob offered. "Just go."

"Train is taking on fuel even as we speak. I told them to wait for you," Morris offered. "They weren't too happy, but when I explained the situation, they agreed to hold off until you got back. They'll be pleased to find it'll be just minutes instead of hours."

Adrik nodded. "Sounds good. I'm indebted to both of you."

Morris grinned. "I have a packet of papers for you to

deliver once you reach Seward. That way you won't have to lie to your missus. Jacob can tell your Karen that you were needed on official railroad business."

Adrik's laugh bellowed across the otherwise quiet countryside. "I see you've thought of everything."

"The light's nearly gone," Jacob said with a glance at the skies. "You go on. I'll tend to this. Morris and I will make short work of it."

Adrik nodded. "Don't forget to give Karen the ledger. She'll see to it that my figures are entered right."

"I'll do it. Just go."

Jacob watched as Adrik gathered his things from the back of the cart. He seemed happier than Jacob had seen him in ages. *I think he brought Ashlie home as much for himself as he did for Karen,* Jacob mused. Ashlie was the light of her father's life, and Adrik spoiled her terribly. Jacob supposed if God ever blessed him with a daughter of his own, he'd do likewise.

Jacob walked into his cabin well after dark. He felt an overwhelming urge to collapse at the kitchen table, but he knew he smelled pretty bad. He pulled off his heavy parka at the door and hung the fur on a peg before bending over to pull off his muddy boots.

"I have a hot bath waiting for you," Helaina called.

Jacob noticed the tub sitting in front of the fireplace. "I don't deserve such kindness, but I'm thankful for it." He grinned up at his wife and noted the sparkle in her eyes. She seemed to be in an unusually good mood.

"I'm working on supper. I figure to have elk steaks and fresh bread. Canned vegetables too. Oh, and Karen shared part of an apple cobbler she baked."

"That sounds almost as good as the bath." He chuckled and finished pulling off his boot. "Almost."

She came toward him, but he held her off. "You don't want to get too close. I smell worse than ten men."

Helaina pinched her nose and leaned forward with a quick kiss. "Then get thee to thy bath." She headed back toward the stove. "So what did you do today?"

"Adrik and I worked on those felled trees. We cut them into manageable pieces, stripped some and loaded them. I delivered them just before coming home."

"Sounds like you'll be nursing some sore muscles. I have more of that liniment Leah made. I can rub your back later," she murmured.

Helaina busied herself at the stove while Jacob shed his filthy clothes and climbed into the tub. He eased into the hot water and sighed. Life just didn't get much better than this. A beautiful wife fixing supper in the kitchen, a hot bath to soothe his weary muscles, and a good house to hold them safe and warm. Jacob had always known God's blessings, but now he knew God's abundance.

"So what did you do today?" Jacob asked after several minutes of silence.

"Oh, I kept very busy. Karen and I gathered evergreens for Christmas wreaths and trim. We visited a little with Leah and shared news. Karen heard from her friends—the ones you knew in the Yukon. They all seem to be well."

"That's good. Peter's the one I told you about—the one who owns the shipping company. If we decided to get serious about starting a mercantile, he'd be the one I'd talk to about supplies."

"I remember," Helaina said, coming to where Jacob sat soaping himself in the tub. "You want me to get your back?"

"Sure." He handed her the washcloth and soap. "I can't tell you how nice this is. Thanks for thinking of me."

Helaina washed his back, giving special attention to his weary shoulders. "Maybe with the extra time away from the railroad work, you could check out some of the details regarding the store. Write some letters to Mr. Colton. You know we have whatever money we need. We could buy up some of the townsite lots and at least plan things out."

"You know how I feel about using your money, Helaina. It's not that I won't, but I don't want to take undue advantage. I want to make my own way."

"I thought we agreed that we would share everything. Money, possessions, good times and bad," she said, handing the cloth back to him. "You know I don't want anything like that coming between us."

Jacob rinsed off and stood to take the towel she offered. "I know that. I don't want anything coming between us either. If need be we'll use your money, but only if we both feel it's where the Lord is leading. I want this to be a good life for both of us, but I want it focused first and foremost on the Lord."

Helaina went to the chest and got clean clothes out for Jacob. He dressed quickly, then pulled her into his arms. "It's so good to be home." He kissed her passionately on the lips, then lingered to plant kisses against her cheek and neck.

"There's something I want to give you," Helaina said rather breathlessly. "An early Christmas present."

Jacob pulled back and shook his head. "No. We agreed.

No presents until Christmas morning."

"But this is something really special. Something that isn't my gift to you, but rather the Lord's gift to us both." She smiled and took hold of his hand.

"I don't understand. The Lord has given us a gift?"

Helaina nodded and stepped back. As she pulled away, she drew his hand to her stomach. "He's given us a child."

For a moment the words didn't register. Jacob felt her press his hand against her as she continued. "We're going to have a baby, Jacob."

———

Leah was just serving dinner to Jayce when they were both startled by the sound of her brother giving out first one yell and then another.

Jayce met her eyes and it was all Leah could do to keep from laughing out loud. "I guess she told him about the baby."

Jayce chuckled. "I guess she did. Sounds like it met with his approval."

Leah laughed and spooned out peas for the twins. "I'm sure he's quite pleased with himself—and with Helaina."

Chapter Seventeen

I don't know where Adrik is," Karen confided to Leah. "Here it is Christmas morning, and he should have been back by now." She twisted her hands together and pulled back the curtain at the window for at least the tenth time.

Leah turned to her brother. "Do you know anything about this?"

Jacob shrugged. "I know he took some papers to Seward for the railroad. I don't know what else the railroad wanted of him while he was down there, but I do know they aren't working Christmas. I'm sure Adrik will be here soon. He definitely had plans to be celebrating Christmas with his family. That much I know."

Everyone had gathered at the Ivankov house to celebrate Christmas morning, but Karen's mood was far from festive. Leah decided it would be best to keep Karen's attention on something else.

"Karen, I am so impressed by the breakfast you prepared. I would have been happy to come and help."

Karen glanced at the abundant table and shook her head. "I just wanted everything perfect. I was already worried about Adrik. Do you suppose something has happened to him? Should we send Jayce or Jacob to go look for him?"

"Let's give him just a little more time. You never know. There might have been heavy snows between here and Seward. Adrik loves you and the boys more than anything. He'll be here when he can."

Karen smoothed down nonexistent wrinkles on her blue serge skirt. She had dressed with obvious care for the day. "I have a bit of a headache. Maybe I'll brew some more willow-bark tea."

"Now stop fretting. You know he'll be fine. And just look at you. You look wonderful," Leah told her. "I especially love what you've done with your hair." Karen's red hair, now marked with streaks of silver, had been fashioned in a loose bun atop her head. She had taken extra care to curl the wisps of hair that fell gracefully around her face. She looked like a proper Victorian lady, Leah thought. The only problem was, Victoria had died more than a dozen years earlier and a new age was upon them.

"Sorry I'm late!" Adrik bellowed as he pushed open the front door. "Merry Christmas!"

Karen gave a sigh. "He's safe."

Leah squeezed her arm. "Of course he is."

"I've brought my wife a special present," Adrik announced and stepped aside. All gazes turned toward the door, and even the twins were silent.

"Merry Christmas!" Timothy Rogers called to the assembly as he peered around Adrik's broad frame.

Leah couldn't hide her smile. "Timothy! How wonderful to see you. What a great surprise."

Karen shook her head. "I can't believe it. You're finally here to visit, and you pick the dead of winter to enjoy our hospitality? Whatever made you come now?"

He laughed and hugged Karen close. "I had to accompany Adrik's Christmas gift to you."

Just then Ashlie stepped into the doorway. "Merry Christmas, Mama."

Karen's eyes widened and her mouth dropped open in wordless wonder. Ashlie rushed to her mother's arms and gave her a tight embrace. "I've missed you so much."

Leah watched as Karen's shock turned to joy. She embraced her daughter, but her gaze met Adrik's. Leah saw such an exchange of love in those glances. It gave her a warm and happy feeling inside to have shared in that moment. If ever two people loved each other, it was Karen and Adrik Ivankov. How perfect that God should have put them together.

"How in the world did you arrange this?" Karen asked as Ashlie ran to greet her brothers. By now Adrik was at her side, but he only shrugged.

"Did you know about this?" Karen asked Leah.

"I did not. I doubt I could have kept such a secret."

Adrik leaned over and kissed Leah's forehead. "And that is why I did not tell you," he said, laughing.

"Just look at you," Karen said as Ashlie pulled off a long green wool coat. Ashlie was dressed in an impressive traveling suit of blue wool. Her hair was pinned up and trimmed with a smart little green hat that matched her coat.

"I've learned to be quite fashionable," Ashlie admitted. "I don't want to shame my school or Cousin Myrtle. Who, by the way, sends her regards and love. As well as a few gifts."

Leah thought Ashlie had aged considerably since they'd last seen each other. The girl was radiant and charming. Tall and slender, she had Karen's delicate features but Adrik's teasing smile and dark eyes. There was just a hint of her Tlingit ancestry in her features, and they added a rather exotic flavor to her appearance.

"Can we open our presents now?" Christopher asked impatiently. "I've waited a whole year for today to come."

Everyone laughed, but it was Adrik who started the festivities. "I believe it is time for presents. After all, I just started by giving us Ashlie and Timothy."

"That's silly, Papa. People can't be presents."

"Ah, but that's where you are wrong, Christopher. Of course they can be presents. Jesus came to earth as a present for us. Remember?"

This led quite naturally into a telling of the Christmas story. Adrik had long ago memorized the second chapter of Luke and began a recitation even as the adults found their places around the table.

Leah knew she would always remember this day as one of her very favorite Christmases. Everything seemed so perfectly right: Her menfolk were safely home from their perilous adventures; Jacob and Helaina were happily married with a new baby on the way; Jayce and the twins were all Leah could ask for or want in a family, and all were healthy and safe.

That evening as she sat beside Jayce in their home, enjoying the close of the day, Leah couldn't begin to voice her gratitude to God. *I'm so happy, Lord. You've given me far more than I could ask or imagine. Definitely more than I deserve.*

She sighed and leaned against Jayce. He put his arm around her and gently stroked her hair. Only moments before Leah had taken out the pins and brushed through the long brown curls.

"I can't believe we're really here—like this. I'm so blessed," she said, her voice barely audible.

"I was thinking the same thing. Last year I was lost at sea, waiting and watching for the ice to crush our ship and send us out across the frozen ocean. It was terrifying, but the waiting almost robbed us of our sanity."

"I can well imagine. It nearly robbed me of mine," Leah replied.

Jayce gently lifted her face. "Are you happy here?"

She pulled back and looked at him for a moment. "Haven't I just said so?"

"I know you're happy with this day, I'm just wondering, however, if you're happy here. Do you miss Last Chance?"

"Of course I miss Last Chance. I miss Emma and Sigrid and Bjorn and the children. I miss Oopick and John. I especially miss Ayoona, but I know I'll see her again someday in heaven. I loved Last Chance Creek. But it was the people who made it particularly special. I miss them most of all."

"I know. And we don't have to stay here if you find it unbearable."

Leah shook her head. "It's not unbearable. In fact, I feel blessed by God for bringing us here. What about you?"

"What about me?" He seemed genuinely surprised by her question.

"Are you happy here? Do you want to stay and call this home?"

He smiled, and it made Leah feel weak in the knees. This man always had a way of transforming her worries and concerns to feelings of comfort and security. "My home is wherever you and the twins and any other children we might have are. You are my home, Leah. I never really had a home until I married you."

"But I want you to be happy in your work. Karen has told me over and over that men must find satisfaction in their job choices. It's important to the entire family. I won't have you miserable just because you think I'm happier close to my loved ones. Please promise me you'll always be honest about such things."

Jayce laughed and pulled her close again. "I promise. And you promise me that you'll always be honest about such things as well. I find I can endure a great deal of misery when I know you are waiting for me at the end of the day."

"Leah! Leah!"

It was Ashlie calling—no, screaming—from outside the door. Leah and Jayce jumped up so quickly they nearly took a tumble. Righting each other, they hurried for the door.

"What is it?" Leah questioned, pulling Ashlie into the house as soon as Jayce had the door open.

Ashlie was crying, and it was clear that something was terribly wrong. "It's . . . it's . . . Mama."

Leah looked to Jayce and back to Ashlie. "Something's wrong with Karen?"

"Yes!" Ashlie took hold of Leah. "You have to come. She collapsed on the floor, and she won't wake up."

Chapter Eighteen

Jayce remained with the children while Leah hurried to the Ivankov house with Ashlie. The girl was so distraught, Leah couldn't imagine what had happened to Karen. She was perfectly fine when Leah had headed home with Jayce and the twins. Karen had been suffering a headache, but the day had been exhausting and Karen had worked very hard to make sure everyone had a good time.

"What happened, Ashlie?" Leah asked as they approached the house.

"I don't know. She said . . . oh, she said that her head hurt. I didn't think anything about it. I should have. I should have seen that something was wrong." She stopped and shook her head vigorously. "I should have known."

Leah halted her steps and turned. "Why?" Leah asked, hoping the matter-of-fact question would cause Ashlie to regain some composure. "You're not a doctor."

"I know. But she's my mother."

"I wasn't much younger than you when my mother died; should I have known enough to keep her alive—to prevent her death? Is it my fault that my mother is dead?"

Ashlie calmed just a bit. "Well . . . of course not."

"And neither is it yours that your mother is sick."

"She seemed fine. She really was happy." Ashlie began walking toward the house again. "She was getting ready for bed. She told me how happy she was to have me home, and then she got a funny look on her face and fell to the ground."

Leah pushed open the door to the Ivankov house without knocking. "Papa went for the doctor," Oliver announced.

Leah gently touched his shoulder. "How long ago?"

"Just after Ashlie went for you."

"What's wrong with our ma?" Christopher asked.

Leah shook her head. "I don't know. Let me check on her."

Leah went quickly to Karen's room and found that they had managed to get her into bed and her nightclothes. She touched her hand to the unconscious woman's pale brow. She didn't feel feverish or clammy. "Karen, it's Leah. I'm here. Please wake up."

Leah took hold of Karen's wrist and felt for a pulse. The beat was weak. "Karen, I don't know what's happened to you. Please wake up." Ashlie had mentioned Karen's headache, and earlier in the day Leah knew Karen had suffered enough discomfort that she had brewed some willow-bark tea to ease the pain.

"Do you know what's wrong with her?" Ashlie asked as she came into the room. Leah saw that the boys were fearfully standing guard at the door, listening for whatever answers Leah might offer.

"I don't know. Sometimes people have spells that cause them to lose consciousness. Some are very bad and others are less so. I wish I could tell you which case this was, but I can't. Your mother seems very weak, although nothing was previously wrong."

"It was her head," Oliver said quite seriously. "She told me earlier to pray for her because it hurt."

Leah let out a long breath. "She might have ruptured a vessel in her head." The thought of an aneurysm came to mind. She had once talked with a doctor about such things when she still lived in Ketchikan. The doctor explained that sometimes vessels in the brain would rupture and cause extensive bleeding, and there was very little they could do to help the patient. In some cases, he had explained, holes could be drilled into the skull to drain the blood, but the risk was great.

It seemed to take forever before Adrik returned with the doctor. The man came quickly to Karen's bedside and demanded everyone leave the room.

"I'm Leah Kincaid. I have some training in medicine," Leah offered. "I could act as your nurse."

The middle-aged man eyed her up momentarily, then nodded. "Everyone else out."

Adrik led Ashlie to the door. "Come on, boys, let's let them work. They'll tell us what's going on as soon as they know something." His gaze met Leah's, as if to confirm this.

"Of course we will. I'll come out just as soon as I can," she promised.

Once the door was closed, the doctor looked to her. "What can you tell me?"

Leah shrugged. "She's complained of a headache all day. Apparently it was bad enough to ask her son to pray about it. She also took some willow-bark tea earlier. Karen's always been a very strong woman, and when she stops to take a remedy of any kind, I know that it's because there is a strong reason. Still, she didn't really show any other signs. Do you suppose it's an aneurysm?"

"It could well be. I've seen it before and the symptoms sound quite similar."

He checked her pupils and listened to her heart. Leah watched and waited, feeling very unnecessary. She longed for Karen to open her eyes and announce to them that she felt perfectly fine, but something inside told Leah this wasn't going to be the case. For the first time since Ashlie came to the door crying for help, Leah began to fear for Karen's life.

"She's not doing well," the doctor said as he pulled the stethoscope from his ears. "Her heart is very weak and her breathing is quite shallow." He reached for his case and took out several instruments. "I'll check her reflexes, but I'm afraid there's little we can do. It may be a ruptured artery, as you suggested, or she may have had a stroke."

"A stroke?"

"Her body isn't responding as it should," he said, pointing to her left side. "The nerves show little or no reaction."

"What does it mean?" Leah bit her lip and met the man's stern expression.

"Only time will tell.... We have no way of knowing whether she'll recover from this or not."

"So she could . . . she might . . . die?"

"That is a strong possibility. I'm sorry. I know Mrs. Ivankov to have a reputation for kindness and generosity. Her husband too."

"What can we do?"

"Little but wait. I'll check in on her in the morning. If there's any change in the night, you can send someone for me." He put his instruments away and got to his feet. "I don't want to discourage you, but I've seen situations like this before. The outcome has never been good."

Leah nodded. She looked to Karen and then to the closed door. "I understand."

When they came out from the bedroom, Jacob and Helaina had joined Adrik and the children. The doctor looked at Adrik and shook his head. "Mr. Ivankov, I'm sorry. It appears your wife has suffered a major trauma to her brain. There is no way of telling at this point in time whether she will recover."

"What are you saying?" Ashlie asked, her voice shrill and unnatural. "Is she going to die?"

Christopher and Oliver looked at each other in disbelief, while Ashlie began to sob. Leah went to her side. She put her arms around the girl and pulled her close. "We need to pray for your mother. We don't know what God has yet planned for her, but prayer is always the best way to help someone."

The doctor nodded and looked back to Adrik. "I'm sorry. You may send someone for me if her condition changes." He left just as quickly as he'd come, leaving the family in stunned silence.

Adrik looked to Leah as if to will the truth from her. The questioning in his eyes left her uneasy. She wanted so much to reassure him, but she had no words for it.

"This is all my fault," Ashlie said as she broke away from Leah and went to her father. "I should have been here. She's had to work too hard."

"It's not your fault," Adrik said, putting his arm around her. "Your ma would work hard whether you were here or not. We don't know why this has happened, but it has."

"Leah, do you have any idea of what can be done?" Jacob questioned. "Are there any native remedies?"

Leah shook her head. "If there are, I don't know them. I can ask around, but I don't know that it will help."

"Do whatever you can," Adrik said. Gone was the usual strength in his voice and demeanor. To Leah it appeared that Ashlie held him up as much as he supported her.

"I will," she promised. "I'm going back to tell Jayce what's happened, then I can come here and sit with her so that you can sleep."

"No. I'll take care of her. She's my mother," Ashlie stated, pulling away from her father. "I'll send for you if I need you."

Leah thought to protest but then nodded. "Please do. I'll come in the morning and relieve you and cook breakfast for everyone."

"I'll come help as well," Helaina offered.

Adrik followed Leah outside, much to her surprise. "Look, if you know something more . . ."

"I honestly don't," she said before he could continue. "The brain is a queer thing; doctors know so very little on how to treat problems related to it. It could have been a ruptured vessel, in which case she's bled into her brain. Or it could be a stroke, in which case the chances for recovery would be better." She touched his arm, feeling the warmth against the chilled night air. "Adrik, I'm so sorry. I wish I could say that things will be all right, but ..." Her voice trailed off as tears came to her eyes.

Adrik hugged her tightly. "I didn't know she was sick. I didn't know anything was wrong. She was so happy today. So happy to have everyone here and Ashlie home. I would have been here if I'd known something was wrong. I would have let Timothy bring Ashlie here by himself if I'd thought Karen needed me."

"You didn't do anything wrong, Adrik. She was happy and healthy. What happened is no one's fault. You mustn't be hard on yourself. Of what I know, there is usually little warning. Sometimes nothing at all. Don't blame yourself."

"But I know she was worrying these past couple of days with me gone. That could have been avoided. I should have just told her the truth. I should have been here."

Leah pulled back and shook her head. "You taught me long ago that we cannot live on 'what if's' and 'should have been's.' Adrik, we need to pray and remember who is in control. God knows what His plans are, and we do not. It isn't easy, but the alternative is much worse."

Adrik nodded. "I know. But, Leah, I cannot imagine my life without her."

Leah whispered, "I can't either."

———

The days passed by without any sign of Karen recovering. Leah took her turn by Karen's bedside remembering both the good days and bad they'd shared. Her most frequent thoughts were of Karen's love and faithfulness. When the rest of the world had deserted her, Leah had known Karen would be her constant. She was a good second mother and a dear friend.

"And now I'm losing you," Leah whispered. "I can't bear that you won't be here to see my children grow up—to offer me advice—to comfort me in sorrow and to share my joys."

The room was dark, except for a single lantern atop the dresser Adrik had made. The light cast strange shadows on the walls of the room and bathed them in an eerie yellow glow. In a few hours everyone would wake up and welcome in a new year.

Leah yawned and dozed off and on in the hard wooden chair, then startled awake at the sound of the bedroom door opening. Adrik came in quietly and looked to Leah for information.

"She's resting easy," Leah offered. "Nothing has changed."

Adrik sat down on the bed beside Karen's still body. "I thought I'd ask the doctor about taking her to Seattle. Maybe a large hospital would know how to better help her. After all, we're always hearing about the progress made in medicine."

Leah wanted to offer him encouragement. "That's true. There are always new treatments. Perhaps Seattle would offer something good. I'm sure the doctor might have an idea about it."

Adrik took hold of Karen's hand and gently stroked it as he continued. "I'm grateful for all you've done. I know it hasn't been easy."

"Jayce has been good to stay with the children. He loves being with them and doesn't mind at all. He knows how important Karen is to me—to all of us. He loves her too."

Adrik smiled sadly. "Who could help but love her? She's done nothing but give of herself since the day she was born. She's always helping someone with something."

"No one knows that better than I do. She was such a blessing to Jacob and me. You were too, Adrik. We wouldn't have made it out of the Yukon alive had it not been for the both of you. I hate to think where we would have ended up. I probably would have been forced to marry some grizzled old prospector, and Jacob would probably be dead. You and Karen kept us safe and became the parents we no longer had."

"I don't know what I'll do without her, Leah. She's been my everything. If she dies, how will I go on without her smile? Without her touch?" He looked at her as if she honestly might offer answers. "What will the boys do? They're so young. And Ashlie. Poor girl. She blames herself for this. She's sure that if she'd stayed here, her mother would still be healthy and happy."

"I know. I've tried to talk to her. Guilt is an awful thing to try to overcome."

An hour later the doctor showed up. He was in between delivering a baby and setting the arm of a man who'd had a nasty run-in with a stack of cut wood. He quickly examined Karen, then turned to Adrik and Leah just as Ashlie joined them.

"I wondered," Adrik started before the doctor could speak, "if I should consider moving her to Seattle? I could arrange to have her on the next ship. I could even wire my friend to send a ship. Would the hospital there be able to help her?"

"I'm sorry," the doctor said, his eyes downcast. "I can't advise that." He looked up, regaining his façade of strength. "I don't expect that she'll last the day."

"No!" Ashlie cried out and rushed to her mother's side. "You can't say that. We've taken good care of her."

"The care she's received has little to do with the situation," the doctor said softly. "Just as there was little that could be done to prevent the condition, there is nothing to be done to prevent her passing. I'm so sorry. Medicine has much to offer in this modern age, but unfortunately, treatments for the brain are still limited."

Ashlie sobbed against her mother's neck while Leah shuddered at the chill that washed down her spine. Adrik stood silent as the doctor made his way to the door. "If time permits," the man said, "I'll return to check on her again."

"I should never have gone away," Ashlie sobbed. "All of this is my fault. If I'd stayed, Mama would be just fine."

"That's not true," Adrik said, coming to his daughter's side. He took hold of her and turned her to face him. "You must stop this. Your brothers will not understand. They will be frightened more than ever if they see you falling apart like this."

"I don't want Mama to die." Ashlie leaned against her father's chest. "I don't want her to go."

"Neither do I." Adrik barely managed to speak the words.

"No matter what happens, I'm staying here to take care of my family," Ashlie suddenly declared. She pushed back and wiped her eyes. "If Mama . . . if she . . . I'll be here to take care of you and the boys. You won't have to worry. I won't ever leave my family again. Never!"

Later that afternoon Leah joined her brother and Adrik and Ashlie at Karen's side. The boys had gone to be with Helaina to help pick up some things in town, and Jayce was again watching over the twins.

"Her breathing has slowed a great deal," Adrik told Leah as she took her seat.

"She's not in pain, is she?" Ashlie asked Leah.

"No, I don't see any signs of that," Leah replied. "Usually there are ways to tell. Your mother seems quite at peace."

Ashlie was stoic. "She deserves so much better than this. I don't understand how God can be so cruel."

"Sickness and death are a part of life, darling girl," Adrik said, putting his arm around her. "Your mother loves the Lord. She knows that He loves her as well. She wouldn't consider Him cruel in this and neither should you."

"Karen once told me long ago that her only fear of dying young was to leave her children without a mother. She had asked me if I would see to helping your father raise you should anything happen," Leah said as she took hold of Karen's hand. "I promised her I would."

"I remember that," Adrik said. "I asked the same of you, Jacob. Remember?"

"I do," Jacob replied. "We are here for you, Adrik. For you and the children. You are the only family we have on this earth, besides that which we are making anew."

"I can take care of my brothers," Ashlie said, her tone quite serious.

"Your mother wouldn't want you to bear this alone,

Ashlie," Leah said. "No one is meant to take this on by themselves. That's what family is for."

"I can handle the job by myself." She straightened in the bedside chair and kept her gaze on Karen.

Leah decided to let the matter drop for now. She would try to talk to Ashlie when they were alone; now was not the appropriate place or time.

"I think we should sing," Leah said without thinking. "Karen loved the hymns in church. I think she'd like it if we surrounded her with music."

"'I am Thine, O Lord, I have heard Thy voice and it told Thy love to me,'" she began, singing Karen's favorite song. The others joined, except for Ashlie.

"'There are depths of love that I cannot know till I cross the narrow sea; there are heights of joy that I may not reach till I rest in peace with Thee.'" Leah felt an odd sensation as the words of the chorus permeated the room. "'Draw me nearer, nearer, nearer, blessed Lord.'"

She gripped Karen's hand, feeling as best she could for a pulse but finding none. Leah knew her friend was gone. She looked across the bed to where Adrik sat. When their gaze met, Leah knew he already knew. She didn't need to say a word.

The words of the song faded just as Timothy came into the room. He looked across to where they had gathered. "The doctor has come," he announced.

Adrik put his arm around Ashlie. "Tell him . . . tell him there's no need. Tell him my beloved has gone home."

Chapter Nineteen

Two weeks passed with a series of blizzards and heavy snows. Leah felt Karen's loss deeply but tried her best to offer encouragement to Adrik and his family. Ashlie, in particular, seemed impossible to reach. As best Leah could tell, Ashlie was waging a battle within herself, divided by guilt over not having been home sooner and a fierce desire to leave again.

Ashlie was so like her mother; tall and slender, athletic in nature. Had it not been for some of her father's darker features, she might have been a strong replica of Karen in her youth. Ashlie also inherited her mother's outgoing nature and bold spirit. Very little frightened her—except the death of her mother. Losing Karen had sent Ashlie into a dark place. She refused to talk to anyone and usually kept herself hidden away working at one thing or another. A few days after Karen's death, she had requested that the others stay away from the cabin to allow the family some time alone. While Leah disagreed, she had conceded. She decided to let Ashlie have her way—at least for a short time.

To her relief, however, the situation didn't last long. Leah finally began to see hope for a return to normalcy when the girl showed up one morning asking for a lesson in making her father's favorite dried berry cobbler.

"I heard that Timothy is planning to return to Seattle."

"Yes. He's leaving at the end of the week," Ashlie said, looking away as if completely disinterested.

"What about you? Will you go back? Surely school has started again."

"I suppose it has, but I have responsibilities here with my family."

"Ashlie, have you talked to your father about this?"

"Why should I? He needs me. He's so sad over losing Mama. I have to help him."

"Ashlie, I've been very worried about you. You and I used to be close. I thought to help you share your grief."

"How do you share this?" Ashlie looked at Leah with a befuddled expression. "This is exactly why I didn't want to have you all at the house. I don't feel like talking and answering a lot of questions, and I don't want anyone trying to change my mind. I owe it to my family to be here for them."

"It's admirable, and I don't fault you for wanting to help them," Leah admitted. "I know you feel obligated to your family, but I think you should also think about what they need and want too."

"Meaning what?" Ashlie finally took a seat but still refused to look Leah in the eye.

"Meaning that they don't need you to replace your

mother. No one can do that. Not you or me or Helaina. They also don't need you to stay, only to grow bitter at all the things you've had to give up. I know you don't want to be here, but you feel you have to be here."

Her head shot up. "My family is here and they need me. Of course I want to be here. How dare you say I'd grow bitter?"

Leah shook her head. "Please don't be angry with me. I'm on your side."

Ashlie's expression contorted. "I'm all they have. They need me to stay here and help. My brothers are too little to be without a mother."

"You're too young to have lost your mother as well. But you won't give yourself that much consideration." Leah leaned forward to touch Ashlie's arm. The girl stiffened, but Leah refused to pull back. "I want you to drop all the pretenses and façades related to what you think you're supposed to be right now. I want you to just talk to me honestly—openly. I'll keep your confidence, but it's important that you open up and be truthful about your feelings. You can't just keep them buried inside."

Ashlie bit her lower lip so hard Leah was certain she'd draw blood any moment. The tension in her body never eased, even when she finally spoke.

"My father needs me to take my mother's place. My brothers need me. My selfishness killed my mother. I owe it to them to be here."

Leah nodded. "All right, let's talk about this one issue at a time. First of all, your father loves you. He enjoys your company and wants only the best for you. But he does not need for you to take your mother's place. He's grieving her loss, just as you are. He isn't looking for a replacement. He needs for you to be his daughter and for your brothers to be his sons. Would you honestly thrust your father's responsibilities on the shoulders of Oliver or Chris if he'd died instead of your mother?"

"Well . . . no, but I'm older. I'm nearly grown. A lot of girls have had to take over their mother's duties. Why should I be any different?"

"Because your father has me. He has Helaina. We are here by choice to begin with, making our home in Alaska. You left because you felt called to something else. You wanted a different kind of experience, and apparently your parents saw the validity of that desire. Would you discredit them for their thinking?"

"But that was then," Ashlie began in earnest. "That was when everything was perfectly fine. I went away when things were good and everyone was happy."

"I know that, but their reasons for sending you to Seattle haven't changed." Leah had spoken with Adrik only the day before and knew that he worried about Ashlie remaining at home. He feared that she would relegate herself to being an old maid, watching over her mother's children and husband, instead of having a family of her own. He didn't want to force her to leave, but Leah knew his wish was that Ashlie should not give up her life on his behalf.

Ashlie seemed to consider Leah's words. When she looked up, Leah saw the tears that had formed. "I want to do the right thing for them, Leah. The boys are so sad. They can't believe Mama is gone. I can't either, but at least I'm old enough to know that these things happen and that they are a part of life. Christopher worries constantly that our father will die as well. Oliver too. They watch him as if he might disappear before their very eyes. I'm so glad he hasn't had to work for the railroad since Mama died, because I don't think the boys could bear it."

Leah nodded. "I know. But God has provided, Ashlie. And He's provided for you as well. It will be hard to see you go, but you need to be a young woman with the liberty to seek your own future—not just assume your mother's role. I admire your willingness to stay more than anything you could have done, but, Ashlie, I want you to have your future. Your very own future. Your father wants it too." She paused and added, "And, Ashlie, I know your mother would want it."

"I don't know what to do." The words made her sound so lost.

"Ashlie, you just need to sit down and talk with your father. He wants you to be happy, and he's worried about you giving up your dreams."

Ashlie began to cry. "But if I go ... if I go ... what will happen then?"

"Life will go on," Leah said softly. "It always does. People come and go in our lives; sometimes they stay for a long while and other times they are here just a brief period. The important thing is that we cherish them while we have a chance. I don't tell you to go without grave consideration to the matter—your father would say the same. It's a dangerous world; there's a war going on in Europe, and Americans are a part of the fight. But Myrtle needs you as much as anyone here. Your schooling awaits you. And who knows where it will take you and what interests you might find? Don't give it up, Ashlie. I'm afraid you'll always regret it if you do."

"But being here for my family is the right thing to do," Ashlie said, seeming to regain some composure. "I've always been taught to put my family first. That family is the one thing that lasts."

"I agree, and if there were no one else to be here for your father and brothers, I would tell you to stay. I promise you, I would." Leah smiled and gently rubbed the back of Ashlie's hand. "Your heart is full of good motives. It's full of love. That doesn't change just because you make plans to go away."

"But won't it be hard on Chris and Oliver? To see me go after losing Mama?"

Leah leaned back and crossed her arms. "It will be hard no matter what. If you stay, it will be hard because you aren't their mother. They might even resent you for trying to take her place. If you go, they will feel another sense of loss and miss you. Either way, there will be some degree of pain. But, Ashlie, life is full of pain and misery. Sorrow dogs our heels and refuses to let us be. But God has also promised that we can overcome everything in Jesus. Jesus said, 'In the world ye shall have tribulation: but be of good cheer; I have overcome the world.'"

"I don't understand that. Of course Jesus overcame. He's God. What does that have to do with me?"

"You belong to Him. He loves you and He cares what happens to you. Because you have given Him your heart, He lives in you. Therefore, you have also overcome. It doesn't mean that bad things won't happen, Ashlie, but it does mean that you have victory before they ever come to roost on your doorstep. You have Jesus. You have only to keep your eyes fixed on Him and let your faith in Him be firmly rooted.

"And, Ashlie, you aren't to blame for what happened to your mother. No one is. Something went wrong inside her head. You didn't cause it. Your brothers didn't cause it."

"But people sometimes die because they work too hard."

Leah smiled. "Your mother worked much harder when you were all at home and much younger. I remember because I was here helping for part of that time. Look, you can't continue to carry this burden, Ashlie. It isn't yours to carry for one thing, and for another, it will consume you and make you old before your time. Your mother died because it was her time to die. Nothing more. Nothing less. You don't have the power of life and death in your hands. Only God does."

For several minutes Ashlie sat in silence. Getting up, Leah decided to check on the twins and give Ashlie some time to consider what she'd said.

"I want to go back to Seattle, but I'm afraid of hurting my father."

Leah ran her hand against the smooth wood of a chair Adrik had made. "Ashlie, I think it would hurt your father more if you refuse to talk to him and share your heart. Why don't you just go to him and explain how you feel? Tell him everything you just told me. He'll understand. I promise."

"You don't think it will just make him sadder than he already is?"

"No. I don't think anything could make him as sad as losing your mother. The worst has happened, and now he's just trying to put his life back together. Talk to him."

Ashlie nodded and got to her feet. "I will. I'll go find him right now."

———

The snows let up and the temperature warmed just a bit the next day. The tall spruce and hemlocks were covered with a fresh frosting of white. Their heavy boughs seemed to reach to the ground, as if asking for help to free them from their bonds. Across the landscape the white coating left everything with a clean, pristine feel. It was like a world untouched.

For all of her time in Alaska, Leah had not really encountered a place like this. In Ketchikan the winters had been mild, with more rain than snow, while in Last Chance the winters had been bitterly cold, with some snow and a great deal of fog and wind. It snowed far more here in the Ship Creek area than she'd even experienced in the Yukon. There was probably two feet of snow on the ground already, and she'd been told there was bound to be a whole lot more before winter ended.

Leah looked at the canvas pieces in her hands. She was always sewing these days, it seemed. Not that she minded. Her mother used to say that the sewing basket told the family's story. Tales of adventures gone awry or of new babies born. Stories of prosperity or poverty played out in the creation of new clothes or the multiple mendings of old ones. The memory made Leah smile.

"I can't believe the way these babies are growing," Helaina, said shaking her head at the twins.

Leah looked at the new canvas trousers she had been working on for Wills. He'd grown nearly two inches taller in the past few months and all of it seemed to be in his legs. "I know. I saw it in other people's children but hadn't expected it in my own." She glanced at the clock and put her sewing aside. "I need to go make sure Ashlie is doing all right getting supper on. Could you keep an eye on the children for me?"

"Of course." Helaina raised her own sewing. "I'm just about finished with this baby gown, but it seems much too tiny."

"It won't be." Leah smiled and pulled on her parka. "You'll see. I thought the same thing when I was making clothes for the twins."

"I just want them to be perfect," she said, studying the piece.

Leah smiled. "I'll only be a minute. The twins should be asleep for at least another hour."

"I don't mind if they wake up. They're good babies. You've been a good mother to them, Leah."

"I hope so. We all come into parenting without the experience that we so desperately need. I helped Karen with her children, but it's not the same. I never remember listening through the night to make certain that Ashlie was still breathing, but I constantly fret over the twins."

Helaina gave a rather awkward laugh. "I haven't had even the experience you have."

"Nonsense. You've been a great help with Wills and Merry. I don't know how I would have survived that first year without you. You'll know what to do—of that I'm certain."

The walk to Adrik's house was a short one, but before Leah arrived there she stopped midstep. A strange noise came from behind the house. It sounded muffled, almost like sobbing. She left the path and walked through the snow to a small shed where Adrik kept tools.

Leah approached the shed slowly and saw the crumpled form of Oliver. He was nestled up against several furs, his face buried in his hands.

"Oliver?"

He looked up as if mortified to have been found. "Go away."

Leah frowned and wondered if she should. Something compelled her to stay, however. "Oliver, you don't have to be ashamed of crying."

He buried his face again. "I don't want to talk about it."

Leah went to where he sat and knelt beside him. Reaching out gently, she touched his head. "Oliver, I want to help."

"You can't help," he said, looking up at her. "My mama is dead. You can't help that."

Leah nodded. "I know. I can't change what's happened. But you need to know that I miss her too. She was like a mother to me, and it feels like there's a hole inside where her love used to be."

Oliver sobered and nodded. "There is a big empty place. It hurts a lot."

"I know, sweetie. I know." She opened her arms to him. For a minute Oliver just looked at her, then just when Leah felt he would spurn her, he dove for her, knocking them both over. Leah just held on to Oliver and fell back against the furs.

Oliver cried softly for several minutes while Leah prayed silently. *Please, God, please ease his pain. It's so hard to know what to do to help him. Please show me.*

Leah tried to imagine what Karen would want her to say to Oliver. How would she word things to help him understand about life and death? Leah drew a deep breath and let it out slowly. Was there ever a good way to talk about something so very painful and sad?

"My mama was a good person, wasn't she?" Oliver asked, easing away from Leah just a bit.

The question surprised Leah, but she tried not to show it. "Of course she was. She was helpful to everyone and she demonstrated love and kindness all of the time."

"She loved Jesus too."

Leah leaned up and smiled. "Yes. Yes, she did."

"I love Him too, but I feel bad 'cause I wish He hadn't taken my mama. I feel real bad inside, Leah. I feel mad at God for taking Mama."

Leah pulled him close and rested back in the furs. "Oh, sweetie, God understands how you feel. He knows it hurts."

"Will He get mad at me?"

"No, I don't think so. But, Oliver, He wants to offer you His comfort. He doesn't want you to be mad at Him. He knows how you feel, and He wants to help."

Oliver stayed in her arms for several minutes before pushing away. "I'm sorry I acted like a baby. I'm trying not to cry in front of Christopher or Papa. If I cry it will scare Christopher."

"You don't have to be strong for everybody else, Oliver. You miss your mother. That's going to stay with you for a long time. I know. It stayed with me a long time. Sometimes I still miss my mother."

Oliver wiped his face with the back of his coat sleeve. "I gotta go. Christopher is waiting for me to help him with the dog sled. We're going to do some errands for Papa."

Leah got up and smiled at the boy. "You know I love you, Oliver. You've always been like a little brother to me. I'll always be here for you, and you don't have to be afraid of crying around me. I won't say a word to anyone, if that helps."

Oliver nodded. "I just don't want Papa to worry about it. He's got enough to worry about right now."

Leah hugged him, then let him go. How she wished she might take away his pain. She looked to the skies overhead through the canopy of trees that surrounded Adrik's land. "Lord, this is so hard. My father used to say that life was full of death. I guess I'm seeing that more now than ever before. It's a hard lesson to learn, much less to know what to do with."

———

"I appreciate your writing to Grace and Miranda," Adrik said later as Leah presented him with the two letters. "I don't think I could have done it justice."

"It wasn't a problem. I know they'll be shocked and heart-broken by the news, just as we are."

"I still can't believe it's happened. I think back to how just a few short weeks ago we were laughing and making plans for Christmas." He gave a harsh laugh. "I was feeling all smug for my plans. Now I don't feel anything but a sort of numbness—a disbelief that any of this could have happened." He continued to stare at the letters. "When you lose a man on the job—like we did last week when the log chain snapped—well, you just kind of take it in stride. It's sad and it's shocking in its own way, but you know the risks are there. When your sweet wife falls over dead, never to speak another word—never to hear your words to her, well, that's just not something you think will happen."

"I know. I find myself feeling like Ashlie, wondering if I missed seeing some sign. Was there something more I could have done? But I know the dangers of trying to second-guess a situation. I've learned that much in life."

Adrik looked at the letters for a moment longer, then stuffed them in his jacket pocket. He looked up and met Leah's eyes. "Ashlie came and talked to me. I think I have you to thank for that."

Leah shrugged. "We're all here to help each other, Adrik. Did she talk to you about Seattle?"

"Yes. I'm glad she did. She said that she really would like to go back to school—maybe even college. She wondered if I could bear having her go back at least until summer."

Adrik looked to have aged about ten years since Karen's death, but today he actually looked as though a burden had been lifted.

"And what did you tell her?"

"I told her that I thought her mother would want her to finish her education. At least I didn't lie about that. Karen missed that girl something fierce, but she was so proud of what she'd accomplished in school. Her teacher wrote to say that Ashlie will probably graduate first in her class next spring."

"That is impressive," Leah admitted, then offered a smile. "So what did you lie about?"

"Huh?"

"You said you didn't lie about the fact that her mother

would want her to finish her education. So what *did* you lie about?"

Adrik looked rather surprised for a moment, then came a hollow laugh. "I told her I'd be just fine—that I had plenty of help and didn't need her here to watch over us."

"And that was a lie?"

"I don't know," he said sadly. "Maybe it was about the part where I said I'd be just fine. I don't honestly know if I'll ever be fine again."

Chapter Twenty

Helaina picked her way through the mud and snow as she double-checked her list. They needed a half dozen things, most of which were for the special meal Leah had planned for Timothy and Ashlie's farewell. They would be leaving the next day for Seattle, and Leah wanted to send them off with the best of meals and plenty of warm wishes.

Helaina had to admit she was rather glad for the excuse to leave home. Everyone was still so sad over Karen's passing. Helaina mourned too, but since she hadn't known Karen as well, the others seemed not to recognize her sorrow. She paused in front of the mercantile, feeling oddly misplaced.

"Excuse me," a vaguely familiar voice said from behind her.

Helaina turned to find Cheslav Babinovich, and her eyes widened in surprise. The last time she'd seen this man had been in Nome. She started to greet him, but the man immediately turned and started to flee.

"Mr. Babinovich, whatever is wrong?"

He stopped and turned, eyeing her strangely for a moment as if to ascertain something. But what? "I ... uh ..." His Russian accent was thick and he seemed confused.

Helaina thought perhaps he'd again forgotten her name. "Mrs. Barringer. Although when we first met it was Mrs. Beecham. We met in Nome, remember?" It seemed so strange that every time she'd run across this man since their initial meeting, he seemed to have no recollection of who she was. Perhaps his fears and worries imposed upon his ability to remember.

"Of course. I am sorry for my poor memory. I have traveled so much over this state in my searches, meeting so many people. How might I be of service, my dear woman?"

Helaina thought his entire demeanor rather strange, but she shook off her concerns. "I have heard many troubling things about your homeland. I have thought about you, wondering if you ever managed to help your czar and his family."

Babinovich looked around him in a rather alarmed manner before hurrying back to Helaina's side. "It is best not to speak of them. Circumstances have worked against the family, I'm afraid. They are captive prisoners in the motherland. I fear the Russia that I once knew and loved is no more. The government in power now would see all of the royals killed. In fact, they will see many people killed, I fear."

"I am sorry to hear that. The newspapers have been full of negative stories to be certain. The war has left its mark all over the world."

"That is true. Should the war not have come to Europe, my czar might yet be safe in his palace. Now ..." His voice faded off as he gazed blankly down the street. "These are desperate and sad times."

"So what will you do?" Helaina asked.

"I have no idea. I suppose I will continue to look for ways to get the royal family to safety. There might yet be a way, but God alone knows what that might be."

"And why have you come to this part of Alaska?"

"Ah, that is simple. I had heard of this growing railroad and desired to see it for myself. I thought it might be useful to my needs should the czar and his family be able to sail as far as Seward."

"But there are far more favorable areas in Alaska where Russians would feel very welcome. I am told that Sitka is still predominantly settled by the Russians. There are families there who can trace their ancestry back several generations to a time when your motherland still owned the property."

He nodded but leaned closer and whispered. "But that area could also be filled with enemies. We would have to see for ourselves if the population would be favorable toward the czar and his family. I have men checking into such matters even now."

Helaina felt her feet growing numb with cold. She felt equally sorry for Babinovich whose boots showed signs of irreparable wear. No doubt he had walked all over the territory in search of a hideaway for his beloved czar.

Just then Helaina got an idea. "I was just about to pick up a few things. We're having a grand meal tonight. A couple of family members are heading to Seattle tomorrow. Why don't you join us for supper? There will be plenty of food."

Babinovich seemed to consider this for a moment. He

rubbed his mustache with the back of his index finger. "Such a meal sounds quite inviting to a weary pilgrim such as myself. I will accept with great happiness."

"Good. If you wait for me, I'll take you to my home. You can stay and visit and warm yourself by the fire. Later, my husband can bring you back by dogsled. Where are you staying?"

"I only got here this morning. I haven't really arranged for myself."

"Then you could stay with us if you like," Helaina offered. She wasn't sure what drew her to the man, but she longed to know more about him. "There isn't much to offer in the way of housing; most of the railroad men lived in tents, and now they're gone."

"It seems the area is less settled than Nome and Seward," he said, looking around the little town.

"It's almost deceptive. The area is growing, and there are far more people here now than there were just months ago—despite the railroad releasing their workers. I would expect to see this entire area boom. Especially if they were to find gold or silver."

"And do they expect to do that?" Babinovich questioned with sudden interest.

"There have been some finds—some rumors of big deposits—but nothing has been found as of yet to prove that true."

"It sounds promising."

Helaina smiled. "The thought of gold always sounds promising, but I wouldn't count on anything until you actually hold it in your hand." She turned. "I'll only be a minute, and then we can make our way home. You're welcome to join me."

She waited for him to decide. Finally he shook his head. "You go ahead, Mrs. Barringer. I'll wait here."

Helaina hurried into the store and went quickly to retrieve the items needed. She was quite pleased to learn that one of the native women had brought in a few eggs. They were frozen, but Helaina thought they would surely thaw so she could make a cake. She made certain to see the two eggs were wrapped in cotton batting before she tucked them gently into her purse. The other things went into her large canvas bag.

"I hope you are not frozen through," she told Babinovich as she emerged from the store. "I should have insisted you come in, although it was scarcely any warmer in the tent."

"I am not surprised. I do not know how people exist in such cold."

"But you have cold in your country as well, do you not?"

Babinovich took the bag from her as they turned to walk. "We have wonderful places where the cold is not so bad. Siberia, now that is different. That place is like a frozen death. Some parts are not so bad, but others are . . . well . . . I would not want to be there."

"Tell me about your home in Russia. Where did you grow up? Are your parents still there?"

Babinovich shook his head. "My parents are dead. My life there centered around my service to the czar. We are family, of course, but distantly so. I served him and serve him now. It is all I have known."

"Did you enjoy the privileges of such a life?"

He nodded but stared straight ahead. "I have known great

wealth. Such parties—such foods and clothes. They were magnificent."

Helaina heard a tone of regret in his voice, but whether or not it was for the wealth of bygone days or simply missing the days that had once offered him so much, she was not sure. As they neared the place where Adrik had chosen to build their little family village, Helaina motioned to the largest of the three houses.

"That is where we'll go. The cabin to the right belongs to my sister-in-law and her husband. The one to the right of that is my home with my husband, Jacob."

"And whose home is this?" he asked as they approached the larger cabin.

"This is the home of dear friends. The man's wife just passed away, but he lives here with his two young sons. His daughter, Ashlie, is one of the people returning to Seattle. She's not yet eighteen and is returning to school."

"I see." He followed Helaina into the house but said nothing more.

"I found everything you needed and then some," Helaina announced as Leah looked up from the stove. "They had three eggs and I bought two of them." She reached into her purse and pulled out the treasures.

"Real eggs? Real eggs in January in Alaska?" Leah questioned. "That is a marvel." Just then she noticed Babinovich. "Oh, you've brought company?"

"Yes," Helaina said, handing Leah the eggs. She then turned around to take the canvas bag from the man. "This is Cheslav Babinovich. I met him in Nome some time ago. He just arrived in the area, and I—"

"Took pity on me," Babinovich interrupted. "She was quite kind to invite me to your supper and to take refuge here from the cold."

"He will stay with us a day or two," Helaina announced as Ashlie came in from the back room.

"Who is staying a day or two?" she asked.

"Mr. Babinovich. He's from Russia and has been traveling for some time. He just came to this part of the country and I encouraged him to stay with us a short time. Mr. Babinovich, this is Mrs. Kincaid, my sister-in-law, and Ashlie Ivankov."

"Ivankov?" he asked with a look that almost seemed akin to fear.

"Yes, her father is of Russian descent, like yourself," Leah explained. "However, he was born in this territory and also shares some Tlingit Indian ancestry."

"I'm sure you'll enjoy my father's company. I'm pleased to make your acquaintance and glad you could join us. I'm sure my father would love to hear your stories of Russia. He has never actually been there, but his grandfather lived there most of his life before coming to Alaska."

Babinovich rubbed at his mustache nervously. "Yes, well, the stories of our motherland are not at all pleasant these days."

Leah took the eggs to the kitchen and Helaina followed with the bag. "Just make yourself comfortable, Mr. Babinovich. Rest and warm yourself by the fire."

He nodded and moved toward the hearth, while Ashlie joined the women in the kitchen. "I'm packed," she announced. She sounded forlorn. "I hope I'm doing the right thing."

"We will miss you," Leah said as she went to work pulling things from Helaina's bag, "but I know you'll visit us in the summer."

"I've been thinking about something," she said, casting a quick glance toward the fireplace as if to make sure Babinovich wouldn't overhear. "What if Papa and the boys came with me?"

"To Seattle?" Leah asked in disbelief.

"Yes. I mean, the railroad work has stopped for the winter. I know Papa said some tasks could be done, but other things would have to wait for spring. I just think it might be nice for Papa and the boys to come back with me. I know Cousin Myrtle would love it. She owns a huge house, and there are more than enough rooms for all of us. The boys could go to school down there, and just think of what a diversion the city would be for them."

Leah looked to Helaina and then to Ashlie. "It would probably do them all a great deal of good, but it's such short notice. I don't know that your father would even consider it."

"But I could try, couldn't I?"

Helaina pulled off her coat and crossed the room to hang it by the door while Leah continued to speak on the matter with Ashlie. She felt sorry for Babinovich, who looked rather uncomfortable with his own company.

"I'm sorry we can't sit and visit properly," she said, smiling. "I'll be happy to fix you a cup of tea if you would like."

"I would like that very much," Babinovich responded. His accent sounded less thick as he relaxed.

"I'll have it ready in just a moment." She took a step toward the kitchen, then stopped abruptly as she felt something strange in her abdomen. Helaina put her hand to her belly and gasped. "I felt the baby move."

"The quickening," Leah said, coming to her side. "Isn't it marvelous!"

Helaina held her hand against her barely rounded stomach. "It's miraculous."

"I did not realize you were with child," Babinovich said. "Congratulations."

Helaina felt her cheeks grow hot. Such matters were generally not discussed with strangers—especially men. "Thank you." She knew she should go about her business, but she hated to move. Even though the moment had passed and the flutters were gone, she hated to lose the essence of what had just occurred.

"It will come again," Leah assured her with a smile.

Nearly an hour later, Adrik, Timothy, and the boys arrived. Supper was just being put on the table and Leah's cake cooled on the counter.

"Well, I see we have a visitor," Adrik announced. His boys were on either side of him, like shadows that refused to leave.

"Adrik, I hope you don't mind, but I ran into Mr. Babinovich in town. We had met in Nome. He's from Russia, and I thought you two might enjoy a chat."

"It's always good to have a brother join us," Adrik offered in their native tongue. "I'm glad you've made yourself welcome."

Babinovich shook his head—his expression one of great alarm. "Please do not speak so. I have vowed to speak only English."

"But why would you do this?" Adrik asked, again in Russian.

Helaina spoke Russian proficiently along with several other languages. She put her hand on Babinovich's arm and spoke also in his native language. "You have nothing to fear here. We want only to offer you hospitality and perhaps a bit of familiarity."

Babinovich seemed nearly panic-stricken. He looked at Helaina as if she'd suddenly sprouted horns. "I beg you both. Do not speak my mother tongue. It is not safe. There are spies everywhere. Men who would see us dead."

Adrik laughed and looked to his sons, who were wide-eyed. "He's not serious, boys. There's nothing to fear. Go wash up for supper."

Oliver looked warily at the visitor. Helaina could see there was some degree of fear in the boy's expression as he reached for his brother. "Come on, Christopher." They went to the kitchen washbasin, Oliver continuing to cast suspicious glances over his shoulders.

Adrik lowered his voice. "Mr. Babinovich, I would ask you not to say such things in my house. My boys have just lost their mother, and they aren't yet recovered from that horrific event. I don't need to have you fill their head with stories that have no foundation or basis in truth. We are quite safe here. Safe to speak Russian or not." He looked at the man oddly and added in Russian, "If you truly can speak the language."

"I cannot stay," Babinovich said, taking up his coat. "I have too much at stake. My life would mean nothing if I were to remain here." He headed for the door quickly and promptly ran into Jacob, Jayce, and the twins as they entered the cabin.

Jayce turned away with the twins in his arms to avoid Babi-novich crashing into either one.

"Whoa, there. What's the hurry, mister?" Jacob asked. "You'd think the house was on fire."

Helaina went to her husband's side. "This is Mr. Babinov-ich. I had invited him to dine with us, but he is rather upset."

Jacob eyed him in a questioning manner, but Babinovich only pushed past him. "My apologies to everyone," he called as he hurried away into the night.

"Well, that was strange," Jayce said, shaking his head. He put the twins down and laughed as they immediately ran to the door as if to see what had happened to the strange man. Jacob gently pulled them away and closed the door. Wills started to protest, but Leah quickly came to distract his atten-tion. Merry happily followed.

"Strange, indeed," Adrik replied. "Helaina, where did you say you met him?"

"In Nome, actually. He told me a strange tale of how he was related to the royal family in Russia. He said he was here trying to find a place for them to hide, as politics were not boding well for them."

"Rumor has it the entire family is held prisoner in one of their palaces," Adrik said. "I read it some time ago in the newspaper."

Helaina nodded. "Yes, Babinovich said the same. He has always been one for secrets and queer concerns. He begged me to buy some of the royal jewels in order to help him finance his endeavors."

"And did you?"

"At first I didn't," Helaina said remembering the time

only too well. "The next time we met I could not help myself. I purchased several pieces. They were quite lovely, and I figured if they helped the man, it was of little consequence to me."

"Where are those pieces now?" Adrik asked.

"In our cabin. Mr. Babinovich begged me not to show them to anyone or tell anyone about them. He said if word got back to those holding the czar and his family hostage, they might suffer more. After all, the jewels technically belong to the country, I suppose. I could show you the pieces, if you like."

"Yes, get them. I know a thing or two about jewels. You learn a lot during gold rushes when people are bartering anything and everything to get supplies. I was involved with quite a few trades in those days that included jewelry. I can tell you if the pieces are quality, but I wouldn't know what the value would be."

"I'll go get them right now."

"I'll go with you," Jacob said, taking hold of her arm. "It's snowing again. I wouldn't want you to fall."

Helaina relished the feel of his protective hold. They hurried to retrieve the pieces, with Jacob stopping only long enough to kiss her soundly as soon as they stepped inside the house. Helaina wrapped her arms around Jacob's neck and pulled his face close for another kiss as soon as the first one ended.

"I felt the baby move," she whispered against his lips. "Just a little while ago. It was the most marvelous thing. I wish you'd been there."

He pulled away and looked into her eyes with wonder. "Truly?"

Helaina giggled. "It was such a precious fluttering—almost too faint to know for sure, but it was clearly the baby."

Jacob hugged her close. "I wish we could just stay here and forget dinner."

Helaina kissed his neck and wished the same, but she pushed away, shaking her head. "This is Ashlie's and Timothy's last night here. We're expected to celebrate with them."

"I know." The disappointment was clear in his tone.

Helaina winked. "It doesn't mean we have to celebrate very long."

She went to her trunk and brought back a small bundled scarf. Arm and arm they made their way back to the Ivankov cabin, both smiling as if they knew a very special secret.

Once she uncovered the pieces and spread them atop the scarf, Adrik sat down and gave each one consideration. A ruby necklace was the largest piece. There were some twenty-five gems of reputable size. The pieces were set into heavy gold that fell in a half circle from a thick, braided chain of gold. Within a few moments he looked up with a frown. "I hope you didn't spend much to acquire these. They're fake."

"What?" Helaina shook her head. "Are you certain?"

"Definitely. These are not real—not the gems nor the gold. They are quality costume pieces—the kind you might see in the theatre or for those who want to appear to be from the upper classes of society but can't afford the price of the actual product."

"How odd. Why would Babinovich create such a story?"

"My guess from the way he acted," Adrik offered, "is that

he's faking more than the jewels. I don't believe him to be Russian at all. My guess is that he's a confidence man selling these fake jewels to finance his living."

"Why would he come to Alaska?" Leah wondered aloud. "It seems so far removed and of little consequence. It's not like wealthy people linger on every corner."

"Which is probably exactly why he chose the location. The railroad officials informed me that many wanted men are venturing north. The law seems less likely to catch them up here, and information is not as easily had regarding criminals. Even our legal system is sorely lacking, as you well know. My guess is Babinovich saw a chance to play upon the pity of good-hearted people. He probably created the story about helping the czar, realizing that word of his plight could easily be had from the newspapers, but checking it out in any depth would be impossible due to the distance and the war."

"Well, I suppose that's the last of him that we'll see," Leah replied. "What a strange man."

A sense of rage washed over Helaina, and in that moment she made a silent pledge to investigate and find out the truth about Babinovich—or whoever he was. She, of course, would say nothing to Jacob or anyone else for that matter. No one would approve of a pregnant woman occupying herself with such things.

"So, Papa, what do you think about my idea?" Ashlie asked as her brothers came to join her.

Helaina tried to act natural—as if Adrik's announcement meant little to her. Jacob sensed her frustration, however, and put his arm around her in a supportive manner.

"You've only just mentioned the idea. I've hardly had time

to consider it, Ashlie," Adrik said.

"Consider what?" Jacob asked.

"Ashlie suggested that the boys and I join her in Seattle—at least for a short visit. However, I had already talked a similar idea over with Timothy, and I believe it would be better for us to visit in May." He turned to Ashlie and added, "During your graduation. I hope you won't be too sad or disappointed. It just seems that for now we should probably stay here."

Ashlie smiled. "It will give me something to look forward to. How special to have you there when I graduate. I can't be sad." She went to Adrik and hugged him tight.

"I don't know about the rest of you, but I am starving," Jayce announced. "I think we need to get this party started."

Leah laughed. "I think Wills and Merry would agree with you," she said, pointing to the table. The twins had already climbed onto the bench and were reaching for whatever food was closest.

Adrik took up the pieces of jewelry and rewrapped them. He handed them to Helaina and offered a warning. "I'd be cautious of Mr. Babinovich in the future. He appears to be the kind of man who preys on gentlewomen. If he tries to approach you again, find one of us."

Helaina nodded and took the bundle. She would be cautious of Mr. Babinovich, but her kind of caution was probably different than what Adrik Ivankov had in mind.

Chapter Twenty-one

Winter passed into a muddy, wet spring. The railroad began work again, keeping the men busier than ever and leaving the women alone more than they liked. As the line moved north, the men were gone for longer and longer periods, and Leah hated the separation.

When May developed into an unseasonably warm month, Leah decided to plant a little garden despite the possibility of losing it all to late frost and even snow. They would need the vegetables, and the risk seemed worth it. She also ordered several crates of chickens from Peter Colton's shipping company. Her thought was to have fresh meat through the summer but also to keep a couple of laying hens. Perhaps she could get Jayce to build her a small attachment to the house so that they could keep them through the winter. It would be so nice to have eggs year round.

Working the land around her cabin gave Leah a sense of

permanency and belonging. The twins were nearly two years old and were happy to wander at will in the forested area around them. Leah, however, was not so enthused and worked constantly to keep track of them. She tied bells to them, attached rope leashes to them, and even tried to fence them in, but nothing worked. She was forced to keep them under her surveillance at all times.

Glancing up to check the children for the fifth or sixth time, Leah was surprised to see her brother and husband walking toward her. She brushed the dirt from her hands and stood, while Wills and Merry ran for their father.

"I wasn't expecting you so soon," Leah admitted. "Although I'm quite pleased." She pressed her face between the laughing twins in order to kiss her husband.

"I know. We caught the last ride down. Adrik stayed up north again. There are big plans for lines running up through the mountains, and he's pretty interested to hear what the surveyors say about the area."

"I figured now that they were connected to the coal fields, Adrik might actually start thinking about staying home more or even heading back to Ketchikan."

Jayce put the twins down and shrugged. "I couldn't tell you. You know he's not been much of a talker since Karen's death. I try sometimes to get him to just talk about the old days, but he works himself hard, then cleans up and goes to bed."

"I know. Even when he's here he doesn't do much else. The boys aren't doing well either. Christopher has horrible nightmares. He wakes up screaming at least two or three times a week. Oliver will talk to me on occasion, but he's always filled with worry about his father and brother. He just wants to go home."

"Home? To Ketchikan?"

"Yes. But I think it's more that he just wants things to feel like they used to," Leah admitted. "I don't think it would really matter where he lived, so long as he could have his mother back and his father and brother happy. He's such a deep little guy."

"He's not that little. Adrik said he was asking about working with him."

"He's not yet fourteen. He needs an education, not a job."

"I agree," Jayce said, holding up his hands. "You don't need to convince me."

Leah watched as Wills tried to ride Champion. The dog patiently let the boy climb all over him, but when Wills climbed on Champion's back, the dog merely crumpled to the ground and let out a howl of protest. Leah smiled and shook her head. How she wished Adrik's boys could find such simple contentment.

"Well, if Adrik comes back soon," Leah began, "I'm going to insist he sit down and talk to me. I need for him to understand what's going on."

"Don't be too hard on him, Leah. I can't imagine how I'd be if I lost you." He put his arm around her. "I know I'd never be myself again."

"But those boys need him. Even though we've moved into their house to see to their needs, it's not easy on them. They resent their father's absence and my presence. I know it, although they have never said as much."

"Give them time. They all need time. It's the only thing that will help," Jayce said.

Leah knew his counsel was true; she'd said the same thing over and over herself. She also wrote letters of encouragement to Ashlie, who penned long letters about her loneliness and sorrow regarding her mother.

"When do they leave for Seattle?" Jayce asked.

"Next week. Unless Adrik has changed his plans, they'll head out on the twenty-second."

"The trip will help. It will be something fresh and different. It will see them removed from Alaska and all that is familiar, and they will be forced to come out of their cocoons and talk to each other. It's going to be all right. You'll see."

Leah hoped her husband was right. She'd watched Adrik withdraw little by little throughout the winter, and when the railroad called the men back to work, it seemed the perfect excuse for him to completely lock himself away. Leah knew that everyone had to grieve in their own way, but this had been going on now for months, and it wasn't helping anyone.

The next few days brought even more trouble, however. Newspapers reported a hideous round of influenza in the Nome and Teller areas of Alaska. They called it Spanish influenza but said little more about where it had come from or what its symptoms were. It seemed that the deadly sickness took hold in the winter months and rendered entire villages dead.

Leah was desperate for some word from her friends. She

had waited patiently through the winter but now felt anxious for some good news to arrive soon. She wanted to know about Emma and the children, as well as how John and Oopick were doing. There were so many people she cared about, and she longed to hear from them.

A letter arrived from Grace with the sad announcement that her son Andrew had joined the army. Grace also wrote of her desire to come north and see Adrik and the boys. She felt a need to see them without Karen in order to make the woman's death seem real. Her letter stated, *From so many miles away, it's easy to pretend she is still with us.*

Leah didn't have that advantage. Every day she felt Karen's absence. She supposed part of it was living in Karen's house. The arrangement had just seemed easier for everyone, given that the men were gone for longer and longer periods of time. Leah and the twins took up residence in the room Adrik had intended for Ashlie. When he'd built the house, he'd made sure there was space for his daughter, just so she wouldn't feel any excuse to stay away.

At first, whenever Adrik returned, Leah and the twins would head home to their own cabin, but after a time it just seemed stressful for all concerned and Leah and Jayce moved in with Adrik and the boys. But when everyone was gone or asleep, Leah would find it particularly lonely. She could almost hear Karen's voice and envision her working in the kitchen or at the table. Due to the frozen earth and heavy snow, they had only recently been able to bury Karen. The funeral had only served to reopen the wounds of loss.

"I'm glad you'll be staying in the house," Adrik said as Leah and the others gathered for dinner a few days after his return from up north and the night before he and the boys were to head to Seattle. "I think you'll enjoy the bigger space, what with those rambunctious twins of yours." He chucked Wills under the chin and leaned over to kiss Merry. The little girl squealed with delight as Adrik's kiss trailed down her neck and then turned into a loud chopping sound. It was a game Adrik used to play with her and hadn't done in some time.

Leah was glad to see Adrik seem a little more like himself. "We'll miss you. I suppose next thing I know I'll get a letter stating that you'd decided to stay in Seattle."

Oliver looked up with a deep frown. "We won't stay there."

Adrik shrugged. "What if we like it more than we like it here?"

Oliver pushed back his chair so quickly that it clattered to the floor as he stood. "I don't even want to go to Seattle. Nobody asked me!" He ran out of the room, leaving Adrik looking rather stunned.

Christopher got up slowly and shook his head. "I don't want to go either." He followed his older brother to their loft bedroom.

"Well, I seemed to make a mess of that," Adrik said, looking rather dejected.

"They're really suffering," Leah said. She spooned some mashed up vegetables into Wills' bowl and handed him a spoon. Merry was still happily gnawing on a piece of sourdough bread with butter and had hardly touched her vegetables. Buttering bread for Wills, Leah continued, "I've been meaning to talk to you, but—"

"But I'm never home," Adrik inserted. "I know, and I'm sorry. I've allowed my work to occupy me so that I don't have to think or feel Karen's absence. I knew it was wrong, but . . . well . . . things will be different now. I've been very selfish in all of this. Jacob and Jayce helped me to see that much."

"We did?" Jayce questioned. "When did we have time to do that?"

"You did it by your actions. Every time I turned around, you were wanting to come home and be with your family. I wanted to be with the boys but wanted even more to be with Karen, and I knew she wouldn't be here. Further, I knew the boys would have questions, and I would have to deal with their heartache on top of my own. I wasn't up to it." He shook his head. "I'm really sorry, Leah. It was selfish of me, but I intend to do better. I'm hoping this trip will give us a chance to really talk to each other and work through some of the pain."

"You owe me no apology. I was just worried about you—about them too. They haven't been doing well, Adrik. Christopher suffers from nightmares and Oliver worries incessantly about everything. They both ask me about you constantly, always wondering and worrying if you'll meet with some horrible fate."

"I didn't know." Adrik looked upward toward the loft. "I'll talk to them—help them to understand." He started to get up.

Leah touched his arm gently. "Why don't you give Oliver a little time to calm down? He'll be more inclined to listen to you once he stops being so angry."

"I doubt the anger will stop anytime soon. Not if he feels like me," Adrik said, retaking his seat. "But you're right. I'll go up after supper."

Oliver and Christopher listened to the things being said as they huddled together in their bed. Oliver shook his head and turned to Christopher. "I know what he'll say. He'll tell us that we'll have a great time in Seattle and that we won't miss Mama there as much as we do here, and before you know it he'll be buying a house and getting a job. Then we'll be stuck there. Well, I've made up my mind. I'm not going to Seattle. I'm going home."

"To Ketchikan?"

"Yes. That's where we were the happiest. That's where I want to be."

Christopher's expression turned quite serious. "I'm going home too. I want to go back to our old house. But, Oliver, how will we get there? Ketichkan's a long ways off, and we don't have any money."

"If we take the train down to Seward, we can find a boat to take us to Ketchikan. I've been asking some questions; I know all about this stuff. The fishing boats will take us so long as we work. We know how to do that kind of stuff. We'll be home in less than two weeks if we're lucky."

"You'll take me too?"

Oliver put his hand on Christopher's shoulder. "I won't leave you here. I'll take care of you, Christopher. I promise."

"And I'll take care of you," he replied.

Oliver didn't want to hurt his brother's feelings by explaining that an eleven-year-old boy could hardly take care of himself, let alone anyone else. "We'll make it, Christopher. Together we'll do just fine. Now, come on. Let's go to bed. When Papa comes to talk to us, we'll pretend we're asleep. That way we won't have to lie about our plans."

Christopher hurriedly pulled off his heavy flannel shirt and put on his nightclothes. "When are we going to leave?"

"As soon as everyone is asleep." Oliver had everything planned out in his mind. He'd been working on this ever since his father had made the Seattle plans known. He had originally figured to part ways once they'd arrived in Seward, but maybe he'd be better off to head out now. He knew there was a freight train that would come through sometime in the night. It was the train returning to Seward for supplies needed on the rail line up north. They always stopped to take on water in Ship Creek. If he and Christopher were very careful, they could probably sneak on board and make their way south. He'd watched the train cars on many occasions. Most of the time the doors were left open. It should be easy enough to hide inside one of them for the trip south. At least he hoped it would be.

Leah hurried to get breakfast on the table while Adrik called to the boys for the third time. "Come on, guys, we'll be late for the train if you don't get your things and get down here right now."

He shook his head when there was no response and headed for the ladder. "They were so tired last night they were already asleep when I went to talk to them. No doubt they're worn out from their grief and worry. I'm really sorry I put all of that on you, Leah."

"I was glad to be here for you, Adrik. You know that. Don't blame yourself or be upset with the situation. It's just the way things go."

"I think I'll go up and talk to them before they come down. That way, maybe I can explain the way things are."

Adrik went up the steps while Leah turned to retrieve the coffeepot. The front door opened, and Jacob and Helaina entered. Leah couldn't help but smile. Helaina moved ever so slowly under the heavy burden of her child. For weeks they had discussed whether the baby was a boy or a girl, and both concluded it was a son, due to his rowdy activity in the womb.

"How are you feeling?" Leah asked as she pulled out a chair for Helaina with one hand and placed the coffeepot on the table with the other.

"I slept pretty well. As I mentioned, the baby has been less active. The doctor said that's due to his saving up his energy to be born. He doesn't think it will be long."

"Neither do I," Leah admitted. "You've really dropped since last week. I believe it will be any day now."

"Leah, have you seen anything of the boys?" Adrik asked as he came back down the ladder.

"No, not since supper. Why?"

"They're gone. They're gone and so are some of their things. They packed knapsacks to carry on the trip. Those are missing."

"Do you suppose they had a change of heart and decided to head over to the train station early—maybe to show you that they were willing to go?" Jacob questioned.

"I don't know. I guess I should head over there and see."
He scratched his bearded face. "I've got a bad feeling about
this."

"Why?" Leah asked. "What's wrong?"

"Is any food missing?" Adrik asked.

Leah shrugged and went to the cupboard. "I hadn't really
noticed." She began to look around. "Well, several bags of
jerky are gone—you know the stuff you put up last winter?
And it looks like all but one loaf of sourdough bread is missing as well." She looked up fearfully. "They've run away,
haven't they?"

Adrik nodded and went to the door for his coat. "That's
what I'm thinking. I don't know where they think they're
headed, but—"

"We'll help you look," Jayce said, as he and Jacob stood.
Jacob reached over and grabbed a piece of toasted bread and a
few pieces of sausage to make a sandwich. Jayce took note and
did likewise.

"Let us know as soon as you find out anything," Leah
declared. "Chances are they're still close by. They wouldn't
have any means of getting too far."

An hour later Leah had finished cleaning the kitchen, and
still there was no word from the men. She worried about the
boys and had stopped to pray for the entire party over a dozen
times. It was just so hard to imagine the boys out there by
themselves. They were smart children, however, she kept
reminding herself, and they had grown up learning to fend for
themselves. Surely they would be all right.

"Leah, I think the baby is going to be born today,"
Helaina said rather nervously.

Leah noted that she was holding her stomach. "Are you in pain?"

Helaina looked up and nodded. "They've been coming off and on since early this morning. I thought at first it was like some of the other times, but this is different. These are getting stronger and coming more often."

Leah glanced at the clock. It was a little past nine. "Well, we should prepare. Since we don't know what's going to happen with the boys or our men, I would like to put you up here. Would that be all right?"

"I certainly don't want to be alone right now," Helaina admitted.

"Do you feel well enough to go home and get a few things, or would you rather stay here with the twins while I go?"

"I think I'll be all right." She got to her feet slowly. "What do I need?"

"Bring a clean nightgown and blankets and clothes for the baby. I have the rest." She smiled at Helaina's worried expression. "Don't fret."

"I just don't want anything to go wrong," she said. "The doctor said he lost a mother and baby last week." She fell silent.

Leah came to her side and hugged Helaina. "Don't consider such things. You'll be fine. Let's not worry until there's something to worry about."

Helaina put her hand to her abdomen and grimaced. "Seems to me that giving birth to a new individual is something to worry about."

Just then Wills ran full steam into Leah. "Mama. Mama. Look see."

Leah laughed as he held up one of his toys. "Giving birth is the easy part. Raising them up—now, that's something that causes worry."

Helaina took her leave ever so slowly, while Leah reached down to ruffle her son's hair. Her hand touched the warmth of his forehead, causing her to frown. She put her palm to his head and realized Wills was running a fever. She knew the twins were teething so she put away her concern. No doubt Merry would be feverish too. She went to her daughter and checked. Sure enough, Merry's head was also warm.

"Well, looks like I should get you two some rawhide to chew on and something to bring down that temperature." But before Leah could see to that, Helaina returned. Her face was as white as a sheet and her expression told Leah something was wrong.

"What is it?" Leah asked.

"My water just broke."

Chapter Twenty-two

Jacob could see frustration and worry etched on Adrik's face. No one at the railroad or in town had seen Christopher or Oliver. It was as if the children had simply disappeared off the face of the earth.

"They couldn't have gotten far on foot," Jacob told Adrik.

"I tracked them here to the railroad," Adrik said, shaking his head. "If they came here in the night, they might have managed to get on the freighter headed south to pick up supplies in Seward."

"But why would they head to Seward without you?" Jacob said shaking his head. "They didn't even want to go to Seattle. Wouldn't it make more sense that they'd just hide out somewhere around here until they thought you were gone or had changed your mind about the trip?"

"I don't know. I think I'd better go back to the house and get some gear. Then I'll catch the train south just like I was going to do. That way if they have made their way to Seward, I'll be able to look around and find them there. You and Jayce could keep looking around this area."

Jacob nodded. "You know we will."

Jayce came trotting from down the road. "Nobody's seen 'em at the water," he called. The inlet wasn't all that good for ship traffic, but there were smaller vessels that could make it through the channels.

"Adrik thinks they've taken the supply train south."

Jayce looked to Adrik as he came to stop in front of the two men. "Why?"

"I tracked them here. There's no sign of their leaving the area on foot. No sign of a wagon in the area where I see the signs of their boots. Just railroad tracks. I don't know why they would do this. I just don't understand."

"Understanding can come later," Jacob said. "Let's go back to the cabin and figure out how we can help you the best."

They began walking back to the house. Jacob wished he could offer some encouragement, but he knew how awful Adrik felt about the situation. If Jacob had a son and he disappeared, he would be frantic. There would be no comforting him.

"You can get word to me by telegraph," Adrik said. "If you find them, just wire me in Seward. I'll check in periodically at the telegraph office."

"You're going to Seward?" Jayce asked.

"I don't see as I have a choice."

"We'll keep searching the area," Jacob promised. "We can hire another man to help with hunting and just devote ourselves to the search until we hear otherwise from you."

"I really appreciate your help. I don't know what I'll do if—"

"Don't borrow trouble. We'll find them," Jacob said.

They were nearly to Adrik's house when a scream tore through the air.

Adrik turned to Jacob. "What in the world was that?"

The scream came again.

"That's Helaina!" Jacob said. He made a mad dash for the house. "Helaina!"

He practically knocked the door off its hinges as he burst into the room. "Helaina!"

Leah came from the bedroom she'd been sharing with Jayce. "Calm down. You don't have to yell."

"What's happening? What's wrong?"

Leah smiled. "Nothing's wrong. You simply have a son."

Jacob stopped in midstep. "A what?"

Leah laughed. "I said you have a son. A boy, Jacob. Helaina just had the baby. It's a boy."

Leah watched as Jacob carefully took his son from Helaina. He looked at her with such love that Leah thought she might burst into tears.

"What will you call him?" she asked the couple.

"Malcolm Curtis Barringer," Jacob declared. He studied his son in apparent wonder. "Malcolm because we both like the name and Curtis for Helaina's maiden name."

"That's a good name," Adrik declared. "I wish I could stay and get to know the little guy better, but my little guys need me."

"I won't stop looking either," Jacob promised. "The baby doesn't need me right now as much as Oliver and Christopher do." He looked at Helaina, who nodded.

"You have to help them," Helaina said firmly. "I'll be fine here."

"Leah," Jayce said, coming into the bedroom, "something's wrong with the twins."

"What do mean?" She dropped the blanket she'd been holding.

"They're sick, Leah. I went to check them like you asked, but they aren't waking up. They're burning with fever."

Leah felt her stomach clench. She pushed past Jayce and went into the room where the twins shared a bed. Reaching to touch their foreheads, she pulled back in alarm. They were decidedly hotter than when she'd checked them only an hour ago. "We need the doctor. Can you find him?"

"I'll go right now. What do you think is wrong?"

Leah could only think of the newspaper accounts of influenza on the Seward Peninsula. "I don't know. I pray it's not influenza."

Leah refused to leave her babies until Jayce returned with the doctor. The man appeared quite grave as he examined each child. "It could very well be influenza," he told her. "There are several cases in the area that seem similar. I have no way of knowing for certain. At this point, their lungs are clear, and that's a very good sign."

"What can be done?" Leah asked, wringing her hands together. Jayce put his hands on her shoulders and pulled her close.

"You should work to get that fever down. I recommend

tepid vinegar baths and aspirin powder. I don't have much on hand and I have none of the new tablets. I'll leave some of the powder," he said, reaching into his bag. "I'll look in on Mrs. Barringer, then check back on everyone later this afternoon."

Leah watched him leave, feeling completely helpless. In the other room Helaina was recovering from childbirth, and baby Malcolm was vulnerable to whatever sickness the twins were suffering. As soon as Helaina felt up to it, Leah would encourage her to go back to her own cabin. Maybe she would even suggest Jacob move his wife and baby there right away.

"Tell me what to do," Jayce said after seeing the doctor out.

Leah shook her head, feeling so overwhelmed. "Undress them and I'll get the vinegar bath ready."

She went into the kitchen to find the things she'd need. Tears came unbidden and before she knew it, Leah was sobbing into her hands.

"Leah, what's wrong?" It was Jacob. She looked up to see him standing only a few feet away. He reached for her, but she shook her head.

"Don't. The babies are sick and may have influenza. We don't know. They're burning up with fever, though. You should probably move Helaina and the baby to your cabin. I'm so sorry."

"The doctor is seeing her and the baby right now."

"Good. I pray they're all right. There's no telling what they've been exposed to." Her voice broke, and she began to cry again.

Jacob ignored her protests and pulled her into his arms. "Leah, please don't worry. I'll take care of Helaina and

Malcolm, but is there anything I can do for you—for the children?"

"No. Nothing. This just couldn't have come at a worse time." She pushed away from him and regained her composure. She hurried to pour water into a small tub. "I didn't know they were sick. When Helaina got closer to delivering, I put them to bed. They were so tired and while they were feverish, I thought they were only teething."

"How are they now?"

"Much worse. The fever is high, but the doctor said their lungs are clear. He'll be back this afternoon to check on them."

She found the vinegar and poured a generous amount into the tepid water. "I have to go." She started to lift the tub, but Jacob took hold of the bath and motioned her to the room. "Go on. I'll bring this."

Leah saw little change in the twins' condition throughout the day. The doctor came again and left without any word of encouragement. She sat rocking and praying, never feeling more worthless in her life.

Why can't I make them well? Why did this have to happen? They're just little babies. She gently pushed back the hair on Merry's forehead. Her fever still raged. Why wouldn't it come down? Merry seemed so pale—so still. Leah lifted the baby into her arms and rocked her. Tears blurred Leah's vision. The thought of losing her daughter was more than she could bear.

"Please, God, please don't take her away from me. Don't take Wills. I love them so much." She thought back to her worries of old—of whether the children were Jayce's or Chase's. None of that would ever matter again. Never. They were hers. They were more important to her than Leah could have ever imagined.

She rocked Merry until her arms could no longer bear the weight. Carefully tucking the baby back in bed, Leah leaned down and kissed each of them on the head. Neither stirred, and her heart constricted as she realized her babies might die and there was nothing she could do to stop it.

"Oh, God, show me what to do."

She sat by their side through the night and into the day; Jayce joined the vigil from time to time. As Leah dozed she thought of life in Last Chance Creek. She still hadn't heard from Emma or Sigrid. She was desperate to know if they were well or sick, dead or alive. She wondered if Emma sat beside her babies, feeling the same hopelessness that threatened to strangle the life out of Leah.

In her dreams, Leah was taken back to working with an old Tlingit woman who had taught her much about healing. She watched the woman work, tearing the leaves of a large palmy plant.

"Use the skunk cabbage leaves, Leah. You won't cut your hands on devil's club if you do."

Leah reached for the protective skunk cabbage, then took hold of the devil's club, with its razor-sharp spiky spine. They used this plant for all kinds of ailments. Karen even called it Tlingit aspirin.

Leah awoke with a start. Her heart pounded hard, as if she'd just run miles and miles behind a dogsled team. She struggled to focus on the dream and the thoughts that had awakened her.

"Tlingit aspirin. Devil's club!" She jumped to her feet

and stopped only long enough to check on Wills and Meredith. They seemed less feverish, but she thought perhaps it was her own wishful thinking.

"Jayce, are you here?" she questioned, coming into the living room. She had no idea how long she'd slept.

"What is it? Are they worse?" Jayce came from the stove, where Leah could see he was busy cooking something.

"No. They're the same. Look, I have to get some devil's club. It's a remedy for fever and pain. I dreamed about it just now and remembered it from the old days in Ketchikan. I think it's exactly what we need."

He touched her face and nodded. "Go. I'll be here."

Adrik breathed a sigh of relief as he caught sight of his sons. They were sitting on the dock, waiting . . . watching. He'd been told by local officials of two boys who were seeking work on the docks. The police officer had tried several times to speak with the boys, but they always seemed to run away before he could catch up with them. Adrik shook his head. He wasn't at all sure why they'd come here or why they wanted to get jobs on the boats. But none of that really mattered right now; they were safe. They were alive.

He didn't want to frighten them, so Adrik called to them, hoping that the distance would give them a chance to accept his presence.

"Oliver. Christopher."

They turned and looked at him momentarily before lowering their heads in complete dejection. Adrik sat beside them, wondering how he could possibly explain to them how worried he'd been—how wrong they were to leave.

"I'm sorry, Pa," Oliver offered first. "Please don't be mad. This is all my fault. Christopher just came because I told him to. Don't be mad at him."

"I'm not mad, son. I was just so scared."

Oliver looked up. "You?"

Adrik nodded. "I couldn't find you. I thought I'd lost you for good."

"Like Mama?" Christopher asked.

"I have to admit," Adrik said softly, "that I was afraid you might get killed."

"Sorry," Oliver offered again. He hung his head and refused to meet his father's gaze.

"Boys, I don't understand why you're here. I don't understand why you ran away."

"We're going home," Christopher offered.

"Home?"

"To Ketchikan. To our real house," Christopher replied.

Adrik shook his head. He didn't understand any of this. "But why?"

"It's my fault." Oliver drew a deep breath. "I don't like Ship Creek. I don't like the railroad. You're never home and we've got no friends."

"And it's where Mama died. It killed her there," Christopher added.

Adrik had known the boys had disliked Ship Creek, but he had hoped they would adapt. But he realized now, with their mother gone, they felt even more alienation toward the place.

For several minutes neither boy said a word, then Oliver looked up. There were tears streaming down his face. "I can't remember Mama's face. Sometimes I do, then it's like she dis-appears and there's just this cloud around her."

"There are pictures of her at home in Ketchikan," Chris-topher said, his lower lip quivering. "Can't we go home, Papa? I was never afraid there."

Adrik realized there was so much he didn't know about his boys and what they were thinking and feeling. He felt like a failure for not understanding their need. "Come here, boys," he said, opening his arms to them. Christopher came imme-diately and hugged his father tightly.

Oliver was slower to respond. He wiped his face with the back of his sleeve and coughed. "I'm too big for you to hug."

"Never," Adrik replied softly. "Even big guys need a hug now and then."

Oliver considered this for a moment, then edged over to his father. Leaning hard against Adrik, Oliver buried his face against his father's neck. Adrik felt the heat of his son's body.

"Oliver, are you sick?"

"We slept outside last night. It was cold."

Adrik put his hand to Oliver's head as the boy began to cough again. "Come on, guys. We're going to get a room at the hotel and see if we can't get you both warmed up."

"And then we'll go home?" Oliver asked.

Adrik held them both at arm's length. "I promise you this—we'll go back to Ketchikan as soon as I can get things settled in Ship Creek. We'll definitely go home before the summer is out, but for now we have to get you well and then go back to take care of business. Will that be all right?"

Oliver straightened and looked his father in the eye. "You promise we'll move back to Ketchikan?"

Adrik nodded. "I promise."

Later that night, long after the boys had fallen asleep, Adrik sat watching and listening to them breathe. Oliver would break into a spell of coughing from time to time. The deep, hacking cough worried Adrik more than he wanted to admit.

"But they're safe," he whispered. He'd been so afraid; they were too young to understand all of the dangers, but Adrik knew them only too well. He could never have forgiven himself if something had happened to them.

Tears came to his eyes as he thought of Karen and how hard it had been these last few months without her. He had never had a chance to say all the things he had wanted to say. He had never given her all of the attention he'd wanted to give. So many times he'd wanted to take her away and share some quiet moments alone, but always life got in the way and he'd put it off for another day.

"But there will never be another day," he whispered. "You're gone. You're gone and I'm here, and nothing will ever feel the same—nothing will ever be quite as good." He looked up to the ceiling, knowing he wouldn't find her there but feeling somehow comforted to just imagine Karen smiling down from heaven.

"I don't know why you had to die. You were my everything ... and now I just feel so empty. So lost." He forced back a choking sob. "Oh, Karen, I miss you so much."

Chapter Twenty-three

J une arrived with mixed blessings. The devil's club tea seemed to do the trick in bringing down the twins' fever. They were still sleeping a great deal, but as their second birthday arrived, the doctor pronounced them out of danger. Leah had never heard words that meant more to her.

"We've had another telegram from Adrik. He said the devil's club is helping Oliver, and Christopher seems immune to whatever the sickness is. Oliver is much better and they hope to be back here in less than a week," Jayce announced, holding up the telegram.

"I'm so glad to hear that." Leah picked up a tray of partially eaten food and glanced at her sleeping babies. "The doctor said the twins will be up and running before we know it. He's so happy with their progress that he's asked me to help him with some other patients."

"What did you tell him?" Jayce eyed her curiously.

"I told him I would make devil's club tea for him, but that I had a responsibility right here. He agreed and was happy for the tea." She smiled and went to deposit the tray in the kitchen. "Of course," she added, "he can hardly believe that such a vicious plant could prove so helpful. He told me only three weeks ago he had to treat a poor man for a leg infection after having a run-in with devil's club. Now it seems everyone will be singing its praises."

Jayce came to her and pulled her into his arms. "I feel as though the world has been quite mad for the last few weeks."

Leah nodded. "I don't honestly know what I would have done without you. I'm sorry for the trouble the railroad had without you and Adrik helping with the regular meat supplies, but I am so blessed that you were here."

"Jacob handled it well. He hired a team of dock rats down in Seward. They've managed quite well. Well enough, in fact, that Jacob is thinking of leaving the business once Adrik is back to run things. I'm thinking of leaving as well."

"And then what?" Leah asked, looking up into his eyes.

"I don't know. Jacob has asked me to consider going into the mercantile business with him, as you know. I'm definitely considering it. This seems like a good place to set up such a thing. People are moving in by the hundreds. The railroad officials told me they believe there to be some four thousand men here. Most are working in some capacity for the railroad."

"That's incredible. I knew there were more people than when we first arrived—more permanent structures too. That's always a good sign. Soon we'll have all the things any other town could offer us." Leah put her arms around Jayce's neck.

"But you know it doesn't matter. I'll go with you anywhere and be happy with whatever you choose to do for a living."

A rap came at the front window. Leah and Jayce looked to find Jacob waving something at them. They'd been careful to have as little contact with the rest of the family as possible. Leah was desperate that Malcolm and Helaina, as well as Jacob, should stay well and free of the influenza.

"Mail," Jacob called. "I'll leave it at the door."

"Thanks!" Leah replied. She could hardly wait to see who had written. She prayed daily for news from Last Chance, having decided that it was far worse not to know their fate than to have to face the truth. She waited until she was certain Jacob would be well away from the door before opening it. There was probably no longer a need for quarantine, but Leah couldn't see pushing things too fast.

There were two letters, and both were addressed to Leah. One was from Grace Colton. The other was from Emma Kjellmann. Leah clutched them to her breast. "Emma has written!"

"Well, maybe now we will finally know what has happened," Jayce said, taking a seat at the table. "Why don't you come here and read it to me? We'll share whatever news together."

Leah closed the door and came to the table. "I've waited so long for this, but now I'm afraid."

"God already knows what's happened," Jayce replied. "What's happened is done—we cannot change it. If the news is bad, we'll face it together."

Leah opened the letter and drew a deep breath. "'Dear Leah and Jayce,'" she began. "'The news from Last Chance is bad. I'm not sure if you've heard anything of our area, so forgive me if this repeats what you already know. Around Christmas last year there were rumors of sickness in Nome and along the coast. We didn't think much of it.

"'I was of course busy with my newest addition to the family, little Samuel. He was born in November, with Qavlunaq and Kimik's son Adam being born nearly two weeks earlier. Christmas seemed all the more special with new babies in our congregation, but soon tragedy struck.'" Leah looked up at Jayce momentarily, then continued reading.

"'Several men returned from Teller to give us the news that the village was full of sickness. We had word come from other villages as well. It seemed no one was sure what had caused the sickness or how to treat it. It started with high fevers and labored breathing. Sometimes fierce coughing developed and sometimes the person just seemed unable to breathe at all. Most were delirious from fever and often unconscious for the duration of their illness. Leah, it was unlike anything we'd ever seen—not even the measles epidemic we'd suffered so long ago could compare. People began dying without even seeming all that sick. They would go to bed feeling poorly and be dead by morning. I nearly lost Bjorn and Sigrid, but they miraculously pulled through. Rachel and Samuel did not.'" Leah gasped. "Oh no, not the babies. Oh, poor Emma."

Tears filled her eyes as she continued. "'Kimik died on the third of January and was soon followed by Oopick.'" Leah could hardly bear the news. Oopick was gone, and Kimik too.

"'So many you loved are gone,'" she read from Emma's shaky handwriting. "'The village had so few people left that we considered heading south to Nome for the remainder of the winter. However, word came that Nome was suffering and the few remaining did not wish to risk getting sick, so we remained here to wait out the winter or at least until we heard that the quarantines were lifted.

"'But what started as an overwhelming situation became even worse.'" Leah shook her head and looked again to Jayce. "I don't see how it could be worse."

"I suppose you should read on," her husband encouraged.

Leah looked to the letter. "'Government officials from Nome showed up here as soon as passage could be made. With them came the news that many villages had been wiped out—that there were now many orphans as well as widows and widowers. The man told the villagers that there were no orphanages for the children and that the people would have to see to adoption. To facilitate this, he further forced the remarriage of those who were now single. Leah, it was awful. People still grieving for their unburied dead were forced to agree to marriage. The men were given the choice of picking a wife from amongst the remaining women in the village. If there were no women, they were told they would have to accompany the men to another village and find a wife there.

"'Poor John and Qavlunaq were beside themselves. Neither had any desire to marry again, but because of the officials forcing the matter, they agreed to wed each other. John said he would never treat Qavlunaq as anything other than the daughter-in-law she was, and Qavlunaq stated she would always care for John as the father of her husband. Still, they are legally married and have taken on two orphaned girls from a village near Nome to raise with Qavlunaq's two sons—both of whom I'm happy to say survived the epidemic.'"

Leah turned to the second page and continued in stunned sorrow. "'Of course, Bjorn did not approve these forced marriages, but the officials didn't care. They had come armed with a sheaf of marriage licenses already filed and filled out with exception to the actual names of the couple and the date of their marriage. After leaving our village, the group was headed to Teller to impose the same thing on those poor unsuspecting souls. I'm so very glad you did not stay here to see this abomination. Bjorn and I will be leaving with the children and Sigrid at the end of the month and heading for a sabbatical with my family in Minnesota. I doubt seriously that we will return to Alaska. Our hearts are so completely broken at the loss of Rachel and Samuel, as well as all of our dear friends. I pray the situation has boded better for you in your part of the territory. I have not heard of sickness in your area; however, as usual we have not had much news of any kind.

"'I will close this letter to further tell you that it has also been decided that the village will be evacuated. Most of the remaining Inupiat are heading to Teller or Wales. A few are going to Nome. Last Chance Creek will be no more.'"

Leah let the paper fall to the table. "I have no words." She shook her head and let out a heavy sigh. She felt as though her tears were dried up and there were no possible explanations that could make sense of anything she'd just read.

Jayce picked up the letter and read, "'I will be in touch and hope to hear from you. I have written my Minnesota address at the bottom of the page. I hope you will all pray for us. Love, Emma.'" He put the letter down and reached out to take Leah's hand.

An eternity seemed to pass with Leah and Jayce doing

nothing more than holding on to each other. Leah tried not to think too much of her old friends—it hurt too much. Her mind seemed to blur, and it wasn't until she felt a tug at her sleeve that she opened her eyes and met Wills' grinning face.

"I eat, Mama." He patted his stomach liked he'd seen Adrik do on occasion.

Leah lifted him in her arms and held him much tighter than she'd intended. She needed to feel his warmth—to hear his breathing. She needed just to know flesh to flesh that he was alive and well. "Oh, Wills," she said, burying her face against his neck.

Helaina read the letter sent by Stanley for the third time before tucking it into the pocket of her skirt. He had finally been able to provide her with information about Cheslav Babinovich. At least he provided information about a man who was notorious for using that alias and posing as a Russian.

Stanley had told her that the man was wanted in several states for trying to defraud a variety of people regarding the sale of faux jewelry, furs of poor quality, and even land deeds. His real name was Rutherford Mills, an actor originally from New York City. He had a list of names he used across the country and seemed to prey particularly upon wealthy women. His latest scheme of posing as Russian royalty raising money for the czar and his family had been seen up and down the coast of California, Washington, and now Alaska.

Worse than his thievery and fraud, however, Mills was considered to be a prime suspect in the disappearance of several women. Women last seen in his company had simply disappeared, leaving no trace of their whereabouts. Mills would also disappear, leaving the authorities no chance to question him. He was considered very dangerous.

Helaina began to pace the small living room space. Stanley had told her there was a good-sized reward for the man if she wanted to get back in her old line of business. Of course he knew from her letters that she was expecting a baby, but he may not yet have received her own letter telling of Malcolm's birth. Stanley's wife, Annabelle, had given birth to a son earlier in the year, and it pleased Helaina to realize that she had become both aunt and mother within a matter of months. Stanley was obviously quite proud of having a son of his own. He'd been completely captivated by his wife's daughter, Edith, a spunky four-year-old whom he'd adopted, but Helaina knew this son meant someone would carry forward the family name. Still, the matter of Babinovich or Mills captivated Helaina.

"Are you ready for a grumpy little man?" Jacob asked, bringing her a fussy Malcolm. "I've changed his diaper, but I believe there is more to the matter." He grinned. "I think he's hungry."

Helaina smiled and took her son. He cried, but there were no tears. "You are such a little duper." The words were no sooner out of her mouth than Helaina thought of Mills. Mills had duped so many. Old feelings flooded Helaina's mind and heart. Yearning for justice, to see people pay for their mistakes—of demanding retribution instead of offering forgiveness. Still, she knew there was a difference between those who sought to change their ways and those who only appeared to change when backed into a corner.

"So what did Stanley have to say?" Jacob asked as Helaina moved to the rocking chair.

"He said that the family is doing well. He's beside himself with joy, thanks to his son, and has felt even closer to Edith as she embraces her new role of sister."

"Did he have anything else to share? Word of the war?"

Helaina shook her head. "I had hoped he would tell us the war was over, but no such luck. He did, however, have some interesting news."

"News about what?"

"About Mr. Babinovich. It seems he's not Russian—just as Adrik suspected."

"If he's not Russian," Jacob began, somewhat confused, "what is he?"

"A confidence man—a trickster breaking the law for his own benefit."

———

Adrik smiled at the young woman making her way through the crowd at the dock. It seemed she'd matured greatly in the six months since he'd seen her.

"Father!" Ashlie fell into his open arms.

Adrik held her tight and just enjoyed the moment. He didn't even mind the more formal address of Father instead of Papa. It was just good to see her—to see the reflection of her mother and the beauty of the young woman Ashlie had become. "I was so glad you could make it home. I hated missing your graduation. I want to hear all about it—including your speech."

Ashlie laughed and pulled away. "Cousin Myrtle cried

bucketfuls. It was rather embarrassing."

Adrik put his arm around her and moved her toward the hotel. "Your brothers are beside themselves waiting for you to get here."

"How's Oliver?" The concern was evident in her tone. "Your telegram was so brief."

"He's much improved. We had planned to return to Ship Creek this week. I'm glad we could arrange for you to come with us. However, I need to let you know that we won't remain long in the area. I promised the boys we'd go back to Ketchikan."

"Honestly? But why? I thought the work was good here."

Several rowdy people pushed past them, causing Adrik to pull Ashlie against him in a protective manner. "Your brothers are miserable." He began to fill her in on the turn of events.

"I can't believe they would run away. That must have been awful for you to face." Ashlie sounded so grown up to Adrik. It seemed she had been just a girl when she'd first gone away, but now a lovely young woman had returned in her place.

"It wasn't easy. Then when Oliver came down sick, I thought for sure I'd lose him. He's better though, and we can head to Ship Creek on the next train if you like."

"I don't mind at all," Ashlie replied. "I had good accommodations on the ship and slept quite well last night. I'm ready to move on." She paused and looked up at her father to add, "But there are a couple of things I'd like to talk to you about without the boys around."

Adrik heard what sounded like caution in her voice. He knew whenever Ashlie took this tone with him in the past that something was afoot. "You have my attention—and my suspicion."

Ashlie laughed. "I suppose you know me too well for me to try and fool you. I suppose, too, that it's best to just come out and tell you what's on my mind rather than to beat around the bush until I've driven everything out but what I intended to reveal."

Adrik shook his head and laughed out loud. "You sound just like your mother. She would reason around a thing rather than just deal with the matter itself."

"I just don't want to give you further cause to worry or fret." Her brow furrowed as she seemed to give the situation deep consideration.

"Stop stalling." Adrik finally said. "What do you want to talk to me about?"

Ashlie drew a deep breath and squared her shoulders. "Two things. My future education and ... well ... a young man named Winston Galbrith."

Chapter Twenty-four

So this man is very dangerous," Jacob said after Helaina explained who Rutherford Mills was and what he stood accused of doing.

"Yes. Stanley says he's the prime suspect in the murders of several women," Helaina replied. "Authorities have been searching for him for over four years."

Jacob rubbed his stubbly chin. "I don't understand why a man like that would come to Alaska."

"Probably because of the isolation. He no doubt feels he can lay low here and then return south after things have calmed and the search has been given up. Stanley says there's a hefty reward for the man's capture. He wondered if I wanted to take on bounty hunting." She grinned.

Jacob shook his head. "Knowing you, you're probably already planning something."

"No." Her tone reassured him. There was no hint of

desire or longing for such a task.

"I suppose I could go to the authorities and let them know what we know. We can give them your brother's information and offer descriptions and details of his approach to women—how he came to you with his sad story about the czar. Apparently he's no fool. He knows enough to keep up with world events and use them to his advantage."

"I know. I thought of that too. Most men like him are very intelligent. It's why they manage to keep at it for so long without being caught. I remember reading a case about a man in Chicago who killed dozens—maybe hundreds—of people. He was a great businessman and people liked him. He had a charm that seemed to get him into places he'd otherwise never be invited."

"It just makes that kind of person more dangerous," Jacob replied. "They aren't suspected and no one sees any need to shy away from them. They aren't perceived as dangerous."

"No, there was nothing of Babinovich that suggested danger. In fact, the man seemed quite mousy and meek."

"My ma always said the devil would come to us as a wolf in sheep's clothing. She said a lot of folks figured the devil to be a monster—ugly and scary and obviously evil—but that the Bible said otherwise. If the devil will come to us as an angel of light, why wouldn't a mere man try the same tactic to gain the trust of unsuspecting people?"

"Exactly. Most of the criminals I've dealt with are that way," Helaina replied. "Mills seemed genuinely concerned about his loved ones, and that seemed to motivate his actions."

"Well, we know now that this wasn't the case. I suppose I

can go to the authorities and take your brother's letter. I can explain his work with the Pinkertons and what we experienced with Babinovich here in Ship Creek, as well as what happened in Nome. If they choose to do nothing, we'll have to take it from there." He eyed her with what he hoped was a stern expression. "Just promise me you'll have nothing further to do with this situation."

Helaina leaned forward and kissed him on the forehead. "I promise. I'm a changed woman."

"Oh, sure. You're so changed that for months you've been trying to dig up information on this man, even while carrying my unborn son. That kind of change is hardly comforting. Knowing you, you probably staked out the man's hotel and lay in wait for him."

Helaina laughed. "Not quite." She picked up an iron from the stove and tested the heat. "I did ask after him, mentioning that I wanted to buy jewelry from him, but otherwise . . ."

Jacob rolled his eyes and got to his feet. "That's enough. I don't think I want to know anymore. Please just promise me that you'll leave this in my hands now."

"Of course," Helaina replied with a sweet smile. "I'm quite happy to turn the matter over to you."

"Uh-huh. I've heard that before."

Jacob left his wife and son and headed to Jayce's cabin. Since Adrik had sent a telegram saying that he and the boys were returning home, Jayce and Leah had decided to move back into their own place. Jayce was in the back sharpening a hoe when Jacob approached.

"There's something we need to talk about," Jacob announced. "I could use some advice."

"Sure, pull up a stump," Jayce said, motioning to the thick log stumps he had yet to cut into firewood.

Jacob did as instructed, then began to tell Jayce about Mills. "I doubt he'll come here or be any real threat to our families. He knows Adrik will discover the truth regarding his Russian heritage or lack thereof, and he might fear Helaina learning the truth about the jewelry."

"But he needs to be apprehended," Jayce said, running the hoe's blade against the sharpening stone. "There's no telling what a man like that will do."

"I agree. I figure we can go to the authorities at the railroad and let them know what's going on. They are the only law in this area right now. They want people comfortable with coming to the territory and settling in around the line. They would surely want to see Mills captured."

"I think that's a good idea. Better than our trying to apprehend him ourselves. I've learned I make a poor law official."

Leah worked the dirt of her garden, feeling great pride in the appearance of new growth. The long hours of sun had worked out favorably for her garden, and she meant to take every advantage. There would surely be enough to can for the entire family.

"Did you miss me?" a female voice questioned.

Leah straightened to see Ashlie standing at the end of the carrot row.

"I didn't know you were coming home!" Leah put down her hoe and ran to where Ashlie stood. "Just look at you."

Leah gave her a hug, being careful not to get dirt on Ashlie's pristine blue-and-white day dress.

"I wanted to surprise everyone."

"Well, you have certainly accomplished that. Your father was quite ornery to keep this from us."

"Don't be too hard on Father. It's my doing."

"You look so grown up. I can't believe it. At Christmas you still appeared so much a child, but now you are clearly a woman—and a beautiful one. You're doing something new with your hair, aren't you."

Ashlie smiled and reached up to touch the carefully pinned creation. "Actually, I am. But I may soon be cutting it all very short."

"Surely you're joking." Leah had seen some women cut their hair short, even in Alaska, but that was usually the result of fever having damaged it or some other such reason.

"I'm not joking. That's kind of why I came out here. I wanted to tell you what I'm thinking about."

Leah dusted off her hands. "Why don't we sit over there?" She pointed to a large bench under a collection of spruce, hemlock, and alder. "Jayce built that for me just a couple of weeks ago. It makes a nice place to sit and watch the children."

"I can hardly wait to see the twins," Ashlie declared. "Father said they were very sick. I'm glad they're better."

"They're napping now. Those times of slumber come in fewer intervals, but I still insist on an afternoon rest. For them and me." She grinned. "So what's your news?"

"I know I didn't write much, but I found myself very busy. Cousin Myrtle was of course so sad about Mama. To my amazement, however, instead of making her more reclusive, it caused her to get out more. It's almost as if seeing Mama die young was an announcement to her that she needed to cherish and use the time she had left."

"That's understandable. It definitely made me more aware of how fleeting our time on earth can be."

Ashlie nodded. "That's why I started doing some serious thinking about what I wanted out of life."

"And what did you come up with?"

Ashlie folded her hands and straightened her shoulders. "I want to be a nurse. I just kept thinking of how things might have been different for Mama if she'd been in a place where there were better-trained people who could have helped her. Of course, I do not say that to make you feel to blame; I know you and the doctor did what you could for her. I just wish there might have been a nice big hospital with the newest innovations and a well-trained staff. As I thought about this, I figured I would do well to be a part of the solution instead of the problem. Then I met someone who really helped to confirm what I was thinking."

Leah leaned back and waited for Ashlie to continue. The girl was clearly excited about her decision. No wonder she seemed more grown up. She was full of adult thoughts and feelings and now was planning a future that would take her into a job of helping people on a full-time basis.

"I'm in love."

Leah hadn't been expecting this. She looked at Ashlie, knowing her expression must have registered the shock she felt inside. "Love?"

Ashlie grinned and nodded. "He's a wonderful man. His

name is Winston Galbrith. Dr. Galbrith. He's been studying to specialize in surgery. He's working now with a physician in a Seattle hospital. He's pledged four years of work with this man and hopes to be a highly qualified surgeon after completing his study. Meanwhile, I'll train to be a nurse at the same hospital."

"Whoa. Back up a little. How did you meet this young man?"

"We actually met at a church dinner. Our church has everyone bring food and share it together once a month. Myrtle decided since it was so blustery outside that this would be a good way to spend the afternoon instead of venturing across town to see one of the relatives. While at the social I met Winston. It was love at first sight for both of us. We sat and talked nearly the entire time, and when the social was over he looked at me and said, 'I feel as though I've known you all of my life. Would you permit me to call on you?' I told him I felt the same way and would very much like for him to call. We've seen each other nearly every day since. He tells me about his cases at the hospital, and he helped me to get into the training program for nurses."

"My, but this all seems so sudden," Leah said, shaking her head. "What does your father say?"

"He's concerned," Ashlie admitted. "However, I've persuaded him to come to Seattle and meet Winston for himself. I even managed to talk those ornery brothers of mine into coming as well."

"That couldn't have been easy," Leah said with a chuckle.

"Well, once I explained how important this was to me and that I couldn't move forward until I had their approval as well as Father's, I think they saw the importance. Father said we will all head down in a couple of weeks. I wish you could come too."

Leah shook her head. "I fear that would be quite impossible. I will look forward to hearing what Adrik has to say about your young man, however. He sounds very industrious."

"He is. And he loves God and wants to serve people. I want the very same thing. And here's the best part: We both plan to come to Alaska after our training is complete. We want to live here and offer the best medical care possible. We'd like to open our own hospital, in fact."

"That is very impressive," Leah replied. She was happy to hear that Ashlie planned to return to Alaska. That would have pleased Karen very much.

"I know it all seems very sudden, but if Father approves of Winston, we'd like to marry right away. Cousin Myrtle wants us to live with her, to help us get through our training without the additional cost of housing."

"I can't imagine you married," Leah said in wonder. "It seems just yesterday you were a little girl in pigtails. Now you're talking of cutting your hair short. Which, by the way, you didn't explain."

Ashlie laughed. "Well, the fashions are changing, but more important, it would be easier for me with my nursing duties. Several of the nurses at the hospital have already cut theirs, and it works quite well for them. I figured that if Winston didn't mind, I might give it a try too."

"And Winston doesn't mind?"

"Not at all. He says that whatever I choose is fine by him, as long as I'm happy." She laughed again with such girlish delight that Leah couldn't help but join in.

"I'm happy for you, Ashlie. He sounds like a wonderful man."

"He is, Leah. He's helped me so much to deal with my grief and sadness. It's like God knew exactly what I needed— before I ever knew it for myself."

"He did, Ashlie. Just as He knows what you need now. We'll pray about this young man of yours and for the future the Lord has for you. But I have a feeling that future is well on the way to being established. Come on. We'll need to start putting supper together."

———

"Well, the plan is to go to Seattle and then return in August or early September to Ketchikan," Adrik told them after supper that night. Oliver and Christopher nodded in unison as if they'd had great say in the matter. "I would be happy if you would all join us there. I know I convinced you to give this area a try, but for my family, it's been anything but ideal."

"What do you have in mind, Adrik?" Jacob questioned.

"I figure to return and start making furniture again. I've already had several of the railroad officials tell me they would be happy to pay top dollar for whatever I might supply. They are working hard to put in permanent housing for some of their officials and stationmasters. Those houses will of course need furniture, and it would be much cheaper to get furnishings here in Alaska than to ship them all the way up from Seattle or San Francisco."

"You'll still have to ship it up from Ketchikan," Jacob replied.

Adrik leaned back with a nod. "I've explained all of that. They like the quality they see, however, and for now they want whatever I can provide."

"Well, it sounds like you'll have a trade," Jacob said. He appeared deep in thought.

"I mainly wanted to extend the invitation so that ... well ... we might remain close to each other." Adrik held up his hands before anyone else could speak. "I know, however, that we all have our own lives to live. I'm not suggesting you have to do this for me. The boys and I will be fine either way."

"Of course you will," Jacob replied. "That has never been in doubt." He reached over and tousled Christopher's hair. "With boys as ingenious as these, how could you not be fine?"

"I ask simply because I want to stay close to my family for a while," Adrik admitted. "I was foolish in spending so much time away. We need each other now more than ever."

"It wouldn't be so different opening a store in Ketchikan instead of here, would it?" Jayce asked Jacob.

"I'm sure there wouldn't be as much business—at least not if this area continues to grow as they've suggested it will. There's already talk of incorporating the town next year; with the railroad and the push for statehood, I can well imagine that this would be a more prosperous area. However, that much said, I loved growing up in Ketchikan. The area is a good place to raise a family and certainly not as given to drifters and rowdies. There's a kind of peacefulness in Ketchikan that I've not known anywhere else in Alaska."

Jayce nodded. "I agree." He looked to Leah. "What do you think?"

She smiled. "I'm happy to live wherever you choose. I simply want to make a good life with my family. I loved my home in Last Chance, but there's nothing left there except empty houses." She stopped for a moment to regain her composure. "I want to look to the future—not the past. Ketchikan would make a good home. It's true your business probably wouldn't be as prosperous, but maybe in time you could have two stores. One here and one there."

"That is a possibility," Jacob said, looking to Leah. "In fact, it just might be the answer. We could start small and work our way up." He looked to Jayce. "What do you think of that?"

"I like the idea of returning to Ketchikan. As for the stores—well, I think if the Lord is behind it we can't fail," Jayce said, grinning. "Ketchikan blessed me before—it introduced me to Leah."

"What say you, sis?" Jacob asked.

Leah smiled, excited to share her own secret. "I loved my life there. I would very much like to have my baby there," she announced. "There are good midwives who know me from my childhood."

Everyone turned in unison to look rather blankly at Leah. She laughed in delight at the expressions. "Surprise! I'm going to have another baby—this time in January. Leave it to me to pick the coldest part of winter."

"That settles it." Jayce shook his head. "Ketchikan will be less cold."

"I agree," Jacob said. "I'm for Ketchikan if that's all right with Helaina."

Helaina nodded. "I think it sounds fine."

"How soon will you be ready to leave?" Adrik asked, excitement in his voice.

"Well, there's nothing to really keep us here. I've been offered money for the cabin on several occasions," Jacob replied. "I know you and Jayce have received similar offers."

"Yes," Adrik said. "The railroad would be happy to buy all three cabins. They have people they'd like to put in them immediately."

"Then I suppose we should arrange the sale and leave as soon as that's concluded," Jacob said, looking to Jayce and Leah for approval.

"I agree," Jayce replied. "Adrik, why don't you make the arrangements. Tell them we can also leave the larger pieces of furniture and the stoves."

"I will. I'm sure they'll make it worth our while. Meantime, when you are ready to head out to Ketchikan, go ahead. You can stay at my place while you see what's available to buy. If there's nothing suitable, you can just stay with us until we can build something else. That house has plenty of room. It's twice as big as this one, and we all managed to live here without too much trouble. Your families can take the upstairs bedrooms, and my family can live downstairs."

Leah felt Jayce reach for her hand. He squeezed it and she glanced up to see the pleasure in his eyes. She had wanted to tell him about the baby when they were alone, but it seemed important to mention the matter here as they discussed their future. It seemed they had come full circle: They had met and she had fallen in love in Ketchikan. Now they would return to live and raise their family. It all seemed very right.

"And you have proof that this man is wanted by the legal authorities in the States?" a stern man asked Jayce. The gentleman had introduced himself as Zachary Hinman and declared himself to be in charge of all legal matters for the area.

"Yes, Mr. Hinman." Jacob handed him the letter from Stanley. "As you will note, my wife's brother is an agent with the Pinkertons. When my wife requested information on the man, he looked into the matter and revealed the situation that I've just told you about."

"This is indeed a find," Hinman said, sitting up a little straighter. "The man who captures this Mills fellow would make quite the name for himself." He stroked his thick black mustache. "I'm intrigued."

"I've asked around," Jacob began, "and it seems people have seen the man in town. Some even remember being approached by him."

"You can be assured, Mr. Barringer, that I'll see personally to this matter. If the man is still in the area, I will apprehend him."

Jacob got to his feet. "As you can see, the authorities warn that he is to be considered dangerous. If he comes near my family, I won't hesitate to take the matter into my own hands."

"Never fear, Mr. Barringer. We have some good men on the payroll. We'll see that this man is captured."

Chapter Twenty-five

Ashlie Ivankov leaned against the rail of the *Spirit of Alaska* and sighed. Soon she'd be in Seattle and once again in the presence of her beloved Winston. Never had she met anyone who intrigued her or gave her reason to care as much as this soft-spoken, humorous man. She thought of his tall stature and broad shoulders and laughed to herself as she realized she'd fallen for a man who was built much like her father.

Ashlie fondly remembered her mother talking of how her father's sense of humor first attracted her—that and his honesty. Ashlie knew the same could be said of her interest in Winston. The man was good to speak his mind but also to hear her speak in return. Ashlie found him attentive to the interests and dreams she held. Not only that, but he was very supportive of her goals. Other men—boys, really—that she'd talked to for any length of time could hardly be said to have any concern for her desires at all. They were generally self-centered—more interested in war and playing soldier than anything else.

But not Winston. Winston detested the war. He wanted to heal and repair bodies, not destroy them. She felt the same way. She'd seen a few of the men who'd returned after serving in Europe. Some were missing limbs, while others were blind or suffering serious lung ailments. Winston said it was because horrible tactics were being used in this war. Men were being gassed—poisoned—as they fought under raining bullets and shrapnel. She shuddered. *It's positively hideous.*

She pushed the images away and focused on dreams of her future with Winston. If things went well, she reasoned, she and Winston could be married before her father and brothers returned to Alaska. Cousin Myrtle was all for having a summer wedding. Her gardens were a delight, and she had suggested to Ashlie on more than one occasion that such a setting would be perfect for a day wedding. Winston had liked the idea very much. His parents were deceased; after becoming parents much later in life, they had passed away in their late sixties only a year ago. First his mother had died of some stomach ailment, and within four months his father had passed peacefully in his sleep. Winston said it was from a broken heart. Given this, and the fact that Winston was an only child, neither one expected to have a large wedding. Although Ashlie had numerous friends from school and church, and Winston shared many of the same acquaintances, neither she nor Winston desired a big to-do.

Ashlie turned from the rail and began moving down the deck. She smiled at a young woman with two small children.

"Someday that shall be me," she murmured under her

breath. *I shall be married to Winston and be mother to his children.* The thought of such intimacy with the man made her blush.

"Excuse me," a man dressed in a fine black suit declared. He tried to hurry away, but Ashlie was certain she recognized him. His hair was combed in a different fashion and he was clean-shaven, but she was sure she knew him. Wasn't he the Russian man who wasn't really a Russian? The one who'd come to her house only to have her father declare him a fraud? *Oh, what was his name? Bab-something. Babcock? Babinokov?* He glanced quickly over his shoulder and Ashlie suddenly remembered. "Mr. Babinovich!"

The man turned, looking rather alarmed. He hurried away without a word.

"How strange. Why would he do that?"

Ashlie thought perhaps the man had heard that his game had been found out, though she couldn't really see the harm in pretending to be someone he wasn't. These were troubled times, and perhaps the man thought that by playing a Russian nobleman, he'd avoid having to serve in the army.

She continued her stroll on the deck. Her father and brothers were enjoying an early lunch, and Ashlie was enjoying the time to herself. Her father was far too protective, watching her every move. The only reason she was able to be alone now was because her father believed her to be resting in their cabin.

Ashlie remembered protesting her father's actions once to her mother. She had argued about his need to always know where she was going. "We live on an island," she had told her mother. "Where could I possibly go?"

She smiled at the memory of her mother patiently

explaining Adrik's protective nature and desire to keep his family from harm. "God has given him a family and the responsibility to provide for and protect them. Your father considers that job to be a great honor ... but also of the utmost importance."

Ashlie took a seat on one of the deck chairs and wiped a tear from her eye. She missed her mother at times like this. She would love to talk to her about falling in love with Winston and about the wedding she had been planning since Winston first declared his love for her. How her mother would have enjoyed helping her make a gown. Instead, Ashlie had already planned to purchase a lovely gown that she'd helped a local seamstress to design. The woman was working on it in Ashlie's absence, in fact.

Oh, Mama, you would like Winston. Ashlie closed her eyes and tried to imagine her mother sitting beside her. *He's so like Papa. So gentle and sweet, yet strong and capable. He makes me laugh, and yet he cares about my tears.*

Her mother had always told her that the most important thing to have in a mate was a man who knew the Lord and loved Him. Ashlie saw that daily in Winston. He loved helping people, because he felt confident that it was what God wanted him to do. He and Ashlie had discussed this more than once. Winston had even made it clear to Ashlie that he would not impose the life of a doctor's wife on her unless she desired to serve in the medical field. Ashlie had laughed, telling him that for ages now she'd considered being a nurse.

Ashlie thought of her mother again. She couldn't help but wonder: If her mother had been closer to proper medical facilities, would she have died? *I'll become a good nurse, Mama. I'll study hard and help save lives. I just wish we could have saved you.*

"Miss Ivankov. I'm sorry that you remembered me. You've put me in a rather difficult spot."

Ashlie opened her eyes and looked up in surprise. "Mr. Babinovich?"

"Mills, actually." With a quick glance over his shoulder, the man reached out to take hold of her Ashlie's arm. "You will come with me."

"I will not." She tried to pull away, but he held her fast.

"If you do not, then I'm afraid something bad will happen to one of your brothers. Perhaps the youngest one. Little boys always have a penchant for getting into trouble."

Ashlie froze. Her heart pounded harder. "How dare you threaten my family!"

"Come, come. Your family has threatened my livelihood and you question me on my actions?"

He pulled again, and this time Ashlie, seeing there was no one nearby to help her, walked with him. "What do you want and who are you? My father says you are not Russian."

"And so he is correct, although I have fooled hundreds, maybe more, into believing I am. My name is Mills. Rutherford Mills. And your family has caused me a great deal of trouble."

"I don't understand. What kind of trouble? How problematic can it be for my father to know that you've lied about being Russian?"

He pulled her toward an inside passage and again Ashlie pulled back. "Miss Ivankov, I grow weary of your games. I am taking you to my cabin. You will either accompany me there of your own free will or I will be forced to do something rather drastic." He opened his coat just far enough to reveal a revolver.

"What? Will you shoot me here and bring everyone running? I do not easily cower, Mr. Mills, and I'm not a stupid child. Tell me now what it is you are after."

"I will tell you in my cabin. I do not wish to bring you harm." He shrugged. "Although you probably do not believe me. Still, I have something to discuss in private. I would hate to hurt you, but this is a life and death matter to me. Therefore the stakes are quite high."

"Life and death? I'm sure I do not understand you."

His grip grew stronger. "I'm losing my patience, Miss Ivankov." He narrowed his eyes and leaned close enough for Ashlie to smell the spirits on his breath. "Do not make me hurt you."

Ashlie weighed the matter briefly, allowing him to guide her down the passage as she considered her choices. She was uncertain at this point what would be best to do. There was no one in the passageway to aid her, and if she began to cause a fuss, Mills might well find a way to harm one of her brothers. Perhaps, she reasoned with herself, it was better to simply see what the man wanted and then if he wouldn't let her go, she would simply wrestle the gun away from him. He didn't know the manner of woman he was dealing with. She was, after all, an Alaskan.

"Get inside," Mills declared, giving Ashlie a push inside his cabin, then locked the door behind him. "I have watched your family closely ever since learning that the authorities were looking for me. You see, I am not inclined to be taken into custody."

"Taken into custody for what? What are you talking about?"

He looked at her oddly for a moment. "So your family didn't tell you?"

"Tell me what?" Ashlie crossed her arms and tried to look bored with the entire matter. "Why don't you just tell me why you've forced me to come here?"

Mills took a seat and motioned her to do likewise, but Ashlie refused. He acted as if it was of little consequence, but Ashlie could see in his eyes that he didn't know quite what to make of her defiance.

"Someone in your family learned of my true identity and turned that information over to the local authorities. They have dogged my heels ever since. When you recognized me, I knew I could not let you make it back to your father. You would alert him about my presence and my circumstance would be known to everyone."

"Why would my father care about your presence on this ship? Why would the local authorities care about your true identity? I know you sold fake jewels to Helaina. Is that what this is all about?"

Mills laughed. "Hardly. That is the least of my offenses as far as the criminal authorities are concerned. You need to understand, Miss Ivankov, I am a wanted man. I had thought to seek refuge for a time in Alaska as many of my cohorts have done in the past. But alas, your friends and family made that quite impossible."

"But whatever are you wanted for?" Ashlie looked at him hard. "Not for the fake jewelry sales?"

He shrugged and looked almost proud. "I'm wanted for murdering foolish women who naïvely believed themselves capable of handling a man like me."

Ashley raised a brow. "Are you suggesting that I am fool-ish or naïve with regard to you?"

"That remains to be seen. I will weigh that matter momen-tarily after I have told you what I mean for you to hear."

"Then please be quick about it. My father will soon be looking for me, and you will have to explain yourself to him."

Mills shook his head. "I do not think so. You see, I saw him in the dining room with your brothers. They were only begin-ning their meal. I had thought myself safe because no one even noticed me, but then I crossed your path on deck. I seriously doubt they will worry over your whereabouts for some time. But I am just as anxious as you to be done with this. Here's the matter as I see it: I managed to slip out of Alaska under the nose of the authorities, but if anyone believes me to have made it this far, they will no doubt have the authorities waiting for me in Seattle. That would prove to be quite uncomfortable for me. Therefore, I plan to utilize your services in two ways."

"Do tell." Ashlie tried her best not to appear afraid. She had no idea what Mills was up to, but the idea of his causing harm to either of her brothers left her feeling both angry and fearful.

"I have a friend on board who is happily assisting me. I spoke to him just moments before coming to you. He will let me know when your father and brothers are nearly done with their meal. He will also help me keep track of you and your family for the duration of our journey. Therefore, do not think that you can return to your father and declare my pres-ence. Ridding yourself of me will not be beneficial. My assis-tant has his orders to slay all of you if any harm should come my way."

"That still doesn't tell me what you want," Ashlie said in what she hoped was her most severe, no-nonsense look.

"I want protection. I want help when we get to Seattle."

"Help in what way?"

"Well, I cannot trust you. You may yet manage to slip a note to someone or get word to the captain about me. This could cause the ship's crew to try something stupid in order to take me hostage. I won't tolerate that. So I have come up with a plan. A rather unsophisticated one, but one that should nevertheless be useful.

"I'm certain that your family will have little trouble passing from the ship to the dock in Seattle. If there are police officers to greet the ship, I will find it more difficult to debark, as you can well imagine. Now, my assistant will have no trouble leaving. He is not known nor expected. He will follow closely by your family and carry out my plan."

"What plan?" She wanted an end to this matter, but Mills just kept dragging it out.

"You will walk a few paces behind your father and brothers. Pretend you have a problem with your shoe or whatever. My assistant will bump into you. You will scream and declare that he is trying to rob you. He will run of course, but you will raise a ruckus that brings every officer—either in uniform or out—running. It will be up to you, Miss Ivankov, to make it appear real and to draw the attention of everyone. That way, I can slip from the ship and safely make my getaway."

"You are quite mad. I would never help you."

"You will help me, or you will be the cause of one of your brothers dying. Let me make the decision less difficult." He got to his feet and came to stand directly in front of her. "You will do this, or I will see your youngest brother dead even yet tonight. Do you understand me? You cannot protect him. I have my means . . . and my friends. It will be very easy to have the boy simply fall overboard."

Ashlie stiffened. Her father would no doubt have beat this man to a pulp for his threats, but Ashlie had no ability to fight him. At least not physically. It would not be a good idea to create a fuss at this point, she decided. "Very well. I will do as you say, but what kind of assurance do I have that no harm will come to my family?"

"You must understand, Miss Ivankov, I hold your family no personal malice. I simply want my own survival. If you do as you have promised, I will have no reason to further concern myself with your family. Otherwise, you have no guarantee— no assurances. I am what I am, and I really have nothing to offer you otherwise."

The man's dark eyes seemed lifeless—his expression void. Ashlie repressed a shiver. "Then I suppose I have no choice."

He smiled, but there was nothing of joy in his look. "Exactly. You have no choice."

A knock sounded three times on the cabin door. "They're finished," a voice called from the other side.

"Ah, we must conclude our business. It would seem your family has eaten their fill. Do you understand what is required of you? We dock in less than twenty-four hours."

"I know what I have to do," Ashlie replied.

Mills nodded and opened his cabin door. "Then you'd best return to your family, lest they believe some harm has come to you."

Ashlie moved quickly out the door and nearly ran down

the passageway. She made her way back up to the deck where her father had booked their stateroom. Mills' boldness irritated her in a way she could not set aside. His threats to Christopher and Oliver were beyond all reason.

Opening the door to her cabin, Ashlie met her father's concerned expression. "Where have you been?"

"You won't believe me when I tell you," Ashlie declared. She looked at her brothers, then back to her father. "We have some trouble aboard. His name is Mr. Mills."

Adrik shook his head. "Mills?"

"He was first known to us as Mr. Babinovich. Remember him?"

"He's here? The authorities are scouring Ship Creek for him. He's a thief and a murderer."

"Yes, I know," Ashlie replied. "He told me after he forced me to accompany him to his cabin."

"What!" Adrik's booming voice caused all three of his children to jump. "I think you'd better explain everything."

Ashlie told her father in vivid detail everything that Mills had related, right down to the knock on the door from his accomplice. She could see her father was enraged, but he held his temper.

"Did you get a look at his assistant?"

Ashlie shook her head. "He merely knocked on the door, then disappeared. I would guess that Mr. Mills keeps him completely removed from his presence."

"Do you remember which cabin Mills has?" Adrik was moving to a trunk at the foot of one of the beds.

"No, I ran out of there so fast, I didn't even take note."

Ashlie paused and looked at her brothers. "Father, I have an idea."

Adrik pulled a revolver from the trunk. "I have an idea too." He checked the cylinder.

Ashlie reached out, gently touching her father's arm. "Mine doesn't involve bloodshed," she said with a grin.

Her father's angry expression softened. "All right. Let's hear it."

"I think we should let Mr. Mills believe he's got the upper hand. Let him think that I'm cooperating with him. The boys and I can stay here in the cabin. After all, we have less than twenty-four hours before we arrive. If you can manage to sneak away to meet the captain, you explain the situation and have him radio the authorities. They can be prepared to meet him when we arrive."

"But obviously he has someone watching us," Adrik said, still considering the situation. "But I suppose we could pay someone to do our bidding—maybe even watch him."

"Remember the cabin steward?" Ashlie asked. "He seemed eager to earn his gratuities. Perhaps he could be persuaded to get a letter to the captain. Perhaps he would even watch Mills and his friend for us. Sooner or later Mills will have to meet with this accomplice in order to issue instructions and get information."

"That's good thinking," Adrik said with a grin. "You are your mother's daughter." He smiled and checked the revolver. "But it's always good to have an alternative plan." He pushed the open cylinder back into place. "This is my alternative plan."

Chapter Twenty-six

B ut why would that man want to hurt us?" Christopher
asked innocently.

Ashlie ruffled his hair and shook her head. "Because some
people are just evil, Christopher. We must do exactly as Father
tells us in order to be safe." She looked out her cabin window
but could see nothing of the docks.

Oliver sat at the door, his father's revolver in hand. Ashlie
knew the boy would do whatever was necessary to protect her.
He felt a huge sense of importance and responsibility when
their father had asked him to perform the task of guard.

The night before, Ashlie had managed to recall the general
location of Mill's cabin. She wrote down the information in
as much detail as possible, and her father managed to get word
to the captain via the cabin steward. The young man was more
than happy to assist for the large sum Adrik offered. The captain sent word back in return that the Ivankovs should remain

in their cabin and that he would deal with the matter utilizing his crew and the authorities in Seattle. When they believed they had the right man in custody, they would send for Adrik to identify him. And that was where their father was at this moment.

Ashlie tried not to appear worried. She knew the boys were already fretting over the situation, and she didn't want to add to the problem. She almost regretted insisting they come to Seattle, given the situation.

"What if he tries to hurt Papa?" Christopher asked.

Oliver scoffed at this. "Nobody can get the best of Pa. Especially when they don't even realize Pa knows all about them."

"Oliver's right, Chris. Mr. Mills doesn't know that I've said anything to Father. He probably thinks that I would be too frightened to tell Father the truth."

"But you weren't afraid at all," Christopher said, admiration in his tone.

Ashlie smiled. "I'm not afraid, but I do believe that it's important to be obedient and cautious. We will be safe here and wait for Father's instructions. That way we won't be in harm's way, and he can focus on the things that are important for the moment."

"Are you really going to get married?" Oliver asked from his perch.

Ashlie had discussed her wedding plans off and on while sailing to Seattle. It seemed only natural that her brother might be curious about the situation. "I am," she replied. "I think you'll like Winston a lot. I'm really excited for you two to meet."

"Will I like him too?" Christopher questioned.

"Absolutely." Ashlie sat on the edge of the bed. "Winston is so much like Father. He's kind and considerate and loves Jesus. He's tall and broad at the shoulder like Papa, and when he smiles it lights up his whole face."

"And he's a doctor, right?"

"That's right, Chris. He's a doctor, and he's studying extra hard so that he can be a surgeon and operate on people who are wounded or hurting. He loves helping people."

"He's probably good, then," Oliver said. "I don't want you to marry somebody who isn't really good."

"And the best part is that we plan to move up to Alaska. I won't be very far away from you."

"Will you live in Ketchikan?" Christopher's expression looked quite hopeful.

"I don't know," Ashlie admitted. "We'll go wherever we feel God leads us."

Adrik listened as the steward explained the situation. "I've not seen him with anyone else. It's just like I told the captain. I think the gentleman is working alone."

"Well, he's no gentleman, but I'm glad to hear it. Still, my daughter said someone knocked on his door to let him know when I finished eating with my sons."

"I know about that," the steward said rather excitedly. "It wasn't an accomplice that did it at all. It was one of the dining room staff. The man was nearly fired for the event because he left his station."

Adrik shook his head. "Are you certain about this?"

"Absolutely. The man requested to be brought before the captain when his superior threatened to fire him. The man explained that he was paid a large sum of money to watch you and your boys. He was to report to Mr. Mills by knocking and declaring you were finished with the meal. I believe he's the only one who has assisted Mr. Mills."

"Then no doubt Mills is hoping that we are the type of people easily threatened—especially Ashlie." Adrik laughed. "He doesn't know my daughter. She's an Alaskan. We aren't easily intimidated."

Six armed police officers from Seattle appeared with the captain just then. Adrik knew from the information he'd been given that the captain had wired ahead and that Seattle was sending the men by launch. With them on board before the ship docked, they could have Mills in hand without involving any of the other passengers.

"Are we ready?" the captain questioned. "I mean to see this thing done."

Adrik nodded. "Let me go first." The police officers assembled on either side of the door. Adrik lowered his voice and leaned toward the steward. "If he asks to know who it is, call to him and tell him you're the cabin steward."

The young man nodded. He seemed so thrilled to be a part of the capture that Adrik nearly laughed out loud. Instead, he controlled his amusement and knocked. The sooner Mills was in custody, the better for everyone.

"Who is it?" a voice questioned from the other side of the door.

Adrik nodded at the cabin steward. The young man looked

to his captain only momentarily, then answered in a loud voice, "Cabin steward, sir."

"What do you want?"

Adrik felt a momentary sense of panic, but the young man was completely under control.

"We're about to dock in Seattle. I'm here to assist with your baggage."

Adrik held his breath, wondering if this would win the day or if he'd end up having to knock down the door. He heard the latch give way and saw the knob turn slowly. As soon as the door was open a fraction of an inch, Adrik forced it back with such power that Mills landed unceremoniously on his backside.

"And I'm here to assist them with you," Adrik said, standing over the stunned Mills. The police rushed in to surround the man.

"What is this all about?" Mills declared. "You have the wrong man."

"No, I don't think so," Adrik said with a smile of satisfaction. "But you certainly messed with the wrong young woman."

The police got him on his feet and dropped their hold as Mills adjusted his coat. "I have no idea what you're talking about."

"Really doesn't matter much. You're a wanted man and you're under arrest. If I thought I could get away with it, I'd belt you just for threatening my children."

Mills' lip curled. He gave a side glance to the officer who prepared to handcuff him. Without warning, Mills pushed the man backward and rushed for the door. Adrik blocked him, however, and the officers wrestled him to the cabin floor.

"Seems he does better down on the floor," Adrik said, eyeing Mills with great contempt. "Maybe you should just leave him there—roll him off the ship like an empty whiskey barrel."

The officers laughed, but Mills was not amused. It was clear he saw his defeat and was not happy. The officer in charge quickly took down information from Adrik, then hurried to follow his associates.

"Thank you for your help in this matter," Adrik said, turning to the cabin steward as the police led Mills from the room. He looked to the captain and winked. "This young man deserves a raise. He thinks fast on his feet."

"I believe you're right," the captain replied. "Perhaps he can be moved to a better position. One that deals with our ship's security."

Adrik reached out and shook the cabin steward's hand. "Thank you, son." He turned to the captain and extended his hand. "And thank you, Captain. I'll rest easier now knowing my family doesn't have to worry about debarking in danger."

———

Ashlie startled as the key sounded in the lock and the door handle turned to admit their father. "The authorities have him in custody," he announced.

"Was there any trouble?" Ashlie jumped up.

"Oh, he tried to protest his innocence, and when he could see it wasn't going to do him any good, he tried to run. He was no match for the police, however. They easily overpowered him. I gave a statement and Myrtle's address in case they needed to talk to us."

"So we can leave now?" Ashlie asked. She was so anxious to see Winston. Surely he would be worried, wondering why most everyone else had left the ship but not the Ivankovs.

Her father gave her a devilish look of mischief. "I don't know. I'm not in any hurry, and the captain said we might wait here as long as we desire."

Ashlie gathered her things. "Well, you can wait here, but I don't intend to."

Oliver handed his father the revolver. "I'm tired of this ship. I want to see what everyone's been telling me about— this great city of Seattle."

"Me too," Christopher said, coming to his father. "Can we go now?"

The big man laughed out loud. "I guess we'd better. Otherwise I'll be standing here alone. Grab your things, boys. We'd best hurry or our Ashlie will leave us in the dust."

Ashlie opened the cabin door and waited impatiently for her family. The boys hurried to take up their small packs, while Adrik leisurely replaced the gun in his trunk, then hoisted it to his shoulders.

"All right. Let's go."

On the dock, Ashlie searched to find the only man she truly cared to see. "There he is!" Ashlie shouted, picking up her pace. She could see Winston standing beside Timothy Rogers. Was it possible that Winston was even more hand- some than when they'd parted company earlier in the summer?

"I thought we'd never get here," she declared as she dropped her things on the dock and threw her arms around the man in a most inappropriate manner. At that point she didn't care what anyone thought. "I've missed you so much."

Winston hugged her close, then set her away from him. Ashlie could see that he'd grown rather uncomfortable in the shadow of the big man who stood watching them.

"Winston, this is my father, Adrik Ivankov."

"Sir . . . I'm . . . I'm . . . pleased to meet you." He extended his hand. Adrik balanced the trunk with one arm and took hold of Winston.

Ashlie's father eyed the younger man with great scrutiny. "Glad to finally meet you. I figure if we're to be family, we need to get right to work."

The tall dark-haired man seemed rather taken aback. "Get right to work?"

"Getting to know each other," Adrik countered. "Ashlie tells me she'd like to be married within the week. Does that set well with you?"

Winston seemed to overcome his surprise just a bit. He looked to Ashlie, then back to Adrik. "She has a way of getting what she wants," he said with a grin. "At least this time I find that it meets very well with my approval. But I would like to ask you properly for her hand and have your approval as well."

A smile broke the sternness of Adrik's expression. "She does have a way of getting what she wants, and I can tell already that I'm going to like you just fine."

———

Leah looked around the large open room and smiled. Earlier she and Helaina had opened every window in the house to air out the damp, stale smell. This was the home she'd grown up in with Karen and Adrik. The Ketchikan cabin had started fairly small, but over the years Adrik had added on to it with first one room and then another and finally an entire second story. It was a beautiful log home that brought back many special memories of her mother-daughter relationship with Karen.

Now after two hours of dusting and mopping, Leah felt the house was in good order. She sighed and leaned back against the front door. Adrik had told them to feel free to live with him as long as they liked. He wanted the company—no, he needed it. Leah knew that it would probably be hard for him to come back to this house and not be lonely.

"You certainly managed to accomplish a great deal," Helaina said, coming down the stairs. She and the baby, along with the twins, had been napping while Leah worked. "You really shouldn't have done so much in your condition."

"I feel fine. Besides, I can get a lot done when there aren't little ones under foot. Not to mention I enjoyed myself. I kept thinking of times when Karen and I cleaned this house together."

"I know you'll miss her," Helaina said. "I'm missing her myself. Sometimes more than I ever imagined." She frowned. "I suppose that doesn't make sense to you."

"Why wouldn't it?"

"Well, I didn't know Karen all that long, but in the time I knew her, I found she had a way of nurturing people. And she made me feel as if my mother were here again. She would come and have tea with me every day if her schedule permitted. It meant the world to me."

Leah went to Helaina and took her hand. "It doesn't matter how long you knew her. Karen had a special heart for people. I know she thought you to be a perfect mate for Jacob." Leah smiled. "We always knew it would take a strong-willed woman to be a good wife for him."

"We have definitely had our moments. Goodness, but when I think back to our first meeting and how I nearly slapped him for running into me on the street, it makes me laugh. We didn't exactly make a positive impression on each other."

"Well, you were too busy trying to hang my husband," Leah teased.

"Don't remind me. I hate those days—those times of being so hard." Helaina put her hand on Leah's shoulders. "I don't deserve the mercy I've received, but I'm so blessed to have it. I don't deserve any of the good things God has given me."

"None of us do," Leah admitted. "But then they wouldn't be so special if they were deserved."

"I never thought I'd be a part of a real family again," Helaina admitted. "I didn't want to be a part of one. I didn't want children because the pain of losing them would have been impossible to bear, and I certainly didn't want to risk having another husband. Now here I am with both husband and son, and I could not imagine my life without them. Not to mention the twins and you and Jayce." Tears came to her eyes. "Leah, the past . . . well . . . it seems like a vague dream—a nightmare, really. I never thought that would be possible. I'm so happy with my life."

Leah patted Helaina's hand. "I am too. And so many years

ago I sat in this very house, crying my eyes out because Jayce rejected my love. How strange it seems to be here now—married with two beautiful children and another on the way." Leah put her hand to her stomach. "I couldn't have ever seen the possibility of this all those years ago. I never thought I could be happy, but here I am."

"Leah!" Jayce called from outside. He came bounding through the front door, Jacob right behind him.

Leah could see they were both quite excited. "What's going on?"

"We are the proud new owners of the Barringer-Kincaid Mercantile," Jayce announced.

"That's wonderful news. I'm so glad things went well." Leah went to her husband and kissed him lightly on the cheek. She had known the men were trying to put the finishing touches on their new business venture but hadn't known for sure that things would be completed that day.

"I've wired Peter Colton and will have a list of supplies delivered up here as soon as he can spare a ship to make the trip north," Jacob said. He lifted Helaina at the waist and twirled her around several times before setting her back down. "Things are finally coming together for our store."

"I knew they would," Helaina replied.

"We'll have to celebrate tonight," Leah declared. "I'll kill one of the chickens and fry it up."

"And can we have potatoes and gravy?" her husband asked.

"And biscuits and fresh rhubarb pie?" her brother added.

Leah laughed and looked to Helaina. "It would appear our work is just beginning."

September brought the grand opening of the Barringer-Kincaid Mercantile. Jacob was proud of what they'd accomplished and knew that, although there would be less traffic here than what he might have experienced in Seward or Ship Creek, Ketchikan had the feel of home to him. Only two days earlier they'd completed the renovations of the rooms above the store, and he'd moved his family into their own home. With Malcolm quite small, Jacob knew it would be some time before they would need to worry about having a bigger place with a yard. For now this was not only very adequate for their needs, it was beneficial for their business. With the store located just downstairs, Jacob wouldn't have to worry about theft in the night. With the town growing ever larger, such matters were always of concern.

Everything seemed perfect. With the store situated right at the docks, Jacob felt confident they would do very well. Jayce thought so too. He pointed out that ships might even begin allowing their passengers time to depart the ship and come to their store to purchase native-made items they could take home as souvenirs of their trip north.

"I think once we figure things up," Jayce said, looking at the ledger, "we will have made a nice profit today."

"That's to be expected," Jacob said. "It was the first day. Folks were curious about the things we had on hand. We won't have that kind of traffic in here on a daily basis. That's why I didn't want to have too big of a place."

"I've been thinking," Jayce began, "in time we might add on to this building and create rental space for additional shops. Think of it."

Jacob could imagine just such a thing. "I had been thinking perhaps we could even buy the places just up the way from us and attach them on to this building with a few places in between. It would be expensive, but just imagine what we'd have when we got done. We could rent out the other buildings and have a nice income."

Jayce laughed. "We think so much alike, it's downright scary."

The bell over the door sounded as a man looking to be in his fifties entered the store. Jacob moved down the counter. "Welcome, friend. We were just about to close up for the day."

"I'm glad I caught you, then." He moved to the counter and extended his hand. "I'm Bartholomew Turner. Bart to my friends. I've come to discuss a matter with you and your partner."

Jayce joined Jacob. "I'm Jayce Kincaid."

"And I'm Jacob Barringer. What did you want to discuss?"

"The fact of the matter is this: I own a store in Skagway. The economy in that area is quite depressed, and it is my plan to be done with the place when my lease is up at the end of October. I was here in Ketchikan to discuss with my brother the idea of leaving Alaska altogether. We are not young men anymore and a warmer climate would be to our liking."

"I don't see what that has to do with us." Jacob saw the man's expression change from serious to rather hopeful.

"I thought you might be interested in buying out my current stock. It isn't large, by any means, but no one in Skagway wishes to secure it because there are many specialty items that are of no interest. Things like musical instruments and cameras. They used to be quite sought after, I must say. I once sold a great many things. Now I do better with the odd bits of furniture, lamps, and of course food staples. We found we had to add food items just to keep our business lucrative."

"Have you had your store long?" Jayce questioned.

"I set up just after the gold rush began," Turner replied. "I had a store at the end of Main called S&T House Goods. We were in a tent for quite a while, but then one of the wealthy townsmen built several buildings, and we rented out space for our store."

"I remember that place," Jacob said. "I was up there during the rush. I was just a boy, but I do remember your place."

Turner beamed. "We had a fine store. My brother and cousin helped to make it a profitable business, but once the rush passed it became very difficult to keep things going. Not only that, but I long for home." His smile faded. "Our mother passed on while we were up here, and our father is nearly eighty. We need to return to Oregon before he dies."

"I can understand your concern," Jacob replied. "I suppose it might be possible for us to take the stock off your hands." He looked to Jayce, who was nodding.

"Maybe we could all have supper together and discuss the details?" Jayce questioned, looking to Jacob.

"I don't know why not," Turner replied. "In fact, you could join me at my brother's place."

"Nonsense. My wife would happily cook for you both," Jayce replied. "Why don't you and your brother plan to come to supper around six? Jacob and his family will be there as well."

Turner seemed quite excited. "I can't tell you how happy this makes me. I'm quite anxious to get back to Oregon before winter sets in. My brother and I will be there."

That night after supper concluded, Leah put her children to bed and returned as the men were finishing up the last of their dessert and coffee.

"Would you have any objection to my traveling to Skagway at the first of next month with Jacob?" Jayce asked. "Mr. Turner figures to have his merchandise inventoried and ready to go by then."

"I don't mind at all," Leah replied, although in her heart she knew she'd much rather neither man leave. "How long will you be gone?"

Jacob met her gaze. "I wouldn't think any longer than a couple of weeks. Maybe three at the most. I figured since Adrik and the boys plan to be home day after tomorrow, I could talk to him about keeping the store for us."

"Helaina and I could certainly tend to that," Leah replied.

"I'd rather you not have to," Jacob said sternly. "The children need you, and besides, some of the men can be quite rowdy. I wouldn't want there to be any incidents while we were gone and unable to protect you."

"Yeah, it's bad enough to leave you here," Jayce replied. "Maybe it would be better for just one of us to go." He looked at Jacob.

"We are perfectly capable," Leah said, putting her hands on her hips in a defiant pose. "You above everyone else know that."

Jacob held up his hand as Helaina opened her mouth to weigh in her opinion. "Hold on. There's no need for either one of you to get excited about this. Let me talk to Adrik, and then we'll figure it all out."

"You can stay with me while you're in Skagway," Turner said as if to change the subject and calm the ladies. "I am happy to extend the hospitality."

"That sounds great." Jacob looked at the calendar. "We'll try to leave around the first of October. If things go well, and depending on ship availability, we might be able to head home before the fifteenth of the month."

"I will do my part," Turner promised. "I'll have everything crated and ready to go. We can nail down the lids after you approve the goods. I'll even arrange to have movers standing by."

"Well, here's to our new adventure," Jacob said, holding up his coffee mug.

Leah felt a chill suddenly run down her spine as the men clicked their mugs together. She didn't know why she should feel uncomfortable, but she did.

After everyone had returned home and she sat getting ready for bed, she voiced her concern to her husband. "I have a bad feeling about this venture of yours."

"A bad feeling?" Jayce looked up from where he was reading in bed. "What are you talking about?"

Leah shrugged. "I don't know." She ran her brush through her long dark curls. "I suppose there's no reason to feel uncomfortable. Turner is obviously a legitimate businessman, otherwise there'd be no reason to go so far as to try and entice you both to come to Skagway."

"Jacob even remembered his store."

"I know. I don't know why I'm uneasy. I just am. The weather is very unpredictable this time of year. It might be rough to travel farther north." She put the brush down and went to crawl into bed. "I suppose I just worry about your safety."

"Well, stop," Jayce said, putting his book aside. He blew out the lamp. "There's no reason to be afraid. Skagway is an all-year harbor—it never freezes over like in Nome. And it's certainly not as risky as the Arctic. We won't be stuck in any ice floes. Besides, Jacob knows Skagway, and we both have decent funds so that if we need to stay in a hotel should Turner's hospitality prove to be less than desirable, we will be fully capable of doing so."

Leah snuggled into her husband's open arms. "You could get sick."

"And sled dogs could fly," he teased. "You need to stop worrying about the possibility of things that might go wrong and pay more attention to other things."

"Other things? Like what?" She tried to imagine what he might mean.

"Like this," Jayce said. He covered her mouth with his.

Chapter Twenty-seven

Leah adapted easily to her new life in Ketchikan. She was amazed at how much the place had grown just since her last visit. There were now four salmon canneries, with another planned for the future, as well as mining and logging industries. The only problem with increased industry, of course, was the expansion of saloons and bordellos on Creek Street. Leah supposed it was one of those unavoidable issues, although she tried at every turn to encourage those she knew to avoid that area at all cost. In church they often talked of ways to reach out to the soiled doves who worked the houses of ill repute, but too much money was exchanging hands to keep the women away for long. This grieved Leah in a way she couldn't begin to explain. The houses had been there even when she'd been a child, but she'd never thought much about the women who worked there. Now, after becoming a wife and mother, Leah's heart went out to these poor souls. They were somebody's daughters—maybe even wives and mothers to someone. What had brought them to such a horrible fate?

Ketchikan remained scenic and beautiful despite the darker side of life. Eagles were abundant, drawn there by the presence of salmon and other good fishing. Leah loved to watch the birds on the beach. Wills and Merry loved them as well. They didn't go to watch them often, but when they did everyone seemed to have the best time.

With Adrik's house removed from the town and set a bit higher on the forested mountainside, Leah felt removed from the sorrows and dirtiness of life. Here it was quiet and lovely with a rich abundance of all they needed. The winters were mild, with more rain than snow, and the summers were warm and beneficial to growing fruits and vegetables. She'd even managed to reconnect with a couple of dear friends from her youth. The life they'd found here was far better than she could have imagined, and Leah felt they'd made the right decision in coming. It would be a good place to raise Wills and Merry and the new baby.

She put her hand to her stomach. Finding herself pregnant again stirred up some concerns as to how this would affect Jayce's love for the twins. Just as she'd overcome her fears about whether Jayce could love the children as his own, new worries came to haunt her. Would he care more about the baby he knew to be his own?

"I'm leaving now," Jayce said. He came and planted a kiss on the top of Leah's head. "I'll be home around four."

She put aside her worries and smiled. "Don't forget to take those things by the door." She pointed to a stack of ready-made shirts, two fur-lined hats, and a muff. Jacob had encouraged her to produce some items for the store since there seemed a never-ending request for such things.

"These are great, Leah. I know they'll sell quickly. We had a man in the store just the other day asking for shirts."

"I'm glad. It'll give me a bit of money to buy Christmas gifts."

He laughed. "That's still a few months away."

"So's the baby's birth," she countered, "but I'm planning for that as well."

He sobered. "It is coming up awful fast. Are you feeling all right?"

His concern touched her. "I'm just fine. Now off with you." Leah got to her feet. She was afraid if they talked much more about it that she might voice her real fears. "Having one baby is much different than having two."

"How can you be sure it's just one?" Jayce winked. "It could be twins again."

"No, when I was this far along with the twins, I was already out to here." She exaggerated, joining her hands in a circle and holding them out well away from her body. "Besides, the doctor believes it's just one."

"Well, either way, we'll take whatever the good Lord sends."

Once he'd gone, Leah refocused on her work. The house was quiet. Since Adrik had returned with the boys, Leah had enjoyed pampering and spoiling them. However, this was a school day and the boys would be gone until the afternoon. Adrik, too, was off working on getting special wood for some of the furniture he planned to build. He was already talking about expanding his workshop and teaching Oliver as well.

Putting her sewing aside, Leah picked up the newspaper Adrik had brought home last night. There were so many sad stories of problems in the world. Czar Nicholas and his family had been murdered by the people who'd taken over his country. This fact troubled Leah greatly. How could it be that royalty could just be murdered without the world rising up in protest?

There were other worrisome issues too. The influenza had once again reared its ugly head, so while the war seemed to be coming to a close, another crisis arose to claim lives. Leah didn't understand how so much death could go on without wiping the human race completely from the world. Hundreds of thousands were dead because of the war, and the influenza might claim that many and more. That seemed impossible to imagine. Leah prayed that the influenza would not come to their shores, but at the same time, she'd already gathered quite a bit of devil's club, just in case.

"I hope you'll never have to know war or sickness," she told her unborn child.

"Mama," Wills called. He came maneuvering down the stairs, as was his routine when awakening in the morning. "Let's eat!" He jumped off the last step and ran for his mother's open arms.

Hugging him close, Leah kissed his neck. "I suppose I shall feed you, my little man. Is your sister awake?"

"Merry playin'," he told her. This, too, wasn't at all unusual. Merry often woke up and played in her bed quietly until Wills started making a ruckus.

"Well, let's get both of you dressed and ready for the day. I have a feeling you're going to keep me busy."

Hours later, when the boys returned from school, Leah felt a weariness in her body that seemed to grow as the new baby grew. She had worked to reorder the pantry as well as sew on several new pieces. One piece in particular, a new quilt for Helaina and Jacob, was taking more time than she'd hoped. She had planned to have it ready to give as a Christmas present and had patterned it after the quilt Karen had given her in Last Chance. Leah had also noticed that Adrik's coat was quite worn. If she could get her hands on a good piece of fur, she could make him a new coat as a present.

"How was your day?"

"We learned more about the Silver War," Christopher told Leah as he put his books on the table.

"The Civil War, you mean," she said matter-of-factly.

He nodded. "Civil War. I always forget. Anyway, a lot of people were fighting each other, and it was like if Oliver and I decided to fight a war. It was brother against brother."

"I remember learning about that myself," Leah admitted. She put out a plate of cookies for the boys. "It wasn't a very good time for our country. There were a lot of hateful people, and a great many innocent people who were hurt."

Oliver plopped down on a chair. It seemed he had sprouted up about six inches overnight. Leah was already hard at work making him new shirts and trousers. No doubt he would be as tall as his father.

"And what of you, Oliver? What are you studying?"

"Nothing I like. We have to memorize a lot of Bible verses, and I'm no good at it." He took a cookie and popped it in his mouth.

"Memorizing is sometimes hard," Leah admitted, "but

your mother taught me a little trick a long time ago. She told me if I could put the verse to music—just make up a little song to go with the words—I could memorize it much easier. I still do that today."

Oliver shrugged. "I remember her telling me that too. I never really tried it, though." He glanced up at the clock. "I have to cut wood. I promised Pa." He grabbed another cookie and headed for the door.

Once he'd gone, Leah looked to Christopher. "And what about you? Don't you have chores too?"

"I suppose so," he admitted, "but I wanted to ask you a question."

Leah could see the twins were happily occupied with their toys, so she turned her full attention on Christopher. "What did you want to ask?"

"Why did God have to take my mama away?"

She had no answers for such a question—a question she'd asked many times herself. What could she possibly tell him?

"My mama was a good woman. You said so yourself. She loved God and did good things. So why did He take her away? Why'd He do that to her?"

"You make going to heaven sound like a punishment."

"Well, dyin' sure sounds like a punishment," Christopher replied. "Dyin's no fun. You don't get to do anything anymore after you die."

"I don't know about that," Leah said, taking the seat directly across from the boy. "I think there are probably all sorts of wonderful things to do in heaven. The Bible says we'll be happy—that we won't have any more tears."

"I still don't like that God took her away. I need her."

Leah nodded. "I know you do, Christopher. I wish I could give you answers. We can't always know why God does things a certain way." She thought back over her own life. There were so many times she'd questioned God about why things were happening a certain way. Sometimes the answers became clear in time, but just as often situations remained a mystery.

"Christopher, I can tell you without any doubt, that your mama loved God and trusted Him for what was best and good for her life and for yours. She would want you to trust Him now."

"But God's scary to me."

"Why?"

Christopher looked at the cookie in his hand. "I don't know. He's just big, and He has all the power. I have to be really good all the time or He won't love me."

"Who told you that?"

Christopher shrugged. "I don't know. Just some people."

Leah smiled. "He is all-powerful and big. He has to be so that He can handle the entire world. But, Christopher, He will love you always—no matter what. He wants your love and obedience, but He loves you even when you mess up. The Bible says that even while we were still sinners, Jesus came and died for us. We weren't good—yet God still loved us and sent Jesus to die on the cross for our sins."

"He's still scary to me."

"Like your father sometimes frightens other people."

"My pa isn't scary."

"He is to some people who don't know him. He's big and very powerful. I've seen people be very afraid of him. In fact, the first few times I was around your father as a young girl, he frightened me."

Christopher looked at her in disbelief. "But my pa is good."

"So is God. Do you have any reason to believe He's not?"

"Well . . . He . . . He . . . took my mama. That wasn't a good thing to do."

Leah felt the boy's pain pierce her heart. "Christopher, I wish your mother could have stayed, but you know we all have our time to die."

"Pa told me that. It's in the Bible that we all have to die once. If we don't accept Jesus as our Savior, then we have to die twice."

"That's right. We would die once in the flesh, and then on the judgment day—if we had rejected Jesus—we would die again. That time it would be forever."

Christopher nodded. "I remember my mama saying that." He sighed and got to his feet. "I'm glad you came here, Leah. I like having you around. You remind me of Mama sometimes." He looked to where Karen's picture hung beside the fireplace. "I sure miss her, but now I can remember her face."

Leah fought back tears as Christopher left the cabin to see to his chores. *God, this is so hard. Please help those boys. Help Adrik. They need your healing touch in their lives.* She looked to where the twins were playing. She had thought she might lose them to influenza. She had worried about losing Jayce and Jacob to the Arctic Ocean when the expedition went missing. So many of her friends from Last Chance were dead. Death was just such a hard thing to bear—even the threat of it could be crippling.

Leah tried to shake off the heavy feeling. She began to hum and then to sing aloud verses she'd memorized from the latter part of Romans eight.

"'For I am persuaded, that neither death, nor life, nor angels, nor principalities, nor powers, nor things present, nor things to come, nor height, nor depth, nor any other creature shall be able to separate us from the love of God, which is in Christ Jesus our Lord.'"

Death would always be a natural part of life, but Leah would not let it defeat her. It would not separate her from God's love. She would not allow it to.

———

"We have passage booked to Skagway," Jacob said, holding up the tickets for Jayce to see. "The problem will be in return-ing. There are only two ships coming into Skagway in Octo-ber. The *Spirit of Alaska* will leave Skagway on the seventh—probably too soon for us to have concluded our business since we won't arrive in Skagway until the third. The *Princess Sophia* will be in dock on the twenty-second."

"That means we'll have to be gone an extra week." Jayce's tone made it clear he didn't like the idea at all.

"I know. I suppose we can push to get things accom-plished as soon as possible. Maybe if we explain to Turner, we can work day and night to see things accounted for and loaded."

"It sure won't give us much time. Maybe we should just plan to return on the *Princess Sophia* and leave it at that. At least we can explain it to the girls and then they'll have time to get used to the idea."

"Get used to what idea?" Adrik asked as he came in from the back room. "I just left some fresh fish upstairs. Helaina is already hard at work."

Jacob smiled. "Thanks. Did you have a good catch?"

"Enough to supply us all. So what idea were you wanting the girls to get used to?"

"Well, I picked up our tickets for Skagway and learned that we probably won't have a chance to head back until the twenty-second. The only other ship that will be available will leave before we'll have time to load all the stock and equipment we're purchasing from Turner."

Adrik frowned. "And you expect me to keep track of the store in your absence? I don't know that I'm cut out to be a storekeeper for almost a month."

Jayce looked to Jacob. "I could just stay here."

Adrik laughed. "I was just joshing with you. I can handle it. The girls will handle it as well. We all do what we have to—right? This is just one of those times when everything doesn't go perfectly our way. But it will be all right. I'm confident that we can get by without you for a time. Maybe you can go visit some of the old places. I hear Dyea is nothing more than a few abandoned buildings and old-timers."

Jacob nodded. "I had thought about visiting the cemetery."

"Your father's grave?" Jayce asked.

"Yes. It's been a long time. Might do me good to visit." The thought had been on his mind ever since Turner had invited them to Skagway.

"So the extra time will serve you well," Adrik replied. "It'll probably end up being a blessing to you both."

Jayce looked to Jacob and smiled. "Probably, but I know it's going to be hard to convince Leah of such a blessing."

Chapter Twenty-eight

Skagway proved beneficial for both parties. Jacob and Jayce were quite happy with the inventory and felt confident the supplies would serve them well. Turner even came down on the original price to compensate for the shipping prices. With the goods headed to the dock to load on the *Princess Sophia,* Jayce and Jacob finished up the paper work at the shipping office.

"You fellas want to insure the load?" the agent asked.

"I hadn't figured to," Jacob replied.

"If the cost isn't too bad, Jacob, it might be wise. There have been quite a few storms of late. Remember Peter sent you that letter about the load he lost to heavy water damage?"

Jacob considered it for a moment. "True enough. The weather's been pretty lousy of late, and with the snows and wind, I suppose it might be a good idea. Why don't you show us what you have to offer?"

The man quickly explained the details of the insurance and the prices available. Jacob and Jayce finally agreed on the coverage and concluded business with the man. In a few hours they would be on their way.

"I still can't believe the way this place has changed," Jacob said as they walked back up the main street of town. "When we lived in Dyea, this place was as busy as Seattle. Maybe not as big, but definitely as busy. People were shoulder to shoulder, and prices were outrageous. Pay was good." He grinned. "I always said the real money of the gold rush was to be had right here. People often journeyed to Dawson by way of Skagway. Packers and laborers could make great money."

The area looked rather like a ghost town now. The buildings were still there, but many were in sad disrepair. There were still people to walk the boardwalks, but the numbers were greatly reduced. If not for the railroad that had been built to take people north to the gold fields, Jacob seriously doubted Skagway would have survived.

"I wonder if it will ever revive."

Jacob shrugged. "I suppose if the politicians in this territory have their way, it will. There's a railroad already in place and a good harbor. If there proves to be a reason to bring people into the area—even if it's like last time and this is just a place to come through on the way to some other destination—then I suppose it might thrive again."

Jayce pointed to the café. "How about we grab some supper? We don't board until around five, right?"

Jacob nodded. "Yeah. We should eat. Oh, and I want to pick up a present for Helaina. She was really good-natured about our coming here for so long. She deserves something special."

"What'd you have in mind?" They went into the restaurant and took seats at the first table by the door.

"Well, Turner told me about a woman who has some great handwork for sale. She creates those nice doilies and such for tables and sofas. You know the ones."

Jayce grinned. "Never thought I'd see the day we'd be buying such things."

Jacob laughed. "Me neither, but I guess I never was quite sure I'd be happily married either."

"I know what you mean, but I'm more blessed than I can express. I love your sister more than life itself, and my children run a close second."

"I can hardly wait to get home," Jacob admitted. "It's gonna be good to get on that ship."

———

Unseasonable cold dropped the temperature nearly twenty degrees as October moved rapidly toward November. Snow covered the mountains and trickled down into the valley to coat everything with a dusting of white.

Jayce and Jacob had been gone for nearly a month. Malcolm had been cranky and missed his father, causing many sleepless night for Helaina, while Leah and the twins did their best to get through each day without Jayce's good-natured humor and attention. Had it not been for Adrik and the boys, neither woman would have fared well at all, as far as Leah was concerned.

Leah, now seven months pregnant, could hardly wait for

the child to come. Even the twins were curious about where the baby was, insisting from time to time that Leah let them put their ears against her stomach so that they could hear their brother or sister. Their antics kept Leah from being completely lonely, but even they couldn't keep her from worrying.

A strong storm blew in on the twenty-third, causing Leah to fret about whether this would delay Jayce and Jacob's return. They were to arrive on the *Princess Sophia* by the twenty-sixth, but weather was always a factor with northern shipping routes. When things dawned calm on the twenty-fifth, Leah breathed a sign of relief. *Just one more day,* she told herself. *One more day and they'll be home.*

"You'll never believe what I've just brought home," Adrik called from the doorway. "Come have a look."

Leah put a lid on the pot of stew she'd been working on all morning. "What in the world have you done now, Adrik?" She gave him a good-natured smile and followed him into the yard.

Adrik pulled back a tarp. "We have enough bear meat here to last the winter."

Leah looked at the mound of butchered meat. "Goodness, but I think you're right. Where did you get him?"

"Up the mountain. Never seen anything so big in all my life. Here, just look at the fur. You ought to be able to make several things out of this." He held up a portion of the bloody hide.

"Adrik, that would make a great new coat for you. I've been trying to find some decent fur for just such a project. Your own coat is nearly worn through."

Adrik sobered. "Karen was going to make me a new coat last winter. She said it was well overdue. I kept telling her not to worry with it."

Leah went to him and reached out to touch the fur. "If Karen were here now, she'd agree with me that this bear fur is perfect. I'll get to work tending the hide right away. Given the way the weather's been acting, you'll probably need its warmth."

"We're almost out of salt for treating the hide. Why don't I take care of the meat, and then we'll head into town? Helaina's been handling the store all morning, and I want to relieve her as soon as possible."

Leah considered this for a moment. The idea of getting away from the house for a little while was appealing. "We could probably get Ruth to come stay with the twins." Ruth was a young Tlingit woman who lived just a quarter mile away. "Would you mind listening for the children while I go ask?"

"Not at all. I'll be close by," Adrik assured her.

Leah returned shortly thereafter with Ruth in tow. The woman had a new baby—her first—and didn't mind at all coming to stay with Leah's children. Ruth's mother had been a good friend to Karen when Leah had been a girl.

"We shouldn't be long," Leah told Ruth. "If they wake up, just feed them some of the stew on the stove. It should be done by then. You be sure and eat as well."

The dark-eyed woman nodded as she placed her sleeping baby on a pallet by the fireplace.

"Leah, you ready?" Adrik called from the door.

"Yes. I'm coming." Leah pulled on her parka.

"We'll take the smaller cart and let the dogs help us with

the load," Adrik announced. He'd fixed a team of Jacob's huskies to the wheeled cart. Adrik had taken over the animals' care since Jacob was now living in town. "These guys will be grateful for the exercise. I'm sure they miss the long trips with Jacob." He helped Leah into the cart.

"I'm sure that's true. They do love to run."

Adrik moved them out once Leah was settled, but he kept the dogs at a slow trot. Leah appreciated this, knowing that the animals would much rather move fast. The entire trip only took ten minutes. Downhill was the easy part, but coming back would be a little slower.

When they'd arrived in front of the mercantile, Leah allowed Adrik to help her down. She stretched and put a hand to the small of her back. To her surprise, Helaina came bounding out the front of the store. She looked fragile and pale, her expression suggesting something was wrong. Her eyes looked as though she'd been crying.

"Leah, there's been trouble."

Leah looked to Adrik, who'd tied off the dogs and was now coming to join the women. Leah looked back to Helaina and asked. "What is it? What's happened?"

Tears came to Helaina's already reddened eyes. "There's been word by telegraph. The *Princess Sophia* is sinking on a reef somewhere in Lynn Canal."

———

Leah didn't remember what had caused her to faint, but when she woke up to Adrik's worried expression and Helaina fanning her, she knew it must have been quite bad. Then little

WHISPERS of WINTER

by little the memories flooded in and Helaina's words returned to haunt her.

"The Princess Sophia *is sinking...."*

"Tell me everything," she said as she struggled to sit up.

"Don't you think you ought to just lie there for a little bit?" Adrik questioned.

"I want to know what's going on," Leah demanded and pushed Adrik away.

"Apparently there was a fierce storm—a blizzard," Helaina told her. "I don't know much else except that the ship began to sink after a time. They weren't too far from Juneau, and rescuers were on the scene to help, but I haven't heard anything else. I learned it this morning but had no way to come to you. I was just about to close up the shop and walk out to the cabin with Malcolm when you pulled up."

Leah sighed. "Well, we need to hear the latest and find out what's happened. Who would know?"

"We might start at the telegraph office," Adrik said. "That'd be the logical place."

Leah nodded. "Let's go there, then."

"Why don't you stay here with Helaina and I'll go," Adrik offered. "You really shouldn't risk your health. You've had a big shock."

"I need to find out for myself," Leah said. "I didn't like the idea of their going in the first place. There are always accidents and tragedies in the water. Just look at the placards in every coast town—memorials to those who've been lost at sea. I don't care if I never get on another ship."

"I'm closing the store," Helaina said. "I'll get Malcolm and come with you."

Leah looked at the woman who had become as dear as any sister. "Hurry, then."

Helaina ran upstairs, leaving Leah and Adrik to talk. "I know you don't want me to go," Leah began, "but I need to do this. Please understand. I'm not trying to be purposefully defiant."

Adrik gently put his hand on her shoulder. "I know you aren't. I'm just concerned about you and the baby. I promised Jayce and Jacob that I would look after the both of you."

Leah shook her head. "First we lose Karen and now this." She looked Adrik in the eye. "I don't think I can survive another loss. I don't think I can bear the pain."

"God knows what we can and can't bear," Adrik said softly. "I didn't think I could bear losing Karen, but my boys and Ashlie needed me. Remember how I tried to hide from it all? You were the one who stood by me—helped me to see the truth. Now I'll be there for you—no matter the outcome."

"But surely if they're close to Juneau and rescuers are on hand, the outcome shouldn't be too bad," Leah said, trying to convince herself. She still couldn't shake images of when she and Jayce had nearly lost their lives when the ship *Orion's Belt* sunk in the ocean off Sitka.

"That's my thought. We have to have hope."

"We're ready," Helaina said, adjusting a hat atop Malcolm's head.

"I wish you'd both wait here," Adrik said, giving them each a hopeful look.

"You know better." Leah headed for the door. "Come on."

There was a crowd already gathered at the telegraph office by the time Leah and the others arrived. She pushed her way through several men, using her femininity and pregnancy to gain their compassion.

"Excuse me, please." She put her hand to her expanding stomach and offered a smile she didn't feel. Her mind reeled with thoughts and images of her husband's and brother's circumstance.

Lord, she prayed silently, *I need you now more than ever. I truly cannot bear this alone. Adrik said you know what I can endure, but I know I cannot handle losing them. You brought them back to me once, please bring them back to me now.*

"If everyone will settle down," a man announced, "I have the latest word from Juneau."

Leah froze in place. She looked to the people around her and drew a deep breath before fixing her gaze on the man. She didn't know how Adrik had managed it, but he was suddenly at her side, his arm firmly wrapped around her shoulders.

"The *Princess Sophia* ran into trouble in a fierce storm," the man began. "Apparently they radioed for help and received rescue boats from Juneau. However, the storm prevented any help. Apparently the storms also kept the *Sophia* from lowering lifeboats. For quite some time the rescue was attempted, but it was to no avail. The *Princess Sophia* sank with no reported survivors."

This can't be happening. They can't be dead.

Leah and Helaina sat at the table in Adrik's home. At his insistence Helaina and Malcolm had come home with them. The shock had been so great that neither Leah nor Helaina had cried. They'd simply walked away from the crying, enraged crowd in a state of disbelief.

"I tried to telegraph Skagway for confirmation of the men boarding the ship," Adrik said as he came through the door. He and the boys had been in town trying to get more information.

"And?" Leah asked hesitantly as Christopher and Oliver moved to their bedroom. Obviously Adrik had told them to leave the adults to talk.

Adrik shook his head. "They won't send it. The lines were ordered to be kept open for the Coast Guard and those helping with the *Princess Sophia*'s situation." He took his coat off and hung it by the door. "I gave them instructions to send it at the first possible moment."

Leah heard his words but could hardly comprehend them. She tried to pray, but words failed her. Helaina had opened her Bible, but she seemed unable to read.

What will we do? Leah refused to vocalize the words, but it was the same question that had haunted her since learning about the *Princess Sophia*. She knew Adrik would offer her a home with him and the boys. He would probably offer Helaina one too, but it didn't matter. That wasn't the point of her question.

Adrik sat down between the two women. "There's always a chance that those reporting the situation don't have all the information. It's rare that a ship would sink without any survivors. Even the *Titanic* had survivors, and they were more ill prepared than the *Princess Sophia*."

"Do you really think there's a chance that passengers made it off safely?" Helaina asked. "I mean, why would the reports say no survivors if there was hope some were saved?"

"I don't know. The world is full of doomsayers. Let's give it a few days and see what happens. Either way, I want you both to listen to me."

Leah looked up and met his gaze. She saw nothing but compassion and love in his eyes. "I'm listening."

"You know you've been like a daughter to me and Jacob like a son." He turned to Helaina. "I've come to love all of you like family. I want you to know that no matter the outcome of this situation, you have a home with me. In fact, I want you to just keep the store closed until we can find out the truth."

"You're good to care so much for us," Helaina said, shaking her head. "I can't even begin to think about the store or anything but Jacob and whether he's safe."

Leah nodded. Helaina had taken the words right out of her mouth. She could barely register rational thought and care for the twins. To have to worry about anything else would be impossible.

"We're family," Adrik stated, reaching to take hold of each woman's arm. "You helped me deal with Karen's death. I want to be here for you—to see you through this. I feel confident God has put us all together for just such a time."

"I don't understand any of this," Helaina began. "I want to trust God, but I'm angry. I'm angry that after everything we've gone through—after everything that they've suffered—we should all be up against another ordeal. I hope this doesn't seem shocking, but God seems very unfair."

Adrik lowered his head and seemed to consider her words. "There are always times when God seems unfair. I wish I could

355

give you answers—explain why this had to happen. But it wouldn't hurt any less if you knew the reasons."

"It might," Helaina interjected. "If I knew why, then maybe I could rationalize it all in my mind. Why should I have lost one husband to tragedy only to remarry and lose another? Have I not learned something God wants me to know? Am I being punished for something?"

Leah had asked the same questions and knew in her heart there were no answers. "Sometimes," she said softly, "life doesn't make sense. The war in Europe, the influenza wiping out whole villages, children losing their parents, husbands losing their wives." She looked to Adrik. "Sometimes answers don't help. Sometimes life just hurts too much to make sense."

Chapter Twenty-nine

The next few days passed ever so slowly for Leah. She often thought of the plans she had made with Jayce . . . little things and big. They had talked of building their own home in the spring. They had both looked forward to the new baby, as well as seeing the twins begin to do new things.

Walking alone in a light rain, Leah struggled to make sense of the events that had just taken place. *It seems so unreal. How in the world do I make sense of this? We were happy, Lord. Really happy. And now this. What am I supposed to do?*

She thought of Adrik's generous offer to have them all remain under his protection and care. It reminded her of the Last Chance villagers being paired off with a new spouse in order to see to the welfare of the children. Leah knew there was money to support the children and herself, however. Jayce had always been clear on the money he held in savings and stocks. Helaina was far wealthier than Leah and would have no trouble at all in seeing to Malcolm's needs. Still, there was so much more to life than money. More to surviving than material items.

"Leah?"

She looked up. "Christopher, what are you doing out here? It's cold and wet."

He shrugged. "I saw you walking and thought maybe you could use a friend."

She smiled at the boy. For such a young man his heart was always sensitive. "I can always use a friend—but especially if it's you."

He came alongside her and matched her pace as they headed up the forest path. The thick covering of spruce and fir kept much of the rain from them. "Leah, can I ask you something?"

She nodded and shoved her hands deep into her parka pockets. "What would you like to know?"

"Is God scary to you now?"

She stopped and looked at Christopher in surprise. He gazed up as if embarrassed. "I just mean ... well ... since Jacob and Jayce's ship sank. I wondered. . . ." He fell silent and looked back at the ground. "You don't have to answer."

Leah thought about the question for a moment. "I won't lie to you, Christopher. This is very hard. It's probably the hardest thing I've ever had to bear."

"Like me when my mother died?"

"Yes. Exactly like that." Leah started walking again, thinking that perhaps the action would help her to reason an answer. "I don't understand why it had to happen this way. So much had already happened."

"It doesn't seem fair—just like with Ma," he threw in.

"No. It definitely doesn't seem fair."

They walked a ways without speaking. The sounds of rain falling gently against the supple spruce branches and their boots against the path were the only noises.

"I guess it's hard for me to put into words," Leah finally said. It wasn't that Christopher couldn't understand; she simply wasn't sure she understood her emotions well enough to convey the matter in words.

"I've never known a time when Jacob wasn't in my life. He's my older brother, so like for you with Ashlie and Oliver, he's always been there. And with Jayce, well, I fell in love with him a long time ago. To imagine my life without them seems almost impossible for me."

"Like me with my mother," Christopher admitted. "Sometimes when I wake up in the morning ... well ... sometimes I think for just a minute that she'll still be there. That her dying was just a bad dream." He shrugged his shoulders. "Guess that sounds silly, huh?"

"Not at all. I felt that way many, many times when Jayce and Jacob were in the Arctic. I kept hoping I would just wake up and find that I had imagined the whole thing—that they were safe in the village and that there was nothing to fear."

"But they're in heaven with Mama," Christopher said, stopping to look at Leah. "Right?"

Leah knew Christopher needed to hear the right thing from her, but she felt completely inadequate to the task. "Yes. I would imagine they're all in heaven." She felt tears come to her eyes and turned to look upward. The canopy of trees overhead, along with the rain clouds, blocked out more and more of the light.

Turning to head back to the cabin lest they run into some kind of animal trouble, Leah tried to regroup her thoughts. "To answer your first question, I don't think God is scary. In fact, right now, He's offering me the only real comfort I can find. I know He loves me. I know He has my life in His hands, just as He had your mama and Jacob and Jayce. He's good, Christopher. Even in bad times, when we think He's stolen what we love the most. He's good, and He loves us."

"Leah, you've been real good to me and Oliver. We love you a lot."

She smiled and put her arm around Christopher's shoulder. It wouldn't be that long before he shot past her in height. "I know you do, and I love you too."

"You've been doing stuff for us like Mama would do. You've been helping us and helping Pa. I want to help you. You're being like a ma to me. I guess I want to help be like a papa to Wills and Merry. I know I'm not a real pa, but I want to play with them and keep them safe. I just want you to know that I'll do that for you."

Leah couldn't keep the tears from her eyes. She pulled Christopher close and hugged him for a long time. He didn't pull away or act embarrassed; instead, he wrapped his arms around her and held on to her as though his life depended on it.

After several moments Leah spoke as she pulled away. "That is the sweetest thing anyone has ever offered me. Thank you, Christopher. I'd be very proud to have you show the twins that kind of love."

"I just don't want them to be sad," Christopher replied. "I don't want them to miss their papa like I miss my mama. I don't want them to hurt in their heart when they grow up and wonder why he went away."

———————

Helaina sat at the table staring at the same piece of sewing that she'd struggled with all morning. Malcolm slept soundly by the fire in a beautiful cradle Adrik had brought from the storage building, while the twins were with Leah in the kitchen. Leah had decided to give them some dough to play with, and Helaina could hear them laughing.

"This is a waste of time," she said, throwing down the material.

"What's the matter?" Leah asked, coming to the table.

"What isn't? Nothing is right. Nothing will ever be right again." She got up and shoved the chair in so hard that it hit the table and rocked backward. Teetering for just a moment, the chair finally fell forward into place.

Leah seemed surprised by Helaina's outburst, but Helaina had no desire to apologize. They were all being so very good. . . . They were all so very calm. It wasn't human. It was completely contrived.

"I don't feel content or comforted," she replied. "I know God has absolute control of this matter, but that's what grieves me most. He has control and yet this . . . this abomination has happened."

Leah nodded. "I know."

"You can't possibly or you'd feel the same way," Helaina ranted, knowing the words were unfair even as she spoke them.

"Just because I'm not throwing a temper tantrum in front

of you doesn't mean I don't feel the same way. I have plenty to say to God in private. Right now I'm trying hard not to say it in front of everyone else."

"But why? Are we Christians not to feel? Can we not hurt and suffer and admit to such things? Will doing so somehow decrease or invalidate God's sovereignty and love and put our faith in doubt?" Helaina paced to the hearth and stared down at her son. "I am a widow for the second time. I vowed never to marry again in order to never again suffer this pain. I thought God understood. I thought He cared, and yet I cannot see how He could and still let this all happen to me. I'm confused, Leah. I don't understand this at all."

Leah stood and hesitantly reached out and took hold of Helaina's hands. The sticky warm dough that still clung to Leah's fingers seemed to knit them together. "I don't understand either," Leah admitted. "But, Helaina, what else can we do?"

Helaina looked away. "I'm lost and so alone, Leah. I'm awash on a sea of my own creation. A sea of tears and sorrow so deep that I will surely drown."

"You aren't lost, Helaina. He knows where you are—He's right here with us. And you aren't alone. I'm in this with you. You are my sister, remember?"

"We were sisters. We were sisters only because I married your brother."

"No," Leah said shaking her head slowly, "we are sisters first in God. And second, we are sisters in heart. My heart is bound to you—not just because of Jacob. You befriended me and helped me so much when Jacob and Jayce were in the Arctic. Will you abandon me now?"

Helaina embraced Leah tightly. "No! I will never abandon you. I'm sorry if I made it sound otherwise. Oh, Leah, I know that you care for me and for Malcolm. I know that. I'm sorry to make it sound so trivial."

Leah pulled away. "I know your heart. But more importantly, He knows our hearts. He's all we have right now. I won't turn from Him in hopes that something or someone else might offer better refuge. I know from experience that they won't."

Helaina nodded. "I know that too. I want to be strong, Leah, but it's just so hard. When the officials came and said that the recovery of bodies had begun, I wanted to die. When they said they would send Jacob and Jayce back to us once certain identification could be had, I wanted to scream. How could they sit there so calm and indifferent? There was no more emotion than if they were reading the inventory for the store."

"I know, but what would you have them do? Weep and cry out? We were already doing enough of that for everyone." Leah squared her shoulders. "We can't give up on life. We have children who need us. We have others who need us as well. We cannot grow bitter and hateful."

"Bitterness is something that seems to come quite naturally to me in times of disaster," Helaina replied. "I shall count on you to help me avoid its fetters."

"And I'll rely on you to help me avoid the shackles of hopelessness," Leah replied. "Both would see us prisoner, and neither would do a thing to keep us alive and well. Now come on. I need some help bringing in firewood. The twins are busy and Malcolm is sleeping. I don't think we'll have a better opportunity."

Helaina cast a quick glance at her son and nodded. "Let's go."

They opened the door to find Adrik on the other side. His hand was extended as though he were about to take hold of the door latch. Leah jumped back, startled, but Helaina held fast, captured by Adrik's expression. He was stunned by their appearance, but there was something in his countenance that suggested an entirely different matter.

"What are you doing here? It's only midday," Helaina said.

"I . . . I . . . that is . . . I came to share something," Adrik said, stumbling over his words.

"What is it, Adrik?" Leah asked. "We were just going out for more wood."

"I think you'd both better sit down," he said softly. Moving forward, he turned the women toward the front room.

"Why?" Leah asked. "What have you heard?" Her face grew ashen, and she put her hand to her swollen abdomen. Adrik helped her to the couch.

Helaina felt almost numb. What could Adrik possible say that could be worse than what they'd already endured? "What's happened?" she finally asked.

"Just sit." Adrik motioned her to take the place beside Leah. "I promise you won't regret this surprise."

Just then the door pushed back in full, and in walked Jacob, followed by Jayce. Helaina's hand went to her throat as she choked back a cry.

"We didn't know how else to tell you," Adrik said. "They

just arrived, and we ran all the way to get here."

Leah shook her head back and forth as if seeing a ghost. Jayce came to kneel down beside her. "It's all right. I'm home. I'm here."

Helaina was on her feet. She threw herself into Jacob's arms. He smelled of sweat and fish, but she didn't care. She didn't know how this miracle had taken place.

"Papa!" Wills bounded across the room with Merry right behind him. "Papa!" He squealed and dove toward Jayce.

Helaina could see it all from where she stood. It was like something from a dream. She pulled back and stared into the face of her exhausted husband. "They said there were no survivors. No survivors."

"There were no survivors on the *Princess Sophia*," Jacob admitted. "We weren't on the *Princess Sophia*."

"But why? You telegraphed that you would be."

Helaina turned to look at Jayce and noted he had his left arm in a sling. Leah sat beside him in stunned silence. "What happened?"

"We had just finished eating and had plans to head over to a place where I'd been told I could buy some nice handwork. I wanted to get you a gift," Jacob said, smiling. "We were just crossing the street when a team of draft horses broke away from their driver. Jayce pushed me out of the way, but he was knocked unconscious—broke his arm as well. I carried him over to the doctor's office, and by the time he regained consciousness and was well enough to travel, the *Sophia* had already sailed."

"We were upset to say the least," Jayce picked up the story. "There wasn't another ship due in for over a week. I didn't want to wait that long but figured we had no choice. By that time the telegraph office was closed for the night, so we went back to our hotel and went to bed. Come morning our efforts were again thwarted when they informed us that the telegraph wasn't working due to the bad snowstorm that came in."

Jacob continued. "So we made arrangements to book passage on the next available ship. We didn't find out about the *Princess Sophia* until a small fishing vessel came into port and announced the sinking. We knew you'd be sick with worry, but no one seemed to be able to help us. That's when Jayce hit upon an idea."

"What idea?" Helaina asked, looking to Jayce.

"We hired that same fishing vessel for an outrageous amount of money to get us as far as he could. He took us to Juneau. We had to stop several times because of the weather, but we finally made it. From there we tried again to send a telegram, but it seemed that three hundred other people were trying to do the same thing, and the only ones being allowed were related to the rescue and recovery efforts for the *Princess Sophia*. We left our money and message, and they told us they would get it out as soon as possible."

"But Adrik told us there had been no word," Jacob added. "I'm really sorry. We figured you'd at least have that much."

"I can't believe you're here," Leah said. Her gaze had never left Jayce's face. Helaina could see that the color was finally returning to her cheeks. "We thought you were dead."

Jayce shook his head. "Guess God had other plans."

"Yeah," Jacob said. "A broken arm and concussion."

"But you're both alive while everyone else perished," Leah

said, looking finally to her brother. "You would have been dead if you'd made it to the ship on time."

"The way we figure it," Jayce said, "is that God must have something else for us to do."

"Or that we're too ornery to die right now," Jacob said, laughing.

Helaina felt a sense of peace settle over the house for the first time in over a month. She could scarcely believe what God had done—despite her anger and questions. Despite her fears and lack of faith.

"Well, you can't imagine how I felt when these two came walking into the store. I'd gone there to get a few items I thought we needed, and here they come. I just about passed out right there. I think we've had enough excitement to last us for a lifetime," Adrik said.

Leah suddenly moaned and clutched her stomach. "Oh no . . . the baby." She gasped for breath. "It's too early."

Helaina went immediately to Leah's side. "Jacob, help her to bed. Jayce, you go sit with her. I'll see to the children and Adrik can go for the doctor."

The doctor arrived nearly a half hour later. The pains had subsided for the most part, but Leah was scared. She didn't want to lose the baby, not when she'd just managed to get Jayce and Jacob back.

"You'll have to stay in bed until the birth," the doctor told her in a fatherly manner. "If you don't, you will most likely lose the child."

"She'll stay right here," Jayce promised. "I'll see to everything else."

"I'm glad to hear of your survival. Chances are the shock of this entire matter has just been too much for your wife. She needs to remain calm and rested."

Leah couldn't help but laugh as she heard a loud crash and Wills yelling at the top of his lungs for Merry to stop it. "Calm and rested in a house with twins. That should be easy."

Chapter Thirty

B ut I'm tired of sitting in bed all the time," Leah argued. "I feel perfectly fine."

"That's because you've been sitting around in bed all the time. Just like the doctor ordered," Jayce countered. He gave her a look of utter exasperation.

"Look, I know you're bored. I've tried to get you as many books as possible, and the doctor has even allowed you your sewing. But getting up is just too risky. You would hate yourself if you insisted on it and then lost the baby because of it."

Leah sobered and fell back against the pillows. "I know." Her tone held all the dejection she felt.

"It won't be long now," Jayce reminded her. "Just a few more weeks. It's nearly Christmas, and after that the doctor said you should be out of danger. The baby can come anytime after the first of the year."

He came to sit beside her on the bed. "I know this has been hard on you."

Leah shook her head. "No harder than thinking you were dead. I have decided that you and ships do not mix. You were the common denominator in every ship problem I can think of with exception to the *Titanic,* and for all I know you may have been on that one as well."

Jayce laughed heartily. "I assure you I was not on the *Titanic.* But I agree. I think I'm land-bound for a time. I remember when we were stranded in the Arctic, I just kept thinking that if I'd just curbed the wanderlust and remained with you and the twins, I could have avoided that misery all together. Having a family makes you much more cautious."

"I think about that too. I never used to concern myself with things that others thought dangerous. I accompanied Jacob on the sleds for long trips, never thinking about the risk. Now it's all I consider."

Jayce took hold of her hand. "I love you more than life. When I sat on that fishing boat thinking of you suffering—believing me dead—well, it nearly did kill me. I kept wishing some of those old Tlingit legends about ravens or eagles flying down to swoop up folks and carry them away might be true—at least if they could fly me home to you."

"Jacob said there are people already trying to make plans for air service in Alaska, so maybe next time you can just fly and avoid the water completely."

"As long as we live in Alaska—especially Ketchikan—we'll always have to deal with the water," Jayce reminded her. "But I hope you know that I will be more cautious. For you and Wills and Merry." He let go of her hand and gently touched her swollen stomach. "And for whoever this little one might be."

"We haven't talked much about that," Leah said, covering his hand with hers. "If it's a girl, I'd like to name her Karen."

Jayce nodded, his expression quite serious. "I think that would be fine. What about if it's a boy?"

"Well, I thought you might like to pick the name. I'm partial to Michael and Paul, but I really don't mind something else."

"Like Hezekiah?" Jayce asked with a grin.

"Well, I'd rather not call my child Hezekiah," she said with a frown. "And I'm not too keen on Ezekiel or Methuselah."

"Those were my next favorites!" he teased.

"I'll try to be content no matter what name you give him—if it is a boy."

"Well, I'm proud to give him the name of Kincaid. He will be mine, just as his older brother and sister are mine."

Leah felt such a peace in her heart at those words. Jayce seemed always to know how to put her fears to rest. "I love you."

He leaned over and gave her a brief kiss on the lips. "I love you very much, Mrs. Kincaid." He got to his feet. "Can I get you anything else before I go rescue Helaina from the twins?"

Leah sighed. "No. I have my Bible and my sewing. I think I'm set."

After he'd gone, Leah tried to get comfortable. Christmas was just a few days away, and because she could do nothing out of bed, she had sewn presents for everyone. Jayce had helped her tuck most of them away, with exception to his own gift. She'd even managed to work out the pattern for Adrik's coat, and it was nearly finished. Leah knew the bearskin coat would be a real surprise for Adrik. He had known her original intentions but had also admonished her not to worry about him. He wanted her to rest, and Leah had followed orders.

"But I can't sleep all the time," she said aloud, taking up the new trousers she was making for Oliver.

She felt a twinge in her side and thought nothing of it until several minutes later when it came again, only this time it seemed to spread further toward the middle of her abdomen.

"It's the twentieth of December," she murmured. The doctor had told her it would be best for the baby not to be born until after the first of the year. At least by his and Leah's calculations.

Leah put the sewing aside and tried to relax. She closed her eyes and pictured herself in Last Chance Creek, sitting atop a small hill along the shore. She tried to imagine the warmth of the sun on her face. She tried to remember the smells and sounds.

The pain came again, however, and forced her to realize the truth. The baby was going to be born soon—maybe even today.

"Jayce?" she called. "Jayce, are you there?" She knew he had plans to retrieve the twins from Helaina. They were spending the afternoon with her and Malcolm in town. Leah also knew, however, that Jayce would not leave her by herself.

"Is anyone out there?"

No one responded. The thought of being alone and in labor filled her with a sense of apprehension. Leah sat up slowly. She drew a deep breath and waited for the contraction that she knew was sure to come. When nothing happened, she gently moved her legs over the side of the bed and got to her feet. Without warning, her water broke. There would be no waiting on the baby now.

"Did you call, Leah?" Oliver stepped in the room, looking rather surprised. "You aren't supposed to be up."

"It's the baby, Oliver." The pains came again and Leah pressed her hands to her stomach. "Jayce just left to get the twins from Helaina. Can you run after him and stop him?"

"Sure!" He turned and ran from the room, obviously happy to be free of any other obligation that might include delivering Leah's baby.

She would have laughed out loud at the situation had the circumstances not seemed so grave. "Lord, you have always held this child in your hands. I don't know why he or she wants to come so soon, but I trust you for the outcome. Please, please, keep my baby safe."

She went to retrieve a towel to wipe up the floor. There was no sense in remaining bedfast now. To her surprise, Leah was taken back in time to when Ashlie was born in this very house. Leah had been there at Karen's side along with a midwife from the Tlingit tribe. She had been honored to help in Ashlie's delivery.

"Oh, Karen. I miss you so much. I wish you could be here now to help me with this baby." She smiled to herself even as she spoke the words. In so many ways, Karen was with her in the memories and things she had taught Leah.

Pain ripped through Leah's body. This baby was not going to be slow in being born. Already she could feel the child moving lower.

"Leah!" Jayce called as the front door slammed against the wall.

She maneuvered back to the bed and sat down just as he came into the bedroom. "I'm still here," she teased.

"Oliver said that the baby was coming. I sent him for the doctor." He came to her side and saw where the floor was still wet. "Your water broke?"

"Yes. I guess there's no stopping this Kincaid." She patted her stomach. "I think she's coming fast."

"So you've decided it's a girl, eh?" He helped Leah ease back into the bed. "No doubt you're right, for all the trouble she's causing."

Leah grimaced and gripped Jayce's arm hard. "If the doctor doesn't hurry, you'll be delivering this baby yourself."

Jayce paled but squared his shoulders. "What do I need to do?"

Leah pointed to the trunk. "There are blankets and diapers, clothes for the baby in there. We'll need a couple of wash basins, some hot water, and scissors." She clutched her stomach. "Hurry ..." She barely managed the word against the pain.

Just then Christopher came to the doorway of the room. "Where's Oliver? He was supposed to help me with the wood."

"I sent him for the doctor," Jayce said as he worked to pull a stack of things from the trunk. "Leah's going to have the baby."

Christopher looked at Leah in awe. "Truly? Right now?"

Leah nodded. She bit her lip to keep from crying out and frightening the boy. She was surprised that he didn't look in the leastwise uncomfortable with the situation, unlike Oliver, who had clearly been disturbed by the turn of events.

"Do you want to help me?" Jayce asked.

"Sure, Jayce. I'd do anything for Leah and you. What should I do?"

"Get the scissors and bring some hot water."

The boy ran without another word to do Jayce's bidding. Leah smiled and took a couple of ragged breaths. "He'll be able to help you deliver the baby."

Jayce looked at her as though she'd lost her mind. "He's just turned twelve."

Leah nodded. "But he's got two good hands and doesn't seem at all bothered by this." She felt the urge to bear down. "Jayce, I have to push. It won't be long now."

"Here, Jayce. I got the water and the scissors. What else do you need?"

Jayce frowned and looked as if he were trying to remember. "Washbasins."

"And some twine, Christopher," Leah managed to speak before the need to push once again took her focus.

Jayce came to the bed and adjusted the bedding to better facilitate the birth. Leah gritted her teeth and panted against the pain. "I see the head," Jayce told her.

Christopher came back with the basins and nearly dropped them at this declaration. "Are we really going to deliver the baby? Right now?"

Jayce pushed up his sleeves and nodded. "Right now. I need you, Christopher. Are you sure you're up to this?"

The boy nodded. "I can do it, Jayce. You can trust me."

Leah could no longer focus on the conversation. She knew

these were the final moments of her baby's birth. She bore down on the pain and pushed with all her might, feeling the child slide from her body. She fell back against the pillows and gasped for breath.

"Quickly," she said, pointing toward the baby Jayce was now turning over. "Tie off the cord in two places and cut in between."

"Here's the twine," Christopher said, handing the ball to Jayce. "And the scissors." He was very efficient and matter-of-fact.

Jayce went to work doing exactly as Leah had told him. Once the cord was cut, he looked up and awaited further instruction.

"Clean the face and clear out the mouth. You need to hang her upside down and hit her bottom a couple of times to get her crying."

"She's so tiny," Jayce said, lifting the rather lifeless child. He did as instructed, hesitating only when it came to the spanking of this tiny infant.

"Hurry, Jayce. She's got to breathe."

He smacked the baby's bottom lightly at first, and then a little more firmly. This sparked life into the child, and she began to cry in an almost mewing fashion. Soon the cry built to a crescendo, and the wailing sound made Leah smile.

"Welcome to the world, Karen Kincaid," Leah murmured.

Christopher looked at her oddly. "You named her after my mama?"

Leah nodded. "I couldn't think of a better name or way to honor someone I loved so much. Is that all right with you?"

Christopher nodded. "I think Mama would like that very much."

Jayce wrapped the baby in a couple of blankets and moved the rocking chair beside the stove. "Here, Christopher, come hold her and keep her warm. I need to finish helping Leah."

The boy looked with wide eyes at Jayce and then Leah. "Me? Are you sure you want me to hold her?"

"Absolutely," Leah encouraged. "She needs to get warm, so hold her close and snug."

Christopher went to the rocker and sat. "I don't want to hurt her."

Leah smiled. He seemed so grown up sitting there waiting for Jayce to deposit the baby in her arms. "You won't hurt her if you're careful," Leah said. She watched the pleasure that crossed Christopher's face as Jayce handed him the baby.

The boy was immediately smitten. "She's beautiful," he murmured.

Jayce looked at Leah and smiled. The look of love in his eyes was quite evident. "Yes, she is."

———

"I can't believe you helped deliver a baby," Oliver told Christopher after the doctor had come and gone. Everyone had gathered in Leah's room to get their first official look at the infant.

"He was as good as any doctor," Jayce declared. "We made quite the team. Maybe we should take it up as a living. What do you say, Christopher?"

"I might want to be a doctor," he replied. "I'm thinking it would make Mama proud."

Adrik patted his son's back. "It would at that, but your mama would be proud at any profession you chose so long as you put the Lord first in all you did."

Oliver looked at the tiny baby in Leah's arms. "She's really little."

"Yes. She's a bit early, but the doctor said she's breathing well and her lungs are clear. That's a good sign."

He reached out to touch Karen's tiny fingers. "She was almost a Christmas present."

Leah laughed. "Almost. At least this way, I can be up and around with everyone on Christmas morning. What fun that will be."

"Mrs. Kincaid, I specifically remember the doctor telling you to stay in bed for a week."

Leah looked at her husband and shook her head. "No, he told me to rest for a week. I promise, I will rest on Christmas morning, but I will do it with everyone else in the front room, sharing a wonderful breakfast and opening presents."

Adrik laughed. "The women in this household have always tended to the stubborn side. I wouldn't argue with her. We can surely make provision."

"Is there room for a couple more?" Jacob called from the door.

Leah turned and saw her brother. Helaina stood directly behind him, Malcolm in her arms. "You know you're welcome. Come see your new niece."

He came to her side and leaned down to view the new baby. Oliver moved away to afford him a better view. "Well, she's mighty pretty. Going to break a few hearts, no doubt."

"If she takes anything after her namesake," Adrik said,

"she'll be a handful to be sure."

"I can't believe you delivered her, Jayce. That must have been quite the experience." Jacob was in complete awe. His voice dropped a bit as he added, "Our mother died in childbirth, you know."

"I had forgotten, but I suppose Leah never did."

"Actually, I hadn't really thought of it," Leah admitted. "I was too busy."

Everyone laughed at this, but it was Adrik who spoke. "I think it's probably time for us to let you and the baby get some rest." He came to Leah's bed. Leaning down, he kissed Leah on the head. "Thank you for naming her after Karen. She'll be a special blessing to all of us." He turned and looked to his boys. "Come on, fellows, we have some cooking to do. I don't know about you, but I'm starving."

Jacob took Malcolm from Helaina. "We'll be just outside if you need anything. Adrik invited us to supper. He's making 'surprise meat' pie. At least that's what he promised. Remember the old days when he'd make those for us?"

Leah smiled. "I do indeed. Has he told you what meat he's picked out?"

Jacob shook his head and smiled. "Nope. Hasn't even hinted. Guess we'll all be surprised."

Helaina reached down and gave Leah's hand a squeeze. "I can't imagine having a baby out here without a doctor or midwife. You are very brave, Leah. I hope I can be more like you. I'll have Jacob move my things here so that I can take care of you and the twins, and of course this little one." She gently touched her finger to Karen's face.

"I'll look forward to it," Leah replied. "It will be like the days when we all lived together. Just one big happy family."

After everyone had gone, Jayce came to Leah and knelt beside the bed. "Mrs. Kincaid, you are a wonder. I think back all those years to that sweet kid who told me she thought she was falling in love with me. I can't believe I said no to that love then. I can't imagine even being able to live without it now."

"Everything in its time, Mr. Kincaid. A wise woman once told me that."

"Who? Ayoona?"

Leah shook her head. "No. Karen. Karen waited until she was considered well past a marriageable age, until true love found her as well. When I despaired of ever finding another love to match what I felt for you, that's what she told me, 'Everything in its time.'"

Jayce took hold of her hand and kissed her fingers. "The war has ended, we're all safe and healthy, and we have each other. The blessings we know are abundant."

"Among many sorrows we have indeed been blessed." Leah shifted the sleeping baby to lean closer to her husband. "I thought after nearly losing you that I would grow afraid each time you walked out the door. I thought I would dread those moments when you had to be out of my sight—to the point where I would make us both crazy. But God has given me such a peace about life."

"How's that?" Jayce asked, his gaze never leaving hers.

"I've had weeks to lie here praying and reading the Bible. God has been good to meet me here. Perhaps it was the only way He could get me to be quiet long enough to hear Him."

Jayce grinned but appeared to know better than to speak.

Leah continued. "I heard Him speak to me, Jayce. As clearly as if you or Jacob had been here talking to me. He assured me that I would never be alone—that the future was something He had already seen—already taken care of. No matter what happens, God will walk with me—with us. I know it might sound silly; after all, we've heard it said many times that we need to put our trust in God. But somehow it's more real to me now. More understandable."

Jayce nodded. "I think I can understand it too. Seeing Karen born—feeling the breath come into her body as she took her first cry . . . well . . . it did something to me. I was praying so hard to do all the right things and in the end I knew there was nothing I could do to give her life or keep her alive. Only God can do that. And just like He'd preserved my life so many times, He faithfully brought us a new life."

Leah sighed and gave Jayce a smile. "Whether in the glory of summer or the whispers of winter, He has ordained our path. It doesn't mean there won't be uphill climbs or rocky roads, but it does mean we can count on Him—believe in Him—hope on Him. We have only to trust our hearts to Him . . . and to each other."

Jayce leaned down and kissed her ever so gently. "And we'll do just that—in good times and bad."

"For better or worse," she whispered.

"For so long as we both shall live."

TRACIE PETERSON is a popular speaker and bestselling author who has written more than seventy books, both historical and contemporary fiction. Tracie and her family make their home in Montana.

Looking for More Good Books to Read?

You can find out what is new and exciting with previews, descriptions, and reviews by signing up for Bethany House newsletters at

www.bethanynewsletters.com

We will send you updates for as many authors or categories as you desire so you get only the information you really want.

Sign up today!